RETRIBUTION

SECTOR 64 BOOK TWO

DEAN M. COLE

CANDTOR PRESS

Retribution: Sector 64 Book Two

Published by CANDTOR PRESS

Retribution: Sector 64 Book Two is a work of fiction. Names, characters, places, and incidents are either the products of the author's imagination or are used fictitiously. Any resemblance to actual persons, living or dead, events, or locales is entirely coincidental.

Cover Art © 2018 Rafido

ISBN: 978-1793359285

Also by Dean M. Cole

Get *Solitude: Dimension Space Book One* Today!
(Read the *Solitude* sneak peak at the end of this book.)

The Martian meets *Gravity* when Earth's last man, Army Captain Vaughn Singleton, discovers that the last woman is stranded alone aboard the International Space Station. Commander Angela Brown could reverse the event that swept humanity from Earth's surface ... if only she could get there. If you like action-packed, page-turning novels, you'll love the electrifying action in this award-winning, apocalyptic thriller.

Blurbs

What the critics are saying about the Sector 64 series.

Huffington Post - IndieReader.com - Top Ten Science Fiction

Kirkus Reviews

"Cole tackles the first-contact scenario with bombastic flair. [He] delivers the high-resolution imagery of a Hollywood blockbuster ... A technologically riveting dream for sci-fi action fans."

LiquidFrost - Amazon Top 500 Reviewer

"This series moves into the Space Opera world, officially ... Retribution moves (even) faster than Ambush ... Hits the ground with destruction; ends with destruction, with destruction in-between. So yes, it is a heartwarming tale full of rainbows and kittens."

AudiobookReviewer.com

"SECTOR 64 was a highly imaginative action-packed apocalyptic assault on your mind."

IndieReader.com

"SECTOR 64 is an engaging book from the very first page to the final words of the Epilogue."

Audiobook-Heaven.com

"His descriptions of aerial battle and military procedure are accurately detailed and his knowledge of the aircraft themselves fascinated me ... Sector 64 is a great read."

The Complete *Sector 64* Series
  1947 - *First Contact a Sector 64 Prequel Novella*
  Today - *Ambush - Book One of the Sector 64 Duology*
  Tomorrow - *Retribution - Book Two of the Sector 64 Duology*

(Read the sneak peak of *Ambush* at the end of this book.)

PART I

"Infuse your life with action. Don't wait for it to happen. Make it happen. Make your own future. Make your own hope. Make your own love. And whatever your beliefs, honor your creator, not by passively waiting for grace to come down from upon high, but by doing what you can to make grace happen... yourself, right now, right down here on Earth."

— Bradley Whitford

CHAPTER 1

"This cold is going to be the death of me," Remulkin Thramorus said as he trudged through another waist-deep snow dune. Pulling the nanobot-enhanced parka tight around his ears, he lowered his head into the frigid gale. Buffeting him, it threatened to blow Remulkin back to the empty transport hovering to his rear.

Leaning into the wind, the scientist looked through his eyebrows. Ahead, a jagged rock protruded a few stories above the ice plain. Buried under the polar ice cap, a huge mountain, hundreds of times taller than the visible portion, spread out beneath the camp.

Only a month earlier, a construction crew had finished boring a science station into the mountain's exposed triangular peak. The camp's sole entrance lay ahead of Remulkin. Behind and to the sides of the lone scientist, the white plain stretched to the horizon, disappearing into the pole's perpetual night. Interrupted only by the snow dunes that always seemed to occupy the space between him and his destination, the surface was otherwise perfectly flat.

Anchored at the pole of the newly settled planet, this part of the ice field sat motionlessly. Sub-zero temperatures and a thick, stable ice sheet that insulated the site from the planet's iron-rich surface made it the perfect region for Remulkin's experiment.

One snow dune later, the scientist trudged up to the smooth outer skin of the camp's entrance. With the sound of tearing paper, a rectangular opening appeared in its seamless surface. A force field-entrained bubble of heated atmosphere ballooned out and wrapped him in its warm embrace.

The scientist stepped through the hatch-shaped opening, an action that breathed life into ancient memories of his brief military stint. A lifetime ago, a much younger Petty Officer Thramorus had haunted the vast halls of an Argonian-manned battlecruiser.

Dusting the frost from his ample belly, he frowned. In the years since his three-year, all-expenses-paid tour with the Galactic Defense Forces, his forehead had become a five-head, and his six-pack looked more like a twelve-pack.

Remulkin stepped through the inner door into the compound's main room. In mercurial rivulets, billions of nanobots streamed from his bib and parka. No longer needed for insulation, the omnifunctional microscopic robots flowed into the mottled gray floor, rejoining the facility's matrix. The parka and bib morphed to their normal volume and function as a day shirt and pants.

Excited to share the bounty of data garnered at the pole, Remulkin forgot about the day's isolation.

He dusted the last of the frost from his shirt and looked around.

His smile faltered.

Why was it so quiet? Why was the common room empty? At this hour, it should be bustling with activity.

Thramorus shook his head. "I'm back," he said, yelling toward the back rooms. "Is everyone on break?"

Silence.

Raising his voice, he said, "I go away for one day, and you all take a holiday?"

Nothing.

"Hello?"

Anger—and the first hint of concern—chased away his good cheer. "Guys, this isn't funny."

All he heard was his voice's fading echo floating in the still air.

Determined to find someone, he walked and then jogged through the subterranean compound.

"Hello?"

Still no answer.

Now panting, he ran from room to room.

They were all empty.

He even checked the ladies restroom.

As Remulkin turned to exit, he saw movement. After a confused moment, he realized the scared, middle-aged, portly man was him.

Blinking and wheezing, Remulkin studied his reflection in the vanity mirror. His normally pale, freckled skin was ruddy, glowing above and below his ring of red and gray hair. His mother had once told him that you never really *see* yourself until you think you're looking at someone else.

He shook his head and turned from the unsettling image.

Finally catching his breath in the camp's elevation-thinned atmosphere, Remulkin exited the restroom and walked to the last door, his quarters.

Shaking his head after a final confused glimpse back toward the entrance, he stepped into the room ... and jumped right the hell back out.

A body had popped into existence in front of his face.

In the middle of his private room!

"Damn holograms!" he screamed, once his pounding heart and hitching breath permitted speech.

"Sorry about that, Mr. Thramorus," said an uncharacteristically dour-looking Falinch Meklem. His assistant—usually jovial to the point of annoyance—stared grimly from the pre-recorded hologram.

Annoyed at the intrusion into his quarters, holographic or not, Remulkin searched for the deactivation key.

"I know how much you hate these things, but I don't have time for anything else."

There it is, he thought as he found the virtual shutoff key floating on the front right corner of the hologram. Remulkin reached for it.

As if reacting to the scientist's movement, his assistant held up a hand. "This is important, sir. You'll want to hear it."

His finger hovered over the virtual button. Then Thramorus pulled it back as if he'd touched a hot surface.

What the hell was he thinking? His disgust with the invasion of his privacy had banished all other concerns. Remulkin's wife would have loved that one. She was always saying he was too stuffy, too worried about privacy and personal space. She had begged him to let them connect their Electro-Organic Networks to the colony's matrix. Then they could use the neurally implanted EONs to stay in constant contact.

Oh, joy! Remulkin thought.

In the hologram, a running man bumped into Falinch. The assistant lunged forward. Remulkin heard a shouted apology. Regaining his feet, the man pushed his tousled blond hair out of his eyes and appeared to stare at Remulkin.

The uncharacteristic seriousness in the young man's eyes had Remulkin's short hairs standing on end.

Meklem pointed a thumb over his shoulder. "The sensor network detected a Zoxyth fleet entering our galactic sector."

"My Gods," Remulkin whispered.

The assistant continued. "We're all leaving to be with our families. Everything should be fine. The Galactic Defense Forces can't be far behind."

Another person ran through the image. "Sorry."

Falinch waved at the person and then continued. "We tried to call you in, but couldn't detect your terminal."

"Shit!" Remulkin shouted. A sinking feeling struck his gut as he recalled disabling his hand terminal's external link during the experiment.

Falinch continued speaking as Remulkin worked to activate his terminal.

"Sorry for the short message, we have to get on the transport. As soon as it drops me off, I'll set its autopilot to return for you."

"Anyway, I'm sure this is an overreaction. The GDF has those green-blooded, ancestor-worshipping lizards on their heels ... Don't they?"

As holographic Falinch began to dematerialize, Remulkin saw a look of trepidation leak through the man's brave facade.

"No, no, no," Remulkin said, growling in frustration. Hunched over the hand terminal, he tapped furiously. "Come on!"

The scientist shared his assistant's apprehension. They *were* at war with the Zoxyth. The fanatical leader of the reptilian race had declared a holy war against all Argonians. He had sworn to right an ancient wrong, to avenge a supposed Argonian attempt to wreak genocide upon their sacrosanct Forebearers. The visceral Lord Thrakst had vowed to eradicate every last Argonian from the galaxy.

A chill ran down Remulkin's spine.

Finally, his terminal finished its digital handshake and connected to the station's network.

A multi-pitched storm of audio alerts announced a flood of messages and warnings. Red, strobing icons streamed across his screen.

"Oh Gods." This was bad, real bad.

Remulkin scrolled through the news updates and government alerts in sequence. Most had timestamps more recent than the assistant's message. They painted a picture of a rapidly deteriorating situation.

City after city in this newly settled world had fallen silent.

The arrival of an enemy ship preceded each event.

Reports of a brilliant light.

Then nothing, all contact with the area lost.

On the final newsclip, Remulkin watched as the godsdamned aliens closed in on the last settlement.

His new home town.

In this new colony, everyone lived in or near a town.

Whatever the bastards were doing, they had done it to every settle-ment, every man, every woman, every child.

Save his.

Now Remulkin's home was in their sights.

7

The last item on his terminal, a recorded video message, opened.

"Baby, I'm scared," his wife said. "Why won't you pick up?" Farene's eyes pleaded. "I need you, baby!"

In the background, daylight streamed through the windows of their home. Suddenly they darkened as if a black cloud had passed overhead.

"Oh my Gods! They're here now!" she said, her voice cracking with fear.

Remulkin touched the image of her face. "Farene!"

His pounding heart threatened to burst from his chest.

To either side, his son and daughter clutched at their mother. At nine years old, their son, Wilby, stood taller than his younger sister, Freena.

His wife stared into the camera he'd mounted over the kitchen door. She'd asked him to put it there. That way the scientist could watch his wife's experiments with cooking—just one of the many things they'd both had to learn as colonists on a new settlement.

"Remulkin?" she said, her eyes pleading. "Why aren't you answering?"

Through tear-muddled eyes, he saw unnatural light burst through the room's window coverings—curtains Farene had painstakingly selected for their new home.

"Baby!" his wife screamed as she doubled over. Collapsing at her feet, both of their children cried out, writhing in pain.

The yellow light's brilliance—and his family's shrieks—grew until the image completely washed out.

"Farene!" Remulkin screamed. "Oh Gods!"

"Wilby!"

"Freena!"

"No!"

Remulkin stared helplessly into the whited-out image.

"No," he said again in a weak whisper.

The light streaming through his splayed fingers faded and then disappeared, taking their screams with it.

And then there was deafening silence.

"Farene?" Thramorus said through his constricted throat.

Pulling his hand away, he watched as color and shadow returned to the image. Three unrecognizable, multicolored clumps sat where his family had been.

Trying to blink the tears from his vision, Remulkin pulled the screen closer.

Still arranged as they had been when their wearers had fallen, his family's emptied garments lay strewn across the kitchen floor.

"No, no, no," Remulkin uttered between whimpers.

Clutching the terminal to his chest, he rocked back and forth.

Then, keening like a mortally wounded animal, the last man on the planet collapsed to the floor.

CHAPTER 2

Under a three-quarter moon, an angular, white space fighter flew through a vast field of tumbling ghost ships. Ahead of the weaving vessel sat a swelling black void, a hole cut into the field of stars.

Inside the small starfighter, United States Air Force pilot Captain Jake Giard squinted, trying to resolve some detail, hell, anything within the wide, gaping maw of starless space. He could almost imagine they were flying into the event horizon of an elongated black hole.

But it was no rift.

No, this was a ship.

A damned big one.

As they neared the enormous stealthy carrier, it blotted out a sizable portion of the universe. None of the crisp, brilliant stars that crowded the rest of the sky reflected off of its light-absorbing skin.

Named the *Galactic Guardian,* the three-mile-long alien carrier hovered two hundred miles over the North Atlantic, defying gravity.

For now.

A few hours ago, thousands of Argonians had lived aboard the mammoth vessel.

Like the hundreds of other vessels crowding this moon-sized region of space, it, too, was an empty ghost ship.

And Jake needed to find a way to board it.

If he didn't get in there soon, things were going to get significantly worse.

Considering the day's events, that was saying a lot.

The colonel had crammed Captain Giard into the small space behind the single-seat fighter's sole ejection seat. Now his legs were going to sleep. Jake shifted his weight to return circulation to his numb extremities.

In front of him, the squared-off gray and white flat top that protruded above the ejection seat twisted left and right.

"Son of a bitch!" Colonel Zach Newcastle said, shaking his head.

Tugging at the ejection seat's shoulder harnesses, Newcastle managed to turn his upper body. Regarding Jake with his left eye, the colonel cocked a salt-and-pepper eyebrow. "I thought the enemy ships were huge." He pointed through the fighter's bubble-shaped canopy. "I knew it was damn big—you could see that when they showed up." He paused. "But God, there must've been thousands of people in there."

Facing forward, Newcastle settled back into the seat. He shook his head. "Shit," he said again in a hoarse whisper, drawing the word out into two syllables.

"Yes, sir," Jake said with a nod. "The whole thing is royally fucked."

Newcastle rested his elbow on the spacesuit helmet he'd stowed on the left console. The big man scratched his head. Thick fingers left short-lived furrows in the stiff bristles of his graying flattop.

Casting a nervous look over his right shoulder, Jake scanned the battlefield.

Several kilometers behind them, a broken and burned asteroid hung motionlessly against the backdrop of stars. It was the tattered dead remnant of the only remaining enemy ship.

Every time he looked that way, Jake half-expected to find the asteroid bearing down on them, the alien face sculpted across its hundred-meter width glaring at him.

A mental image of spraying arterial blood crowded out his thoughts.

Jake shook away the memory, forcing out the unbidden image.

He focused on the enemy ship. It still wasn't following them, but he knew it never would. Jake and his wingman, Captain Richard Allison, had searched the interior of the hollowed-out asteroid.

There weren't any enemy aliens left, none living, anyway.

Of course, there weren't any friendly aliens left either.

A few weeks ago, Jake had been a simple fighter pilot, just an Air Force officer training for another combat deployment to the Middle East. In preparation for the air war against ISIS, Jake and a wingman had taken a pair of F-22s out on a night training exercise over Las Vegas's Nellis Air Force Base.

Events of that night had led to Jake's presence here today.

Now he and Colonel Newcastle—an officer he hadn't known until a few hours ago—drifted across a cluttered battlefield in a human-made spaceship—a space fighter that Jake hadn't known existed before this morning.

Hundreds of tumbling ships of varying sizes drifted around the mammoth *Galactic Guardian*, all of them undamaged. They were also fully functional.

And completely devoid of life.

As far as Jake knew, the two of them were the only living souls in Earth orbit.

Captain Giard shook his head.

No, not orbit.

Hell, things would have been a lot easier if they had been in orbit, if the battle hadn't taken place at a relative hover.

One of the first lessons a fighter pilot learned was that, in aerial combat, speed and altitude are the currency of life. Without one or both, a fighter pilot wasn't long for this world.

Here they had altitude, had it in spades, but in space, the lack of orbital speed rendered said altitude a liability.

Gravity drives held every one of these ships aloft. A reverse-engineered version of the same technology even held their small space fighter up here as well.

As Jake had already seen, if a ship's gravity drive failed, the vessel would drop like Wile E. Coyote one second after he'd chased the Roadrunner over the cliff's edge.

During the battle—far below a geostationary altitude, and nowhere near orbital speed—anything that had lost its protective gravity bubble had fallen like a homesick rock.

In the aftermath, small drifting space fighters didn't pose much of a threat to the planet below. However, hundreds of incredibly massive ships hung two hundred miles above the North Atlantic Ocean like the hammer of God stayed by a slowly unraveling technological thread.

Only gravity drives and their currently unmonitored power systems held the enemy asteroid ship as well as the Argonian carrier and its complement of stadium-sized battlecruisers at bay. Without one of the two, they'd instantly drop into the planet's gravity well.

A lesson Jake had relearned only a few minutes earlier.

After he and Captain Richard Allison had finished sweeping the alien asteroid, they had parted ways. Newcastle had instructed Richard to take a small spaceship called the *Turtle* back to Nellis Air Force Base for supplies and personnel.

Yes, if you squinted just the right way, the ship looked like a turtle —sans head and legs—albeit a very, very fast turtle.

Anyway, the two ships had no means of coupling. Without a docking connector, Jake's transfer to the colonel's ship had required a spacewalk.

From the *Turtle's* airlock, Captain Giard had saluted the colonel.

"Permission to board, sir?"

Newcastle had returned the salute, then waved impatiently. "Let's go, Captain."

After a moment to estimate the vector and necessary force, Jake pushed off of the *Turtle*. As soon as he had cleared the round-topped ship, he'd foolishly notified Richard of the fact.

Unlike its namesake, the *Turtle* was fast, the now-you-see-it-now-you-don't kind of fast.

Jake slowly floated across four feet of open space with his hands extended toward Newcastle's fighter.

He felt a brief flutter in his abdomen, and the colonel's ship rocketed upward. To his right, Jake saw the speed-blurred image of the *Turtle* blazing toward the western horizon.

Richard had left for Nevada.

He shifted confused eyes to Newcastle's fading fighter.

"Uh ... Colonel Newcastle? Where are you going, sir?"

Then Jake saw another problem. Every ship in the battlefield had flown away from him.

"Oh shit!"

He had swapped one zero-G frame of reference for another.

Jake was falling.

Of course, he'd felt like he was falling as soon as he stepped out of the *Turtle's* one-G interior field and into its external zero-G buffer.

But now he was truly falling.

And truly fucked if nothing changed.

Like Wile E. Coyote, Jake fell feet first into Earth's gravity well. He could almost see the cartoon swoosh above his head. Unlike said cartoon character, Jake didn't have a *Help!* sign to hold up.

So he screamed it.

"Help!"

Nothing. No one responded.

As far as he knew, his suit's radio was only designed for short ranges, although this was the first day he'd ever used one.

"Richard!"

No reply.

"Colonel?"

"Hang on, Captain. Almost there," Newcastle, sounding maddeningly calm.

Jake's body had rolled forward a few degrees—that might've had something to do with his flailing arms. Craning his neck, he looked upward again. A bright point of light moved against the backdrop of stars. In seconds, it expanded into a space fighter.

"Thank God!"

Hyperventilating and not wanting to look down, Jake focused on the fighter. With a hundred and fifty miles of empty space between him and the upper reaches of the atmosphere, he didn't want to think about how fast he'd be going when he got there.

So of course, it was all he could think about.

His heart pounded in his ears. Wide-eyed, he watched as Newcastle matched his acceleration. Then the Air Force colonel overtook him and slid his ship under Jake. From Jake's perspective, the colonel's fighter had swooped in from above, but now it hovered under him.

"Holy shit!" Jake screamed.

The Atlantic Ocean already looked closer.

"Don't look down, Captain," Newcastle said. He pointed two fingers at his own eyes. "Focus on me."

Jake did as the officer said.

After a moment, he reined in his breathing and stopped flapping his arms.

"That's better," the colonel said.

The space fighter slid a few feet closer.

Jake felt a flutter in his abdomen again. For a second, he floated a couple of feet above the fighter. Then, the ship's internal one-G gravity field pulled him onto the ship's outer skin.

The smooth metal surface sloped toward the ship's edge.

Jake started to slide toward the precipice.

"Oh fuck!"

The fighter's bubble canopy shot upward. A vice-like hand clamped down on his forearm.

Before Jake knew what was happening, the big man had dragged him into the cockpit.

After a few seconds, he caught his breath. Swallowing hard, Jake fought to rein in his racing heart.

His suit's helmet retracted as the cockpit pressurized.

"Sorry about that, Captain," Newcastle said, his Texas accent even thicker in person. "My fault. Should've let Allison know that my gravity bubble doesn't reach as far as the *Turtle's*."

"I can't believe Richard didn't come back."

"He didn't know. I didn't radio him. Figured I could get you."

Jake blinked. "I'm glad you were so sure, sir."

Newcastle twisted his helmet and removed it. Setting it on the left console, he gave Jake a crooked, sideways grin and winked. "You're welcome, Captain."

That had been several minutes ago. Now they were back, flying through the field of slowly tumbling ghost ships.

Jake's stomach knotted up again as his thoughts returned to their final battle in the Zoxyth ship. Every time he thought of the short, close quarters battle, the image of Victor's spraying arterial blood filled his mind's eye.

Captain Giard shifted his gaze outside. The real-world image of an emptied Galactic Defense Force fleet pushed out the memory and the doubts it fed.

A GDF starfighter tumbled past them. The ship was a smaller, sleeker version of the *Turtle*. Not unlike the vessel he'd encountered less than three weeks earlier, during the training flight.

The fateful events of that night had embroiled Jake in a decades-long well-intentioned global conspiracy.

The world was going to change for the better!

And Jake was going to be part of it!

Apparently a lost colony of Argonians—or humans, as we call ourselves—had been stranded on this planet tens of thousands of years ago. In the intervening millennia, we lost touch with that past and integrated with or eliminated the indigenous populations—as witnessed by the disappearance of Cro-Magnon man and the recent finding of Neanderthal genes mixed with our own.

But humanity was no longer a lost colony.

After detecting nuclear detonations in backwater Galactic Sector 64, the Argonian leadership of the United Galactic Federation sent agents to establish first contact.

The emissaries arrived in the year locally designated as 1947. They soon discovered the planet was inhabited by Argonians.

Their initial foray into Earth space ended in tragedy, an incident popularly known as Roswell.

After recovering from that unfortunate event, the emissaries met with world leaders of the day. They laid out a seventy-five-year plan to incorporate our world into the galactic government.

In spite of our genetic relationship, the Argonians decided to follow their standard integration protocols. During the intervening decades, the process had streamlined our global culture and economy for inclusion in galactic society.

As Jake had learned, we were approaching the point of disclosure, the time when the entrusted governments could reveal the secret to the world.

Then Zox happened.

This morning, a fleet of sixteen city-sized asteroid ships showed up on our doorstep.

The Zoxyth, an ancient reptilian race with a deep-seated hate for Argonians, attacked Earth. They'd used a new weapon of a type and capability that even the GDF hadn't anticipated.

The whole thing had been a coup de main, a ruse to draw the Galactic Defense Forces into an ambush.

Jake shook his head as he considered the tragic irony.

Our genetic lineage had made us the perfect pawn. The bastards had hit us with a genocidal weapon that eradicated anyone with Argonian genes.

Unfortunately, the GDF had been late to the party.

In less than an hour, the fleet of sixteen asteroid ships depopulated most of the world's capital cities.

Jake had seen the aftermath firsthand. The weapon left nothing but a pile of clothes where the person had been. Everything else remained untouched: birds chirped, banal elevator music maddened, driverless automobiles and unpiloted airplanes met fiery ends.

You know. Typical end of the world shit. Shit for which even dozens of apocalyptic movies and books hadn't prepared Jake.

He shook his head again.

A lot of good that integration plan and our genetic lineage had done.

Too bad our ancestors hadn't mixed with a few more Neanderthals. Maybe a little more genetic diversity would have rendered the enemy's gene weapon ineffective.

Jake pointed at the *Galactic Guardian*. "Would it have killed the bastards to give us a little heads-up? A simple *Oh, by the way, there's a race of giant, pissed-off reptiles out there. Here are some ships to defend yourself* would have been nice."

Without responding, the colonel leveled off the fighter a few feet above the carrier's hull.

Jake still hadn't seen an access point. He pointed over the colonel's shoulder. "I think their fighters launched out of the back of the ship."

Newcastle nodded. "That's where I'm headed."

Below the space fighter's belly, the *Galactic Guardian's* skin flowed like black mercury. To Jake's left and right, curled protrusions of unknown purpose scrolled past like frozen waves on a sable river.

"You know," Newcastle said softly. "They did ultimately give their lives."

"What, sir?"

"Those bastards you mentioned. They sacrificed themselves ... for us."

Jake felt his face flush.

The reason these ships were now empty was because the Galactic Defense Forces had stayed in the battle, even after Jake had warned the GDF commander about the effects of the enemy's weapon.

Ultimately, the commander and his troops had sacrificed themselves to save Earth.

Jake wanted to shout at the colonel. Yeah, a lot of Argonians had died here today, but down there, millions more had lost their lives.

Jake ground his teeth together.

The image of Victor's head falling to the floor followed a second later by his body flooded Jake's reddening vision.

"Son," Newcastle said in a paternal tone. "I know what's really eating you. I told you not to kick yourself."

"Excuse me, sir?"

"From what you told me, Lieutenant Croft died a hero."

Jake's head snapped back as if the colonel had slapped him.

In a day chock full of fucked-up shit, somehow Victor's death weighed heaviest on him.

The colonel was right.

Jake shook his head, and his shoulders slumped as the fight left him.

"If I had acted quicker, sir, he might still be alive."

"Quicker? You were the one who realized it was a ruse, that the Zox were using our genetic ties with the Argonians to draw the Galactic Defense Forces into a sneak attack. If you hadn't figured out the enemy's plan when you did, they would've wiped out the GDF."

"My call didn't do them much good." Jake pointed at the empty *Galactic Guardian*. "They still got wiped out."

"Yeah, but not before the good guys hit first. Your quick thinking allowed them to take out all but the last ship. If you hadn't warned them, the Zoxyth would've fired that damned weapon with their entire fleet still intact. How many millions or billions more would've died?"

Jake turned from Newcastle and looked at the battle-blasted remnant of the enemy ship. The colonel's words sent a chill down his spine.

The Zoxyth vessels weren't as big as the carrier, but they'd dwarfed the GDF's battlecruisers. All sixteen had been unique, each a collection of hollowed-out asteroids held together by trusses and skyscraper-sized metal structures. Serving as the ship's bridge, a huge, sculpted Zoxyth bust with a human skull clenched in its jaw headed each, literally.

After Jake had warned the Galactic Defense Forces, the Argonians opened fire, hitting the Zoxyth fleet with a continuous laser barrage. The GDF commander, Admiral Thoyd Feyhdyak, told them that an enemy ship under an active shield couldn't fire the gene weapon.

They had to keep the enemy pinned down.

No matter the consequences, they had to keep the Zoxyth ships under constant fire.

The humans had remained outside of the gene weapon's range. However, the Argonian fleet was trapped between the enemy ships and the planet. They couldn't get out of range, not without leaving Earth unprotected.

As some of his lasers diverted to vaporizing debris falling from the hovering enemy fleet, the GDF admiral had requested assistance from Colonel Newcastle's space fighters.

The combined firepower of Argonian lasers and human nuclear bunker busters had peeled back the defending ships like layers of an onion.

Finally, only the scorched bridge section of the commander's ship remained. However, as the last missile closed in on the unshielded ship remnant, the bastard had fired the gene weapon. In the millisecond between the failure of the last shield and the impact of the missile, the genocidal weapon's energy wave surged across the battlefield, completely enveloping the GDF fleet.

In the blink of an eye, every Argonian in the Galactic Defense Force's hundreds of ships ceased to exist.

Hovering in the middle of the surreal scene, the intact alien face chiseled into the front of the enemy bridge glared across the battlefield.

The final bunker buster had passed through the hollowed-out asteroid without detonating.

Jake, Richard, and Victor had boarded the ship remnant, armed with only pistols and shotguns. Inside, they met no resistance. At first, only mangled enemy bodies greeted their arrival. Then they found their first and last living Zoxyth on the top floor of the bridge.

The massive, heavily injured reptilian beast had attacked with a ferocity Jake hadn't thought possible. Unscathed by multiple shotgun blasts, the monster attacked Richard.

In an instant of uncharacteristic valor, Jake's junior wingman, Lieutenant Victor Croft, charged the beast.

Looking over the colonel's shoulder, Jake consulted the fighter's clock.

Only two hours earlier, the enemy commander had beheaded his friend and wingman.

Jake hadn't reacted fast enough to save him.

"Hell, son," Newcastle said softly. "I owe you a great debt. Because of you, I'll get to see my grandchildren again." Not waiting for a reply, he patted Jake's protruding knee. "Now let's get back to work."

After a long pause, Jake nodded. "Yes, sir."

CHAPTER 3

"Nellis Tower, this is Turtle One, over," said Captain Richard Allison.

"Roger, Turtle One. This is Nellis Tower. I don't have you on radar. Please state aircraft position and type."

"Nellis Tower, I'm currently fifty miles south, descending out of flight level two thousand five hundred."

After a pregnant pause, the air traffic controller returned with a condescending tone. "Lieutenant, you're either at flight level twenty-five, that's twenty-five hundred feet, by the way, or you're at flight level two-fifty, which is twenty-five thousand feet. Otherwise, son, you're in outer space. I think your training aircraft would have a little trouble operating at two hundred and fifty thousand feet."

Having just survived the longest day of his life, Richard was in no mood to deal with this asshole.

"Nellis Tower, you're right, I'm not in space … anymore. I'm now descending through flight level one thousand, and yes, that's one hundred thousand feet. I'm twenty-five miles south with airport information: Charlie. I'd like to land directly to Alpha ramp. Please notify General Pearson that I'll be landing in two minutes."

After another pause, the air traffic controller's suddenly very accommodating and nervous voice returned. "Roger, Turtle One. You're cleared directly to the ramp. Say type, please."

"Nellis Tower, that'll be self-evident in a moment."

"Uh … roger, Turtle One. Cleared direct to the ramp," the tower controller repeated. "Please advise when you have the landing area in sight."

In the background, Richard heard a second, more animated voice tearing the controller a new asshole.

"Uh, Turtle One, I've been … advised that a vehicle is there waiting for you."

"Roger Tower, good copy. Cleared direct. I'll report landing area in sight."

Reaching a relatively low altitude, the *Turtle* leveled off at a thousand feet. Approaching Las Vegas from the southwest, Richard began a gradual deceleration as he steered the ship toward Nellis Air Force Base on the far side of the city.

Barely discernible in the dark, the *Turtle's* light-absorbing skin rendered it a virtual black hole. Lost in the city's significant light pollution, the ship should be all but invisible from the ground, the only evidence of its passing a sequential eclipsing of the few background stars bright enough to penetrate Las Vegas's glowing atmosphere.

Richard watched through the ship's forward view-wall as McCarran International Airport passed on his right. He was thankful for the late hour and the ship's stealthy features. Considering the day's events, he knew there'd be no shortage of people willing to take pot shots at anything alien, and the *Turtle* was truly alien.

The Air Force captain looked over his shoulder at the shrouded body lying on the floor. The junior officer of the team, Lieutenant Victor Croft, had given his all in the battle. Victor's actions had saved Richard and enabled their final victory over the eight-foot-tall enemy commander.

Captain Allison turned his attention back to the city.

In the *Turtle's* roomy first floor, he stood between the ship's three-foot-wide center column and the four-foot-tall control panel that lay halfway to the *Turtle's* forward perimeter.

His fingers danced over the pedestal's concave glass surface. The commands activated a room-spanning hologram. A vortex of swarming pixels coalesced into a three-dimensional rendering of the city and its surrounding topology. Richard's upper body protruded above the hologram like a man wading through an ocean of sand.

In the image, a miniature version of Sunrise Mountain stood on his right, well east of the airport. To the west, the steep, jagged cliffs of Red Rock Canyon National Conservation Area framed the left side of the display. Rendered in various colors that signified elevation and differentiated man-made from natural features, the display made the long runways and low military buildings of Nellis Air Force Base easily identifiable.

With his index finger pressed to thumb, Richard reached into the hologram with his right hand. Touching the center of the holographic rendering of the Base's runway complex, he spread his fingers apart. As it would with a multi-touch smartphone display, the gesture magnified the image. The airfield expanded. The enlarged rendering clearly showed individual runways and taxiways.

Richard made a rotating gesture, and the display spun one hundred and eighty degrees, bringing Alpha ramp to the forefront. Spotting his desired landing zone, Richard extended his index finger and poked it into the virtual tarmac. The double click of an oilcan pop echoed through the fifty-foot-wide interior. Concentric rings radiated across the hologram from his point of touch.

Now that the autopilot's approach was programmed, Richard shut off the display. The pixels fell to the floor and faded away.

Looking through the *Turtle's* uni-translucent forward view-wall, he watched Vegas's ocean of sparkling lights spool under the ship. Named because of its distinctive shape, the *Turtle* was roughly sixty feet wide and thirty feet tall. Girdling its widest point, a horizontal, three-foot-thick bulge ringed the entire ship, delineating its flat-bottomed bowl of a belly from its domed top.

The *Turtle* had three interior levels. An airlock formed the only traversable portion of the belly. Above that, the main floor spanned the entire interior width of the ship. Only a closet-sized airlock access and the central column interrupted its open space.

Additional features—like the now present control pedestal—emerged from the floor's networked ocean of nanobots on an as-needed basis.

The ceiling ten feet overhead formed the floor of the utilitarian upper deck. The vertical walls of the main floor tied into the pointed dome that formed the walls and ceiling of that top level.

From behind the control panel, Richard looked up at the ten-foot ceiling and then back at the shrouded body behind him. It seemed like a lifetime had passed in the hours since Jake, Victor, and he had stood under that upper deck's uni-translucent dome watching the Moon's desolate surface scroll under the *Turtle*.

When all hell had broken loose, they had been on an orientation flight around the Moon. Richard had taken them to its far side to demonstrate the *Turtle's* speed and capabilities. Having watched Earth pass peacefully behind the Moon's limb, they'd had no idea that when next they saw the planet, an alien armada would be bearing down on it, preparing to launch an apocalyptic attack.

Richard stared at Lieutenant Croft's shrouded body. "Sorry I was such an asshole, Victor."

Thrust into combat, nervous almost to the point of cowardice, the young lieutenant proved courageous in the end. During the final battle, Victor had saved Richard from certain death and sacrificed his own in the process.

Captain Allison shook his head. "Thanks, asshole. I treat you like shit, and you go and save my life."

Colorful lights cascaded through the *Turtle's* interior, drawing Richard's attention outside.

He sighed and turned back to the control console.

Below, the brilliant Las Vegas Strip passed under the ship. Ahead, the Base's runway complex slid into view.

"Nellis Tower, Turtle One has the landing zone in sight. I'll be on the ground in about five seconds."

"Roger, Turtle One. I still don't have you on radar or visual. I ... wait ... holy shi—" the controller cut out mid-word. Then he returned. "Uh ... Turtle One, you're clear to land."

Illuminated by myriad vehicles and portable light towers, the designated section of ramp glowed as if a midsummer sun shone on it. Richard cast a final glance at his fallen comrade. He nodded toward the front. "There's your welcoming party, Lieutenant."

Extending the landing gear, the captain flared the ship and executed a perfect touchdown in front of the airmen and their small fleet of support vehicles.

Through the view-wall he recognized several of the personnel from the Area 51 underground hangar facility that usually housed the *Turtle*.

"Nellis Tower, thanks for your assistance. I'll see you on the way back out."

"Roger," replied the tower controller in an awed voice.

Richard shut down the *Turtle's* systems. With a final glance at Victor's shrouded body, he walked to the airlock. Stepping in, he heard the soft, static noise accompanying the closing of the door behind him. After the airlock had lowered him into the belly with no apparent movement, a rectangular section of the exterior skin vaporized with the same sound.

Richard squinted into the flickering, multicolored blinding light streaming into the small space.

Beyond the opening, two security police sergeants in full dress uniform waited with an ambulance stretcher. At its center sat a folded US flag. In the moments he'd taken to shut down the *Turtle,* the remaining personnel had fallen into two groups facing each other across a five-foot-wide path that led from the ship's airlock to the waiting ambulance. Each officer, sergeant, and airman stood at rigid attention.

One of the police sergeants commanded, "Present arms!"

In unison, the gathered military personnel saluted.

Standing at attention, Richard returned the salute. "At ease."

They lowered their hands. However, everybody remained at attention.

Understanding, Richard waved the two SP sergeants forward, gesturing into the airlock. "This way, Sergeants."

Breaking from their rigid posture, they grabbed the stretcher and rolled it into the *Turtle*. Richard followed them.

A few seconds later, now on the *Turtle's* main deck, the sergeants stepped to the side of the lieutenant's body.

After staring at the seamless silver foil that enshrouded the young lieutenant, the two men exchanged concerned glances. Then they gave Richard a questioning look.

"That's pretty thin foil, sir," said the one to Richard's right. "It's not going to hold."

"It'll hold," Richard said flatly. He took the folded flag off of the litter.

"Is it Mylar, sir?"

"Something like that," he said impatiently.

The medics exchanged glances again. Finally, they bent over and grabbed the corners of the nanobot-formed body bag. After a tentative pull had proved it wouldn't tear, the sergeants lifted Victor over the stretcher. Then they gently lowered him into the US Air Force standard-issue body bag resting on its white sheets.

With respectful reverence, the sergeant by the lieutenant's foot began zipping the black body bag closed.

Richard and the other sergeant saluted.

As the zipper neared the end of its travel, something moved inside the bag.

Both of the medics jumped back.

The nanobots that had formed the foil shroud streamed through the narrow, puckered opening at the top of the zipper. Undulating like a mercurial python, the silvery snake flowed back into the floor's nanobot matrix.

Both sergeants stared wide-eyed as the bots merged with the floor.

Richard lowered his salute and handed the mute men the flag. Following his lead, both snapped out of their trances.

After zipping the bag closed, the sergeants stood at attention. With military precision, they unfolded the US flag. Standing at opposite ends of the litter, they held Old Glory taut a foot over Victor's body.

Richard saluted again. "Thank you for your sacrifice, Lieutenant. I, hell, the whole world owes you a great debt."

As if in slow motion, the flag drifted down. A moment later, it covered the entire body bag. The two security police officers adjusted it until the red and white stripes ran straight and the corners presented square angles.

After a silent pause, the medics rolled the ambulance stretcher into the airlock.

Richard joined them.

A few seconds later, they exited the ship. As they emerged into the stark lights, someone yelled, "Present arms!"

Again, the rigid right hand of every person snapped to their brows. In respectful silence, the officers and airmen held the salute as the two sergeants rolled Victor's flag-draped corpse down the makeshift aisle.

Standing in the ship's opening, Richard held his salute until the sergeants pushed the stretcher into the back of the waiting ambulance and closed the doors.

The vehicle pulled away from the formation. A captain near the front shouted, "Order arms!" Snapping their right hands back to their sides, each person returned to attention. Then the officer commanded, "Forward, face!" Simultaneously, the half to Richard's right executed a left-face, while the group on his left executed a right-face.

"Present arms!" shouted the officer that stood opposite Richard.

With an audible crack, a hundred impeccably rendered salutes regarded Captain Richard Allison. Not a single dry eye peered from the assembled personnel. Few actually knew the lieutenant, but all of them obviously took his loss hard.

Richard realized the sight of Victor's flag-draped corpse served as a symbol for everything the Zoxyth had taken that day, the untold millions of vaporized bodies, their emptied garments strewn about population centers across the globe.

The image wavered as Richard shed silent tears.

Standing at attention, he returned their salute. Making a point to look each airman and officer in the eye, Richard nodded at those he knew. Behind their tears, he saw another emotion take root.

With apparent pride and even admiration, every man and woman looked directly at him.

Their veneration made him uncomfortable. He didn't deserve it.

Richard lowered his hand, self-consciously looking down.

The same officer said, "Order arms!"

Richard looked up and said, "At ease." This time everyone relaxed.

He stepped from the airlock and the organized assemblage collapsed on him, the swarm of cheering men and women nearly tackling him.

"What the hell?"

"You don't know, sir?" said a sergeant from his Area Fifty-One ground crew, his voice barely audible above the din.

"Know what?"

"You're a worldwide hero!" he said pounding Richard's shoulder. "All three of you. Well, they don't know your names yet, but it's all over the news."

"I'm no hero," Richard said softly. He shook his head. "Wait, how could the news networks know anything about what we did? What did you hear?"

"We didn't hear it, sir. We saw it. An observatory on the East Coast was piping a live feed from its telescope to the news channels." He slapped Richard on the back. "It was a little blurry, but the moment we saw something slide from behind that enemy ship, we knew it was the *Turtle*. Those bastards were still firing their lasers, but you guys slipped right in. You should have heard the cheers. After a while, the lasers stopped, but we were on pins and needles until we saw you pull away an hour later." The tech sergeant slapped Richard's shoulder again. "Great job, sir!"

In stunned silence, Richard absorbed the sergeant's words. He scanned the crowd, studying their proud, eager faces.

Uncomfortable, he looked at the sergeant and shook his head. "I'm no hero," Richard repeated softly.

After a moment, he sighed and winked at the tech sergeant. "Fuck it. Let's get this show on the road."

A smile chased away the sergeant's uneasy look.

Richard raised his voice. "We've got a lot of work to do, folks. Let's get this thing loaded up."

The group's excited chatter ceased, and everyone nodded soberly.

Richard pointed at the *Turtle*. "I want the entire top floor filled with supplies." He turned to Airman Johansson, the team's medical specialist. "Make sure we have a full complement of med supplies. Plan to support at least a hundred personnel for two weeks. That should be enough for now."

The airman nodded. Saluting smartly, he turned and departed.

Richard addressed the sergeant in charge of logistical support. "Load up enough food and miscellaneous supplies for the same number."

The sergeant snapped a quick salute and headed off with his subordinates in tow.

The remaining personnel constituted *Turtle* ground support. Richard turned and addressed them en masse.

"Well, folks, you guys know your jobs," he reached over and patted the dark, light-absorbing skin. "Run your diagnostics. Make sure our baby is ready for the next flight. And make sure all of our little nanobots are happy. I'm heading upstairs to get out of this." He gestured at his spacesuit and cocked an eyebrow. "I'm going to change back into my flight suit. So, unless you want an eyeful, I suggest you wait to check that floor until *after* I come down."

"Can we go a little faster, sir?" Captain Jake Giard said.

"I'm trying to look non-threatening," Colonel Newcastle said. "I know the carrier is unmanned, but it might have a fail-safe defense system."

Jake nodded. "Fair enough." He had seen the ship's lasers in action. He was in no hurry to have his body reduced to its constituent atoms.

Looking for a way to board the Galactic Guardian, he and the colonel continued to work their way aft. The carrier's starfighters had deployed from that area.

As they approached the stern of the mammoth ship, Colonel Newcastle oriented the nose of the space fighter toward the ship's surface. The empty Argonian ship filled the fighter's forward field of view. Its aft end slid into view overhead.

"Figured I'd give us a better view of its skin. Maybe we'll spot an access hatch. How are you doing back there?"

"Actually, sir, I'm getting a bit nervous. I'm not sure that pointing our guns into the carrier's center of mass is in spirit with the whole looking non-threatening thing." Jake tried to shift his position. "Otherwise, aside from not being able to feel my legs, I'm not too bad."

"Oh shit," Newcastle said. He pushed the fighter's nose away from the carrier. Now the ship's black skin scrolled overhead with the fighter's nose pointing in the direction of flight.

Jake managed a smile. "Hopefully, somebody left a door open for us. Once we find it, I'm sure there'll be plenty of legroom in there."

He didn't even know if they could get aboard the *Guardian*. And if he did manage that small feat, he didn't know if it could remotely control the other vessels. However, as the fleet's largest ship, it seemed a good place to start.

They didn't know if other Galactic Defense Forces were inbound, much less additional enemy ships. The same unknowns had driven Jake to lead Richard and Victor on that last-ditch effort to defang the sculpted asteroid. After it had killed Lieutenant Croft, the enemy commander fled deeper into the vessel. Ultimately, Jake tracked down and killed the bastard, stopping its systematic destruction of the emptied Argonian ships and attaining a measure of revenge.

Beyond the tragedy of its lost crew, the GDF fleet represented a crucial asset. If Earth's militaries could gain control of it, they might stand a chance against further Zoxyth attacks.

The colonel slapped Jake's jutting knee and pointed through the fighter's canopy. "It looks like we're almost to the back of the ship."

The long, thin carrier had a pointed bow and a wide stern, giving it a wedge-shaped aerodynamic appearance.

Just like the *Turtle*, the skin of the huge ship absorbed starlight, earthshine, and almost all of the sunshine that fell upon its surface. The effect gave the impression they were flying over a hole in space. However, a new, closer horizon now appeared ahead. In the direction of flight, more stars became visible as the squared-off stern began to slide into view.

As Newcastle rounded the back of the massive Argonian carrier, a huge opening came into view.

"Yes!" Jake said.

As they continued drifting aft, a second opening appeared to the right of the first. The small portion of the interior that he could see at the oblique angle gave the impression of a vast hangar facility.

Inside, Jake saw dozens of landing pads and several structures. Spread throughout, pieces of apparent ancillary equipment still sat waiting for the fighters to return.

Jake pointed over the colonel's shoulder. "It looks like we should be able to fly right in." After a brief pause, he added, "As long as one of your hypothetical self-defense laser batteries doesn't vaporize us at the slightest misstep."

Colonel Newcastle nodded. "We'll try not to look too menacing. Let's give it a shot." Decelerating, he maneuvered the space fighter toward the center of the left bay door.

As they neared it, the hangar opening slowly expanded to fill the forward field of view, gradually eclipsing the stars visible around the ship.

Just as Jake was about to say they were in, the ship bounced back. Aside from the visual change, he did not sense the course reversal. The fighter's gravity drive isolated their inertia, preventing them from perceiving the vector change. The small fighter's hull creaked in protest but otherwise seemed undamaged.

"I thought that might happen," Colonel Newcastle said. "The

Argonians probably have a system in place that prevents non-Argonian equipment from entering."

Jake nodded. While he had hoped for the best, he'd suspected the same thing.

He looked down to the fighter's lower right. "I've got an idea." Pointing, he said, "The hangar floor extends outside of the force field. See? It forms a lip below us. I'll bet there's a gravity field generated on it."

"Yeah, but how's that going to help?"

Jake pointed to his chest. "I'm wearing an Argonian spacesuit. Hopefully, it has IFF built into it," Jake said referring to the US military's ubiquitous Identify Friend or Foe computer transceivers. They prevented friendly fire … most of the time.

It was then that Jake noticed that laser cannons adorned all four corners of each bay door, all eight of which appeared to be aimed at the space fighter.

Not wanting to point, Jake said, "Um, sir, I think your slow approach was a good idea. Take a look at the corners."

"What cor …? Oh shit."

"Well," Jake said. "We're still alive. So far, so good."

Newcastle nodded. "Hopefully, their computer remembers that we were an ally during the battle."

"From your lips to God's ears," Jake said. "Mind lifting the lid, sir?"

Newcastle turned halfway toward Jake and gave him the fisheye again. "Are you sure about that, Captain?"

Jake nodded.

After a long pause, Colonel Newcastle nodded as well. Then he grabbed something off of the far panel. "Take this." He passed a handheld radio back to Jake. "Keep it as a backup. It probably has greater range than your suit radio. Try to find a way to drop the hangar bay's force field. Otherwise, you're going to have to do this on your own."

Taking the radio, Jake nodded.

"Deploy your suit's helmet," Newcastle said. "I'm going to pump the air out."

"Go ahead, sir. It activates automatically."

Newcastle shrugged his shoulders. After donning his spacesuit helmet, he pressed a button.

In spite of the assurances he'd given the colonel, Jake held his breath.

A hiss superimposed over the popping in his ears. Then the clear dome of his helmet flowed into position like a reverse time-lapse video of melting ice.

Jake released the breath. Then he stuck the radio to his right hip. The suit's intuitive nanobots held it like velcro. It stuck next to the pistol he still carried. The empty shotgun he'd used to kill the Zox commander was on the *Turtle* with Richard.

All sound followed the atmosphere out of the cockpit. Newcastle's voice shattered the deafening silence as it blared over the suit-to-suit radio. "Well, son." He paused, gesturing to the nearest laser turret. "Don't come crying to me if that thing zaps you into a pile of smoking ash."

Jake grinned sardonically. "Thanks, sir. I'll try to remember that."

Colonel Newcastle's reflection smiled. Then the canopy shot open.

Both Jake and the colonel twitched.

Fortunately, the laser had not.

"Son of a bitch!" Newcastle said. "I really need to talk to the engineers about slowing that down a bit."

Jake climbed over the colonel. Since the fighter had its own gravity well, Jake easily climbed out of the cockpit and onto the small craft's smooth titanium skin. As before, its internal gravity caused him to start sliding toward the edge. However, this time Jake didn't fight it. He let the slide take him over the precipice.

When he reached it, the Argonian ship's gravity field took over. He landed firmly on his feet.

Casting a wary eye at the nearest laser turret, Jake turned and gave the colonel a thumbs-up.

As the fighter's canopy lowered, Newcastle returned the gesture.

Taking a moment to enjoy the view, Captain Giard nervously inched toward the ledge's rear edge. Standing as close as he dared, Jake braced himself against the fighter and craned his neck. Peering down, he looked at the Atlantic Ocean two hundred miles below his feet.

As Jake had learned all too well, if he stepped from this stationary ledge, he'd fall straight down.

A chill ran up his spine. His heart pounded out an echoing cacophony audible over his rasping breath.

He shifted his gaze up, to the top of the planet. Ahead of him, beyond the horizon, lay the north pole. To his front left, the southern tip of the snow-covered island of Greenland cut a jagged white notch into the arcing blue horizon. On his lower left lay the east coast of North America. To his lower right, Spain, the Strait of Gibraltar, and North Africa finished the image. To his distant right, across a couple of hundred thousand miles of space, the Moon peeked from behind the back corner of the massive ship.

"Anytime now, Captain."

Jake nodded and waved his free hand—his other still had a death grip on the edge of the fighter.

After a cautious backward step, he released it. He was almost surprised that his fingers hadn't left indentions. Jake flexed blood back into them.

Turning from the panorama, he walked toward the hangar's opening.

As he approached the point where the force field had blocked the fighter, he extended two querying hands.

Squinting his eyes, Jake spotted the membrane. Barely perceptible, a thin, milky film stretched across the bay door. His gloved hands passed through it without resistance.

Flickering electrical discharges formed a ring around each finger and then his hands.

In spite of the suit's protection, Jake felt a pressure differential across the plane of the force field.

He pulled his hands out. Stepping back from the paper-thin membrane, he shook his head. Somehow the force field held back the massive atmospheric pressure applied across its significant surface area without deforming. It was a perfectly flat plane.

Holding his hand at eye-level, he studied its metallic covering. It looked normal. The force field hadn't damaged his spacesuit.

"My hands passed through the force field. There's atmosphere on the other side," Jake said over the radio. "Now's as good a time as any. I'm going to try to step through."

"Roger. Call me back from the other side." After a chuckle, he added, "If it doesn't fry you to a cinder."

Turning his back to the colonel, Jake waved. "Thanks again, sir."

He faced the opening. After a brief pause, he took a deep breath.

"Here goes nothing."

CHAPTER 4

"Admiral, all ships report battle-ready," said the *Helm Warden's* tactical officer.

Admiral Ashtara Tekamah gave her a single nod then returned his attention to the display. He studied the holographic rendering of his fleet and the rapidly approaching star system.

He shook his head. There were too many damned unknowns.

Sector 64 had gone dark, and now the Chuvarti system in Sector 19 had followed suit.

"I hate blindly flying into a potential battle!" he said for the third time.

In his EON's virtual vision, Tekamah toggled Admiral Feyhdyak's icon. "Any contact with your bio-half?"

An hour earlier, the computer-based portion of the commander he'd sent to intercept the Zoxyth fleet in Sector 64, Admiral Thoyd Feyhdyak, had informed him of a loss of continuity. He reported they had been seconds from dropping into Earth space when the disconnect occurred.

"Nothing yet, sir," computer-based Thoyd said. His synthetic voice had a panicked edge. Disconnected intelligences usually did.

As a combat commander, Ashtara communed with disjointed

personalities all too often. They always seemed on the verge of panic, as if the time separated from their organic id would lead to irreparable psychosis.

Tekamah knew it wasn't an idle concern.

Long term, untethered parallel existence could create a permanent schizophrenic duality. It happened, and the longer the separation, the rougher the reconnect. Bonding with a fresh, tank-grown body was easier than re-merging with a divergent copy. He'd seen relief in the virtual face of more than one computer-based personality when they'd discovered their bio-half had indeed died.

The practice of placing copies of combat personnel into the network began for the obvious reasons. To prevent that duality, they had dedicated a percentage of each ship's nanoscale wormhole communication link to enable real-time galaxy-wide connections between network-based and organic-based ids. Otherwise, the loss of continuity rendered one merely a copy.

If a person's body died while connected to its computer-based self, his or her stream of consciousness continued without disruption. Their consciousness remained intact within the network.

If someone died during a period of disconnection, the individual experienced true death. The portion of their id residing within the network continued as a separate person.

An earth-based Argonian from the 1970s or 80s would ask, *Is it live, or is it Memorex?*

Computer-based Thoyd's virtual eyebrows hoisted higher. "I've consulted with my subordinates. None of them have heard from their bios either." Feyhdyak's panicked tone matched his rendered face. "What do you think happened, Ashtara?"

"Calm down, Thoyd," Tekamah said. He'd known the man for over a century. Ashtara found Thoyd's uncharacteristic trepidation disconcerting, corrosive to his own calm.

"I'm sure there is a reasonable explanation," Tekamah said. "You were still in parallel-space. The Zox don't have anything that could touch you there."

Admiral Feyhdyak's avatar looked ready to say more, but Tekamah held up a virtual hand. "Thoyd, I have to go. We're approaching Chuvarti. Hang in there, friend. I'll let you know as soon as I hear anything."

Thoyd nodded.

Ashtara closed the connection.

He turned to the communications officer. "Have we received any further distress calls from the Chuvarti system?"

"No, sir, nothing since the initial call. It's fortunate we were so close to Sector Nineteen."

Tekamah nodded, but he knew fortune had nothing to do with it. The intel he'd received placed half of Thrakst's fleet in this sector, while the other half had deployed to the far side of the galaxy, to remote Sector 64. He had a nagging feeling there was more to this situation than met the eye.

"Place all battlecruisers on a weapons-free status," ordered Tekamah. "All fighter squadrons are to launch as soon as we drop out of parallel-space. If we're flying into a trap, I want the Zoxyth to regret it."

He studied the fisheye lens of the squeezed star field in front of the formation. The fleet's superluminal speed compressed all light from the front half of the visible universe into a sphere Tekamah could cover with a hand held at arm's length. The light of the stars to aft traveled too slowly to catch up with the ship, rendering a virtual black hole of the rest of the universe. Brightest at its center due to the Doppler-shifted starlight, the fisheye faded at its edges, shifting through the visible spectrum like a round rainbow, finally dwindling to red and infrared at its periphery.

A tiny, bright blue point at the fisheye's center, the planet Chuvarti, grew into a discernible sphere as the fleet closed.

The navigation officer broke the silence. "Normal space in three, two—"

The undersized Zoxyth crewmember nervously peered at Thrakst from behind the communications console, unease evident in the way his dark green, horn-shaped ears folded flat against his scaled skull.

The razor-sharp talons of Lord Thrakst's right hand curled into a fist. "What is it?" he roared.

That a communications officer cowered before him came as no surprise—after all, the pitiful excuse of a Zoxyth had chosen a non-combatant position—but Thrakst couldn't abide weakness in any form.

"No response from Commodore Salyth, my Lord."

With lithe fluidity, Lord Thrakst's massive bulk exploded from the cool embrace of the carved black-rock throne and flashed across the damp stone floor of the *Tidor Drof* bridge. Sliding to a stop, he allowed the mottled gray-green scales of his forearm to graze the idiot's neck, grinning internally as the coward flinched away from a retaliatory blow that didn't land.

Raising the forearm to eye level, Lord Thrakst watched its black, razor-sharp dewclaw talon extend and retract, the underlying muscles of his huge arm rippling its sheath of dark scales. Shifting his focus beyond the claw's gleaming sable edge, he glared at the visibly shaking officer.

In spite of his evident unease at the Lord's proximity, the officer held his ground and repeated his report. "Commodore Salyth has not replied to our calls," he swallowed hard, "my Lord."

At least the fool stood his ground. Had he not, Thrakst would've used his dewclaw talon to relieve the junior officer's shoulders from the burden of carrying the idiot's head.

After a moment of silent menace, Thrakst retracted the talon and returned to his high-backed, black cathedra. Dropping his enormous bulk into the dark throne, he said, "This is *our* day. I will deal with Commodore Salyth later."

To the right of Lord Thrakst, his long-time friend and confidant, Raja Phascyre, growled. The deep rumble rattled through the wizened warrior's massive chest. Turning his scarred face to Thrakst, the Raja grinned. However, the expression didn't reach his sole eye. In the mixed tones of the Zox language, Phascyre's voice rumbled and screeched as he whispered, "I don't trust Salyth. Too eager to ascend, that one."

Thrakst nodded. "His silence concerns me as well."

The Raja's smile evaporated. "I told you he thought his time had come. I fear he has overreached, my Lord." Looking forward, he said, "You should've let me take the hatchling down a notch when I offered."

Nodding again, Lord Thrakst turned from Phascyre and scanned the bridge. Images of his fifteen dreadnoughts filled monitors across the bridge of the *Tidor Drof*. The first fourteen asteroidal vessels had already completed their attack. Displayed on monitors across the cavernous room, they lifted from the planet, hammering vertically through the thinning atmosphere, a roiling trail of superheated plasma in their wake.

Thrakst turned his attention to the primary display. The fifteenth dreadnought hovered over the last target, blocking most of the Argonian settlement from view. As with the *Tidor Drof*, the dreadnought's intimidating bulk came from its collection of massive ferrite asteroids held together by enormous trusses and iron works. Matching the rest of the fleet's ships, a grinning face glared from the vessel. Chiseled into the likeness of a Zoxyth Forebearer, an arena-sized head with an Argonian skull clenched in its jaw formed the dreadnought's bridge.

Modified to provide living space and moist, breathable air, the multilevel interior of the giant, hollowed-out iron boulders felt like the home world. The zoxaformed environment rendered the decks of the asteroid an adequate simile of Zoxa's huge caves and humid atmosphere.

Thrakst's steel-reinforced talons scratched longingly at the wet floor. Its slimy surface reminded him of home. Studying the layer of green algae covering the cathedra's armrest, he thought of all the blood spilled in the fruitless war with the Argonians.

After the loss of his wife and son—a loss that Thrakst blamed on Admiral Tekamah—he had sworn to avenge them.

Even when the High Council had ordered him to withdraw back into Zoxyth space, he'd struck at the heart of the enemy. But the GDF quickly reversed his early victories. Star systems started falling back into enemy hands.

However, in spite of the loss of all but the last thirty-two dreadnoughts, victory now lay within Thrakst's reach.

As the first phase of the two-pronged attack drew to a close, the Zox dreadnought that currently dominated the image presented on the primary display prepared to deal the final deathblow to this colony. The events to follow should bring the Argonians to their scrawny knees.

All Zoxyth would soon be home, especially if Salyth had realized the same level of success in Earth space as Thrakst anticipated in Chuvarti's.

The Lord cast a sideways glance at his old friend.

As if reading his mind, the Raja said, "I hope the hatchling didn't squander his opportunity."

Through Phascyre's words, Thrakst saw something disturbing flicker across the warrior's face. It almost looked like hope.

"We should fallback, my Lord."

Thrakst froze. "What?"

The Raja pointed at the main display. "We're all but finished with this world, my Lord. The Argonians may have discovered a defense for this weapon."

Recovering, Thrakst laughed. "If I didn't know you better, old friend, I'd think you afraid."

The Raja bristled at the Lord's suggestion, his ears standing fully erect.

Thrakst raised a hand. "Calm yourself, my friend. You are a wise warrior. However, we have come too far to stop now."

Phascyre's ears lowered a shade, but he continued to glare at Thrakst.

"The coordinated timing of our and Salyth's attacks, as well as the measures we took to suppress communications in both systems, have made it impossible for the GDF to formulate a defense against this weapon."

"The Galactic Defense Forces should be here soon. I guarantee you, Tekamah knows nothing. See for yourself," Thrakst said as he gestured at the ships portrayed across the bridge's video displays. "Even if Salyth attacked too soon, even if he failed, the Argonians in this sector did not know of our weapon."

The thought of the coming battle had Thrakst's salivary glands churning. The pointed tip of the Lord's black tongue dabbed frenetically at his dripping silver fangs.

His eyes twitched from the dreadnought to the tactical display.

Standing, Thrakst raised his voice. "Speaking of the saraph, where is Tekamah?"

"No sign yet, my Lord," replied another officer.

"I hope he gets here soon. I wouldn't want him to miss out on all this," Thrakst said with a broad, sweeping gesture toward the main display.

"Lord Thrakst, we're picking up a new distress call from the surface."

"Is it a subspace signal?"

"No, my Lord. We're still jamming all subspace communications," replied the nervous officer.

Lowering his voice, Thrakst turned to the Raja. "The GDF won't know what happened until it's too late," he said through a toothy grin.

He returned his glare to the undersized communications officer. "So *where* is the signal coming from?"

"It is an in-system video message, my Lord."

Thrakst's grin widened, and he sat up on the rocky ledge of his throne. "Show me!"

On the main display the hovering Zoxyth dreadnought disappeared. The image of a disgusting Argonian female with her whining cubs clutching at her skinny legs filled the monitor. The high-pitched whine of the breeder and her whelps abraded his nerves. "What is it saying?" he growled at the communications officer.

After a nervous twitch, the officer entered a couple of commands into his console, and a deep, melodious Zoxyth translation replaced the abhorrent squeaky Argonian voice.

"Oh my Gods! The Zoxyth ship is ... is overhead now!"

Thrakst smiled. "Put this Argonian bitch and her cubs out of their misery," he said coldly.

The tactical officer nodded and forwarded the command. The image of the ship hovering over the settlement returned to the display.

With a brilliant flash, the glorious, cleansing light wave of the genetic disruptor erupted from the dreadnought's bridge.

～

The sphere of stars ahead of Tekamah's ship blossomed two seconds early!

Like a sparkling, circular waterfall streaming from the orb's center, a perfectly symmetrical wave of red-shifted stars expanded across the black dome of space. The racing front quickly encircled the GDF formation. In its diminishing wake, the wave deposited its bounty of stars in their normal positions and usual colors as, no longer outrunning light, the fleet fell into regular space before the scheduled time.

"... one, zero ..." the navigation officer said, finishing his countdown with a confused tone.

Multiple icons within Tekamah's virtual vision shifted to red, half of his awareness falling away as if a laser had cleaved his soul. The expressions crossing the faces of the bridge's complement of officers mirrored Tekamah's feelings. While the men likely thought it a temporary disconnect, the admiral knew better.

Whatever had knocked them out of parallel-space had also closed their communications wormhole.

"Report," Tekamah ordered as he evaluated the data streaming from his few still active EON channels.

"All fighters away," Tactical announced through a bewildered tone.

Tekamah looked at her and shook his head. The information pumped into his EON interface showed that local space was empty. Nothing that could threaten his ship was in the area. "Recall them. We dropped out of parallel-space early. We're still tens of light seconds out. There's no sense in our fighter pilots spending the next hour in their cockpits."

"I don't understand, sir. Why don't we just short-jump our way in from here?"

Considering the loss of communication with Feyhdyak in Sector 64, Tekamah already knew the answer, but he pointed to his navigation officer. "Tell her."

The officer nodded. "There's a Zoxyth fleet here all right, but now I know why we haven't received calls. Someone dropped a subspace picket across the sector. That's why we've lost Omninet connection as well."

The nav officer's face twisted with confusion. Turning to Tekamah, he said, "But sir, that doesn't make sense. Why would we place a disruptor field across the system?"

Tekamah shook his head. "I assure you, we did not."

The subordinate pointed through the view-wall. "It couldn't have been the Zoxs. They don't have that kind of technology."

"Apparently they do now," Tekamah said. "But the biggest question is why would they use it here?"

From behind the tactical console, the other officer said, "If they've gained the tech, it's a fairly standard ploy—"

Cutting her off, Tekamah pointed at the helmsman. "No, he was right the first time, it doesn't make sense. Once the Zoxyth fleet knew they had a big enough head start, they made no secret of their destination. Hell, a first-year Academy student could've tracked them here. So why wouldn't they want us to see their attack on our outpost? With that much lead time, they could've finished the attack and jumped back out of the system before we arrived. As we blazed toward the system at top parallel-space speed, still unable to intervene, why wouldn't they want us to receive subspace messages from colonists begging for our help?"

Through narrowing eyes, Tekamah studied the distant planet. *What are you up to, Thrakst?*

47

CHAPTER 5

T he pressure differential made stepping through the barrier feel like slipping into a vertical pool of water. First, Jake's right arm and his left leg penetrated the force field. Then his visored face pressed into its surface, the flickering light of the accompanying static discharges glowing red through his closed lids. Finally, the rest of his body passed through the membrane.

He'd made it! He was inside.

Jake stopped. The bay's illumination appeared brighter in here than it had through the force field. More light than he'd expected burned through his squinting and blinking eyes.

Jake twitched as the suit's helmet retracted into the neck ring with startling suddenness. Realizing he'd been holding his breath, he tentatively sipped the air. Other than a faint ozone odor, it smelled and tasted normal.

His eyes slowly adjusted to the increased luminosity. Jake looked back at the hangar's force field. It must limit the amount of interior energy allowed to bleed into space. That's why it had looked darker in here from out there.

The opening through which Jake had passed was roughly sixty feet tall by ninety feet wide. Almost eight stories overhead, the entire surface of the ceiling beyond the bay door glowed, providing the hangar's illumination. Where ceiling met wall sixty feet to his left or port, a gently curving radius joined the perpendicular surfaces. The ceiling's glow faded out halfway through the transition. Beneath it a collection of white rectangular panels with their short ends on top and bottom like vertically oriented bricks formed the left wall. A thin gap between each panel created a grid pattern that foreshortened like railroad tracks as they continued to the back of the huge hangar. The back wall appeared to be about two football fields away, deeper into the ship.

A path or taxiway cut through the center of the wide hangar, apparent landing decks lining both sides all the way to the back. Several pieces of equipment sat next to many of the pads. Spacecraft of varying designs remained on some of them.

Jake didn't see exits along either of the side walls. Focusing his attention on the far end, he saw something that might be a door. He turned and looked back through the rear hangar opening. Silhouetted against Earth, Newcastle's fighter now hovered two hundred yards aft of the carrier.

"I'm in, sir," Jake said. When Newcastle didn't respond to the suit radio, Jake pulled the handheld radio from his hip. He pressed the side-mounted transmit key. "How do you read me on this radio, sir?"

"Not very well, Captain," the colonel replied, his voice distant, barely discernible above the radio's background static. "I copied all, but be advised, you're coming in extremely weak."

"Got you the same, sir." Jake pointed behind him. "I think there's an opening in the far wall." He scanned the perimeter of the large hangar door. "I don't see anything that looks like a control panel on this end. I'm going to head forward and see if I can find a way to let you in here."

"Keep me up to date," Newcastle said. "In the meantime, I'm trying to buy us some time. My pilots are using their ships to marshal the farthest fighters. Like a bunch of space cowboys trying to regroup a herd, they're *gently* bumping and pushing them back toward the formation," he said, emphasizing "gently".

Jake keyed the radio and waved his left arm. "Roger, sir, good idea. I'll try to keep you up to date, but I doubt the radio signal will get any better. The back wall is quite a way into the ship. What are your orders if I don't find anything there?"

"Continue your search. If you haven't found anything within an hour, return to the hangar and check in."

He snapped a quick salute. "Yes, sir."

Turning, Jake started jogging toward the back and stumbled over something on the floor. Looking down, he stared into the face of an empty spacesuit. He'd missed it earlier. The floor was the same milky, metallic color as the garment. Jake looked around and spotted several additional articles haphazardly strewn about the expansive hangar. Some were gathered around the pieces of equipment, while others appeared to have been cut down mid-step while crossing the hangar.

Looking at the poignant reminder of the day's tragic losses, Jake shook his head. "Fuck!" An involuntary shudder ran through him. Dragging his eyes from the faceless victim, he resumed his trek to the back of the hangar. En route, he passed the few remaining ships. The first couple looked like the sleek fighter versions of the *Turtle* that had encircled the enemy fleet before the battle. However, the farthest ship was much bigger. Near the back of the hangar, it was easily fifty feet tall by sixty-five feet wide and three times that lengthwise. All of them had that liquid metal-smooth, light-absorbing skin that he'd first seen on the *Turtle*.

A faint sound froze Jake in his tracks. Had that been a voice? Then it returned. No longer masked by the sound of his shuffling feet, he clearly heard words this time. "...eed to the EON maintenance facility for EON replacement."

Jake snapped his head in the direction from which the voice had issued. It sounded like a woman was calling to him. Barely perceptible, speaking in the Argonian language, it came from somewhere near his destination. He was still about a hundred and fifty feet from the now obvious opening. His spirits rose. However, as Jake drew closer, the voice repeated.

"Your EON is out of service. Please proceed to EON maintenance for EON replacement."

An automated message, it obviously wasn't intended for him.

"Shit." Jake shook his head and continued toward the rear door. A pointed arch framed its tall opening. In the apparent corridor beyond, antiqued bronze surfaces contrasted against the hangar's bright white walls. Pulsing rhythmically, a pair of glowing, green strips streamed down its dark floor, flowing like a river away from Jake.

Louder and more insistent, the automated voice returned. "Your EON is out of service. Please, follow the marker lights to EON maintenance for EON replacement."

"Whatever an EON is," Jake responded in Argonian, "I've got other things to take care of right now, like interfacing with that damn force field." He scanned the area around the opening. Nothing looked like a control console. Remembering the *Turtle's* nanobots, he realized he probably wouldn't be able to see it. Likely, the controls didn't exist until needed. "How do I tell this ship what I need?"

The computer voice answered. "You will be unable to interface with ship systems until your EON is functional. Please follow the marker lights to the EON maintenance facility for EON replacement."

After a shocked pause, Jake whispered, "Okay, you have my attention now." He stared into the incredibly long hallway. Like railroad tracks extending to the horizon, its parallel lines and flashing floor lights extended so deep into the ship that they appeared to converge.

He turned to look outside and toggled the radio. "Vampire Six, I may have found a way to interface with the force field, but I'll have to head deeper into the ship."

Colonel Newcastle's voice came through extremely broken and barely legible. "Roger Capt … you're coming … even weaker now … copied that you … going deeper. If you haven't gained access within … hour, return … check in, over."

"Roger, sir. Captain Giard, out."

Releasing the transmit key, Jake studied the radio for a moment hoping that the colonel had heard him. Shifting his gaze to the distant fighter beyond the force field, he saw it wag left and right. Then it drifted back from the opening and departed, probably to help with the herding efforts.

Now completely alone in the ghost ship, Jake felt another chill creep down his spine. He turned back to the massive hallway's arched opening.

"Your EON is out of service. Please, follow the marker lights to EON maintenance, for EON replacement," the computer repeated, emphasizing "please" with almost human impatience.

Jake resisted the urge to query the computer-animated voice directly, afraid it might ask its own questions, like: 'Who are you, and what the hell are you doing on this ship?'

Instead, he muttered, "I'm going, I'm going."

After a brief hesitation, he shook off the chill and stepped through the opening. The apex of the bronze, pointed arch towered forty-five feet over the twelve-foot-wide doorway. Stepping through brought Jake into a twenty-foot-wide by sixty-foot-tall passageway, the graceful beauty of its architecture reminiscent of a Gothic European cathedral. Fluted casings surrounded the opening. A criss-cross pattern of the same design continued the pointed arch motif down the ceiling of the long hall.

To the limit of Jake's vision, the corridor continued unchanged, tapering to a point like a railroad track, its parallel lines appearing to converge in the distance. Starting a few yards from where he stood and continuing as far as he could see, ornately trimmed openings periodically interrupted the lines of the left and right walls. The moving lights that apparently led to the EON maintenance facility seemed to run to the distant end of the passageway.

"Holy crap," Jake whispered as he considered the length of the ship. Shaking his head, he began jogging, following the light.

As he passed openings, he stole glances into the rooms beyond, wishing he had time to study each. Jake caught glimpses of massive halls, some exceeding the size and grandeur of the Vatican's St. Peter's Basilica. In another room, a massive terrarium featured alien vegetation growing from niches positioned high and low, some even issuing from the ceiling. The sound of falling water accompanied screeches and chirps of unseen fauna, although Jake did glimpse one leathery-winged animal gliding amongst the flora.

As room by room scrolled past, he half-expected Argonian troops to pop out and ask what he was doing on their ship.

As he started to wonder if the hallway ran the entire length of the vessel, the passage of openings accelerated at a pace out of sync with his jog. Jake stopped running, but the rooms continued zipping by him as if the floor moved under his feet or at least the strip upon which he stood. He saw no conveyor, no seam or edge, although the floor's perfectly smooth and featureless surface rendered movement, or lack thereof, indiscernible. Knowing the vast length of the ship, he resolved himself to be drawn into its depths. Adding his own speed to the trek, he began jogging again. Jake hoped it was a two-way street. Otherwise, he'd never make the one-hour check-in.

In the distance, he saw where the moving lights appeared to angle into an opening. Jake broke into a sprint for the distant room. Doorway after doorway zipped past on both sides, too fast to differentiate the contents of the rooms beyond.

Deeper in the ship, it became obvious that some force, not a conveyor belt, propelled him down the corridor. Jake dodged motionless uniforms and alien apparel strewn along his path, the inane clutter still the only evidence of the day's tragedy. Many times he almost tripped as he negotiated areas where the weapon's awful effect had vaporized large groups. More than once he had to peel garments from his lower legs.

Quickly closing the gap, he slid to a stop in front of the doorway through which the lights disappeared. The virtual conveyor halted as well. Jake stood staring into the opening, hopes dashed against the vision of another long corridor.

"Crap!"

Shaking his head, Jake looked back in the direction from which he'd come. The vast distance concealed the bright hangar at the passageway's far end. Jake couldn't even see a white dot where the door had been. Sighing, he turned, his eyes following the flowing lines into the perpendicular hall where a new detail drew his attention. While it appeared that the hallway continued to the far right side of the ship, the lights didn't reach that end. Amidship, they disappeared.

"Your EON is out of service," the obviously impatient computer repeated. Jake tried to detect its source, but the feminine voice seemed to come from everywhere. "Please, follow the marker lights to EON maintenance for EON replacement."

"I'm going," he said, resuming his jog.

In spite of the exertion and the comfortable temperature of the air, a chill ran through Jake as he dodged another pile of empty clothes. Again he abandoned his controlled jog for a sprint. Assisted across the ship's narrower width by the resumed conveyance force, he quickly closed the gap. Ahead, the lights turned left into another opening. Approaching it, Jake reached out for the near side of the doorway, using its fluted trim to brace himself. Releasing it, he slid to a stop in the center of the opening.

He stared into the maw of an empty vertical shaft. The site generated a foreboding déjà vu. Even without a damaged car partially obscuring its door, the elevator shaft reminded Jake of the one they had used to access the enemy's bridge.

Suppressing the dread that threatened to freeze him in his tracks, Jake stepped into the shaft. Unlike its Zoxyth analog, this one had normal gravity. Confused, Jake looked around. Then an invisible force identical to the one in the *Turtle* gripped his lower extremities and lifted him. Accelerating upward, he soon flew in formation with the flowing lights.

The ceiling rapidly approached. Just before he slammed into its solid surface, the metallic panel evaporated. Passing through the opening, he emerged into an empty room. The ceiling-turned-floor rematerialized, and Jake gently landed on its reconstituted surface.

Looking up from his spacesuited feet, Jake whistled his relief. The room's white walls softly glowed. Overhead, the gently arched ceiling formed a flat dome.

Again, the sound of static filled his ears. Worried the floor was dissolving under his feet, Jake leaped to the side, but the sound continued from behind him. He spun around in time to see a table and control panel manifest out of the floor.

"Gotta love those nanobots," Jake said as he stepped up to the pedestal. Multiple arcane controls covered its concave surface. However, one glowed and pulsed with the same color and frequency as the lights that had led him to the room. An Argonian word sat at its base: Activate.

With no other apparent options, he haltingly reached for the control. "Here goes nothing." After a slight hesitation, he toggled it.

Unexpectedly lifting Jake off his feet, an invisible force cocooned his entire body and propelled him across the empty room. Rotating him into a prone position, it drew his rigid body toward the new table. He futilely struggled to free himself from its iron grip.

With mounting horror, Jake felt consciousness slipping from his grasp. "Oh my G—" he began but never finished. The black, velvet-lined abyss of unconsciousness wrapped its icy fingers around Jake and sucked him into its cold embrace.

CHAPTER 6

R ed light flooded the otherwise dark, dank bridge.
"Lord Thrakst, I have multiple targets exiting parallel-space," shouted the communications officer. After a brief pause, he looked up, eyes burning with excitement. "It's the *Helm Warden* and fleet, and they're still ten standard units out, my Lord."

"Just as I planned: perfect timing and distance! The Forebearers smile upon us," proclaimed Thrakst. "Order the fleet to form on the *Tidor Drof* in a standard defensive formation. I will have the head of any commander whose ship takes offensive action!"

"Yes, my Lord," said the communications officer as he bowed deeply.

Turning to the weapons officer, Thrakst growled, "What is the status of the fleet's gene weapons?"

"Lord, eighty percent report recharged and ready for deployment."

With a satisfactory nod, Thrakst returned his attention back to the view-wall.

The gene weapon's only pitfall was its long recharge time. He turned to Raja Phascyre: the wizened Zoxyth warrior posted on his right. "Thank the Forebearers we staggered the attack to preserve our combat readiness. I hope Commodore Salyth had the foresight to implement the same."

The Raja nodded. "As do I, my Lord." He drew a long, raspy breath. "The silence screaming from Sector Sixty-Four makes one wonder."

Shaking his massive head, Thrakst growled through clenched silver fangs. "Don't make me come out to that Forebearer-forsaken corner of the galaxy, Salyth."

"Lord, the *Helm Warden* is trying to hail us on an in-system frequency."

Forgetting Salyth for the moment, Thrakst grinned at Phascyre. "So, they've noticed our subspace jammer." Raising his voice, he turned to the officer. "Do not reply."

"They're also trying to call the planet, my Lord."

"Are they receiving a response?"

The communications officer studied his station. After checking the entire electromagnetic spectrum, he said, "No, my Lord."

Sitting back in his black throne, Thrakst threw his head back and laughed. "The planet is dead, Tekamah. You're too late!" His manic laughter echoed off the cavernous bridge's damp stone walls.

"Admiral, the Zoxyth are not responding to our hails," reported the communications officer.

Tekamah stood from his force field chair. With his EON, he accessed the bridge section's holo-generator. A new holographic rendering of the Chuvarti system coalesced in the air above the elevated bridge section. Following another EON command, the point of view zoomed in, and the planet filled the display. Through the translucent rendering, Admiral Tekamah counted sixteen enemy ships around the globe.

Depicted in red, they streamed from various points above the planet. Scanning the group, he quickly picked out the *Tidor Drof.*

"There you are, Thrakst."

The rest of the enemy fleet moved to take up defensive positions around the bastard's ship—a standard Zoxyth tactic when faced with overwhelming force. Glaring at the gathering enemy formation, Admiral Tekamah said, "What about the planet?"

"Nothing, sir. Aside from a few automated beacons, I'm receiving *no* non-natural transmissions coming from the planet."

"What? That's not possible. Zoxyth never had subspace jamming capability. Even if they do now, jamming the relatively narrow band of subspace is one thing, but the Zoxyth can't jam the entire electromagnetic spectrum."

"No, sir, they're not jamming it. Aside from our fleet's internal radio chatter and the same from the Zoxyth, there are *no* radio transmissions coming from the planet."

Scanning the data streaming through his EON, Tekamah came to the same conclusion.

"Damn it, Feyhdyak," Tekamah whispered to himself. "I could really use a little intel here. This is shaping up just as your last report described."

When he'd received a report that the Zoxyth had split their forces —half to this Sector and the other half to Sector 64—Admiral Tekamah had dispatched a task force headed by Admiral Thoyd Feyhdyak aboard the *Helm Warden's* sister ship, the *Galactic Guardian*. Simultaneously, he'd led the other half of the Galactic Defense Forces here.

Now the *Galactic Guardian* was a day late in reporting back. Their last report had drawn a very similar picture to what now lay before Tekamah.

"Order the fighter squadrons to perform a standard encircling maneuver," Tekamah ordered through his mounting concern. "I want those dreadnoughts boxed in."

"Yes, sir," responded Tactical.

Tekamah monitored the commands as they flowed across the battle network. Manipulating the hologram, he zoomed in on Thrakst's command ship. Shaking his head at the all too familiar sight of the Argonian skull clamped in the Zoxyth's jaw, he panned down to Chuvarti's surface. Over the blue and brown planet's equator, it appeared Thrakst had taken up station, hovering in space directly over the settlement's capital city.

"Maneuver two battlecruisers between the enemy fleet and the city below," the admiral ordered. "If this standoff turns hot, I want it protected from falling asteroids."

Tekamah felt his short hairs standing on end. *Why are they dropping into a defensive position? They reserve that for dire, fight-to-the-death circumstances.*

"Any response from the surface?" he asked again.

"No, sir."

"What areas of the planet have they attacked? The capital looks unscathed."

"None, sir," replied the officer with a confused tone.

"What?" Tekamah asked with matching confusion as he watched the first fighter squadron begin to take up position around the enemy fleet. "That makes no—"

"Admiral! We are receiving a transmission from the surface now," interrupted an officer from the communications console.

"Thank the Gods! Whoever it is, tell them I want this planet's governor on the horn now!"

The officer shifted uncomfortably. "There's a problem, sir."

"What?" Tekamah asked shortly.

"It's better if you see for yourself, sir."

Not waiting for the officer, Tekamah snatched the data stream with his EON and fed it directly into the holoprojector. Expecting to be addressing a military commander or planetary dignitary, he was shocked into silence by the image of a sobbing middle-aged man.

"Who is this?" Tekamah demanded.

Looking like he might collapse, the weeping man only shook his head.

"Son, please calm down," Tekamah said.

The stranger continued shaking his head. Between sobs, he whispered, "They're all dead."

"What? Sir, please. This is Admiral Tekamah of the Galactic Defense Forces. *Who* is dead?"

After the agonizingly long seconds it took the message to make the round trip, the man replied, "They're all dead." Between sobbing gasps, he added, "My family, my coworkers ... everybody. They're all gone." Finally drawing himself up, he said the last part with conviction, anger apparently edging out the man's despair.

"I'm very sorry to hear about your family. What's your name, sir? And what do you mean? How many died; where did it happen?"

As he waited for the light-speed-limited signal, he again wondered how in the hell the Zoxyth had gotten their talons on subspace jamming technology.

Looking down, no longer weeping audibly, the man appeared to be trying to collect himself. In the holographic rendering, only his chin protruded from the parka hood's shadow.

Steadied, the man's voice returned. "My name is Remulkin Thramorus." As his head slowly raised, the distant room's light chased away the hood's shadow. A hate-filled fire burned from the man's holographically rendered eyes.

It was a look Admiral Tekamah knew too well. He took an involuntary step back as his sense of foreboding quadrupled.

"*Everybody* is dead!" he growled. "The whole godsdamned planet has been wiped out. I think the only reason I'm still alive is because of this," he said with a gesture to the walls. "It's an uncharted polar science station. They didn't know I was ... here."

Remulkin swayed mid-sentence. The sound of a tremendous explosion blasted from the display and his holographic image rocked violently.

"The Zoxyth are firing on the planet's northern ice cap," shouted the female officer at the tactical station.

The holographic man shook his head. "Guess they know I'm here now."

"Do we have any ships close enough to cover him?"

The tactical officer also shook her head.

Tekamah saw small rocks falling through the image. Flinching, Remulkin placed an arm over his head.

"Mr. Thramorus, I still don't understand," Tekamah shouted over the din of the Zoxyth attack. "What you're saying doesn't make sense, son. There's no sign of attack anywhere on the planet."

His sense of foreboding and frustration mounted as Tekamah waited for the reply.

Shouting over another barrage of enemy fire, Remulkin said, "All I know was one moment my family was there. Then, after a blindingly bright flash, they were gone. Nothing left but their godsdamned clothes lying empty on the floor ... as if my wife and kids had been ..." Thramorus paused. Tekamah saw and heard the man swallow down a sob, then the holographic man's tortured eyes glared from the image. "As if they'd been ... vaporized."

Tekamah froze: it was only a second, but it was a second that would haunt him for the rest of his days.

The crushing realization of the trap he had sailed into buckled his knees. A seat raised from the floor to catch him, but Tekamah pushed off it, leaping into action.

Turning to his tactical comm, he shouted, "Fall back, fall back, fall back! All units are to break contact with the enemy."

Several officers stared back in bewilderment.

"Now!" he screamed.

Torn from their momentary paralysis, the officers dove into their assignments.

Knowing that the light of the fighters he was looking at was several seconds old, Tekamah feared what may have already happened.

He watched with mounting horror as the message took too long to propagate. The subspace jamming was limiting their communications to the speed of light. The farthest ships, the fighters surrounding the enemy formation, wouldn't get the message for a few more seconds. The sheer size of his fleet and the volume of space it occupied compounded the problem.

Lasers wouldn't help either. They had the same speed of light limitation, couldn't get there any faster than the message, and at this range, they'd barely warm the hulls of the enemy ships.

He could only hope the Zoxyth would hesitate.

CHAPTER 7

A tremendous roar echoed off the wet bridge's stone walls as an infuriated Thrakst blazed across the room, sparks flying from his armored talons. His arm flashed past the tactical officer's neck. Green mist sprayed the adjacent console. Frozen in place, the officer stood motionless.

Turning his back to the fool, Thrakst glared through the view-wall. A leisurely backward kick sent the dead officer's body sailing while his severed head rolled off its shoulders and fell to the floor.

Raising his forearm to eye level, Thrakst flicked out his black tongue. Licking green blood from his retracting talon, he said, "You failed."

The offensive, squeaky voice of the betraying human echoed across the bridge.

"Why am I still hearing that vile thing? Where is that signal coming from?" Thrakst roared.

"It's coming from the planet's closest polar region!" shouted an excited junior officer at the communications console.

"I have it," replied a fierce, older voice from behind Thrakst.

An energy beam shot from the *Tidor Drof*, striking the planet's ice cap.

Thrakst turned back to find his old comrade and friend, Raja Phascyre, had taken over the failed officer's weapons station.

Raja fired again, and another energy beam sought out the damned Argonian.

Thrakst nodded his thanks. "Send him to be with his Gods, Phascyre."

Feeling the element of surprise slipping through his talons, Thrakst turned his attention outside. All of the enemy ships in the magnified view of the *Helm Warden's* arrayed fleet appeared to turn away in unison.

The spread-out waves of enemy fighters occupied several light-seconds of space. From the camera's point of view, the only way all of the ships could appear to turn simultaneously was in response to an order from the *Helm Warden* at the far side of the enemy formation. The image of their response and the radio signal that generated it both radiated through the formation (and toward Thrakst) at the speed of light. Each ship reversed course as soon as they received the order. While they turned in the staggered order caused by their distance from the *Helm Warden* and the speed-of-light-limited transmission, the apparent image of them turning in unison could mean only one thing.

"Tekamah knows!"

Spinning on Commander Phascyre, he shouted, "Fire the gene weapon! Now!"

Phascyre hesitated.

"Now!" Thrakst roared.

Having reversed direction, the enemy squadrons blasted away from his gathered fleet.

"Firing now, Lord," Phascyre said finally. His grizzled hand slammed down on the weapon's activator.

The glorious and cleansing energy wave burst from the *Tidor Drof*, quickly closing on and then enveloping the closest wave of the fleeing cowards.

"Come on!" Admiral Tekamah growled. In the magnified display, he watched the retreat order propagate through the waves of fighters at the agonizingly slow speed of light. Finally, it reached the formations closest to his command ship—2nd and 3rd Squadrons. In sequence, they each instantly reversed direction.

"Thank the Gods."

An eternal second later, the fighters of 1st Squadron also received the order and zipped away from the enemy formation. Before Tekamah could take a breath, a brilliant white sphere of energy exploded from the center of the enemy fleet.

Like the spreading maw of a ravenous monster, the ball of light expanded behind the silhouetted fighters of 1st Squadron. The sphere quickly filled the narrow field of view and became a wall of light. Tekamah issued an EON command. The image zoomed out, and the rendered wave of light returned to its true spherical shape. Like a miniature supernova, the ball of energy continued to swell. An instant later, the monster swallowed 1st Squadron's fighters. Appetite unsated, it reached for the retreating ships of 2nd and 3rd Squadrons. Just as the sphere began to fill the expanded field of view, as it closed on the tiny black silhouettes of the fighters, it faded to black.

The holographic ships continued their mad dash for safety. However, behind them, the green renderings of 1st Squadron began to tumble across the void.

In a dry croak, Tekamah whispered, "No."

A roar echoed off the bridge's stone walls. Falling silent, Thrakst glared at the partial victory manifest across the main display.

Like daggers jabbing into his ears, the Argonian's shrill voice again blared from the radio, shattering the silence. The Lord turned a burning red eye on his weapons officer and growled. "Send *Ancestral Nemesis* to vaporize that planet's pole!"

Turning from the officer, Thrakst dropped into his cathedra and gestured to Raja Phascyre.

As the warrior approached, Thrakst drew him close. "Now Tekamah knows our ability and plans." Pausing, he glared through the display.

The Raja nodded. "Yes, my Lord. They won't let another ship within firing range." Turning from the image of the fleeing enemy ships, Phascyre's sole eye gave Thrakst a questioning look. "What are your orders, my Lord?"

"They won't let us get close," Thrakst said again. Suddenly his eyes widened. "Unless they don't see us coming."

Turning his gaze from the Raja, Thrakst looked into the main display and glared at the magnified image of the *Helm Warden* where it hovered at the far side of the enemy formation. A menacing grin spread across his scaled lips. His black tongue flicked a thin thread of saliva that threatened to drip from a silver fang. For a moment it lingered, probing the tooth with nervous excitement.

Finally, Lord Thrakst nodded. "Raise the *Redeemer*. I need to speak with her commander."

Suddenly, Tekamah felt the familiar presence of his network-based half re-establish its link. At the same time, the Helm Warden's communications officer looked up with wide eyes.

"Admiral, the enemy's disruptor field collapsed."

Before he could digest the news or consider its ramifications, movement in the enemy formation snapped Tekamah out of his trance.

"Admiral, a Zoxyth dreadnought just peeled away from the main formation!" reported the sensor officer. Looking up from his console, he added, "It's headed for the planet's pole!"

"Get a fix on Remulkin's position. I'll be damned if I'm going to let that man die." Not waiting for a reply, he turned from the officer. Knowing the image of movement was a precious light-second old, he activated a direct EON connection with the commander of the battle-cruiser closest to Chuvarti.

When a holographic rendering of the captain materialized in front of him, Tekamah nodded to her. "Commander Bazil, micro-jump to the planet's pole and extract the scientist." Pausing, Tekamah cast a questioning look at his sensor officer. The man tapped a command into his holographic interface and nodded to the Admiral. Ashtara turned back to the battlecruiser's captain. "His coordinates are in your nav computer." He pointed at the red hologram of the enemy ship. "Fire on them the instant you exit parallel-space. Don't give the bastards a chance to fire that weapon."

The commander would have no idea what "that weapon" was, but Tekamah was pleased when she didn't question his order. In spite of her evident confusion, the commander nodded. "Yes, Admiral."

Bazil's holographic visage vaporized. At the same moment, the battlecruiser disappeared from the display, dropping from regular space. For a long second, it was nowhere. Then the image of it over the pole finally reached his sensors.

Tekamah winced as white-hot light from a near source burned through the bridge like an erupting supernova. In spite of the view-wall's auto-dark feature, the blinding light flooding the bridge washed all color from the room, casting everything in monochromatic white.

While the image outside was too brilliant to differentiate, the hologram's sensor told the horrible truth.

The rocky, red holographic rendering of a Zox dreadnought now lay buried in the smooth green lines of one of his battlecruisers. The two ships had melded perpendicularly across their centers like conjoined twins. In the computer-generated image, the Zoxyth dread-nought's rocky protuberances jutted inelegantly from the sides of the sleek battlecruiser.

Outside, the light faded, revealing the grinning, skull-crunching reptilian visage that constituted the dreadnought's bridge.

Tekamah's eyes widened with sudden comprehension. "One of the bastards parallel-jumped into our formation!" he yelled.

Parallel-space travel allowed ships to pass through matter. Traveling in a parallel dimension, they passed through ordinary material with no interaction. Navigators chose jump entry and exit points based on their complete lack of matter. The enemy's uncharted jump had, upon exiting parallel-space, inadvertently placed it in the same real space as the doomed battlecruiser, generating the massive, blindingly bright energy release.

Watching various sections of each ship detonate along the conjoined lines, Tekamah finally recognized the threat posed by the enemy ship's proximity.

"Retreat, retreat, retreat!" the admiral screamed. Fearing that his slow recognition of the enemy's tactic may have cost him everything, Tekamah activated a fleet-wide EON broadcast. "All commanders! Self-execute fallback scenario Alpha! Now!"

Then he followed his own orders. Through a direct EON link, Tekamah activated the *Helm Warden's* parallel-space drive.

Simultaneously, a glowing sphere of energy exploded from the enemy ship.

Tekamah doubled over in agony as the abhorrent, expanding energy wave reached for his command ship.

～

Remulkin Thramorus waited for a final blast or another flash of the enemy's light to take him to be with his family.

So far the science station's hollowed-out mountain peak had proved a durable bunker against the enemy's bombardment. However, the blasts were taking a toll. Many of the prefabricated ceiling and wall panels had been knocked loose. Rock fragments of various sizes and shapes littered the floor of the base.

Looking nervously at the ceiling's recently exposed rock, Remulkin wormed toward his desk, seeking cover. Before he reached the sanctuary, rock the size of a transport calved off the ceiling and crushed the desk. Blinking, Remulkin stared at the jutting corner of the boulder. Its jagged edge lay mere centimeters from his face.

Coughing in the dust-filled air, he tore his eyes from the chunk of mountain. As he glanced warily at the ceiling, another blast shook the station. Fresh cave-ins elsewhere in the station shook the floor under his hands and knees.

Suddenly, a new sound joined the cacophony. Like a giant monster grinding its teeth, creaking and groaning noises emanated from all of the science station's walls.

To Remulkin's right, a prefabricated wall panel cracked and buckled then shot violently from its position. With mounting horror, he watched as a spiderweb of cracks marched across the exposed rock wall.

The station was collapsing!

Discovering that he wasn't ready to die after all, Remulkin jumped to his feet. As he scrambled out of his room, a cloud of dust enveloped him. Another huge section of rock had broken off behind him. The rush of air and dust shoved him forward.

With rocks raining down right and left, he ran toward the station's exit. Detecting his intentions, the smart floor's network of nanobots began to stream into his garments. His bib and parka gained a little more mass as each running footfall permitted a fresh wave of the microscopic robots to board his fleeing form.

Still running, Remulkin was a meter from the exit when the station surrendered to the enemy's onslaught and the planet's gravity. Starting from the deepest section of the compound, the cascading collapse formed an atmospheric pressure wave that shot him through the exit like a cork fired from a pressurized bottle.

He flew through the air. A snow dune cushioned his face-first landing. Remulkin rolled onto his back, brushing ice crystals from his eyes. Looking into the star-filled sky, he saw the silhouette of the enemy ship hovering over the crumbling mountain peak, the irregular lines of its asteroidal shape blotting out the backdrop of scintillating stars.

A dense plume of rock dust radiated out from the mountain's collapse, obscuring the dreadnought. While the billowing cloud blocked his view of the ship, Remulkin knew it offered little protection from Zoxyth sensors. His rapid departure hadn't allowed sufficient time for the normal complement of nanobots to merge with his smartsuit. The chill passing through his incomplete parka told him his body heat was leaking out. With nothing for Remulkin to hide behind, his thermal heat signature would glow like a light source in the infrared spectrum of their sensors.

The transport! he thought, remembering the hovercraft he'd ridden to and from his polar experiment. Turning, he searched the nearly dark horizon. A thin crescent sliver of light from one of the planet's small moons cast a dim glow across the featureless plane. The soft light revealed a smoking hulk half-melted into an ice crater. A Zoxyth laser had already blasted the transporter.

"Shit!" Remulkin shouted.

But then he saw an opportunity. Hoping the transport's still hot hulk might mask his body's infrared signature, Remulkin scrambled across the ice and slid behind the smoking husk.

As he looked back, his breath hitched. The enemy ship plowed through the dust cloud. The Zoxyth dreadnought flew straight toward him. In the crescent moon's glow, he could see the evil, grinning alien visage chiseled into the lead asteroid. The huge face appeared to glare down at him as the now motionless ship towered surreally over the destroyed mountaintop.

Surrendering to his anger and the futility of his concealment efforts, Remulkin stood. Rising to his full height, he defiantly raised both fists toward the Zoxyth ship. "Fucking worthless lizards!" he shouted. "You've killed my family and my world." He raised the two middle fingers of both hands–a derisive Argonian gesture. "Finish the godsdamned job!"

Remulkin flinched as a brilliant laser shot from the mouth of the alien bust. But it blazed over his head and crossed the horizon behind him.

Closing his eyes, Remulkin Thramorus waited for the end. A moment later, the light flooding through his closed eyelids intensified, but somehow he was still alive.

Remulkin opened his eyes to an incredible sight. The laser that had shot from the sculpted mouth now fanned up and down. White-hot, molten rock sprayed from the vertical line cut by the vibrating beam.

Suddenly, a brilliant explosion bisected the ship. As it ruptured, the two halves flew apart, revealing an Argonian battlecruiser closing on his position.

Blasting through the fire-filled space vacated by the destroyed enemy ship, the Argonian cruiser sailed toward him. Then its tractor beam yanked Remulkin from the ground. As he accelerated vertically toward the massive warship's gleaming nose, his EON sparked to life.

"Sorry for the abrupt pickup, sir," said a female voice. "But we've just received an order for an immediate withdrawal from this star system."

Remulkin passed through a port and into the ship's nose. Across the still open line, he heard the GDF officer speak with someone else. "Another one? Already?" she said. "Oh Gods! Emergency jump, now!"

Inside the airlock at the front of the ship, the normal glow of the small room's walls suddenly intensified.

Gripped by a gut-wrenching wave, Remulkin doubled over. An all-consuming fire seemed to burn through him as if it were boiling every cell in his body.

With a sickening realization, he understood that this was the same light that had stolen his family. Remulkin latched onto a mental image of them. Through his grimace of pain he smiled. Finally, Thramorus surrendered to the light. His knees buckled, and he fell to the floor.

CHAPTER 8

"Captain Allison, the general is waiting for you at HQ," the airman said as he snapped a sharp salute.

Richard raised hand to brow, returning the greeting.

Lowering his arm, the airman pointed to the passenger seat. "Hop in, sir. I'll take you there."

Captain Allison nodded and climbed into the roofless and doorless Hummer's right seat.

The airman jumped into the driver's seat. He threw the vehicle into gear, but then paused, looking over his shoulder at the *Turtle*, an odd look on his face. A moment later, he turned forward and stomped down on the Hummer's accelerator. Tires squealed their protest as the vehicle roared away from the busy scene.

Richard looked over his own shoulder. Squinting into the predawn light flowing from behind Sunrise Mountain, he studied the surreal setting. Military support vehicles and personnel now surrounded the clearly alien ship.

Since he'd finished changing back into his flight suit, personnel had swarmed in and out of the space vehicle. After they had got to work, their initial excitement waned. Richard had seen shock hovering just behind their eyes. In the space of half a day, they'd gone from relative innocence—and for most of them, believing we were alone in the universe—to being drawn into an apparent galactic civil war. Then there was the scale of it all. The losses were unimaginable.

That thought triggered a deeper understanding of the emotions he'd glimpsed bleeding from everyone's face. How bad was it? How many family members and friends had each person lost?

Steering the Hummer onto the base's palm tree-lined main road, the driver stole a sideways glance at Richard. In the young man's eyes, Captain Allison saw the odd, haunted look again. This time, he recognized it as the same look he'd seen in those of the personnel now prepping the *Turtle*.

The airman appeared to want something, some reassurance from him, but Richard had no desire to share a "moment" with the man. He'd been an only child. His parents had passed years ago. His few friends were in the military. Richard's personal exposure was limited to the guilt at how Lieutenant Croft had died.

Everybody else was in mourning, all suffering from survivor's guilt at some level.

Richard ground his teeth together. He hated those sentiments. Since his parents' passing, he'd associated those feelings with weakness. He shook his head as if doing so could banish the emotions.

No, there sure as hell wasn't time for it now.

The driver turned on his blinker, then pulled the Hummer up to the curb in front of Base headquarters. Stopping across from the main entrance, he turned to Richard, snapping a sharp salute. "Sir, I just want to thank you for what you did up there. Wish I could've given those sons of bitches some payback."

"Watch what you wish for," Richard said. "You just might get your chance." He returned the salute. "Thanks for the ride."

Before the airman could reply, Richard leaped from the truck. He turned toward HQ's main entrance in time to see General Pearson and his entourage emerge from the building. They made a beeline for Richard. The older man walked as if a great weight rested on his shoulders.

Richard supposed it did.

Standing at attention, he saluted the general. "Captain Richard Allison, reporting as ordered, sir."

The general returned the salute, briefly allowing a thin smile to interrupt his stern look. "Captain Allison, indeed. Welcome, son," Pearson said. His eyes darted skyward, and then he gave Richard a meaningful look. "Good job up there."

"Thank you, sir."

As he lowered his arm, the stoic look returned to the general's face. "Let's move to the conference room."

Pivoting on a heel, the big man spun his large frame around, motioning for Richard to walk next to him.

Caught flatfooted, Richard stutter-stepped into a jog. Quickly closing the gap, he pulled abreast of the general.

As the captain fell into place, the base commander spoke again. "Colonel Newcastle gave me a quick debriefing of what y'all encountered up there. He also briefed me on our present situation. On top of that, I have satellite and observatory data. Hell, half the world watched the battle live on their TV sets. But what I need from you is your feel for what we'll be up against if we encounter more of these … What did Newcastle call them?"

"Zoxyth, sir," one of the general's aides chimed in before Richard could reply.

"Right, Zoxyth," the general said. He turned back to Richard, a questioning look on his face.

Before he could respond, another aide darted past them and opened the large, frameless glass entry door. Cool air and elevator music spilled from the opening. They walked through the main entrance into a large, circular vestibule. Twin stairways bracketed an information desk at the back of the expansive foyer. Left and right of the desk, the stairs followed the curving wall up to the second floor.

Richard lost a step as the serene normality of the scene struck him with disorientating surreality.

The base commander walked toward the right staircase.

As they neared the stairs, the general looked back at him and gave him the "go ahead" look again.

Richard picked up the pace. They mounted the stairs. The captain cleared his throat and said, "Well, sir, the only one we encountered was already gravely injured, covered head-to-toe in green blood."

"Green blood?" the general said. "Holy hell."

"Yes, sir," Richard said as they crested the stairs.

General Pearson turned and led the procession into a conference room. "But even with all of his injuries, he came at us with incredible ferocity and speed. The thing killed Lieutenant Croft with lightning quickness and extreme violence. Even after three point-blank shotgun blasts, we still had to chase him down."

As he rounded the end of the room's long table, the general stopped so abruptly Richard narrowly avoided running into the man.

"Point-blank! Was he wearing body armor?"

"No, sir. I think the thing was naked. Before it killed Lieutenant Croft we had hit its unshielded body three times with twelve gauge shotguns."

"Three times!" the general said. "And it kept going?"

Richard nodded. "Yes, sir. Actually, it was hit a couple more times. It didn't stop until Captain Giard managed to drop a huge stone statue onto it. Crushed the bastard. But it still took a shotgun blast through the mouth to kill it."

The general remained on his feet. They now stood between two American flags.

"Jesus ..." the general whispered, digesting Richard's words. "Sounds like these monsters won't give up easily. We'll need to plan on more of them showing up."

He turned to one of his aides. "Get Admiral Johnston on the horn."

Orders received, the aide turned and darted out of the conference room.

General Pearson turned back to Richard and pointed up. "Son, we've got all of those assets just floating around up there. For the time being, with the Joint Chiefs and the rest of the Pentagon out of commission, I'm heading up the effort to put together a space defense force."

"I'd like to hope the Argonians got out a distress signal, and that the cavalry is on the way. But we have to assume they were caught by surprise and didn't make that call. So we're going to take the proverbial bull by the horns—if this bull will let us." He said this last part almost to himself, his eyes taking on a distant look.

After a moment, General Pearson shook his head and focused on Richard again. "I'm placing naval officers in charge of the large ships. Figure they have the tactical experience for maneuvering large vessels in combat. Although they'll have to adjust to operations in three dimensions. I plan on manning all those Argonian fighters with all the fighter pilots we can muster in short order. We'll combine them with our existing Vampire fighters. Hopefully Colonel Newcastle and your friend, Captain Giard, are having some success getting the empty Argonian fleet under control."

He paused, giving Richard a hard look. "That brings me to the other reason I wanted you here, Captain."

With a quick look to the nearest aide, Pearson held out his hand. "You have them with you, right, Major?"

"Yes, sir," the officer said. The major gave Richard an odd smile and dropped something small into the general's open hand.

Turning back to Richard, the base commander said. "Stand at attention, son. This is the first time I've done this. So let's try to make it look official."

Confused, Richard complied with the general's order, snapping to attention.

Captain Allison saw one of the officers begin to video the general.

The base commander studied Richard's flight suit. "Well, I guess we'll pin these on your collar for now. You can have them sewn onto your shoulder later." After a brief pause, the general continued. "Hold out your left hand, palm up."

Richard complied, and the general placed two small, metallic items on his palm. Still at attention and staring straight ahead, Captain Allison couldn't see them.

Pearson retrieved one of the items and grabbed one of Richard's flight suit collars.

"Son, I'm giving you and Captain Giard battlefield promotions to

Lieutenant Colonel. I discussed this with Zach Newcastle. I'm putting Colonel Newcastle in charge of all space fighters. We decided that your heroic actions against these aliens, coupled with your familiarity with Argonian systems, make you two our best candidates to head up the integration of the Argonian space fighters." After pinning the silver oak leaves to Richard's flight suit collar, General Pearson stood back and saluted Richard.

"Congratulations, Lieutenant Colonel Allison."

Richard finally snapped out of his dumbfounded trance and returned the general's salute. "Th-thank you, sir."

Lowering their arms, the men shook hands.

Richard's head spun. He couldn't believe it. A two-rank promotion! As he considered the responsibility the general had just dropped on his shoulders, the lieutenant colonel rank insignia suddenly seemed to weigh a thousand pounds.

"Thank you, sir," Richard finally said, his voice cracking. "I won't let you down."

"You had better not, *Colonel.*"

CHAPTER 9

S tanding in the dark, the Fifth Columnist stroked the back of his head.

"Fifth Columnist," he whispered, trying the title on for size.

He liked it.

Considering the term came from Earth—likely a dead planet, although they still awaited news on that matter—he thought the title appropriate. He wondered if his contacts would know its meaning, understand the irony.

He doubted it.

The Fifth Columnist—the enemy within—stroked the back of his head again. Still it brought no relief.

He needed to take action. Worlds ... hell, entire species were at stake. But the last time he took action, so much was lost.

A family.

A world.

A war.

He wouldn't contact them.

He had to.

He wouldn't.

He will.

CHAPTER 10

"Neural mapping complete. Please initiate EON function check." Opening his eyes, Jake blinked against the bright light and looked around. Disoriented, he thought he was back on the *Turtle*. Sitting up, he rubbed his eyes, then froze. Slowly, Jake lowered his hands and looked down. Where his head had been, a small drop of blood shrank then disappeared. Looking at the now spotless white surface, he probed the back of his head. Finding a tender area, Jake withdrew his hand to discover a single spot of blood smeared across the tip of his middle finger.

"What the ...?" Jake whispered. His eyes widened as images flashed through his mind: lights flowing through seemingly ancient bronzed halls, a strange, empty white room, a table growing from a floor. Something had swept him off his feet. Then a black void had swallowed him.

"Shit!" He leaped from the table. "What the *hell*?" Landing in a crouched fighting stance, he remembered a voice had woken him, but he couldn't recall what it had said.

As if reading his thoughts, the feminine voice returned. "Neural mapping complete, please initiate EON function check."

Jake jumped then shook his head. It was just the ship's automated voice, but this time its words sounded strangely flat as if the walls were absorbing the sound waves, robbing the voice of its normal echo.

"Neural mapping complete, please initiate EON function check."

Again he wondered what the hell an EON was.

"EON is an acronym for Electro-Organic Networking modem," the same voice replied.

"Well, that answers one question," Jake said, marveling at how seamlessly his implanted Argonian language algorithms converted the alien language and even its acronyms. *It would be nice if the damn translation included the knowledge of what the hell an EON is,* he thought.

"The EON facilitates integration with the ship's network and computer systems."

Jake looked around the room. *That's spooky, almost like the computer read my mind.*

"Actually, Captain Giard, the EON's interface reads your thoughts, analyzes their content, and then transmits pertinent issues to me for resolution."

Startled at hearing the computer refer to him by name and confirming his concern that the ship was reading his mind, Jake spun and yelled at the walls. "What did you do to me? Where is this EON?"

"The EON is a nanoscale brain implant—"

"Implant!" Jake screamed. Remembering the spot of blood, he ran a hand over his head again. Aside from the slightly sensitive area behind and below his left ear, he found nothing.

"The med-sys uses a transcranial injection to insert the nanites into your cerebrum," the feminine computer voice announced. "Once in position, they self-assemble into a network, harmlessly establishing neural communication pathways and protocols. After becoming operational, the EON safely communicates with the ship's network through non-ionizing subspace frequencies."

Jake continued to rub the sore spot, realizing that it must be the injection site. "The ship's network? How do I interface with it, and what can it do for me? And why does your voice sound so flat?"

"Now that your EON is functional, I am no longer employing

external speakers. There is no aural output. I am communicating with you directly through your EON."

In his head or not, the computer's feminine voice took on a confused tone. "These are highly unusual questions for a uniformed Argonian. You should already be quite familiar with the EON and all of its functions."

Jake looked down at his spacesuit. "I'm not Argonian, although genetically I guess I am. I—"

A tearing paper sound filled the room. The opening in the floor closed again. It had shut after he initially entered the room. It must have opened while he was on the table. The thought reminded him about the one-hour check-in with Colonel Newcastle. Consulting his watch, he saw fifty-five minutes had elapsed.

The computer's Argonian voice interrupted his thoughts, its tone now authoritarian. "Non-Argonian, you are an unauthorized intruder. I have sealed off the room and notified security."

"Good luck with that," Jake said.

"I did not understand that language. Please restate in Argonian."

"Just read my thoughts," Jake responded in Argonian.

"The network protocols limit outputs to a synchronization carrier, data queries, and computer commands. I am unable to access your thoughts unless the EON determines you desire access to the afore-mentioned protocols."

"So, why did you lead me here?"

"When I detected no carrier from your life sign, I analyzed your gene code. Finding you were Argonian, I sent you the aural alerts that led you here. If you're not Argonian, as you claim, I'm unsure how you got past security, but I'm sure they will rectify it."

"I wouldn't count on that," Jake said in Argonian.

After a brief hesitation, the automated voice said, "Strangely, I am not receiving a reply."

"Haven't you noticed things are very quiet on your network?"

"Yes. However, I assumed it was an extension of the Zoxyth disruptor field."

This thing doesn't even know it's alone, Jake thought. "Do you have the ability to do a life sign search?"

"Of course I do," the computer responded with an indignant tone.

So you have emotions, Jake thought. *I wonder if you're sentient.*

"Your query has been received. I am not sentient, as you would define it. I am programmed with logic and self-protection protocols. However, the Argonians built in strict limitations to prevent computer self-awareness."

Her words gave Jake an idea. "Listen, you and your entire fleet are in grave danger. Do a life sign scan. The ship is empty! Your entire Argonian crew has been wiped out by the Zoxyth."

The computer's voice came back less sure. "Stand by ... scanning ... scanning."

"Scan the entire fleet," Jake said.

"Scan complete. As you stated, aside from your life sign, I can find no others within the entire fleet."

"We need to take immediate action. Some of your ships are getting dangerously close to reentering the atmosphere."

"Argonians are required to be involved in all fleet-wide commands. I have very limited authority over the fleet's ships."

"Your ships are about to start a long tumble into the ocean below. We're not at orbital speed, but who knows what's going to happen to your drifting ships when they fall into our atmosphere. Hell, they might not make it to the ocean. The jet stream could send them crashing into mountains."

"Argonian protocols only give me the authority to prevent their destruction."

"I believe I have a solution."

"I'm all ears," it said with a sarcastic tone.

Jake paused at the apparent joke. Was this thing programmed with humor, too?

"Yes, I was."

"What? Shit, never mind. Listen, you already know that genetically I am Argonian. What you don't know is that I'm part of a lost Argonian colony that inhabits this planet," Jake said, pointing through the floor. "The GDF came here to defend us from the Zoxyth. So, in all the ways that matter, I *am* Argonian. You need to release me from here and give me access to bridge functions. Then I can give my people access to the fleet."

"I cannot hand over control without Galactic Defense Force authorization," the ship's computer said, more unease creeping into its electronic voice.

"You said you have self-protection protocols built in, right?"

"Yes. Although I don't see how that is pertinent to the discussion. Instituting said self-protection protocols, I placed the fleet's ships in a safer position after you told me of their peril. They are safely away from the planet's atmosphere."

"That's a good start," Jake said with a sigh of relief. "But what will happen to your ships when the rest of the Zoxyth show up? My people are putting together a large task force to ensure the protection of the fleet. However, without your assistance we may all be doomed. The next wave of Zoxyth ships will destroy this fleet and do the same thing to this planet's Argonians as they did to this fleet's."

The computer fell silent. Jake worried he'd pushed it too far, that he'd been cut off and was now a prisoner in this egg-shaped, inverted oubliette.

"Hey, do you—?"

The familiar white noise of an opening door cut off his question. Jake turned and found the floor hatch had reappeared.

"Your logic is sound," the computer announced through the EON connection.

"That's great," Jake said, but his excitement faltered as a mental tingling and disorientation swept over him—the same sensations he'd experienced when the late General Tannehill implanted the Argonian language algorithms into his brain. For a horrified moment, Jake grabbed his head with both hands. Could the edification encoder be reversed? Was the computer de-edifying him? Had she placated him just long enough to wipe his memories?

Then the sensation faded. "What did you do to me?!" Jake said as he blinked his eyes back into focus. He found he could still remember Rita Johnson, his first kiss, so hopefully the rest was still there, too.

"I upgraded your EON access and integrated it with the ship's systems. You'll find ship maps and function keys."

Jake nodded. "That's great, but from now on, I'd appreciate a little heads-up. Please let me know before you put anything else in my brain."

"I'll try to keep that in mind," the computer said sardonically. "Now I'll give you command override authority," she said in a patronizing tone as if talking to a six-year-old. "However, to employ it, you will need to proceed to the bridge."

Jake was about to call the computer a smart-ass, but the disorientating mental prickle returned and just as quickly ceased. Performing a quick inventory, he discovered a complete mental map of all ship functions and commands. Jake's irritation with the computer's patronizing tone evaporated. "This is awesome! Thank you."

Using his now full understanding of the EON and its abilities, he accessed the ship's communication center. Jake made firmware modifications, enabling one of the Argonian radios to work on the correct range of frequencies.

"Vampire Six, this is the ..." Jake paused, pulling up the ship's name. "The Galactic Guardian, over."

"Captain Giard," came a relieved voice. "Where in the hell have you been? You're late for your one-hour check-in."

"Sorry, sir—"

"Hell, son!" the colonel interrupted. "You've done great! I don't know how you did it, but all of the Argonian ships have regrouped around the carrier."

"I, uh ... made contact with the ship's ..." Jake paused. Looking at the ceiling, he tried to think of the right words. "... computer intelligence. Convinced it to give me access to its command functions." Not waiting for the colonel's questions, he stepped toward the opening in the floor and continued speaking. "But I can only execute the important ones from the bridge. Once I'm there, I'll bring the fighters into the hangar. Then I'll let your squadron in as well."

"Good job, son!" the colonel said. "I can't wait to hear how you're doing all that, but for now, I'll stand by for your signal."

"Roger, sir. Galactic Guardian, out."

Air Force Captain Sandra Fitzpatrick dropped the blood-covered flight suit into a red plastic biohazard bag. After tossing in the rest of her soiled garments and boots, she kicked the whole mess into the tiled corner of the command center's shower room.

The bag came to rest next to a full-length mirror. In it, Sandy studied her nude visage. She gently probed the sealed wounds on her right waistline where the corpsman had dug out the two pellets. He'd told her she'd been lucky that it had been a ricochet and that it had only been two. Wincing, she didn't feel lucky, but she knew it could've been much worse. Sandy slid her hand to her flat stomach. The baby bump remained a future development; the corpsman had confirmed she was still pregnant in spite of the best efforts of hostile aliens and drugged-out looters.

A fog spread across the top of her reflected image, tugging Sandy from her thoughts. She stepped into the already running shower. Its jet of hot water coursed through her gore-stained hair. Gray bits of brain matter and ochre blood sluiced off of her and streamed across white floor tiles. As the meth-head's effluence washed from Sandy's body, the water faded to pink. Finally, the last of what-the-fuck-Buck ran down the drain, and it ran clear.

Sometime later, Sandy stepped from the room in the new uniform General Pearson's aide had supplied. The flight suit fit perfectly, but the boots needed breaking in. She planned to give them plenty of exercise. Sandy had no plans to slow down, not with all that had happened. The corpsman had tried to convince her to report her pregnancy, had even threatened to do it himself. However, Sandy had issued her own threats, promising the young corporal serious bodily harm if he breathed a word to anyone. After a glance at the splattered blood and brains of the last person who had crossed her, he'd clammed up.

Walking toward the Base's Command Control Center or C3, Sandy tried to minimize the limp she'd earned when she'd ejected from her doomed F-22. The knee brace the corpsman supplied worked better than the aluminum strut she'd fashioned into a splint, and its slim lines were barely noticeable under the flight suit's baggy legs.

Stepping into the C3, Sandy spotted General Pearson. The female major at his side, his aide, nodded at her. Sandy approached and then stood at attention. When the general noticed her, Sandy saluted.

"Captain Sandra Fitzpatrick, reporting for duty, sir."

"Attention!" shouted an officer as Richard entered the briefing theater. The large chamber was full of pilots. All of them stood and snapped to attention.

Stepping up to the podium, Richard scanned the room. The assembled personnel stood on arcing ledges, each higher than the row in front of it, like a theater with stadium seating. Most of the faces staring back at him were no older than he was.

Suddenly self-conscious, Richard raised a hand. "Please, take your seats ... Take your seats."

Slowly, the officers sat. A nervous silence fell across the room. The American contingent filled the left half of the theater. Russian aviators occupied the right third. Pilots from Europe, Australia, Africa, and the Middle East filled the rest. All of them had segregated themselves by geography. Richard knew he'd have to do something about that. He stifled a smile when he saw the Israeli and Saudi contingents eyeing each other warily.

A wide spectrum of emotions radiated from the assembled pilots. Apprehension, excitement, dread, and eagerness stared from a thousand faces. Realizing these men and women needed more than just deployment orders, he changed his plan.

"Ladies and gentlemen, I came in here with the intention of briefing you on our short-term plan for staffing the abandoned fleet. However, by the looks on your faces, I think it would be worthwhile for us to take a moment to discuss our situation first. I'm sure you've all heard varying versions of what we're up against and the events that transpired during the 'Battle for Earth' as the news networks are calling it."

The change in the room was palpable. The men and women began to focus on Richard's story and less on their own concerns. He described the events from his personal perspective—providing nuances and angles not available in a news report. He effectively personalized the situation, giving the officers ownership of the struggle. Richard was planting the seeds that, he hoped, would lead to the formation of a cohesive unit.

Finishing the narrative, he scanned the room. Richard still saw hints of apprehension and dread, but the vast majority of the faces staring back at him now looked resolute, determined, ready to receive their orders.

That, or they were just tired of his voice.

Either way, it was time to hand out shuttle assignments. There were way too many people for the *Turtle* to carry on one or even ten trips. The stack of papers in front of Richard had all of the pilot's names. The admin officer that had handed him the two-inch-thick pile of documents said that he had sorted the personnel by country.

Looking across the geographically segregated theater, Richard smiled. On the podium, he cut the ream of papers like a deck of cards and began to shuffle the sheets.

Stepping over another vacated uniform, Jake entered the bridge and was immediately overwhelmed by its breathtaking scale and grandeur. The EON had provided him with mental images and detailed specs on the operations command section; however, seeing it with his own eyes was far more impressive.

The bridge's interior was roughly the size of a high school gymnasium, both horizontally and vertically. A huge, floor-to-ceiling view-wall filled the long, forward-facing side like a curved, two-hundred-foot-wide, super-ultra-high-definition television screen. It looked similar to the one inside the *Turtle*, but significantly larger. The other three walls had the same ancient, antiqued bronze look he'd seen in the ship's expansive halls and passageways. Something akin to an earthly bird of prey, like an eagle or a hawk, adorned the upper corners. Each appeared to be caught in a perpetual dive toward the center of the bridge—their talons outstretched, beaks thrust into the onrushing air, their wings pinned back.

With the EON's assistance, he accessed the bridge's hologram controls. As Jake activated it, he almost fell forward. Earth's surface suddenly filled the lower rear portion of the bridge, immersing Jake knee-deep in a sloped rendering of the Atlantic Ocean. The size and clarity of the hologram, coupled with the planet's odd angle, momentarily disoriented him.

Regaining his balance, Jake looked up from the ocean to see a rendering of the GDF fleet hovering overhead. He also saw small green icons that the computer identified as the Earth-based Vampire Squadron. It looked like the rest of Newcastle's fighters had rejoined him in space. Like a malevolent overseer, a red rendering of the Zoxyth ship remnant hovered some distance to the left of the fleet.

Jake knew the bridge contained another level, an invisible elevated command deck. He walked up to one of its dedicated lift points. As he stepped into the yellow ring of light, he began to rise. A moment later, the lift gently deposited him onto the clear force field-generated floor. As soon as he landed on the translucent surface, Jake gained access to an enhanced range of controls. This elevated deck served as the main control point for all fleet-level commands.

Staring into the hologram, he magnified the rendering. Using thoughts instead of gestures to adjust the display, he zoomed in on the fleet.

"Wow!" he whispered. A crooked grin curled one corner of his mouth.

Inventorying the empty Argonian fighter fleet, he discovered their institutional framework. The GDF had organized their units in a hierarchal structure that any human military officer would recognize. Jake left the ship unit assignments unchanged and directed them to their standard parking pads. No need to reinvent the wheel.

Standing on the elevated deck, Jake watched hundreds of green holographic fighters stream into the ethereal *Galactic Guardian* that now floated just over his head.

As the last fighter disappeared into the carrier's aft section, Jake turned to Vampire Fighter Squadron. With a mental command, he assigned them to a specific hangar location. One thought later, they joined the fleet's organizational structure.

This is awesome, Jake thought. He looked at Newcastle's seventeen fighters. Eight to port and seven to starboard, each vessel hovered oriented on the twin hangar bay openings like prison guards monitoring returning inmates. Stepping closer, Jake kicked something. When he looked down, his excitement died. He frowned at the empty Argonian uniform crumpled at his feet. His EON identified its rank insignia as fleet admiral.

Admiral Feyhdyak, Jake realized, shaking his head at the insanity of the day's events.

Dragging his gaze from the vacated uniform, he turned his attention back to the holographic Vampire Fighter Squadron. The process of getting them to their assigned hangar space took a few more steps.

He activated the modified radio. "Vampire Six, this is Galactic Guardian Bridge, over."

"Galactic Guardian Bridge, this is Vampire Six. Hot damn, son! You're doing a fine job! The Argonian fleet just flew into the hangars!"

"Thank you, sir," Jake said. "I've given access to your squadron. The *Galactic Guardian's* tractor beam has been set to guide your ships to their assigned pads. Figured I'd better alert you, so you're not surprised when your ships start moving."

"Roger, Guardian," Colonel Newcastle's gruff voice crackled over the radio. "I've just received word the *Turtle* will be lifting shortly with its first contingent. I want you to remain on the bridge for now. I'll link up with the senior commanders, and we'll meet you on the bridge for a debriefing."

After a quick consultation with the EON, Jake responded. "Copy, Vampire Six. I've set up an illuminated pathway, a set of moving lights that will lead you to the bridge from the exit at the hangar's forward wall."

"We'll see you there. Vampire Six, out."

CHAPTER 11

Just as Remulkin was sure his body would surrender to the energy burning through it, the light evaporated, chased away by the familiar sensation of parallel-space entry. A moment later, his guts wrenched again. Not the burning, family-stealing fire this time, only the regular yank from superluminal speed.

After a short jump, the ship had apparently dropped back into regular space.

Thramorus struggled to his feet. Hunched over, he tried to shake off the sensations that threatened to overwhelm him. Breathing heavily, with hands on his knees to support his upper body, he looked around the airlock.

The ship seemed normal. Its interior walls now glowed with their usual intensity. The parallel-space jump had only lasted seconds, but considering the vessel's superluminal speed, he knew an appreciable chunk of a light-year now sat between them and the enemy. He knew that the GDF took steps to make their emergency egress parallel-space jumps untraceable. So they were safe from the Zoxyth's weapon, for now.

Finally able to stand upright, he stumbled to the airlock's inner door.

Tucked into the bottom of the battlecruiser's nose, the small room's location placed him a good distance from the bridge. Having spent a sizable portion of his short military career assigned to a deployed carrier, Remulkin knew his way around the fleet's complement of ships. While he'd never served on a battlecruiser, he knew the ship's logistician would be waiting on the other side of this airlock door. The officer's duties would include tractor beam operations.

As he drew close, the door opened.

Remulkin froze.

Something was very wrong.

Instead of the anticipated post-jump bustle, deafening silence oozed through the open door. Only a slow staccato drip pierced the ominous quietude.

"What the fuck?" Remulkin whispered.

Lying across the floor as if cleaved at an odd angle, a man's upper torso blocked the exit. His extended right arm looked like it was reaching for the door. Below the elbow, his left arm was gone. With surreal clarity, Remulkin watched as a swelling drop of blood desperately clung to the stump's lowest point. With a quivering release, it lost its battle with gravity and fell into the waiting puddle of blood. The loud report of its splashdown caused Remulkin to spasm as if he'd been shocked.

Beyond the halved body of the man—likely the logistics officer—long, bright red streaks of arterial blood adorned every surface, even the ceiling.

With growing horror, Remulkin stepped over the officer's extended arm. The dead man's empty pants—sitting in the spreading pool of blood and half-covered with unrestrained entrails—lay flat where his lower torso should have been.

Closer now, he realized the officer's upper torso was tapered. The shape under his tunic showed the man was cut along an angle extending from his central back, just below the shoulder blades, down and forward to just above his pelvis. Visible in a gap between his shirt and pants, only entrails and blood extended below the bisecting line.

Remulkin realized that the man had been bending at the waist when it happened.

Empty socks extended from empty shoes into empty pant legs.

Positioned between the tractor beam control panel and the airlock door, the only portion of the officer's body still present was that part closest to the airlock's inner door, the portion closest to the nose and apparently farthest from the enemy weapon.

In the nose of the ship with his back to the airlock, Remulkin faced aft and considered how much of the battlecruiser lay behind that line.

He already knew the answer.

All of it.

"Oh shit!"

Just as fast as it leaped into the emergency parallel-space jump, the *Helm Warden* dropped back into real space. As it did, the compressed fisheye of stars ahead of the ship's nose blossomed to surround it.

Still doubled over, Admiral Tekamah gripped his command console. The internal voice of his resynchronized network id still screamed for his attention. *Not now*, he sent to his other half.

With a massive application of will, he stood upright, bracing himself against the console. Through withering pain and clenched teeth, he ordered, "Report!"

The tactical officer struggled to her feet. "Checking, sir."

As the woman consulted the data streaming through her console, Tekamah surveyed the scene beyond the view-wall. Signaling the fleet's arrival, hundreds of flashes illuminated the bridge. Each pulse of the ethereal light signaled the arrival of another ship as it dropped back into regular space.

"Sir, the fleet has rejoined."

"How much of it?" Tekamah asked in a cracked voice.

"All but *Monarch's Stand* and 1st Fighter Squadron, Admiral." In a choked voice she added, "They still haven't checked in. I can't see their subspace transponders either. The enemy must've reactivated the disruptor."

"It doesn't matter. We've lost them," Tekamah said flatly. Glaring through the view-wall, he studied the white point of light of Chuvarti's star and pointed at the woman. "With that subspace jammer back in place, we can't transmit the self-destruct command from here. Send a fighter back in. Tell them to fly into the Chuvarti system until they get close enough to transmit the self-destruct code via the backup radio channel. They are to keep their distance from all enemy ships, and if the disruptor field goes down, they need to perform an immediate emergency egress."

"But sir, you can't know they're all gone," she said. "There might be survivors on those—"

"No," Tekamah said, turning from the display and cutting her off. "They're gone. Now, transmit the order, Major."

After the briefest hesitation, the officer complied.

Tekamah shook his head. He should have recognized the dropping of the disruptor field for what it was, should've ordered the emergency fallback that instant.

The woman looked up from her console. "What was that light, sir?"

"A godsdamned banned weapon!" Tekamah shouted.

The woman's head snapped back as if he'd slapped her.

"Sorry, Major," he said.

She blinked her confusion. Myriad questions blossomed across her face.

The admiral shook his head. "No time," he said softly. "I'll brief everyone later."

"Yes, sir," she said after a brief pause.

Tekamah activated a small hologram recording of the moments before the fleet had jumped out of the Chuvarti system. In the paused video, the image of the doomed *Monarch's Stand* and the dreadnought that had destroyed it coalesced before him. Melded perpendicularly across their mid-sections, the two ships expanded until the battle-cruiser was about the size of a man.

Tekamah stepped closer. His face glowed red and green. The

majestic lines of the Argonian ship contrasted sharply against the rocky protuberances of the dreadnought's cobbled together asteroids.

Activating the three-dimensional video, Tekamah watched as the weapon's energy wave erupted from the melded ships, instantly enveloping both.

Verbalizing his EON commands, he said, "Slow playback a thousand times. Magnify Zoxyth bridge section to max resolution. Replay from one millisecond before weapon detonation."

His electro-organic network issued the commands.

Tekamah stepped back.

The holographic representation of the enemy ship's bridge grew to fill the space between the command deck and the high ceiling. Its cold, red light washed across the bridge.

The admiral rotated the enemy ship. The carved asteroid's Zoxyth face glared down at him, its fangs forever frozen in the act of crunching an Argonian skull.

"Play," Tekamah ordered through his EON interface.

The alien's partially opened mouth started glowing. Even at the incredibly slow replay speed, the energy wave raced outward, quickly expanding out of view.

"Reverse," Tekamah ordered.

The energy wave shrunk back and disappeared into the Zoxyth ship's bridge. Extrapolating the motion, Ashtara placed the weapon's location at the sculpted asteroid's geometric center.

The tactical officer interrupted his thoughts. "Sir, the *Liberator* hasn't checked in."

Tekamah looked at her. "You said all other ships had checked in!"

She nodded. "Their transponder is responding to pings, sir. But I can't raise anyone on her bridge. They're not responding to radio or subspace hails."

He deactivated the display. Turning from the dissolving hologram, Tekamah said, "That's the battlecruiser I sent to pick up the scientist. Keep trying them."

"Yes, sir."

Turning from the officer, Tekamah accessed the *Liberator's* data.

Nothing.

The battlecruiser had been well into enemy-held space.

He tried to open a direct EON connection with its captain.

Commander Bazil didn't respond. Her icon remained grayed out.

The *Liberator* was as silent as a cemetery.

Tekamah instantly regretted the analogy.

At least cemeteries had occupants.

Leaving the horrific scene behind him, Remulkin walked out of the ship's tractor beam control room. As he traveled aft from the vessel's nose, the circumstances in each consecutive room confirmed his worst fears. In every compartment, empty uniforms lay strewn about in random patterns. He saw no other partially vaporized bodies. These crew members had completely vanished. The doubled-over and curled-up positions of all the person-shaped articles painted a picture of pre-death agony.

Breathing heavily, he hurried through the sections. Passing deeper into the ship, he found more of the same.

"Shit!"

Now running, Remulkin quickly passed from room to room, working toward the ship's central lift. His heart raced as his panic mounted. He slid to a stop in the lower deck's central chamber. Wide-eyed, he stared at its hundreds of empty uniforms.

Mounting panic threatened to overwhelm him. It felt like his heart would soon burst from his chest. Bent over, Remulkin struggled to breathe, but every breath just brought him closer to vomiting. His unnerved sprint hadn't helped.

"Oh Gods," Thramorus whispered. He closed his eyes, but the vision of blinding light swallowing his family chased him out of that dark refuge. Facing that agony now would finish Remulkin just as assuredly as would a plasma bolt to his heart.

The scientist stared at the floor. "Have to move!" he said between gasps.

A few labored breaths later, the giant fist squeezing his pounding heart seemed to relax its grip. Presently the ringing in his ears subsided.

Finally, Remulkin stood upright. When he didn't pass out, he walked on trembling legs toward the lift. It opened, revealing two bodies. The crew members floated slack, unmoving in the lift's gravity-free zone. Their backs were turned to him. Hidden behind their slumped-over uniforms, it looked like their heads were hanging down. Extending his right arm, the scientist reached into the tube's weightless environment.

"Hey," Remulkin said as he reached for the nearest crew member's shoulder. "Are you—?" His hand closed on empty fabric. Stifling a scream, he yanked back his arm. The empty uniforms tumbled out of shape and began to float around in the zero-G environment of the lift's interior. Without gravity and disturbing drafts of air, they had maintained their shapes and positions despite the absence of their former occupants.

Panic tried to take him again.

Bending over, he inhaled deeply. When he could no longer hold it, Remulkin released the pent-up breath in a long, cursing exhalation: "Fuck, fuck, FUCK!"

Holding the grab bar adjacent to the lift opening, the scientist inserted his arm into the gravity-free cylindrical space. He quickly swept it through the drifting clothes as if their owners might return at any moment. As they passed into the central chamber's normal gravity field, the empty articles fell into a pile just outside of the lift.

Avoiding the heaped uniforms, Remulkin leaped into the tube too fast. He ricocheted off the lift's interior walls twice before arresting his weightless inertia. The man held an interior handhold and extended a trembling hand toward the lift's controls. His third attempt activated it. The scientist began to rise toward the distant bridge level. His body accelerated up the narrow tube. Speed-blurred deck markings flashed past him. As he neared the top of the lift tunnel, their passage slowed. Then he stopped just below the tube's upper limit.

The markings confirmed that this was the command deck, but nothing happened. The door didn't open.

"Damnit!"

Holding onto a grab bar, he jabbed at the manual door controls.

Still nothing.

With mounting anger, he jabbed at them again. Then he remembered something from his military days.

"Godsdamnit!"

Shaking his head, Remulkin toggled the lift's controls. Returning to the previous room, he searched through the strewn uniforms. Finally finding what he needed, he returned to the lift. As he raised toward the bridge level, he studied the item.

From his years in the Galactic Defense Forces, he knew that the small, metallic badge contained a transponder. While the EON was the primary way to access most compartments, appropriately cleared individuals used these devices to access sensitive areas. They worked even if EON connectivity failed.

This time, the hatch opened as soon as he returned to the lift's bridge level. Waves of light and sound burst through the opening. Using the grab bars, he launched himself onto the bridge's command deck. He landed inelegantly and dropped to his hands and knees. During his days in the military, he'd done the maneuver hundreds of times without falling. Of course, back then he hadn't had the expansive mid-section.

Clambering to his feet, he stepped over another vacated uniform. Standing, he scanned the battlecruiser's bridge.

Hundreds of holographic ships filled its voluminous overhead space. Remulkin was thankful to see that all of them were green, although red combat lighting still painted the bridge in its night vision-preserving lambency. When the battle had ended, no one had been left to deactivate them.

Through the cacophony of bells and klaxons, he heard voices coming from a nearby control panel. "Liberator, this is Helm Warden. Please respond."

He stepped to the console. Remulkin remembered enough about

its operation to recognize that the transmission was coming in on a private channel. So this ship must be the *Liberator,* and the *Helm Warden* was trying to raise it.

The communicator wouldn't respond to his EON. Remulkin's trembling hand pressed the manual override. "Hel-Helm Warden, th-this is the Liberator."

"Liberator!" the woman said with evident relief. "What is your status?"

Remulkin looked around the bridge. His eyes fell on the vacated uniform of the ship's apparently female captain draped across the command console. He shook his head. Angry and with a horrible sense of déjà vu, he said, "Everybody is dead!"

"Everybody?" the officer said in a confused tone.

"Yes!" he said, starting to grind his teeth. "Everybody aft of the forward airlock was vaporized!" The scientist felt something in him snap. He wanted to throttle the idiot. "They're all fucking gone!" he screamed. "I'm the only godsdamned survivor!"

After a long pause, the stupid woman's tentative voice returned. "Oh my Gods … Is this Remulkin Thramorus?"

"Got it in one!" he shouted. Slamming a fist into the communicator, Remulkin terminated the connection.

Turning from the console, he stared up into the field of holographic ships.

They should've left him on Chuvarti. Why hadn't they just let him die? Tears tried to burn their way into his eyes, but he brusquely wiped them away.

Remulkin glared at the wavering green rendering of the *Helm Warden,* Tekamah's flagship.

"Thanks for nothing, asshole!"

CHAPTER 12

Heat waves shimmered like a silver lake levitating above the baking tarmac. On the eastern horizon, Sunrise Mountain buttressed an azure ocean of air. The image reminded Richard of his drive with Victor and Jake across the Area 51 tarmac.

Good God, that was just a day ago, he thought. After everything that had happened, it felt like a lifetime had passed. Lowering his face to study the gathering personnel, Richard realized his perception was correct. A lifetime had indeed passed. When a large chunk of the world's population had vanished, it had taken that previous life with it.

The odd mix of service members finished forming up. They regarded Richard silently. He smiled and nodded to the few he knew.

Each person had dropped off their equipment and bags. A chain of Air Force airmen had whisked the stuff into the *Turtle's* airlock. Once full, the lock would seal itself and lift the items to the vessel's main floor. On that deck, another chain of airmen would transfer it to the *Turtle's* top floor.

Outside, the assembled formation consisted of personnel of all types. Fighter pilots represented more than half of the group currently staring at Richard. Various combat and support types filled the rest of the first flight's slots. Navy SEALs and Army Special Ops constituted the majority of the expedition's frontline forces. Everything else from cooks to doctors rounded out the tally of collected personnel.

Richard's deck-shuffling stunt had ensured the multinational face of the first wave of pilots. However, for logistical simplicity, American military personnel filled the rest of the positions.

Well at least we aren't taking any lawyers, he thought.

Finishing his scan of the group, Richard decided they were ready.

Receiving his nod, the senior sergeant snapped to attention and shouted, "Task Force, ATTENTION!"

The well-disciplined, highly motivated group followed his lead, snapping to attention in unison.

The sergeant did an about-face and saluted sharply. "Colonel, Wave One of Task Force Swift Vengeance present and ready for duty."

Standing at attention as well, Richard returned the salute. "Thank you, Chief."

The man lowered his arm and moved to his station behind and right of the colonel.

"At ease," Richard shouted, permitting the group an opportunity to relax while he gave them one last pre-flight briefing. "In a moment, the master sergeant is going to have you file into the *Turtle.* The airmen inside will show you to your positions for the transfer to space. Our plan is to have you stand in concentric arcing rows. They will follow the circular shape of the ship's interior. Hopefully, the computer will recognize our needs and provide seating of some sort, although we've never tried anything like this."

"Before we proceed, I just want to take this last moment to tell all of you how proud I am to have this opportunity to work with you. The command contingent will be here shortly, and once we arrive at the main ship, you'll be broken down into your individual units. Regardless of which command you fall under, best of luck, and Godspeed. That is all."

"Task Force, ATTENTION!" the chief master sergeant screamed

over Richard's shoulder. Then he moved to stand in front of Richard again and saluted.

Lieutenant Colonel Richard Allison returned it. "Carry on, Chief."

The chief master sergeant issued his orders, and the task force began to board the ship. Some of the personnel were waving at their loved ones. Richard had decided to allow them access to the departure. Considering the entire world had seen the alien ships attacking the planet, the need for secrecy now seemed like an exercise in futility.

Movement near the tarmac's access gate caught Richard's attention. Turning to investigate, he saw General Pearson's Humvee driving toward the *Turtle*. Three more Hummers followed. The lead vehicle bore two flags: one on each side of the hood. The left one had the general's three-star rank insignia, while the right bore an admiral's rank insignia. Richard guessed it would be the Admiral that General Pearson had referred to during their meeting.

As the last of the task force disappeared into the *Turtle*, the lead Humvee slid to a stop in front of Richard. The driver jumped out to open the door, but the base commander opened it himself and stepped onto the tarmac.

Outside the *Turtle*, scattered personnel continued their work. Someone started to call them to attention. However, the general waved this away. "Carry on."

Richard saluted the base commander. "Good afternoon, General. Wave one of the task force is in place, sir. The personnel are assembled in the *Turtle*."

As the general returned the salute, Richard got his first glimpse of the admiral. He definitely looked the part: tan, lean face wrinkled as if weathered by years at sea—Richard supposed it may have been—hair almost as white as his uniform cut so close it was almost invisible in the area not covered by his headgear.

General Pearson patted Richard on the shoulder. "Good job, Colonel Allison." Gesturing to his right, he continued. "This is Admiral Johnston. He is now Supreme Commander, Space Operations. I will continue to work here to coordinate and oversee all activities between space-based and Earth-based operations." The general turned toward Admiral Johnston. "Bill, this is the officer I told you about."

Pouring from the Hummers that had been following the general's vehicle, a group of fellow Air Force Lieutenant Colonels and Navy Commanders streamed behind the men and into the *Turtle*.

Richard saluted again. "Pleased to meet you, sir."

Admiral Johnston returned it and then offered his hand. Richard shook it.

"Colonel Allison, you've done our nation ... no, our planet a great service. It's a pleasure to meet you. You and your team demonstrated the initiative and drive that will be required of us all in the days, weeks, and God willing, months to come. I'm proud to have you and Giard on my team."

"The honor is mine, sir," Richard said.

They watched as the last of their command staff disappeared into the *Turtle's* airlock.

"Hopefully, none of this will be necessary," Richard added.

"From your lips to God's ears, son," the admiral said with a nod.

They began to walk toward the *Turtle*. The chief master sergeant gave Richard a quick thumbs-up.

Turning to Admiral Johnston, Richard said, "Sir, the airmen loaded your baggage and equipment when it was sent over. It looks like everything is ready for us in the *Turtle*. So, unless there is other business needing your attention, I believe we are ready to depart."

"I'm ready, Colonel," the admiral said and then nodded to General Pearson. "John, I'll be in touch. We'll get things up and running in short order. Then God help those sons of bitches if they decide to show their scaly mugs again."

"Go get 'em, Bill. I know you'll give them what for."

Salutes were exchanged, and the officers parted ways. Reaching the opening, Richard gestured for the admiral to enter the airlock, then followed him in. When the opposite door opened, he heard the chief call the Task Force to attention. The admiral quickly told them to carry on. The chief led the admiral to a seat just behind the control panel. Stepping to the console, Richard scanned the seated personnel.

The chief master sergeant stepped next to him and spoke into his ear. "It was the damnedest thing, sir. As soon as the ship saw how we were filing in, these raised rows of seats just grew right out of the floor. It even adjusted the height of each row, so they all have an unobstructed view of the main display."

"Couldn't have asked for anything more," Richard said. Then he turned and addressed the seated service members. "We'll be departing momentarily. This will be a relatively short flight. As I described in the briefing, the Argonian drive has acceleration that can be visually impressive. However, you won't feel a thing. It can be quite disorienting, though."

They all nodded. Richard smiled inwardly. There really were no words to prepare them for what they were about to experience.

He turned to the control console and toggled the radio panel. "Nellis Tower, this is Turtle One. Ready for departure."

"Turtle One, this is Nellis Tower. You are clear to depart as filed. Good luck up there. We're counting on you."

"Roger, Nellis Tower. Turtle One, cleared as filed."

Richard brought the *Turtle's* drive online and lifted the ship to a hover. While the ship's systems held it stationary, Richard pulled his hand out of the flight controller and activated the hologram. Using hand gestures, he panned the display and zoomed in on the rendered Argonian formation. It still hovered over the Atlantic. Behind him, some of the personnel whispered excitedly.

Selecting a point just aft of the largest ship, Richard made a quick poking motion. The now familiar oilcan pop echoed through the *Turtle's* cabin, and concentric green rings radiated out from the tip of his finger. He toggled a command on the flight console's curved display, activating the autopilot's flight plan.

Trying not to be too obvious, he watched the crowd, grinning knowingly as the ship blasted into the sky, and the entire group twitched and then laughed self-consciously. Even the admiral looked duly impressed.

The ship continued to rocket straight up, its supersonic climb unheard by anyone on the ground. Scientists at Area 51 still didn't know how it did that, why the ship's extreme speed didn't generate a shockwave or a sonic boom. Through the view-wall, he could already see Earth's curvature. The sky rapidly shifted from blue to black.

A welcome familiar voice emanated from the *Turtle's* radio. "Turtle One, this is the Galactic Guardian, over."

"Galactic Guardian, this is Turtle One. Good to hear your voice, sir. I hear you have the red carpet out for us."

"It's good to hear your voice, too. Yes, I do. Just park the *Turtle* a couple of hundred yards aft of the carrier. I'll have the tractor beam bring you in from there."

"Tractor beam?"

"Oh yeah, buddy. There's plenty I need to tell you," Jake said.

Richard glanced over his shoulder. "Roger, Galactic Guardian. We've got a couple of surprises for you as well."

CHAPTER 13

J ake turned to see two armed men step onto the bridge followed by a lone, sharply dressed Navy Commander. He wasn't surprised by their sudden appearance. Through his EON interface, he'd watched the command group's progress from the hangar to his location. Following Jake's trail of neon bread crumbs and bracketed by a team of surly, gun-toting Special Ops types, Richard had led the group through the ship. Following the command staff, a gaggle of support personnel loaded down with gear had tried to keep up as another contingent of armed escorts covered their six.

Along the way, they had paused and stared into several of the expansive halls and massive terrariums. Each of the latter contained unique alien biospheres. Accessing information on them, Jake had been surprised to discover some of those micro-environments could be dangerous. He'd been ready to wave them off; however, none of the group members had strayed off of the path.

Colonel Newcastle had instructed Jake to hand over command of the *Galactic Guardian* and its fleet to the party's senior officer. An order with which Jake was more than happy to comply. The man was exhausted. This had been the longest day of his life. He needed sleep, but first he wanted a hot shower. The odor rising from the neck collar of his spacesuit was making his eyes water. Jake had been very happy to discover that showers did exist on the ship and couldn't wait to climb into one.

Not wanting the command group to find him floating godlike on the transparent force field floor, he had moved to the lower level of the bridge to greet them properly. Presently, he stood beneath the command deck at the center of the room.

As the armed men scrutinized the large chamber for hidden threats, Captain Giard and the Naval officer exchanged salutes. The woman scanned the bridge with unbridled awe, her mouth agape.

Jake heard the rest of the group approaching.

Recovering from her astonishment, the naval commander collected herself and shouted, "Attention on the bridge!" Then Colonel Newcastle and a fresh-looking Captain Allison along with a senior naval officer in a crisp, white uniform stepped onto the bridge. Behind them, the rest of the command contingent stood beneath the entrance's sixty-foot-tall pointed arch and stared in wide-eyed amazement.

Jake recognized the senior officer's rank insignia as fleet admiral. Already standing at attention, Jake saluted. "Welcome aboard the *Galactic Guardian*, sir. The bridge is yours."

The admiral returned the salute and lowered his arm. "No, Captain, I believe you can keep it for just a few more moments."

Hesitantly, Jake dropped his salute. Concerned he'd muffed the handoff, he stood at silent attention. Catching a glimpse of Richard in his peripheral vision, he saw the son of a bitch smirking.

Recovering, Jake said, "Excuse me, sir—"

The admiral held up a hand, cutting Jake off. "The name is Admiral Johnston, but you can just call me Admiral for short." His eyes gleamed humorously.

I'm going to like this guy, Jake thought. He nodded. "Yes, Admiral."

"I know you have plenty to tell us, and believe me, I can't wait to hear it, but there is something I want to take care of first." He turned to the commander on his right and held out a hand.

At rigid attention, still looking straight ahead, Jake couldn't tell what the Navy commander placed in the admiral's hand.

Johnston stepped closer to Jake. "Son, it's not every day that you get promoted two levels in one day, especially when you can say that it happened while you were in command of Earth's largest ship." Opening his palm, he showed Jake a pair of burnished Lieutenant Colonel rank insignia: silver oak leaves.

The admiral looked at Jake's form-fitting metallic suit. "I guess there's nowhere to pin this to your spacesuit without compromising its integrity." He placed the insignia in Giard's hand.

Jake noticed that one of the officers had begun to video him and the admiral.

"*Colonel* Giard," Johnston said, emphasizing the new rank. "In consideration of you and your team's heroic victory over the last of these Zoxyth, and due to your knowledge of Argonian technology," he paused and looked significantly at their surroundings, "coupled with your success here, you and Colonel Allison will each command an Argonian fighter wing."

Jake stole a quick glance at Richard. Sure enough, his old wingman was sporting Lieutenant Colonel rank insignia.

He turned forward to see the admiral looking at him expectantly. Jake nodded. "Thank you, sir, it's an honor."

The admiral shook his hand. "The honor is mine, Colonel."

Newcastle stepped up. Jake saluted him.

He returned the salute and shook Jake's hand. "Colonel," the big Texan said significantly. "The two of you have your work cut out."

"Yes, sir," Jake said, smiling self-consciously.

"Now, if you'll direct us to the EON maintenance facility," Newcastle said, his booming voice echoing in the expansive chamber. "I'll take the command contingent to be implanted." The man winced. "I hate the sound of that."

Jake grinned. "It's not too bad, sir. I'll set the lights to lead you there. The computer is already expecting you. Once you're integrated into the network, it will download the Argonian language to anyone who doesn't already have it." He paused and looked to the admiral. "Of course, it'll give you access to the ship's command protocols, sir."

"Perfect," Admiral Johnston said. "I want you to remain on the bridge until we've completed integration."

"Yes, sir," Jake said.

They exchanged salutes again, and the command contingent turned and left the bridge, leaving only Richard and Jake.

Giard nodded to him. "Wing Commander."

Richard returned the gesture. "Afternoon, Wing Commander."

They laughed and hugged, then stood in awkward silence.

After a moment, Richard said. "I wish Vic could be here to be a part of this."

Jake nodded. "Yeah." He swallowed the lump that was trying to choke him. Finally, he pointed to Richard's rank insignia. "Nice surprise! Would it have killed you to give me a heads-up?"

"If you need a heads-up to appreciate a surprise, then you're really not going to like this one," a female voice said.

Jake turned toward her so fast he nearly snapped his neck. One of the people he'd seen toting equipment in the wake of the command staff stepped onto the bridge. She pulled off a wide-brimmed desert camouflage hat and her long, blonde hair tumbled free.

"Sandy?!"

Jake looked at Richard. "What the hell is she doing here?"

"It's good to see you too, asshole," Sandy said wryly.

After a confused pause, he forgot his protest and sprinted to her. Throwing his arms around Sandy, Jake swept her off of her feet and spun her around. He crushed her lips with a passionate kiss. She returned it fervently.

Afterward, her smile faded as she gently touched the facial cuts and bruises he'd earned aboard the Zoxyth ship. "Are you okay?"

"I'll live," Jake said, then winced.

Seeing his reaction, Sandy nodded. "Richard told me about Lieutenant Croft. I'm sorry, baby."

Jake looked away. Sandy pulled him back to her. "He died a hero, Jake," she said.

He nodded. After a moment, Jake pushed aside the doubts and stared deeply into her eyes. "I love you, Captain Fitzpatrick."

"I know," she said, smiling devilishly.

Jake turned and cocked an eyebrow at Richard. "I can't believe you let her come."

Colonel Allison held up his hands. "Hey, you're the one who decided to fall in love with a hard-headed Irish woman."

"Yeah, but you were already a Lieutenant Colonel. You could have ordered her to stay behind."

"Except for the fact that I like my balls just where they are," Richard protested.

Sandy, still in Jake's arms, grabbed his chin and turned his face to hers. "You know I'm the best fighter pilot you've ever—"

Jake opened his mouth to call bullshit, but she raised her own eyebrow. Giard made a tactical retreat.

Sandy shook her head and added, "There's no way I was staying behind."

Still looking at her, Jake nodded toward Richard. "You'll be assigned to Wing Commander Allison's squadron. Obviously, you can't be under my command."

He looked at Richard. "You brought her up here; so she's your responsibility. I want her to be your wingman."

Richard raised his right hand. "Consider it done, Colonel."

Jake turned back to see Sandy wrinkling her nose. She smiled sardonically and theatrically waved a hand in front of her face. "I hope they hurry up and get back. Someone needs a shower."

Jake laughed and threw his arms around her again. Positioning the neck ring under her nose, he squeezed her to him in a bear hug that sent more of his funk flowing out of the collar.

Sandy squealed and giggled.

Lieutenant Colonel Jake Giard smiled. He might make it through this day after all.

"Here it is," Jake said with a flourish of his hands.

Following him into the shipboard residence, Sandy slowed, trying not to gape. The huge cabin's bronze walls and trim matched the ship's gothic decor. Tall fluted casings framed pointed-arch openings. Beyond them, passages led to other portions of the residence. "This room alone is bigger than my parents' house. Well, bigger than it was, anyway." Considering the portion cleaved from the house by a falling chunk of Zoxyth asteroid, Sandy realized it wouldn't take a very big chamber to eclipse her parents' now diminished residence.

The thought dredged up emotions that Sandy wasn't yet ready to explore. She'd already told Jake of her father's injury. She'd also told him of her deadly encounter with the looters, but had omitted the near rape. The memory sent a shiver down Sandy's spine.

Jake paused and stepped toward her. Apparently mistaking Sandy's reaction, he started to put his arms around her. "Sorry about your dad, baby. I'm sure he—"

Sandy shoved Jake away. "I'm fine!" she said too sharply. After a moment she sighed. "Sorry, Jake. You're right. He'll recover. It could've been a lot worse."

A confused look crossed Jake's face. He hadn't pushed Sandy about the looters, but now she could see him studying her.

Before he could start asking questions, Sandy gestured toward the expansive room. "Give me the grand tour."

When Jake hesitated, Sandy raised an eyebrow.

Jake lifted his hands in surrender. "I know that look." After a final confused glance, he turned back toward the room. "Welcome to your new home."

"*My* new home?" Sandy said. "Why don't we make it *our* new home?"

Jake froze, motionless except for his slowly descending jaw. Sandy reached up and pushed his mouth closed.

He blinked and then said, "Who are you, and what have you done with my girlfriend?"

Sandy waved a dismissive hand. "There's plenty of room. You probably won't even get on my nerves."

"Listen here, Ms. Independent, available space wasn't an issue," Jake said. "I've been trying to convince you to move in with me for a year now. You always said it was too soon."

"Hey," Sandy said through a crooked smile. "It's a woman's prerogative to change her mind." It was all she could do not to look at her stomach.

Jake looked skeptical. "What changed?"

With both hands, Sandy gestured toward the room. "What hasn't?"

Seeing more questions forming, Sandy placed a finger across his lips. "If this day has taught me anything, it's how fleeting life can be. I always thought we had our whole life to take things to the next level, and I still do. It's just that 'our whole life' is now more of a variable. We've both been in combat before. We knew life could be stolen from a person without their knowledge. Death is rarely like in the movies. You don't see it coming; there are no drawn-out goodbyes. One moment you're walking down the street, the next instant you're dead and don't know it, didn't even know you were in peril. You just end."

Jake nodded. "But now it can happen on a much larger scale." A shadow of dark emotions crossed his face. Sandy thought he must be remembering his front-row seat for the day's tragic events, all capped off by the decapitation of Lieutenant Croft.

Sandy stepped closer and wrapped her arms around Jake. "We have a lot of work to do here; we need to maximize every minute of duty time." She gave him a meaningful look. "But I want to make the most of our downtime, as well."

Jake's eyes focused, and a grin slowly surfaced. "On that note, let's begin the grand tour in the bedroom," he said. He reached to pick her up. Sandy held up her hands and wrinkled her nose. "Shower first, Colonel!"

Clad in a fresh spacesuit, Jake stepped from the closet-like cabinet that had grown from the bedroom's floor. "I'm going to head to the hangar and get the bag y'all brought for me." Jake gestured at his spacesuit. "Fresh nanobots or not, I'm really tired of wearing this thing."

After he'd showered, they had collapsed onto the bed. Then they'd made love, a long, passionate exchange that ended with both of them panting and spent. Finally, Jake had risen from the bed and stepped into the spacesuit locker completely nude.

Sandy gave his groin a meaningful look and then consulted her watch. "Including the two-minute shower, you got to take off the spacesuit for five whole minutes," she said facetiously.

Jake laughed. "Five minutes, my ass. That was at least six!"

Sandy smiled wickedly and flipped him the bird. "Go get your bag, Colonel. Then get your butt back in bed. We've both had a *very* long day."

Jake laughed at her middle finger salute, and then his brow furrowed. "Baby, there's so much to do. I need to—"

"No, mister," Sandy said, cutting him off. "You've already saved the world enough times for one day."

Jake opened his mouth to protest.

Sandy raised a finger and cocked an eyebrow. "Are you trying to get kicked out on your first night?"

Jake held up both hands. "I surrender. You win. To the hangar and straight back."

"Good, now that that's settled, is there any way I can contact my mom back in Nellis? I want to check on Daddy."

Jake paused, staring blankly, his eyes unfocused.

Sandy pursed her lips. "Hello?"

He snapped out of his trance. "Sorry, I was accessing my EON."

Suddenly, a chime came from her crumpled flight suit where it lay forgotten on the room's floor. It was her cellphone's incoming text alert.

She cast a questioning look at Jake.

He shrugged a shoulder. "I created a virtual repeater and linked it to a Nellis area cell tower by tapping into its microwave radio link."

"Wow, that's pretty impressive. How did you learn to do that so quickly?" Sandy said.

"I wish I could take credit, but the ship's system is pretty smart. It did all the hard work. I just pointed out your device. It accessed your phone and deciphered the communications protocols. After that, it downloaded the GPS coordinates and frequencies for the most recent cell towers the phone had accessed. Luckily, we're far enough east of Nellis that one of the towers had a microwave communication link that happens to point in our general direction."

"Okay ..." Sandy paused, shaking her head. "Thanks for the telecom tutorial, Captain Techie. You lost me at 'communications protocols.' You could've just said the ship did it."

"Hey, you asked. It's not my fault you can't understand anything that doesn't have nuts and bolts and comes with spark plugs." Jake gave her his patented crooked smile. "And, that's Colonel Techie to you," he said with a wink.

Having collected her phone, Sandy threw her flight suit at him. "Get the hell out of here before I make you go back into that spacesuit locker."

Jake saluted her. "Yes, ma'am."

Sandy grinned and flipped him off again.

As Jake left the room, she unlocked her phone and dialed her mom. To her relief, it started ringing almost immediately, and to her greater relief, her mother answered on the first one.

"Sandra?"

Sandy smiled as an enormous weight lifted from her shoulders. With a single word her mother's voice told her everything she needed to know. The feisty humorous edge to her voice said Daddy was fine.

"Hi, Mom!" Sandy said. "I hope you're behaving."

"Well, I don't give two shits what they think, but those doctors got another thing coming if they think I'll sit by quietly while they ignore my Johnny."

Sandy heard her daddy in the background. "Damn it, woman. I told you I'm fine. Quit pestering them."

Sandy laughed. Even from a thousand miles away, she could picture them bickering. There was no malice on either side, more playful banter than true argument. Her daddy called it 'terms of endearment wrapped in burlap.'

"Put her on speaker, Firecracker," her dad said, calling Sandy's mom by her well-earned nickname.

"Firecracker?" her mother said with a harrumph. "I'll shove a firecracker right up your ass," she added, apparently forgetting her earlier concern for her husband's health. "Listen to Mr. I-still-have-a-flip-phone trying to tell me how to work a smartphone." During the last half of her mother's tirade, her voice gained an echo. The edge faded from her elderly voice as she added, "We can both hear you now, hun."

"Daddy?"

"Pumpkin!"

The returning strength in his voice brought a tear to Sandy's eye. "How are you, Daddy?"

"Oh, I'll live," he said gruffly. "Your mother's nagging will put me six-feet-under way sooner than the loss of a leg."

Several minutes later and after deflecting multiple inquiries as to her whereabouts, Sandy said, "It was great to hear your voices, but I better go. I love you both."

"Bye-bye, pumpkin," her daddy said.

"Just a sec, hun," her mother said.

Through her phone's speaker, Sandy heard the rustle and shuffling of her mother standing and walking. Faintly, she heard her say, "I'll be right back, Johnny."

After the click of a closing door, her mom's voice returned in a whisper. "Does he know?"

Sandy blinked. "Does who know what, Mom?"

"Don't be coy with me, Sandra."

Sandy sat up on the bed. "Wait. How do you know?"

Her mother chuckled. "Oh let's see. I'm not sure if it was the fifth or the fifteenth time your hand went to your stomach while we tried to make our way around that big old rock that hit our street."

Sandy winced. Had she been that obvious? Looking down, she realized even now her hand rested on her abdomen. Self-consciously, she lowered it, resolving to break that unfortunate habit. "Listen,

Mom. I'm sorry I didn't say anything, but I just found out before all this ..." She paused, looking around the alien room.

"Before all this shit happened?" her mother said.

"Yes, Momma." Sandy hesitated again. A tear threatened to crest her lower eyelid. She swiped it away brusquely. It wasn't just this *shit*: the attempted rape at the hands of a couple of white trash meth-heads had scarred her as badly as the day's otherworldly events. The looters had come from a section of California affectionately referred to as Calabama. But those assholes didn't have the sunny Southern disposition she affiliated with the region. What-the-Fuck-Buck and his psychotic brother Leroy had nearly robbed her whole family, baby and all, of their lives.

Before her mother could interrupt, Sandy continued. "But I'll be damned if I'm going to let them pull me from this. We don't know how long this break will last. Hell, we don't know how much longer humanity will last. I won't be doing my baby any favors if I convalesce while the world burns down around my ears."

The sharpness fell from her mother's tone. "No, dear, you wouldn't, but you need to tell your man. Jake deserves that much."

"No, Momma. I don't want him distracted, not any more than my being here already has. Besides, he's just as likely to order me back to the surface or find someone who will."

After a moment's hesitation, her mother said, "Fine, but I suggest you stop holding your stomach like you have a prolapsed abdominal hernia. The little booger won't fall out of your belly ... not for several more months, anyway."

Sandy smiled. "Yes, ma'am."

CHAPTER 14

"Mr. Thramorus?"

Remulkin didn't respond. Seated on the bridge's only combat couch not cluttered with emptied uniforms, he continued staring at the floor.

"Remulkin Thramorus?" the Space Marine said again.

After a second nudge from the female Marine's blaster rifle, Remulkin batted away its muzzle and glared at the woman. "Who the fuck else would I be?" He paused and gestured to the room's complement of piled garments. "I told your admiral that everyone else is … well, they're fucking gone!"

Framed by her closely cropped black hair, the woman's face hardened. "I think I'll be the judge of that, Mr. Thramorus."

"Have fun with that," he said with a dismissive wave. "There's a lovely sight waiting for you in the tractor beam control room. I suggest you start there. Now leave me the fuck alone."

She waved one of her squad members to her side. Jabbing her muzzle into Remulkin's chest, she said, "Keep an eye on the good scientist. If the asshole so much as farts wrong, do me a favor, and shoot the bastard."

"What the hell?" Remulkin said, batting away the muzzle again. "I'm not the enemy here."

"I don't know what you are. Maybe you are what you say: the only man left on the planet, and now the only person left alive on one of my ships. But if you ask me, that's two coincidences too many."

Remulkin glared at the Space Marine. Holding out his empty hands, he said, "Search the damned ship, Lieutenant. Afterward, if you think I'm responsible, feel free to throw me in the brig. In the meantime, fuck off."

Her lined face returned the glare for a moment, then she looked at her subordinate and pointed at Remulkin. "Watch him." Turning from the pair, she gestured to the door through which her squad had entered, and they stormed back out of the bridge.

As silence returned, Remulkin looked at his guard. Pale and skinny, the young enlisted man looked nervous. The Marine couldn't be more than ten years older than Remulkin's son. Thoughts of his lost family threw a fresh wave of grief across Thramorus. Looking from the young man, Remulkin stared at the floor. Hidden from view, tears cast their own waves across the image of the mottled gray deck and its frozen ocean of nanobots between his boots.

To his surprise, a small section of the floor under Thramorus lifted like a finger extending from a viscous fluid. Blocked from the Marine's view, its soft absorbent tip gently dabbed the tears from under Remulkin's eyes.

He shook his head and gently pushed away the assistance of the ship's artificial intelligence. "I'm fine."

"What, sir?" said the Marine.

"Nothing."

A few minutes later, the lieutenant reappeared at the bridge entrance, her face ghostly white. She waved at the nervous private and said, "Quit pointing that thing at him. The way you're shaking you're likely to shoot the poor man at the pop of a micrometeorite hitting the hull."

The young man relented, his weapon's muzzle lowering to point at the floor.

Behind the lieutenant, one of her Marines stumbled into the room. Remulkin noticed a dab of liquid glistening on the man's chin. Before Thramorus had time to wonder about its origin, the Marine, even paler than his commanding officer, doubled over and tossed the rest of his breakfast across the bridge's deck.

After giving the retching man a sympathetic glance, the lieutenant shifted her gaze to Thramorus. "I saw why you're the only one left. It's a good thing you were still in the forward airlock when the weapon hit. Otherwise, we would've lost you, too. I owe you an apology, sir."

Remulkin ground his teeth. "You see a couple of bloody bisected bodies, and suddenly we're best friends? Stuff your apology, Lieutenant."

Surprise at his appropriate use of her rank registered on the female officer's face.

"Yes, *Lieutenant*, I know how to read Marine rank insignia. It's the first thing they teach Space Marines."

At her questioning look, he gave the woman a less than crisp salute. "Staff Sergeant Remulkin Thramorus of the First Space Marines," he said gruffly. "But that was before I attended university. I left that life a long time ago and way behind me." He almost added that it was way beneath him, too, but thought better of it.

Both the private who'd guarded him and the corporal—who had ceased his vomiting—regarded Remulkin with belated admiration. Even the lieutenant's expression changed, but all Thramorus saw was their concern.

He glared at the three Marines and said, "I neither want nor need your godsdamned sympathy."

More Marines stumbled into the bridge. Most were as pale as the corporal. Hearing the scientist's raised voice, they exchanged confused glances.

"There's only one thing I need," Remulkin added.

The lieutenant's eyes narrowed. "What's that, *Sergeant?*"

Her derisive use of his former military rank compounded the apparent confusion of the late arrivals.

Remulkin shifted his glare from the collected Marines to their leader. "You can't provide it, *Lieutenant,*" he said pouring just as much condescension into his use of her junior officer rank as she had into his former enlisted grade. Remulkin paused, his scowl morphing into a grin.

"But Admiral Tekamah can."

~

After being deposited on the invisible raised floor of the *Helm Warden* bridge's command deck, the portly man scanned the scattered officers. Apparently identifying his quarry, the balding scientist locked eyes with Tekamah. The admiral recognized the man from their video conversation during the battle. Quickly closing the gap, the scientist came to a breathless stop in front of Ashtara.

Considering his appearance and pale, mottled skin, Tekamah had a difficult time picturing the scientist as a Space Marine.

"Mr. Thramorus, thank you for alerting us," the admiral said. "If you hadn't called when you did …" Ashtara stopped, not wanting to finish the thought.

A storm of emotions crossed the scientist's face. Beneath it all, Ashtara saw a resolute man whose eyes displayed obvious intelligence. The man stood at something approximating attention, his previous military experience not quite allowing him to be completely at ease in the presence of a senior military officer.

A moment later, a look of determination triumphed, banishing the myriad emotions crossing Thramorus's visage. "I want back in."

Ashtara blinked. "I'm sorry … what?"

Remulkin's jaw clenched visibly, and the scientist stood a little taller. Suddenly he stood at rigid attention and saluted, Space Marine style: elbow straight forward, head bowed slightly, fingertips of his right hand held to the forehead. Loud enough to echo across the bridge, the scientist said, "Sir, Staff Sergeant Remulkin Thramorus requesting reactivation."

Tekamah scanned the bridge. Every eye was on the scientist. After a brief hesitation, the admiral returned the salute. Lowering his arm, he said, "Please come to my quarters, Mr. Thramorus."

Remulkin blinked, "Sir?"

"Let's go to my cabin. We can discuss our options there."

Tekamah had no interest in wasting additional time with the scientist, but he felt he owed the man at least a moment of his time. Gesturing toward the lift, he said, "This way."

A few minutes later, the two men stood side-by-side studying the assembled fleet visible through the admiral's personal view-wall.

After a few moments of silence, the scientist began fidgeting.

Tekamah turned to him. "What do you want, Mr. Thramorus?"

Still looking through the view-wall, Thramorus narrowed his eyes. "Revenge," he said, his voice cold and calculated. Then a shudder passed through the man, and he turned to face Tekamah. "I want the fuckers to pay!" he yelled. The man's eyes widened, and after a moment he sighed. "Listen, I, uh … Damn it! Sorry, sir." The scientist closed his eyes and took a deep breath. After a moment, he appeared to collect himself and said, "Sir, I lost my whole family. They were all I had. Hell, I don't even have my work. Those *scaleheads* took everything from me."

Tekamah winced inwardly at the scientist's use of the denigrating slang for all sentient reptilians.

Apparently mistaking Ashtara's poorly hidden revulsion as agreement, Thramorus nodded and continued. "Anyway, sir, I want a chance to balance the scales."

"I'm sorry, Mr. Thramorus." He paused, casting a meaningful glance at the portly man's physique. "I'm afraid your Space Marine days are too far astern."

Remulkin opened his mouth to protest, but the admiral held up a hand and then gestured outside, pointing to the *Liberator*. "As you know, I am a bit short-handed. In the near term, I'm in no position to turn down assistance. Considering your post-military education, I am issuing a battlefield promotion. You are hereby returned to active duty as Second Lieutenant Remulkin Thramorus," Tekamah said and then thought, *For better or worse.*

Remulkin stared, finally speechless.

"Don't make me regret this, Lieutenant."

Breaking out of his trance, the scientist snapped to attention, the motion sending waves across the man's ample belly. Bowing his head and saluting, he said, "I won't, sir."

Admiral Tekamah shut down his EON's visual overlay and closed his eyes. After dismissing the newly minted Lieutenant Thramorus, he'd tackled the rest of his staffing issues. He'd shifted his command structure to fill the vacated leadership positions. Tekamah had given the new commanders limited authority to recruit personnel from each of the ships within the fleet. Soon, his entire complement of battlecruisers would be operating at their minimum crew levels. At those reduced staffing levels, they would need significant training and drills before the fleet would again be ready for combat.

He rubbed the bridge of his nose. As badly as he wanted to continue to the next sector, he needed to regroup.

Sector 64 was still annoyingly silent. He resisted the urge to call up the network backup of Admiral Thoyd Feyhdyak. The computer-based version had no more data than did Tekamah. And at the moment, Ashtara had no desire to deal with the disconnected personality's unending worries. He'd want closure, push Tekamah to send scouts. The *Helm Warden* fleet wasn't yet ready for another engagement, and any route scouts took, no matter how circuitous, could reveal the weakened fleet's whereabouts. The only thing protecting them now was the nature of their emergency egress from the Chuvarti system. If Tekamah hadn't dropped an egress transponder buoy outside of the disruptor field, the Zoxyth could have followed the signature of their parallel-space trail to the fallback position. It had bought them time. But he would need to find out what happened in Earth space sooner rather than later.

And Tekamah still needed to find an answer for Thrakst's new weapon.

~

"Where are they?!" Lord Thrakst yelled.

The trembling communications officer shook his head. "There's no parallel-space signature, my Lord. I can't track them. The GDF must've dropped an emergency egress transponder."

It was all Thrakst could do not to kill the idiot where he stood. "What about Salyth?"

"Still nothing, my Lord."

Thrakst roared and slammed a clenched fist against the black basalt arm of his cathedra. "Plot a course for Sector Sixty-Four."

Now even the helmsman looked nervous. Bowing deeply, he said, "My Lord, our core is too depleted. If we make another jump, it won't have sufficient power to charge the weapon."

Thrakst glared at the officer.

On the supreme commander's right, Raja Phascyre stirred and turned his good eye to regard Thrakst. "No sense impaling the courier, my Lord." He paused and activated a datapad. A navigational hologram popped into existence ahead of the two warriors. The Raja manipulated the display, quickly zooming into a specific star system within Sector 64. As the individual planets resolved, Thrakst recognized it as the Sol system.

Phascyre dropped a navigational waypoint on the third orbital body and then zoomed out of the system until the portion of the galaxy between Earth and their current location flowed into the display. Closer to the core, Chuvarti occupied the same galactic arm as Sector 64. Cutting a direct path through the river of stars, a red route line now connected their fleet and Earth's star.

The Raja reached into the display and hooked a talon on the glowing line. Caught like an elastic string, the center of the snagged red thread followed Phascyre's claw as he dragged it to the adjacent galactic arm. When the Raja's talon touched a recognizable formation of stars, the line appeared to lock onto a particular point.

Phascyre drew his talon along the line's distinct ninety-degree bend. "My Lord, we can deviate to the Xyglatek system. It's on the edge of Zoxyth space and provides our shortest option. We can be in and out in no time. They have everything we will need to finish off the GDF."

Thrakst turned from the warrior and glared at Sol's floating holographic pinprick of light. He leaned close, as if doing so might reveal to him the location of the missing fleet. In the dank, dark, cavernous bridge, the galactic arm cast its glow across the Lord's scowling face. A deep, rumbling growl emanated from his massive chest. The talons of both hands clenched, relaxed, and clenched again. "What have you done, Salyth?"

The Lord slowly shook his head. Thrakst leaned back. His massive bulk thudded into the rock back of his cathedra. After releasing a long, rumbling exhalation, he looked at Phascyre and gave a single, almost imperceptible nod.

CHAPTER 15

"**P**iece of shit," Remulkin growled as he tugged at the neck of his newly issued battle uniform. In spite of its nanobot-infused smart material, the garments were historically uncomfortable and still required a certain amount of breaking in. Also, he didn't remember the uniform being so snug in the mid-section.

Walking down the long corridor, he approached the door to an office. His EON—newly authorized and augmented with both tactical features and military data—identified the room beyond as belonging to his new commanding officer, First Lieutenant Jenkinson.

Before Remulkin had departed the *Helm Warden*, the carrier's executive officer assigned freshly minted Second Lieutenant Remulkin Thramorus to the *Liberator*—the battlecruiser whose doomed crew had recovered Thramorus. After assigning him, the executive officer had ordered Remulkin to catch a shuttle to the battlecruiser and report to this First Lieutenant Jenkinson.

Technically, the unknown lieutenant outranked Remulkin. However, the scientist damned sure wouldn't allow some wet-behind-the-ears young man to lord over him. He had had more time in the chow line than this Lieutenant Jenkinson had had in the military.

As he approached the door, Remulkin's EON transmitted his identity, but the hatch didn't open. His belly bumped into its surface, and he stumbled backward.

"Damn it!"

A moment later the door finally opened, and a gruff feminine voice said, "Enter."

Thramorus stepped through the opening. Emerging into the room, he froze, realizing the voice had been all too familiar.

"Hello, Thramorus," said his commanding officer—who was neither male nor young. "I see you've been promoted from asshole to second lieutenant."

"You're shitting me!" Thramorus said as he stared incredulously at the woman who'd threatened to shoot him. When she'd first encountered him aboard the emptied battlecruiser, she'd all but accused him of killing everyone on Chuvarti and the *Liberator*.

"I wish I was, Lieutenant. But we're stuck with one another. I know why I'm here, but for the life of me, I can't figure out why a man of your years would want to return to duty."

Remulkin cocked an eyebrow. "You're not exactly a planting season pup yourself, *ma'am*," Remulkin said. His face darkened. "You have no idea what I've been through. I lost everything and everyone down—"

"You think you're the only one to lose someone, Lieutenant?" she said, cutting him off. Jenkinson stood, her face darkening as well. "How do you think this not so young Space Marine became a lieutenant?" She walked around her desk and stood directly in front of him. "Get over yourself, Thramorus. Between yesterday's events and the battles of the last year, everyone on this ship has lost friends, loved ones, and comrades."

Indifferently, Remulkin stared back at the lieutenant.

After a long, silent minute, the woman shook her head and returned to her desk. A chair grew from the floor, and she dropped into it.

"Report to Sergeant Kraiger. He'll set you up with quarters. I've ordered him to get you into the incubator as well."

"The incubator? I-I don't need that!"

She gave his belly a meaningful glance. "That says different."

Incubator was Space Marine slang for the device officially known as the Combat Conditioning and Training Expeditor. Reversing the effect of his years of physical fitness neglect would require significant time in the device. Remulkin's belabored heart went into overdrive as he considered the interminable hours he would soon spend in its claustrophobic coffin-shaped confines.

"Now," she said, "as you so eloquently put it: fuck off."

Lieutenant Thramorus shook his head again. "I told you, I don't want a network backup, don't want another version of me running in your godsdamned system."

In the soft, sterile light of the unit's medical suite, the younger man raised his hands. "But you don't understand, sir," said the sergeant. "It'll run in parallel. With the speed of our network connection, you won't be able to tell where you end and it begins. It's seamless." Sergeant Kraiger shrugged and added, "You need to have a backup running, Lieutenant. The next time the Zox attack, you might not be in the nose of the ship."

Remulkin shook his head and started prying at the bindings on his left wrist.

After Sergeant Kraiger had assigned his quarters, the man had led Thramorus to this room. Apparently acting as the unit's medic as well as its logistician, the young man had guided Remulkin toward a medical device that resembled a torture chair. Remulkin had finally understood the sergeant's intentions when Kraiger began to strap down his left arm.

Presently, he extricated his left wrist from the bindings and closed his eyes. Again the final image of his family within their Chuvarti residence rushed to fill his mind's visual void. This time, he didn't shun it. This was Remulkin's hell to live.

In his mind's eye, the scientist watched the evil, all-consuming light flood through his wife's favorite curtains, turning the umber window coverings ivory. Then, rendered in shades of white, Shikhana and their two children seemed to swim in a lake of blinding light. A shudder rolled down Remulkin's spine as he watched his drowning family disappear beneath the lake's radiant waves.

A year ago, when they'd first discussed traveling to Chuvarti, his wife had used the same arguments as Sergeant Kraiger did now. Remulkin had balked then as well, but for more selfish reasons.

Network backups were usually limited to Argonians assigned to the Galactic Defense Forces. However, colonial governments offered a fee-based version of the service to all new settlers. Thramorus had argued against it. The backup procedure was expensive, and even with the current offering of group plans, the data charges for a family's worth of bandwidth were exorbitant. Remulkin had assured Shikhana that they wouldn't be in any greater risk on Chuvarti than they were on Argonia.

How wrong he had been.

Remulkin opened his eyes and shook his head. "Fucking idiot," he whispered.

Sergeant Kraiger's head snapped back as if slapped. "Excuse me, sir?"

Blinking, Remulkin looked at the young man's reddening face. Still shaking his head, Thramorus said, "Nothing."

He'd made the wrong decision on Argonia, a decision for which he didn't want a second life's worth of regret.

Remulkin swallowed back the lump in his throat and then looked at Kraiger. "Listen, Sergeant. I know you mean well, but I'm not doing the fucking backup."

"Suit yourself," the sergeant said, his tone filling in the omitted "asshole".

Inwardly, Remulkin shook his head and thought, *You don't know how right you are, Sergeant.*

PART II

"The struggle is always worthwhile, if the end be worthwhile and the means honorable; foreknowledge of defeat is not sufficient reason to withdraw from the contest."

— Steven Brust

CHAPTER 16

Inside the cockpit of her Phoenix Starfighter, Major Sandra Fitzpatrick could see in every direction. An immersive, unobstructed, omnidirectional rendering of the external universe flowed across the inside of her fighter's spherical display. Flying while wrapped in its immersive imagery was like sailing through space in a lawn chair—except that Sandy could see through herself.

Today, when she had climbed into the fighter, nanobots programmed to fluoresce in polarized light had covered her body from the neck down. Tucking into the woman's every curve, they covered the portions of her form and the ship's adjacent interior structures that would otherwise obscure her view of the spheroidal display's internal surface. As Major Fitzpatrick flew through space, the glowing nanobots that had flowed around her physique and onto the spacecraft's adjacent surfaces formed an active image. Differentiated by her EON's optical feed, their polarized light generated a three-dimensional display that always pumped out a real-time video optimized for her current viewing angle. Regardless of which way Sandy looked, she couldn't differentiate the image of the external universe painted across her body from the one that flowed across the inside of the spherical display.

Like an automotive rearview mirror, a small EON-generated movable window floated in her peripheral vision. Currently, a front-on view of the fighter flying behind her hovered near the middle of the small display.

Flying through space while suspended in the geometric center of the spheroid, it was easy to forget that an entire fighter surrounded her body. However, visual reminders hung all around Sandy. Flying in formation around her spaceship, teardrop-shaped Phoenix Starfighters lay in every direction. The needle-sharp nose of each pointed at the planet that hung before the squadron.

Beautiful beyond anything she had ever imagined, an incredible panorama filled the forward half of Sandy's spheroid. Knowing she was one of the first humans to see it in person made the image all the more incredible.

Jupiter hung motionlessly ahead of her Phoenix Starfighter. Obscuring half of the star field, it looked closer than Earth did from the altitude of the International Space Station, but they were still outside the orbits of Jupiter's inner two moons: Io and Europa.

Sandy had seen many pictures of Jupiter. Aside from its curvature, the planet's upper atmosphere had always looked flat and two-dimensional, its cloud bands rendered in soft, earthy pastels. However, in front of her fighter, vibrant, brightly colored and visibly churning, three-dimensional bands ringed the gas giant. Within the globe-spanning cloud formations that formed each major band, smaller-scale features boiled and churned. Even from this distance, she could perceive their motion, especially near the Great Red Spot. In places, she could peer between continent-sized cloud formations and see into darker, lower regions. At the giant planet's limb, a faint blue hue hinted at a clear upper atmosphere.

Shifting her mental focus, Sandy studied the virtual hologram that the EON was pumping into her brain's visual cortex. In the tactical display, the perfectly spaced formation of eighteen human-manned Argonian fighters silently sliced deeper into the Jovian system. Europa, one of Jupiter's ice moons, passed beneath the formation as they flew into the space between its orbit and that of Jupiter's innermost moon, Io.

The two moons painted a study in contrast. Scientists believed that Europa's red-striped ice shell hid a global, miles-deep salt water ocean that might support life. On neighboring Io—the most volcanically active planetary body in the solar system—volcanoes, lava lakes, and sulfur-covered plains wrapped the moon in a hellish milieu that outstripped Dante Alighieri's darkest imaginings.

Beneath Sandy, reddish ochre deposits—possibly organic material that had boiled up through cracks in the ice—criss-crossed Europa's white crust. Ahead of her fighter, Io looked like a rotten orange. Various sulfurous compounds covered its mottled yellow surface. Roughly the same size as Earth's natural satellite, the relatively tiny moon appeared to float just above the sharp-edged shadow it cast on Jupiter's vast atmospheric ocean.

Sandy flew in close formation with Richard. As the Commander of 1st Space Fighter Wing, Colonel Allison had also assigned himself as the leader of 1st Squadron. The commanders of the wing's five other units (2nd through 6th Starfighter Squadrons) acted independently, but all reported directly to Wing Commander Allison.

The day after they'd boarded the Helm Warden, Newcastle had promoted Sandy to Major and assigned her to 1st Squadron as Richard's second in command, his Executive Officer or XO for short. 1st Fighter Squadron of 1st Fighter Wing had taken the name of their new starships as its nickname. Using that designation, Sandy's position as the unit XO made her call sign Phoenix Seven. As squadron lead, Richard was Phoenix Six.

In their current configuration, the sixteen other starfighters of Phoenix Squadron cocooned Richard and Sandy's paired fighters in a spherical formation.

Through the use of his EON, Jake had discovered that the original name for the alien fighters came from an ancient Argonian story of a mythical beast that would rise anew from the ashes of defeat. The similarity of the tale to Earth's mythical Phoenix was obvious and made the selection of an English language name self-evident.

As a highly maneuverable and heavily armed attack spacecraft, the Phoenix Starfighter afforded significantly less interior room than the utilitarian *Turtle*. It crammed many of the same amenities into a small, single-floor design. Behind Sandy, a small airlock and spacesuit cabinet sat next to a modest living space designed for use during long-duration flights.

While the ships relied on maneuverability to avoid laser burn-throughs, they also had a protective force field. It turned out the *Turtle* was equipped for one as well, but it had been removed before its arrival on Earth. To bring the utility ship up to specs, engineers had recently installed a spare force field generator.

Capitalizing on their head start in planning and training, Colonel Newcastle and his team had taught the new starfighter pilots how to operate in the three-dimensional battlefield of space. Each pilot had first received a download from the edification encoder. The program helped each man and woman master their Phoenix Starfighter. It also imparted a basic understanding of the tactics of space combat. While the encoder even gave the trainee a level of muscle memory for the learned task, only hands-on training turned a knowledgeable pilot into a proficient combat aviator. And only a live-fire exercise could approximate real-world combat.

Today, for the first time, the fighter wing was about to fire real weapons at an armed target: a modified asteroid that orbited Jupiter. Roughly the size of a Zoxyth ship and apparently a relatively recent acquisition for the Jovian system, the mile-wide moon's orbital eccentricity and inclination were currently carrying it between Io and Europa.

Admiral Johnston had directed them to perform the live-fire exercise in the Jovian system for obvious reasons.

The Phoenix Starfighters had turned out to be devastating war machines. The antimatter-fueled ships sported a pair of incredibly powerful lasers that had punched holes through every test material the scientists placed in front of it. They'd been unable to determine how something that powerful wasn't self-destructive. Its energy output was so intense it should melt the emitter.

Additionally, their long, pointed noses contained an extremely powerful railgun that fired hypervelocity rounds. The projectiles were small, but they were double the weight and mass of a similarly sized lead pellet. The rounds departed the ship's prow with a muzzle velocity of twenty miles per second and slammed into the target with enough kinetic energy to level an office building.

Reckoning that the unit wouldn't get much out of the battle drill if the target couldn't shoot back, Newcastle had sent engineers to the asteroid yesterday. They'd placed targeting lasers all over its surface. Their randomly fired focused beams wouldn't harm the Phoenix Fighters, but any ship that got hit by one of them for anything longer than a millisecond would automatically exit the battle.

Crackling across her tactical radio, Richard's voice broke the silence. "Second through Sixth Squadrons, proceed to your assigned initialization points. I'll take First Squadron to IP Alpha. As briefed, proceed inbound from your assigned IP coordinates at precisely the assigned time."

"Second Squadron, roger."

"Third Squadron, roger."

The last three commanders responded in order.

Across the squadron's assigned frequency, Richard said, "This is Phoenix Six. Turn direct IP Alpha in three, two, *one!*"

As if physically connected to one another, 1st Squadron's eighteen starfighters simultaneously snapped to their new course line. On Sandy's tactical display, the hexagonal formation of six squadrons flew apart like a starburst. Each spherical eighteen-ship formation simultaneously rocketed away from the central point. Their independent vectors soon spread the fighter wing's 108 Phoenix Starfighters across a broad swath of Jovian space. On the new headings, each squadron's sixteen ships raced toward initialization points that ringed the target.

Just as it had during their final drills in Earth space, the choreographed maneuver went off flawlessly.

The navigational portion of her EON's virtual vision fed Sandy position, vector, and velocity information. She was thankful for the edification encoder. Without the intuition-level comprehension imparted by its processes, she would have needed a year in this cockpit to fully understand half of the layered data pouring into her visual cortex. Thanks to the encoder's assistance, Sandy now absorbed the data like a sponge. In this fluid, rapidly developing exercise, she had a high level of situational awareness she wouldn't have thought possible two weeks ago.

The eighteen Phoenix Starfighters of 1st Squadron neared their assigned initialization point.

"Phoenix Squadron, this is Six," Richard said. "Turn IP inbound in three, two, *one!*"

In unison, the squadron's eighteen fighters turned inbound toward the target asteroid. However, an instant before they'd executed the course change, Sandy had seen a problem.

Alarms started going off in her head.

3rd Squadron had turned early!

For this live-fire exercise, the timing was crucial. If one flight fired before the others were in position, the exploding debris field could overtake the other two flights before they could deploy their weapons and change vectors, exiting the blast plane.

She had to alert Richard. "Six, this is Phoenix Seven. Third Squadron turned about a second early!"

"Roger!" Richard said with evident alarm.

"Third Squadron!" Richard yelled over the fighter wing's common frequency. "Break off, break—"

Things were moving too fast. Before the words had left Colonel Allison's mouth, Charlie Flight had fired their weapons.

The asteroid exploded in a brilliant flash. Suddenly, debris and railgun projectiles were flying at them at twenty miles per second.

Her fighter's automatic collision avoidance algorithms had Sandy's ship jumping all over the place. In less than one second, the fighter changed position at least four times, and her shields flashed several more times, as the debris, too concentrated to be completely avoided, impacted her fighter's protective envelope.

"Phoenix Squadron! *Abort! Abort! Abort!*" Richard yelled.

Executing the planned escape maneuver early, each fighter shot vertically out of the asteroid's orbital plane.

As Sandy's ship launched out of the debris field, she saw Richard's fighter tumble out of control. It looked like a huge swarm of tightly packed asteroid chunks had outstripped the ship's maneuvering ability. As Richard's fighter tried to jump out of their path, a glancing blow from one of the tumbling rocks blasted it sideways.

"Phoenix Six, what's your status?"

No response.

"Phoenix Six, come in!"

Still no response.

She did a quick inventory of 1st Squadron. Aside from Richard, all were still with her.

Sandy formulated a quick plan.

"Phoenix Squadron, this is Seven. Continue to the egress rendezvous point and hold. I'm going back for Six."

The expected objections burst from the speakers of her spacesuit's radio. Some of them offered to join her; another said it was suicide.

"The railgun projectiles are well clear by now," she said, cutting them off. "By myself, I can deal with and avoid the largest asteroids. The ship's computer and shields can handle the rest."

She hoped she sounded more certain than she felt.

Sandy turned her fighter in the direction Richard's ship had disappeared. The icy surface of Europa filled her view-wall.

"Oh shit!" she whispered.

Ahead of her fighter, an insane storm of ricocheting, tumbling asteroids plunged toward Europa's frozen surface. Sandy could already see icy geysers erupting as the leading edge of the debris field rained down on the Jovian moon. The tactical display showed Richard's ship in the middle of the storm and falling fast.

"Really?!"

Shaking her head, Sandy dove her fighter headlong into the meat grinder, directly toward the ice-covered ocean.

∼

Richard's ship continued to roll and tumble violently end over end. An insane panorama of alternating red-streaked white and star-speckled black scrolled across the only portion of his display that still worked. The blurred, looping black-white cycle of the outside world visible through its rectangular presentation made it difficult for Richard to get his bearings. If something didn't change, the centrifugal forces would soon rob him of consciousness and any chance of recovery.

Grunting, the pilot bore down, trying to keep the blood from draining out of his brainpan—a technique all fighter pilots used during high-G maneuvers. Unfortunately, it was only useful for short-duration exposure. If he couldn't soon restore power and arrest the spin, he'd first gray out and then pass out completely. And he didn't even want to think about what would come after that.

3rd Squadron's early salvo had launched a city-sized debris field straight at 1st Squadron's fighters. Before he could escape, a particularly crowded swarm of fragmented asteroid had overwhelmed Richard's fighter. He'd almost cleared it. The ship's last-second maneuver lessened the blow, but the rock still slammed the fighter hard enough to knock the gravity drive offline.

When the drive had failed, it took the fighter's inertial dampening with it. Richard guessed that the jolt might have knocked him out for a second or three. One moment the ship had been jinking and dodging around rocks, the next instant he found himself floating in the middle of a tumbling cockpit. When he'd tried to move, Richard discovered that webbing held him suspended, his head in the geometric center of the fighter's now completely hollow spheroidal cockpit. Because of the ship's uncontrolled roll and his head's central position, blood was draining from his cranium and pooling in his legs.

Due to high G-forces and restrictive webbing, Richard was unable to shift his body to a better position. And there was nothing for him to push off of. All of the nanobot-formed cockpit structures had melded back into the fighter's concave floor. He guessed that the constructs had retracted to reduce the threat of blunt force trauma. Fortunately, the repurposed nanobots had encased him in the safety webbing. They'd stopped Richard from becoming a red, lumpy bug stain smeared across the fighter's inside wall. However, the entire thing had happened instantly, in a time frame shorter than the refresh rate of human consciousness; he'd perceived none of it.

Through the insane, spinning image crossing the display's field of view, Richard noticed that each time Europa's icy surface flashed across his small piece of functional display, certain surface features appeared to have grown in size.

"Great!" he said through a grunt. He was falling into the Jovian moon's gravity well. "Fucking wonderful."

Suddenly, an impossible image flashed across the display. He caught a momentary glimpse of a fighter deftly maneuvering through the debris field.

A few rotations later, he saw it again, this time much closer.

Then Richard began to gray out. His eyesight narrowed, peripheral vision fading as his brain was starved of oxygen-carrying hemoglobin.

The emergency radio attached to his hip crackled to life.

"Phoenix Six, this is Seven. Are you still with me, Richard?"

He reached for the radio with a hand that he'd previously freed from the cocoon. Richard tugged at it, but a piece of the webbing had pinned the radio to his leg. The effort exhausted him. Conceding defeat, he released the small device, cursing under his breath. Blindly probing its side, Richard found the textured transmit button and pressed it.

"Get the hell out of here, Major! There's nothing you can do for me." He paused and grunted, fighting to keep his eyes open. "Go, Sandy," Richard said weakly. "I can see Europa getting—"

A series of knocking sounds interrupted him.

"What the hell?" he said through a guttural growl. Then he hyperventilated a couple of quick breaths and bore down in another effort to force a little more blood into his fading brain.

The knocking continued, but its frequency was slowing, as was the spinning of his ship.

Breathing heavily, he felt his body respond to the reduced G-forces. Easing pressure finally allowed his circulatory system to send blood to his oxygen-starved brain. Color and peripheral vision returned to Richard's universe.

Through the rectangular display, he saw an amazing scene. Sandy had pulled her fighter insanely close to his and matched its rotation, but in the opposite direction, meshed together like two counter-rotating gears. Once she had synchronized her roll with his, she had slowed the tumble a little with each rotation. The knocking he'd heard had been the two ships making contact twice per revolution. Two stubby, wing-like laser pods extended from the sides of each of the counter-rotating teardrop-shaped ships. She'd used them like gear teeth. The pods were probably beat to shit now and almost assuredly no longer functional. But her tactic had worked, was working. A few thuds later, the rotation stopped. Then she made a couple of additional surgical impacts and arrested the slower, end-over-end tumble as well.

"Very impressive, Seven, but ..."

"I know. We're not out of the woods yet," Sandy said, finishing the sentence for him.

Outside, their velocity had matched that of the debris field. On the good side, that meant the danger from flying asteroid chunks had subsided. On the bad side, it meant they were falling toward Europa's frozen surface even faster.

His pinned-down emergency radio sparked to life again. "I'm going to position myself under your ship," Sandy said. "I'll try to use my gravity drive to arrest your fall."

Through his EON, Richard attempted to reconnect with his fighter, but the obstinate piece of shit refused to respond.

He pressed the transmit button. "Damn it, Sandy! I appreciate what you're trying to do, but that's gonna be like balancing two bowling balls on top of one another."

As Richard floated weightlessly in the surreally silent and now nearly motionless cabin, Europa's surface crept across his field of view. Then the moon's horizon slid into the bottom edge of the displayed image.

Great! On top of everything else, I'm going in head first.

An image of Major Fitzpatrick's fighter zipped across the display and disappeared overhead, beneath his inverted ship.

"Damn it, Sandy! I said to get the hell out of—"

After an audible thump, he felt his fighter start to decelerate, pressing Richard head first deeper into the emergency restraints.

"I was able to override the safety protocols with my EON. The computer is helping me stay centered under your mass, but it's a *lot* of mass. Hopefully, I can arrest your fall before we hit the surface."

All of the icons in Richard's EON-generated virtual vision remained grayed out. He still couldn't access any of the ship's systems. The impact had apparently knocked out everything except the nanobots and one section of the display.

He keyed the radio. "My ship is completely dead."

Outside, something suddenly fell through his field of view. He pressed the transmit button again. "It's working! We're starting to slow down." The object he'd seen was a small asteroid that had a moment before been flying along in formation, but as they slowed, it hadn't; the rock had fallen away from them and raced toward its date with European destiny. However, through the display, he saw the icy horizon continue to rise as their long fall into Europa's gravity well persisted.

A deafening report came from under his feet. The ship rocked sideways, almost tumbling off of Sandy's fighter.

"What was that?" Sandy asked.

Richard felt the floor shift under him as she corrected for the altered center of gravity.

"I told you to get out of here," he said. "Now that we're slowing, the rocks that were falling with us are still falling." He frowned sardonically. "It's starting to rain asteroids, woman!"

He felt her shift them sideways again. A moment later, a huge piece of asteroid flashed downward through the display's image.

"I guess it was too small to show up on my hologram," Sandy said. "I'm using it to keep us out of the way of the bigger pieces."

"Okay," Richard said, drawing out the first syllable.

The horizon rushed toward the falling formation of space fighters.

From his ever-closing point of view, the surface's reddish-orange fissures gained a depth and breadth not previously appreciable. Many looked like chasms with soft, rolling edges and overhangs. The spaces outside of the canyons looked like gentle plains covered by dirty snow.

Another booming report reverberated through his fighter, this one so loud it left Richard's ears ringing. After a moment, he heard a new noise rise above the ringing: the hiss of escaping air. Through all of it, he heard and felt his ears popping as they tried to compensate for the rapidly dropping pressure.

"That last one breached my—!" His helmet suddenly deployed, cutting off his words mid-sentence.

He toggled the emergency radio. "Phoenix Seven ... *Sandy!* Can you hear me?"

Nothing. Even if she were responding, he wasn't sure he would be able to hear her. Sound wouldn't propagate well in the ship's rapidly thinning atmosphere. Soon hard vacuum would eliminate it altogether.

The last thought reminded him of a contingency he'd heard an astronaut discuss during a TV documentary. In the event of a communication failure during a spacewalk, they planned to communicate by placing their helmet against the skin of the ship. Theoretically, the physical contact would convert the helmet's sound wave-induced vibrations into something people in the space station could hear and understand.

I hope that same theory works with a handheld radio, he thought.

With a mighty tug, he broke the radio free from his hip. Struggling against the safety restraining system, he finally raised it to eye level and planted its speaker firmly against his helmet. Immediately, he heard a tinny, unintelligible voice. Listening intently, Richard slid the radio around until he found a sweet spot. Sandy's words resolved. "... Six, this is Phoenix Seven. Come in, Richard!"

For her to hear him, Richard would need to place the microphone against his helmet, but it sat in a separate part of the device. He slid the handheld radio up until the microphone's smaller grill touched the visor in front of his mouth.

Yelling, he said, "Sandy, this is Richard. Can you hear me?"

As he shouted, he looked past the radio and into the display. Richard's eyes widened. In spite of their continuing deceleration, the surface was rushing up to meet them.

"Oh shit," he whispered as he slid the speaker back to the sweet spot. He found it in time to hear the last part of her response. "... scared me there, Richard. Hold on tight. This is going to be a rough landing."

At the same time, he felt her shift them sideways. Another large chunk of asteroid debris screamed across the display. A brief moment later, a geyser of ice and asteroid shot upward from the surface and crossed his field of view again, traveling in the opposite direction this time.

Then they slammed into the moon.

An ice storm sprayed out in all directions. Debris from their crash-landing mixed with the ejecta from the previous asteroid impact. Their sideways pre-crash jaunt sent the two fighters skidding across the moon's icy surface.

Richard saw Sandy's fighter pinned between his ship and the ice. Through the miraculously still-functioning display—which happened to have ended up pointed in the direction of their continuing skid—Richard stared with wide-eyed amazement as her ship plowed a path through the white field, icy powder spewing laterally from its sides.

From his upside-down point of view, the horizon began to resolve as they cleared the cloud generated by 3rd Squadron's handiwork. If they survived this, Richard was going to have a serious discussion with Major Snead, the Squadron's flight lead.

Weak gravity coupled with the icy surface's low drag coefficient allowed their slide to continue almost unabated, farther than Richard would have believed possible. Then he saw they were riding up an incline. Yard by agonizing yard, the unlikely formation finally slowed in earnest.

Just as Richard began to think that they might actually survive this, they crested the large hill—which he now realized was a ridge line. At the same time, a distant cliff face rose into view. It appeared to run parallel to the ridge they'd crested.

"You're shitting me!" Richard yelled. He pressed the radio button. "It's a fucking canyon!"

Like Olympic class lemmings, they raced toward the edge of the crevice. Apparently having been thrust upwards by plate tectonics, the canyon's far cliff wall loomed. It's sheer wall towered over their side of the chasm.

The vibrations generated by the skidding ships transmitted silently through his ship's hull to the safety restraints holding him securely in place. The frequency of the vibrations steadily decreased as the decelerating pair slid closer to the crevice. Its precipice crept into view as they slid toward the all-too-close horizon created by the ice field's sudden disappearance.

Just as they reached the edge of the chasm, Sandy's ship pitched up on a cornice-like lip.

Finally, the two ships skidded to a stop.

Richard stared for a long, breathless moment. They didn't explode, and the canyon wall failed to collapse beneath them. When neither those nor the other myriad movie tropes currently streaming through his mind's eye failed to manifest, he released his held breath in a long, braying laugh. "Holy shit! I can't believe that just happened!"

The fighter's emergency restraint system gently lowered him to the ceiling-turned-floor.

Rolling onto his feet, Richard squatted and looked into the display. From his partially blocked perspective, he could see Sandy's fighter still pinned under the front of his ship. It appeared to be balanced precariously on the precipice of the ice chasm.

Richard placed the radio against his helmet.

"Sandy! Are you okay?"

"Yeah, just peachy. The impact knocked my drive offline, and I'm hanging like Spider-Man in his freaking web," she said wryly. "I disabled the shields so that I wouldn't have to deal with the balancing bowling balls dilemma." She paused and then added, "The drive still won't respond to EON commands, but the shields are booting up ... now."

Suddenly, a jolt sent Richard rolling across the floor of the fighter.

He heard Sandy string together a series of words that would have left Jake slack-jawed. Then Richard's fighter rocked backward again.

Sandy's voice crackled over the radio. "Oh ...! Oh shit!"

The expanding shields had shoved the two spacecraft apart, knocking Richard's fighter backward. Now lying on the ceiling-floor, he saw Sandy's ship had moved even farther in the opposite direction. It teetered and then cascaded over the rim, disappearing into the icy chasm.

"Sandy!" Richard screamed through his helmet.

She didn't respond.

He stuck the radio to the right side of his suit and headed toward the airlock at the back of the ship. He was relieved to see the appropriate portion of the spheroid's skin dissolve. He stepped into the airlock. A moment later, the lock's outer wall dissolved as well. Richard lunged through the opening. Outside, he stood a little too quickly. In the low gravity—roughly one-seventh of Earth's—his feet left the ground for a moment.

After landing again, he held out his arms and caught his balance. Richard rounded the back of his heavily damaged fighter and hop-walked Apollo astronaut-style along its side. Traversing the surface in long, bounding strides, he approached the precipice.

The colonel slid clumsily to a stop at the canyon's rim. The near side was not the vertical cliff he'd imagined. It sloped steeply away to a point a quarter mile below his current position. There it gradually flattened out and disappeared under the overhanging far canyon wall. Tracking Sandy's long skid line, Richard saw her fighter. Still moving, it had somehow turned right side up and was riding its shield bubble like a giant, invisible sled. As it reached the bottom of the chasm, her fighter slid out of sight beneath the far wall's underturned ice sheet.

Looking over his shoulder, Richard studied his fighter. That thing was never going to fly again. It was toast, and there wasn't anything in it that would help him here and now. Its emergency beacon had started broadcasting the instant he'd lost main power. Someone would find them soon, but Sandy might be in trouble right now.

Richard looked back down into the crevice, frowning and shaking his head.

Finally, he said, "Fuck it," and launched himself down the steep slope.

CHAPTER 17

F lying a few feet above the ice, Richard sailed more than a hundred feet down the steep slope. Even in Europa's weak gravity, the velocity of his slow-motion fall soon built to a disturbing speed. With mounting horror, he watched the slope's surface rush up to meet him. Bracing for impact, he aimed to land on both feet, intent on another lunar-style bounding hop. But as soon as they hit the ice, his legs shot out from under him. The combination of inertia, low gravity, and the slope's virtually frictionless surface shattered his plan.

He slammed hard onto his back. "Shit!" Richard yelled, dragging the word into two syllables. For a moment, his feet shared the sky with a sea of crisp stars as he slid down the steep slope, careening toward the distant canyon floor. Using skidding arms and hands for leverage, Richard lowered his legs and tried to dig his heels into the ice. Even as he did so, his speed increased alarmingly. His arms and legs flailed, but nothing worked; he just kept going faster.

The colonel's heart raced. The initially distant canyon floor now rushed to meet him. As he descended deeper into the chasm, he skipped across raised dark, rough bands like a truck driving down a washboard road.

Still on his back and racing across the ice feet first, Richard steadied himself on his elbows and forearms. Again he tried to dig in his heels. Finally, they found purchase on the roughening surface. He began to slow. Twin rooster tails of spraying ice and dark pebbles sprayed across him. The icy spray and debris soon coated Richard from head to toe. His visor iced over, threatening to blind him to the onrushing terrain. He shifted his weight to one arm so that he could wipe it with the other hand, but a thin strip of material peeled away from the neck ring and began to wipe the visor from bottom to top and back again.

The combination of the fading slope coupled with the textured surface allowed his feet a better grip. Yard by yard, his speed slowed.

Overhead, the visible portion of the sky was shrinking to a narrow ribbon as the far wall towered over him.

"Shit! Ouch, ouch! Shit!" Richard screamed as he traversed a series of spine-jarring ridges. In a cloud of ice spray, he passed under a shadowed ledge and finally came to a stop. Unimpeded by an atmosphere, the tumultuous cloud thinned as its individual components continued to fly away from him.

Looking up through the rapidly clearing sky, Richard saw that he'd slid to a stop just below the same overhanging wall under which Sandy had disappeared. Tectonic forces had apparently sheared off the bottom twenty feet of the two-thousand-foot-tall ice cliff. Two stories above him, the canyon wall's smooth face curled under to form a ceiling of bluish-white ice.

Richard sat up and saw Sandy's fighter. It had stopped forty feet deeper into the cornice-shaped cave. The ship had come to rest wedged into the narrowing sliver of space where curled-under chasm wall met canyon floor.

He scrambled to his feet and reached for his radio.

It was gone!

Turning to face the slope, he visually scanned the long trail he'd left in the ice, but didn't see the dark, rectangular cube.

He hoped Sandy's drive had come back online. If not, they might be in trouble. The steepness of the chasm's walls made getting out that way hopeless. And with Sandy's ship tucked under a quarter-mile-thick ledge of ice, the signal of its emergency beacon wasn't likely to broadcast beyond the floor of the chasm.

Turning back toward Sandy's fighter, Richard started to hop toward her ship, but he tripped over something. Looking down, he saw that he'd stumbled over one of the small ridges. It looked the same as the ones that had jarred his spine during the last part of his skidding stop.

Studying its textured surface, Richard blinked several times. "What in the hell is that?"

He suddenly realized that the dark ridges must be material pushed to the surface from the liquid ocean below because tiny, reddish-brown shells covered each ridge like an encrustation of barnacles. Looking left and right he saw that the brown strata of shells continued down the length of the chasm.

Turning, he walked back to the next ridge. It, too, owed its dark color to the multitude of small, round carapaces embedded in it. Dropping to a knee, he picked up one of the thousands of shells his skidding stop had dislodged. Holding it at eye level, he studied its spiral form. About a quarter-inch wide, it looked like a cross between a nautilus shell and that of a snail. Flipping it over, he searched its opening for signs of its long-dead occupant.

It suddenly occurred to him that the shells had the same color as the red stripes he'd seen from space. Evidence of extraterrestrial life had been staring them in the face for decades.

Suddenly, something touched his right shoulder. Richard jumped. Snapping around, he half-expected to find the creature's big brother towering over him.

To his relief it was just Sandy.

He heard her snorting laugh come through his suit's speaker.

"You nearly gave me a heart attack! I've told you a million times: never sneak up on me when we're stranded on a frozen moon!"

After a final snort, she raised her hand in a mock salute. "Yessir, Colonel Frosty!"

Richard looked at his body. The thick coating of white frost and brown shells almost looked like fur.

"You look like the love child of a polar bear and a grizzly," Sandy said and then dissolved into another fit of snorting laughter.

"I take it you're fine?" Richard said.

"No worse for wear," she finally said after a long sigh.

Richard picked one of the brown shells from his chest and held it out to her. "Did you see these?"

Glancing at it and the band of material, she shrugged. "You ain't seen nothing yet."

She turned and began bounding toward her ship. "Follow me."

He took off after her. Ice spray launched from the surface with each landing. The trajectory of the ejecta reminded him of the old Apollo videos. Unencumbered by gravity or an atmosphere, the spray shot out in all directions from each foot's point of impact, only begrudgingly surrendering to the moon's weak gravity after it had flown a few feet.

"Considering our present situation, you seem awfully chipper," Richard said between hops.

"Well, I know something you don't," Sandy said.

"What might that be?"

"You'll see it when we get in the ship, but first there is something I want to show you over here," she said, pointing to the left of her fighter.

As they went deeper into the dark cave, their suit lights deployed. Sandy's fixture cast a bouncing blue spot over the cave's wall and ceiling. The radiance reflecting off the shiny surfaces cast a swarming kaleidoscope of lights and shadows across the surreal scene.

Slowing to an awkward walk, she went around to the left side and disappeared behind the fighter.

Richard followed. As he passed the ship, he froze in place. Again, he had to blink his eyes a couple of times to make sure he wasn't having a hallucination.

"Oh my God!" he whispered.

Sandy was standing next to a large, frozen carcass that protruded from the point where the two sides of the canyon came together.

After a moment, he was able to unglue his feet from the icy floor of the crevice. As he approached Sandy and the beast, he panned his light from its protruding head to the point where its body disappeared into the ice.

"Holy shit," Richard whispered. "That thing is huge! It's as thick as an SUV and must be at least thirty feet long. And that's just the part sticking out."

Sandy nodded. "I remember watching a documentary about Europa," she said. "These sheets of ice are like tectonic plates. Jupiter's gravity causes them to spread apart, allowing water from deep below to boil up into the gap. But they said it would freeze over instantly. Once the plates move back together, the slush is forced out of the crevice and piled on either side of the chasm." She pointed toward the cave entrance. "Just like the one at the lip of this canyon."

Richard nodded and pointed to the frozen beast. "So this shark-thing got trapped in the gap when the two plates of ice came back together."

He took a tentative step closer to the carcass and shined his helmet light on its head. "Look at those teeth!" He bent in for a closer look. "I don't see any eyes."

Sandy shook her head. "Me neither. Probably too dark under the ice for them to be of much use."

Suddenly, the ice under their feet lunged forward a few feet, knocking both of them down. Frozen spray shot out from the seam where floor met ceiling.

Standing, Richard pulled Sandy to her feet. "I think I'm ready to see the good news in the ship."

"Me, too," she replied and began to head toward the back of her fighter.

Richard bounded after her. He had to push off the ceiling as his adrenaline-fueled leap carried him too high.

In spite of the low gravity, they made good time. Just as they reached the airlock, another tremor shook the chasm. This time, he saw the gap between the roof and ceiling narrow. So far, the ship's shield was protecting it from the crushing weight. He could see it pressing a domed indention into the cavern's ceiling.

He followed her through the airlock. As soon as it cycled, Richard and Sandy entered the fighter's spherical cockpit. As they did, both of their helmets automatically stowed.

Unlike his display, Sandy's still worked. Standing in the middle of the cabin's wraparound immersive video feed, he could no longer see the ship.

Richard took a deep breath. "I hope you've got *really* good news."

"You *have*," she corrected.

"We can work on my English some other ... What the ...?" His EON had connected to the ship's data. All of her fighter's systems had come back online. But when the tactical display pumped its virtual hologram into Richard's visual cortex, he saw the good news for himself.

The *Galactic Guardian* was flying into the Jovian system.

"Hot damn!" Richard said. The two pilots laughed and exchanged high-fives.

For today's exercise, they'd left the carrier and its five other one hundred and eight-ship fighter wings in Earth space. Richard didn't know why it had come here, but he had never been so happy to see the damned thing.

"Thank God!" he said. "Their sensors can see through planets. Hopefully, they see us down here." He paused. Looking up at the domed depression that the shields were pressing into the ice shelf, he said, "I'm not sure how much longer we'll be retrievable."

As if on cue, the chasm began shaking violently.

Suddenly Sandy screamed and pointed forward. "Look!"

Ahead of the ship, slushy ice poured from the crevice's seam. As he watched, the crease opened, and torrents of water spilled out and flowed around the fighter.

The gravity drive wasn't online yet, so he felt it when the ship pitched forward and started to slide toward the gaping maw. Richard reached for Sandy's arm. He yelled, "Get the drive online!" But she was already settling into the cockpit that the nanobots had just formed for her. The fighter continued to tilt into the waiting ocean. "See if you can reverse this slide!"

"The drive still won't come online!" Sandy said. He saw her fingers furiously tapping manual commands into the small control panel that had formed under her right hand.

The fighter tilted again. Now it pointed straight down, forcing Richard to stand on the forward face of the still-functioning spherical display.

As the fighter slid deeper, inky-black water appeared to lap at the outer brim of the display. Richard knew the water was actually lapping at the shields, but the imagery was pretty convincing. It looked like he was standing in a sinking glass bowl.

The dark ocean swallowed more of the light as the ship slipped deeper.

To his left, Richard saw the shark-thing's frozen carcass begin to sink out of sight. Then something even larger and moving with incredible speed emerged from the depths and snatched it, and just as quickly disappeared back into the gloom.

"Sandy! Now would be a good time."

Wide-eyed, she peered between her boots, looking down on him from her unresponsive controls. "The drive still won't come online!" she said plaintively.

The ship slid deeper.

Richard looked straight up. Behind Sandy, a shrinking crown of glowing slush provided the cabin's only illumination.

Then the ship broke free of the ice and began to sink in earnest. The last of the light disappeared.

"Shit, shit, *shit!*" Sandy said. He heard her punch something.

Standing in the dark, Richard still felt like he was in a sinking glass bowl. Then a jolt travelled up his legs. "Did you feel that?" he said.

"Yeah," Sandy whispered. "I think we're hung on a ledge."

Thinking of the shark-thing eater, Richard said, "Try the landing lights!"

"Got it!" Sandy said.

He flinched as brilliant external light suddenly flooded the cockpit. As his eyes adjusted, he blinked and then whispered, "Oh my God."

Over his head and still locked into her seat, Sandy stared outside, her mouth hanging open.

Thousands of small, swimming, multicolored forms surrounded the fighter. Unlike the shark-thing, these apparently had eyes. They swarmed to the lights. Within each of the luminous beams, oddly shaped fins and twisted tentacles periodically protruded from the congregated swirling mass of alien life.

Another tremor rocked the floor. Richard thought they must have slipped off the ice ledge. He was about to say as much, but then light reappeared overhead.

Sandy's eyes widened. "Did we slip off?"

His knees bent as something again tugged them upward, toward the light. Richard shook his head and smiled. "That's a tractor beam. The carrier found us!"

Sandy pumped both of her fists into the air. "Yes!"

Then Sandy looked toward Richard's feet and shrieked in horror.

Richard looked down to see a bus-sized open mouth lined with jagged rows of razor-sharp teeth rising from the depths. The mouth's owner was extremely large and closing on the ship with incredible speed.

This was either the whale-sized carnivore he'd glimpsed earlier, or one of its close relatives.

As the lower half of the starfighter disappeared into the monster's gaping mouth, the landing lights lit up the beast's gullet. Richard suddenly knew how live bait must feel. He resolved to never fish again —if he lived through this.

Then the fighter broke the surface, flying backward out of the water and out of the beast's mouth. Sensing the prey slipping from its grasp, the shark-thing eater gnashed its jaws closed. On the spheroidal display, the monstrous teeth appeared to slam together just beneath Richard's feet.

After a moment of shocked silence, he and Sandy laughed self-consciously. Then they squinted as the fighter emerged into direct sunlight. They accelerated out of the chasm.

Still hanging nose down, the fighter rocketed away from the ice canyon. Over the next few minutes, the chasm's huge, parallel ridges shrank to the apparent size of a railroad track, and then just a thin red line.

Richard's destroyed fighter ascended in formation with them.

Sandy activated the radio. "Galactic Guardian, this is Phoenix Seven, over," she said.

They didn't reply. Which was odd. Flight ops had someone monitoring that frequency at all times, especially during recovery operations.

"Galactic Guardian," Sandy said again. "This is Phoenix Seven. Come in, over."

Still no reply.

"Must be something wrong with our radio," she said.

With the inertial dampeners still offline, he felt the ship decelerate. Then he began to float. "Screw it," Richard said as he drifted past Sandy. He pointed behind her. "There's the *Guardian*. We'll be able to talk to them face to face in a minute."

Looking in the direction he'd indicated, Sandy nodded. Then a confused look crossed her face. "Why haven't they recovered the rest of the fighters?"

Richard looked back to the *Guardian*. Sure enough, it looked like they'd left all of the wing's fighters parked behind the carrier. Aligned in stationary rows, they hung motionlessly, just aft of the bay doors.

Richard shrugged. "Maybe they wanted to recover our damaged ships first."

Gravity slowly returned to the ship's interior. He could now stand next to Sandy. As they approached the back of the carrier, the rear portion of the spheroidal display blacked out, blocking the hangar bay from view. Richard was about to complain about yet another failed system, but then the edge of the Guardian's hangar slid into view as their two fighters passed backward through the bay doors.

He pointed at the inside edge of the door. "We're in, and still nobody is talking to us. It must be our radio. Your little maneuver probably knocked off the antenna."

Sandy cocked an eyebrow at him. "My *little maneuver* saved your life."

Richard shook his head. "No, I would've—"

The ship dropped to the floor with a thud, unceremoniously depositing them just inside of the bay door shields.

"What the hell?" he said. "Why didn't they take us all the way to our regular parking pad?"

"I don't know, and I don't care. I'm just glad to be back on dry ground, as it were," Sandy said as the dissolving flight controls flowed back into the curving floor. Freed from its confines, she stood next to Richard. Extending an arm, she gestured toward the airlock. "Age before hotness."

Richard shook his head and stepped into the airlock. When its outer door opened, the two of them were still chuckling, simply happy to be alive.

Then they stepped out onto the hangar floor ... and suddenly found themselves staring into the muzzles of several Argonian guns. Behind the odd futuristic weapons, armored Argonian combat troops regarded them warily.

A strangely accented Argonian voice broke the tense, silent stand-off. "Who are you?" demanded a distinguished, middle-aged gentleman as he stepped between the guards. He laced together his hands and pointed extended index fingers accusatorially. Rocking on the balls of his feet, the tall man leaned forward and glared down on Richard and Sandy. "And more importantly," he said, his odd dialect adding a twisted lilt to the end of each word, "why are you flying around in *my* ships?!"

CHAPTER 18

A sharp knock interrupted Admiral Bill Johnston's thoughts. Looking across the desk's black onyx top, he studied the section of wall from which the noise had emanated. Framing the door's location, an ornate casing topped by a tall, pointed arch stood out from the bronze wall's smooth surface. Shaking his head, he grinned, amused that, with all the communications technology that events had dropped into their lap, people still preferred to knock rather than simply announce themselves electronically.

"Enter," he said, his voice cracking with the effort. The weeks of training and readying the fleet's personnel had drained the man. His normally gruff voice had a weary edge to it. Casting an eye toward his ancient but reliable clock radio, he watched 3:01 AM roll to 3:02. Looking surreally out of place, it sat on the corner of his desk which in turn occupied the front section of the spacious suite he'd claimed as his command quarters.

The framed section of wall vaporized, revealing an uncharacteristically anxious-looking Lieutenant Commander Levy, the night watch commander.

"Don't just stand there, son," he said with a wave. "Come on in."

Stepping into the room, Levy said, "Sorry to disturb you, sir." The man paused, mild surprise registering on his face. Johnston supposed Levy hadn't expected to find him awake and in uniform at this late hour.

"What is it, Commander?" Admiral Johnston asked impatiently.

Levy flinched. "Sorry, sir. There's something on the bridge that I think you'll want to see."

Rising to his feet, Admiral Johnston stepped from behind the desk and fastened his uniform's top button. He didn't bother to question the lieutenant commander. The man wasn't prone to exaggeration.

With the younger officer in tow, the admiral headed toward the bridge. A few moments later, they entered its expansive chamber. It was bustling with activity.

"Admiral on the deck!" shouted the commander.

Each member of the bridge crew continued with their work as Johnston and Levy walked toward one of the command deck's lifts. The two men stepped into the two nearest yellow rings and began to rise.

As the lifts deposited them onto the force field floor, Levy pointed into the overhead hologram. "We are tracking several ships inbound from the direction of Jupiter."

"Isn't that Colonel Allison's fighter wing?" the admiral said as he moved to the center of the deck. Even as he asked the question, Johnston saw a problem with that possibility.

"That was our first thought too, sir," Levy said. "But there are too many of them. First Fighter Wing only has a hundred and eight fighters. We're currently tracking close to a thousand targets."

Johnston nodded, stoically repressing the surprise and other emotions the news elicited. "What do we have on them? Transponder data? Can the computer recognize their profiles?"

Levy shook his head. "No, sir. They're still too far out."

Hundreds of scenarios ran through the admiral's mind, only a couple of which ended with unicorns and Gummy Bears.

Admiral Johnston lowered himself into the force field-generated captain's chair.

Commander Levy pointed to the medium-sized ships surrounding the *Guardian*. "I've already alerted the battlecruisers," he said. "I also rousted the fighter wings and ordered the combat air patrol to intercept the targets."

Johnston nodded. "Good job, Commander." In the hologram he saw the combat air patrol's eighteen Phoenix Starfighters racing toward the incoming targets. He pointed at the fighters. "Have the CAP hold their position. Bring the fleet to battle stations and start launching the fighter wings."

Levy nodded and returned to his station.

Using his EON, Johnston fired off a quick warning to General Pearson at Nellis: "Moving to intercept unknown inbound force."

Commander Levy looked up from his console. "Second and Third Fighter Wings have launched. The rest will be in the air shortly."

Johnston nodded. Obviously, they weren't "in the air", but as they'd discovered, some habits were too ingrained to break in two weeks. He watched hundreds of fighter icons stream from the carrier's stern.

He turned to the helmsman. "As soon as the fighters are clear, move the fleet to intercept. I want to engage them as far from Earth as possible."

"Aye aye, Admiral."

Johnston turned to the weapons officer. "Let me know as soon as we are in firing range." To Levy, he added, "Tell the combat air patrol that the rest of Second Wing will be joining them shortly. Order Newcastle to keep his squadron in Earth space as a rearguard, and have the remaining wings cover our flanks."

"Yes, sir."

Johnston pointed to the helmsman again. "Begin fleet-wide evasive maneuvers. One per minute, please. I don't want them taking out one of our ships with a potato gun."

The helmsman nodded. "Yes, Admiral."

In addition to laser and plasma cannons, the fleet had kinetic weapons that launched hypervelocity rounds. Johnston imagined that the enemy would have the same tech. In spite of their incredible speed, the high mass projectiles launched by those potato guns didn't currently present much of a threat as long as the fleet made periodic lateral jumps. Each subsequent leap would occur at random intervals, distances, and azimuths. That way, anything an enemy fired at their current position would fly through empty space by the time it had covered the significant distance that still separated the two forces.

Standing and moving to the front edge of the command deck, Admiral Johnston studied the hundreds of unmarked gray icons that filled the far side of the display. Through his EON interface, he accessed the hologram and drew the rendering closer, zooming in on the colorless dots. The point of view raced toward the approaching targets. The formation swelled to fill the command deck, but the icons refused to resolve.

As he stared at the closest symbol, Johnston's eyes narrowed. "Damn it!" he swore under his breath. "Are you friend or foe?"

After a moment, the admiral shook his head. He programmed an alert to notify him the instant that the computer identified the target and then reset the display. He walked back to his station.

Dropping into the force field-supplied Captain's chair, Johnston watched the bridge crew. He admired the collected officers. For the last two weeks, they'd all worked their asses off. As he considered what might lie before them, he felt his blood pressure trying to rise. The admiral took a deep breath and then silently let it out in a long exhalation. Afterward, he looked around the room again. Johnston pursed his lips. He didn't know if they were ready for combat. But events were forcing the issue. And if it were the enemy, they wouldn't give two shits about his concerns.

As they approached the halfway point, Commander Levy looked up. "Sir, all fighter wings are in position."

"Good," Johnston said. He turned to the weapons officer. "How's our firing solution coming?"

"The potato launchers are ready to go, Admiral. I estimate we'll be in laser range in fifteen seconds."

Johnston nodded. "Excellent." He addressed both officers. "Order all stations to hold fire until I give the word. Understood?"

"Yes, sir," they said in unison.

A few seconds later, the weapons officer glanced up from his control panel. "We're in range, sir. I have a firing solution ... wait ... What?" He froze, staring slack-jawed at his console, a look of complete confusion twisting his face.

"What is it?" Johnston said.

The man hunched over and started furiously tapping commands into the control panel. "All my weapons systems just died, sir." He paused and then looked up from his console. "They're offline. I'm locked out."

"Admiral!" Commander Levy said, looking up with wide-eyes. "The fighter pilots are reporting the same thing. Their fire-control computers went dark!"

A message flashed through Johnston's EON. The alert he'd programmed had triggered, but before he could say a word, a familiar voice boomed godlike across the bridge.

"Galactic Guardian, this is Phoenix Six, over."

Every person on the bridge stopped moving. A shocked silence fell over the room. Confused faces turned toward the ceiling. No voices had ever broadcast within this hall. Johnston hadn't known it was possible. A smile spread across his face. He magnified the far side of the hologram. Now it depicted a recognizable fleet of green ships.

"Galactic Guardian," the booming voice continued. "This is Colonel Allison. Greetings from the *Helm Warden*, flagship of the Galactic Defense Forces."

Johnston leaned back into his seat and released a long, relieved sigh. *Unicorns and Gummy Bears, indeed*, he thought.

CHAPTER 19

"Turtle One, this is Departure Control. You are cleared to *Helm Warden* as filed. Godspeed, sir," said the space traffic controller over the flight-following EON channel.

"Roger, Departure Control. Turtle One, cleared as filed. Thanks," Jake said as he maneuvered the small vessel through the hangar's force field and into the vacuum of space.

A three-dimensional holographic rendering of the now doubled fleet floated above the control console. Between the pedestal's concave glass top and the ten-foot-high ceiling, hundreds of ships of every size and shape crowded the display. Jake reached into the hologram with both arms. Grabbing the top and bottom of the largest ship, he spread his hands, and the vessel swelled like an accordion, magnifying the image and zooming in the point of view. Still gripping the virtual carrier, Jake rotated it until the rear hangar entrance of the *Helm Warden* faced the group. As he turned the vessel, the few ships still in the field of view circled the Turtle's interior like rides on a city-sized merry-go-round. When he released the carrier, all of the luminescent green ships stopped and hovered motionlessly. Jake extended his right index finger and poked the hangar entrance. An oilcan pop and a short series of concentric rings radiated from the point of contact.

As the ship began its short journey, Jake announced, "The autopilot is programmed. We are underway, sirs."

General Pearson shook his head. "I wish my F-16 fighter would've had one of those back in the day," he said. "It would've made some of those Desert Storm flights a little less stressful." Turning to the admiral, he lowered his voice so that only Jake and the older gentleman could hear him. "Well, Bill, what do you think we're in for on this Argonian flagship?"

Admiral Johnston's face darkened. "I wish I knew. Jesus Christ, the poor son of a bitch just found out he's lost tens of thousands of people." He paused. After a moment of silent contemplation, the admiral continued. "But I think we're on firm ground here, Charlie. Colonel Allison wasn't able to say much, and we *are* still locked out of the weapons systems, but those are the same measures I'd take in their place."

"Agreed," General Pearson said in his deep East Texas drawl. "If they thought we posed a threat, they could've eliminated us the moment they discovered us aboard their ships. If they can remotely deactivate the weapons, they could've just as easily vented the ship's atmosphere to space—then or at any moment since. Hell, the fact that they haven't boarded us makes me think they're inclined to let us retain control, at least for now."

Admiral Johnston rubbed his thin, weathered face. "I hope you're right, Charlie. I have no desire to sit by idly when the next attack comes."

General Pearson nodded. "You're right about the loss of his people. The biggest variable is the GDF commander's response. Did he already know or, at least, have a clue?"

The three men fell silent. For Jake, the admiral's comment had dredged up memories of their own losses. He supposed it had done the same for the two men as well.

Ahead, the *Helm Warden* gradually filled the *Turtle's* view-wall. It looked like a somewhat larger version of the *Galactic Guardian*. Jake made a couple of minor trajectory adjustments to the flight director's approach profile. Not that the autopilot couldn't handle the maneuver, he just liked to maintain some semblance of pilot input. On final approach, about a mile from the hangar entrance, the *Helm Warden's* tractor beam took over.

Speaking in English, a strangely accented voice addressed Jake over the EON space traffic control channel. "Turtle One, we will bring you in from there."

"Roger ... I mean, okay ..." *Crap!* Jake thought. He had no idea what "Roger" or "okay" would mean to an English-speaking Argonian. Finally, he shrugged and said, "That is acceptable, Helm Warden."

After a brief pause, the amused, accented voice on the other end said, "*Roger*, Turtle One." He emphasized "Roger" in a way that indicated he knew exactly what it meant.

A moment later, the carrier's tractor beam dragged the *Turtle* into the hangar's gaping maw like an insect being drawn into a frog's waiting mouth in slow motion. As they passed into the massive facility, they silently stared through the view-wall. The expansive twin hangar bays looked similar to those in the *Galactic Guardian*, only bigger.

General Pearson broke the silence. "Well, what do you know?" He pointed to an apparent dignitary and his formation of ornately dressed Argonian honor guards. "Looks like we're getting the red carpet treatment after all."

Admiral Johnston nodded. "You weren't kidding about their flamboyant uniforms."

Eyeing the group, General Pearson grinned distractedly and nodded. "Yeah, those are the ones, but I don't recognize the older fella."

At that moment, Jake didn't give two shits about uniforms or who knew who. He was just happy to see Sandy and Richard unharmed. They stood off to the left of the Argonians. He still didn't know the circumstances of their encounter with the GDF, but from the time his wing had launched to intercept an unknown force until this very moment, he'd agonized over Sandy's status. After the initial radio call from the *Helm Warden*, Richard had assured them that they were okay. But Jake had needed to see her with his own eyes. They had only been apart for a few hours, but the relief of seeing her standing next to Richard and the welcoming party sent a huge smile across Jake's face.

While it was impossible for Sandy to see him through the ship's skin, she seemed to peer through it, looking directly into Jake's eyes.

The *Turtle* glided through a ninety-degree rotation. Orienting its airlock toward the left wall, the small vessel nestled into the hangar deck.

Jake shut down the *Turtle's* systems and stepped into the airlock, Colonel Newcastle at his side, the Admiral and General close behind. When the outer hull opened, they exited the small chamber. Richard and Sandy stood at attention directly across from them. Twenty feet to the right of the pair, the apparent honor guard stood motionlessly. Next to them, the tall officer whom Jake had pegged as the commander kept his distance for the moment. His eyes had the glazed-over thousand-yard stare of someone engaged in a silent conversation over an EON channel.

Richard saluted. "Welcome aboard, sirs."

Admiral Johnston returned the greeting and then lowered his arm. "At ease, Colonel." The admiral stepped closer and cast a quick glance at the Argonians. "What's our situation?"

Richard and Sandra's postures lost their rigidity as each followed Johnston's order and took on a more comfortable stance. However, their faces remained inscrutable. Richard said, "Sir, the Argonian commander requested that we allow him to brief you, but I think it is safe to say they are impressed with our progress. Although they're still … adjusting to the news of the loss of the fleet's personnel."

Finally, Sandy gave Jake an excited look that told him all was as good as it could be, given the circumstances. He still didn't know how the *Helm Warden* had stumbled across the 1st Fighter Wing. He couldn't wait to hear about that encounter, not to mention the outcome of their battle drill. He hoped it had gone well.

Speaking in English, an Argonian-accented voice interrupted his thoughts. "I suppose you are Lieutenant Colonel Giard."

Jake turned and came face to face with the stately gentleman he'd seen earlier. The man carried himself with an air of authority. On the surface, he appeared ordinary: slightly taller than Jake, graying at the temples of his mid-length, wavy brown hair. However, his eyes beamed with intelligence and authority.

"Yes, sir," Jake said. Anxious to divert attention from himself, he held out a hand toward his commanding officers. "Please allow me to introduce General Pearson and Admiral Johnston, commanders of Earth's defense forces."

The Argonian commander gave each a curt nod.

The exaggerated colors and flamboyant, almost cheesy cut of the officer's uniform would have looked at home on the set of a 1970s science fiction television series. Smiling inwardly, Jake half-wondered if someone had shown an Argonian uniform to the costume director for *Buck Rogers in the 25th Century.*

The GDF officer turned back to Jake. "I understand you led a small team aboard the Zoxyth command ship. From what Colonel Allison told me, you killed the last Zox warrior before he could scuttle his dreadnought."

"Sir, I don't know that he intended to scuttle the ship—"

"It's Admiral Tekamah," the Argonian interrupted. "And rest assured, had he made it to the Altar of the Forebearers, we would not be having this conversation."

Obviously not used to being upstaged by a subordinate, Jake's commanding officers began to look agitated. Giard decided to redirect the conversation. "Thank you for your concern, sir, but—"

Admiral Tekamah laughed. "I'm sorry. You misunderstand my meaning, Colonel. The fact that two of you made it out alive is not inconsequential. However, your victory and what you found afterward has far deeper meaning than you know."

Several minutes later, they walked into Admiral Tekamah's quarters. Jake looked around. "This is … huge." It looked like someone had stuck a rainforest inside a Gothic cathedral, albeit one with a theater-sized view-wall spanning one side. A waterfall tumbled into the room's back corner, its sound oddly muted. Lush green creeping vines climbed the fluted trim of the room's many pointed arches. Tropical birds flew about the room, apparently nesting in the vines as well as within the various nooks and crannies of the rocks surrounding the full drop of the waterfall. Again, the muted sounds of the scene struck Jake as out of place. The noise of crashing waters and flapping birds barely rose to detectable levels.

Tearing his gaze from the scene, Jake realized the group had stopped, each member staring at the surreal panorama.

Admiral Tekamah shook his head. "Sorry, should have shut that down."

Like matter turned vaporous, the tropical milieu's rocks, waterfall, plants, and birds suddenly dissolved into a rainbow of smoke. Then even the haze vanished.

The admiral smiled mirthlessly at their surprised faces. He moved to stand behind a large, ornate desk. The walnut-colored bureau looked as if it had been carved from a single, ten-foot-thick block of wood.

Jake studied the various pieces of hardware that adorned the wall behind the GDF admiral. As Giard's eyes scanned left, he did a double take. Set alone between the desk and the view-wall, a pair of familiar-looking implements with similar designs appeared to hold a place of significance. After a moment, Jake realized that he knew one of them. Stepping to it, he turned to the Admiral and pointed at the device. "May I, sir?"

The Admiral extended a hand toward the piece. "Please."

Carefully, Jake pulled the weapon from its display rack. Running a fingertip across the six-shooter's decorative engravings, he said, "This is an original eighteen seventy-three model."

The man nodded. "Yes, Colonel. It was the first year Colt made the Single Action Army revolver."

"Where did you get this, Admiral?"

"It was a gift from Harry."

"Harry?" Jake said.

"I believe you'd know him as President Harry Truman," the admiral said in his strange, Afrikaner-like accent.

Jake gave the man an appraising look. "You don't look a day over fifty, sir."

"I assure you, Colonel, I only look *this* old because, even in our advanced society, people still associate one's vintage with wisdom. I could just as easily look your age, but suffice it to say, I am significantly older than anyone you've ever met."

After blinking back his surprise, Jake returned the Colt to its rack. It sat in opposition, muzzle-to-muzzle, with a similar yet unrecognizable revolver. He gestured to it and said, "I don't recognize this one."

"You wouldn't," the admiral said. "Like me, it is much older and comes from a star system far from here."

"Argonia?" Richard said.

Tekamah nodded and raised a hand. "Yes, but I did not bring you aboard to discuss such issues. We have rather more important matters to address."

Each of them nodded somberly.

The Argonian gestured across his bureau. "Please, take a seat."

They fanned out in front of the admiral's desk. Behind each officer, a section of the floor raised, forming an individual seat.

As the group sat, Admiral Tekamah's face darkened. "This was a tragedy for all of us," he said. "I am sorry for your losses, sorry your world got drawn into our war." He looked pointedly at Richard, Jake, and Colonel Newcastle. "I owe you a great deal of gratitude. After we had linked up, I accessed the *Galactic Guardian's* log." Pausing, he pointed at Jake. "Colonel Giard, while it didn't save my people, your quick thinking—" a wry grin lightened his face, "and Colonel Allison's persistence on the radio—prevented an even greater tragedy. Had you not acted when you did, all would have been lost. The fleet would have been wiped out, not just its personnel. The Zoxyth wouldn't have stopped until they blasted every ship into falling slag. Then they would have finished off your planet."

Jake looked at the floor. He still couldn't think of their efforts as successful. So many had died, Victor right in front of him.

When he looked up, Jake saw Tekamah point at Richard and then at Sandy. "It's fortunate for these two that the Zoxyth disruptor field is still running. Had it not been, we would have dropped out of parallel-space too close to Earth to detect their presence in the Jovian system. And, considering their precarious predicament at that particular moment ..." Tekamah hoisted his eyebrows but left the thought unfinished.

Jake wondered what a disruptor field was and how it had led to the events near Jupiter. To his right, Sandy shuddered and paled. Since neither she nor Richard could elaborate at the moment, he'd have to wait for them to fill in the blanks later.

"At any rate," Tekamah said. "We'll rectify that problem soon and reestablish communication with the core."

The Argonian Admiral's face darkened again. Sitting back in his chair, he scanned each of their faces. In those aged eyes, Jake could see the man's years. After a weary sigh, Tekamah continued. "Unfortunately, the Zoxyth aren't done, and I fear they're not done with Earth either."

Each of the room's occupants rocked as if slapped.

Hearing his worst fears spoken as more than just possible, Jake stood. "Then what are we doing sitting here?"

The room erupted with noise as the other officers expressed similar concerns.

Tekamah held up both hands then waved everyone back into their seats. "They won't get here today and likely not even tomorrow." He paused, canting his head and pursing his lips. "Beyond that ...?"

After exchanging glances in shocked silence, the members of the Earth contingent returned to their seats.

General Pearson leaned forward, fire in his eyes. Jake could see the man's jaw muscles working.

"Admiral Tekamah," Pearson said in a measured tone that didn't quite hide the general's anger. "We've already lost hundreds of millions of innocent people to those bastards and their God damned weapon. While I'm thankful that the GDF sent a carrier to our defense, it was too little, too late!" His calm facade crumbled. "Why in *hell* weren't we warned about the Zoxyth?! Why didn't you give us some way to protect ourselves?!"

The GDF admiral maintained his composed visage, but as the man stared back at them, Jake saw pain in his eyes. "I do not know how they discovered your existence. As soon as I received word that they were heading for Earth, I dispatched the *Guardian*. Had I known they had this weapon ..." He paused, shaking his head. Tekamah appeared to stare through them. "You weren't the only one the Zoxyth targeted with this new implement. They attacked one of our worlds. We arrived too late to save the population of that Argonian colony. All but one individual fell to the godsdamned weapon."

"Oh my God," Sandy whispered.

Jake saw General Pearson deflate, the news of the loss of an entire Argonian colony eroding his indignant anger.

Tekamah nodded somberly. "If not for that man's warning, my fleet might have suffered the same fate as the *Galactic Guardian*. Even forewarned by the sole survivor, I was fortunate to get out of the system with only a thirty percent casualty rate."

The faces of Jake's comrades reflected his shock.

"Jesus wept," Admiral Johnston whispered. "You're operating with only seventy percent of your staff?"

Tekamah nodded again.

Jake's mind reeled. Thirty percent was an incredible military deprivation. On Earth, any fighting unit that experienced battle losses of that magnitude was considered combat-ineffective. The cavalry hadn't arrived, more like the French Army following Waterloo. Hell, adding the loss of everyone aboard the *Galactic Guardian's* fleet, Jake knew it was even worse than Napoleon's defeat.

After letting them absorb the news, Admiral Tekamah said, "However, I do have reason for hope." He looked at Richard. "Colonel, please repeat what you told me earlier, the part about the device you and Colonel Giard noticed."

"Device?" Jake said.

In his far left seat, Richard shifted to address the group. He gestured toward Jake and said, "After we killed the last Zoxyth on the

175

enemy ship, Colonel Giard and I searched the rest of the vessel. As you know, we didn't find any other Zox ... none living anyway." Shifting his gaze to the floor, he paused. After a moment, Richard looked up and continued. "But we did find something that looked ... out of place."

Admiral Johnston cocked an eyebrow. "Why am I hearing about this just now, Colonel Allison?"

Richard shifted nervously under the Admiral's stare. "Well, sir, at the time, we didn't think much of it. *Everything* looked alien, but this looked like an afterthought, like it had been retroactively installed. The plumbing and cabling all emerged from holes that appeared to be freshly chiseled through the asteroid's rocky interior."

Remembering the device, Jake nodded. "The sphere."

"Actually, Bill, that *was* in his report," General Harrison said. "I remember a note about an apparently out of place spherical device."

"Oh, yes," Admiral Johnston said, nodding. "As I recall, you found it near the center of the ship remnant."

"Yes, sir," Richard said, looking relieved.

"What you found," Tekamah said, "is nothing less than the Zoxyth gene weapon."

Johnston's face hardened. "That God damned weapon nearly wiped us out, Admiral. My understanding is that you knew of the technology. Who in the hell would develop such a thing?"

Tekamah held up a hand. "We didn't know the Zoxyth had known about the technology, much less developed a weapon." He paused, his eyes momentarily glazing over. Then he shook his head. "Although, in hindsight, I should've realized it."

He told the officers about the refugee caravan that had fallen to a Zoxyth attack. "In spite of obvious evidence that the Zox had boarded each ship," Tekamah said, "there were no bodies left behind, but there were no signs of resistance, either, not a speck of blood anywhere."

"So enemy troops boarded the ships to remove the evidence," Jake said.

Admiral Tekamah nodded. "My scouts found a couple of piles in a remote section of one ship, but ..." The Admiral paused, a series of emotions leaking through his finely coiffed visage. Then his face hardened. "Regardless, we didn't know then, but we do now." He pointed to Jake and Richard. "And thanks to the two of you, we have an opportunity to study one."

Admiral Johnston leaned forward. "That still doesn't answer my question. Why would anyone develop such an obviously genocidal weapon in the first place? Who would pursue such a patently evil thing?"

"Well-intentioned doctors," Tekamah said flatly.

After giving the statement time to spread confusion across the group, he continued. "It started out innocently enough. Even for Argonians, cancer can still raise its ugly head. As you probably know, a malignancy usually begins when a genetic error propagates through uncontrolled duplication. That unchecked growth manifests as a tumor, a clump of flesh with slightly different DNA than the host. Oncologists developed a device that, encoded with the defective gene sequence, could target and eradicate cancerous tumors. It would only affect tissue with the faulty gene sequence. It shifted the targeted tissue into a quantum state incompatible with organic molecules, leaving nothing but an empty pocket where the tumor had been."

"Oh my God," Sandy whispered.

Richard looked at her. "What?"

"Don't you get it?" she said. When nobody answered, Sandy gave the admiral a questioning look.

Still seated behind his desk, Tekamah nodded and held out a hand. "Please."

She looked around the room and then said, "Someone must've figured out a way to boost the signal and focus it on a species' genome."

Jake realized that she had to be right. The epiphany hit him hard. In spite of evidence to the contrary, he'd held a faint hope that they'd find out that the enemy had somehow beamed the humans elsewhere. Looking around the room, he saw the same realization hit each of the gathered officers.

Admiral Johnston sat back in his chair. Shaking his head, he repeated Sandy's words. "Oh my God."

"Yes," Admiral Tekamah said, nodding as he watched the group digest the information. "The weaponized version was never built. As soon as its potential weaponization surfaced, the technology's very existence became a closely guarded secret. Fortunately, the oncologist in question was a government scientist. She had yet to publish her findings and never did."

"Jesus Christ!" General Pearson said. "What in the hell are we going to do if another one of these shows up?"

"Well, General, now that we know they have the tech, there are tactics we can employ. And now that they have one to study, our scientists can look for its weaknesses."

Jake saw questioning expressions cross Johnston and the general's faces as both men leaned forward in their nanobot-formed chairs.

Tekamah held up a hand again. "One moment, gentlemen. There's more."

Admiral Johnston and General Pearson exchanged glances and then leaned back into their seats. The general nodded to the GDF admiral. "Please continue."

"As I mentioned earlier," Tekamah said, "we had our own … encounter with the Zoxyth weapon. Until reinforcements arrive, I'm extremely short-handed. However, those reinforcements are on the far side of the galaxy." He paused, giving each man a meaningful look. "So I'm leaving you in command of the *Galactic Guardian* fleet."

The two men looked both excited and concerned. Admiral Johnston sat up in his chair and said, "More than anyone else, I'd love an opportunity to give those sons of bitches a little payback." He paused and pointed at Richard and Sandra. "But, from your earlier comments, I take it First Fighter Wing's exercise in the Jovian system went less than spectacularly. Their experience shows that we're not ready to face the enemy."

Tekamah leaned back in his chair. "Actually, gentlemen, I'm very impressed with your progress to date. That you successfully boarded and recovered the fleet is far more than I would have expected. The fact that you were engaged in training exercises was unfathomable. Had I not used my command codes to deactivate your weapons remotely, you could've fired on my fleet." He gestured to both officers. "Very impressive, gentlemen."

"Thank you, sir," said Admiral Johnston. "But that doesn't come close to the level of competence we'd need to act as an effective fighting force. The complexity of naval surface operations is a challenge for experienced commanders. To do that in three-dimensional space-based operations is a whole new level."

Tekamah grinned. "Then it's a good thing I have a plan."

CHAPTER 20

Recovering from the momentary disorientation induced by the Edification Encoder, Remulkin shook his head. "I hate this shit."

Through a predatory grin, Sergeant Kraiger said, "Only twenty-eight more modules to go."

"I don't know why I need to go through this. I completed all these training modules twenty years ago."

The sergeant pursed his lips, but before he could repeat the reasoning, First Lieutenant Jenkinson walked into the room. She placed a hand on the sergeant's shoulder and gestured at Remulkin. "Load Earth history and language modules as well. Second Lieutenant Thramorus is going to need them." Turning to Remulkin, she said. "You're being reassigned. Somebody else gets to deal with your shit."

"What?" Remulkin said.

"Apparently, someone thinks you'll make a good liaison."

CHAPTER 21

S qualling cries sang out from the flames. The screeching of his boy—no longer a hatchling, not yet a warrior—joined those of his wife. Thrakst fought to move, struggled to run to their aid. However, a bone-chilling cold turned his massive muscles into flaccid mud. In spite of the fire's nearby heat, the frigid environment robbed his cold-blooded body of energy. Thrakst roared. Heaving mightily, he thrust an arm toward the flames. Then his extended talons found purchase on something. He grasped it with withering strength.

"Lord Thrakst, it's me," whispered a gruff voice.

The Lord opened his eyes to see Raja Phascyre standing over him. Green blood oozed from points where Thrakst's talons still dug into the old warrior's upper arm. However, he displayed no pain. The polished rock bolted into his right orbital socket appeared to glare, but only empathy flowed from the Raja's remaining eye.

"They're still with the Forebearers, my Lord," Phascyre whispered.

"I know, old friend," Thrakst said as he released the arm. "I know." Sitting up, he swung his legs from the stone hearth and stood.

"Now, leave me, Raja."

"Yes, my Lord."

The Raja gave him one last concerned glance and then bowed and departed.

Thrakst walked to his cabin's display wall. At the bottom of the large image, the green world of Zalen hung motionlessly below the *Tidor Drof*. A planet-girding ring station filled the top half of the image. The ring's geosynchronous altitude and orbital velocity matched the planet's rotation, making it appear that they now hovered unmoving over a particular point on Zalen. Unlike the planet's obvious curvature, the ring station—as old as the Forebearers—appeared to continue left and right as a perfectly straight line to the limits of Thrakst's considerable vision. Scavenged from the system's asteroid belt, millions of stitched-together city-sized rocks formed the bulk of the ring structure. Similar to the ships of his fleet, massive trusses linked each asteroid to the next. Thanks to gravity manipulation, their hollowed-out Zoxaformed interiors provided more living surface than the planet they spanned.

Immediately adjacent to the *Tidor Drof's* dock, a tower dropped perpendicularly from the bottom of the ring. The long line drawn by the space lift disappeared in the distance as it continued down into Zalen's gravity well. It was impossible to see from this altitude, but Thrakst knew that the bottom of the tower cut through the jungle and anchored into the planet's bedrock.

Zalen and its massive ring station normally fascinated Thrakst. However, today, the Lord barely registered the scene. The image of his fire-engulfed lair kept burning into his mind's eye.

It was all Tekamah's fault. The bastard had taken the Lord's family. Had the *Helm Warden* not attacked the *Forebearer's Solitude* just before they had retreated into parallel-space, the dreadnought would have dropped into a normal orbit when it returned to Zoxa, not crashed into the planet's surface.

The mental image of his burning family was just that: an imagined image. There hadn't been a lair left for that fire to consume. The crashing asteroidal ship had left only a crater where his ancestral home had lain. Since the days of the Forebearers, a member of the

Thrakst clan had ruled the region. Now only a smoking hole marked its location.

Even after the GDF had taken his family, the Forebearers-damned Zoxa High Council had begged him to accept the Argonians' terms, pleaded with him to end the war.

"The cowards!" growled the Lord.

Before Tekamah had taken his family, Thrakst had started to develop the gene weapon. The doomed *Forebearer's Solitude* had transported the scientific team he'd assembled to develop the device. The Lord had brought his old friend, Raja Phascyre, into the fold and told him of the new weapon. Initially, the warrior had counseled peace, but after *Forebearer's Solitude* had plunged into Zoxa, the Raja had joined him, stood by his side as he'd set off to make the GDF pay for what they had done to their home world, to his family.

And praise the Forebearers, the bastards had paid. Armed with a weapon unknown to the worthless hatchlings of the High Council, Thrakst had gathered his fleet and struck out for Argonian space. First, the test on the fleeing Argonian refugees had proven the efficacy of the gene weapon. Then he'd wiped all but one Forebearers-damned Argonian from the Chuvarti system.

Remembering the voice that had stolen his victory, Thrakst growled, a low rumble that caused the room's few loose pebbles to skitter noisily. Because of that survivor's warning, the Lord hadn't finished the GDF in the Chuvarti system, and he still didn't know what had happened in Sector 64.

A chime yanked Thrakst from his thoughts.

"What do you want?" he yelled. Turning toward the noise, he saw the Raja step into the room.

"Sorry, my Lord. We intercepted a GDF communiqué about Sector Sixty-Four. They haven't heard from the *Galactic Guardian*." With a predatory grin, Phascyre added. "The *Helm Warden* has been dispatched to investigate."

CHAPTER 22

The Fifth Columnist stared at the remote console.
He couldn't send the message.
He had to!
He wouldn't.
But they needed to know about Sector 64!
Bending over its surface, he typed furiously.
A few keystrokes later, he stopped typing and looked down at the screen. The completed message stared back at him, its Send button flashing impatiently.
The Fifth Columnist reached for it and then stopped.
The last time he'd done this, it had only made things worse.
Much worse!
He couldn't betray his own kind.
He wouldn't!
He *had* to betray them, *had* to betray himself.
He …! He …
In the dark room, the Fifth Columnist's shoulders slumped.
He shook his head and sighed.
And then pressed the Send key.

CHAPTER 23

The now familiar wave of vertigo washed over Jake as the edification encoder deposited the latest module of knowledge into his mind. He blinked a few times, and his vision stabilized. A quick mental inventory revealed that he now had a working knowledge of the *Turtle's* upgraded weapons systems. Their abilities astounded Jake. The ship's greater size gave it the capacity to carry weapons even more powerful than those of the Phoenix space fighters. So, as the Commander of 6th Fighter Wing, Jake had taken the liberty of assigning himself to the unit's deadliest ship.

He studied the schematics in his virtual vision. As if floating in midair, the lined three-dimensional rendering rotated in front of him. Using its direct link to Jake's optic nerve, the EON painted the image across his real-world view, creating a hologram that only he could see.

Thanks to the latest download, he fully understood every aspect of each new weapon system. What had previously seemed like an overwhelmingly complex amalgamation of systems now seemed intuitive.

Movement beyond the virtual hologram drew his attention. Through it, Jake saw an unknown male face looking at him impatiently. Using a subvocalized command, he dismissed the schematic. The unobstructed view of the individual only deepened Jake's confusion. Considering his portly physique and receding hairline, the rotund man looked neither military nor Argonian. However, he thought he'd already met all the Earth-based personnel.

Giard gave him a questioning look, but the guy continued his sour vigil without comment. Jake surrendered. "Can I help you?"

"That depends," said the man in an accent that answered one question. He was definitely Argonian. "Are you Lieutenant Colonel Jake Giard?"

"Yes, I am. Who are you?"

The Argonian rolled his eyes. "Gods! The viceroy doesn't know the activities of the exultor!"

The EON fed Jake a quick translation: the right hand doesn't know what the left is doing.

Jake chuckled. "Things are a bit crazy right now. Why don't you tell me who you are and why you're here? Then we'll both know what the other hand is doing."

"Hand?"

Jake raised a questioning eyebrow.

The man rolled his eyes again. "Very well. I am Lieutenant Remulkin Thramorus. I've been assigned as your liaison."

Lieutenant? Jake thought wryly as he cast a dubious glance at the man's generous belly. Apparently noticing it, Thramorus actually sucked in his gut.

"Liaison?" Jake said after a moment. "No one mentioned liaisons."

"Exactly," Remulkin said. "Viceroy … exultant … not communicating. Gods, am I not speaking English?" The man's freckled, pale skin glowed red under his wreath of receding red hair. "Did the idiots download the wrong language module?"

"Don't blow a gasket," Jake said. "We'll figure this out. As a liaison, what are your assigned duties?"

Lieutenant Thramorus shrugged. "They just want me to ride along with your squadron. I am to: *clarify issues should our cultural differences create confusion during the heat of battle.*" He said the last part as if quoting someone else and with more than a little disdain.

Jake didn't care for the man's attitude, but after a brief pause, he smiled and nodded. Extending an arm, he said, "Glad to have you aboard, Lieutenant."

Remulkin ignored the offered hand. Instead, he waved dismissively. "Just stay out of my way, and I'll stay out of yours, Colonel."

What an asshole, Jake thought as he lowered his hand. Shaking his head, he returned to the edification encoder's control panel and reactivated the device. A hologram of his brain sprang back into existence between the two men. Looking into the three-dimensional model, Jake said, "Now, if there's nothing else, I have a few more modules to download." Sparing the asshole a quick glance, he added, "I trust they've assigned you quarters."

Remulkin gestured to his right. "Yes, they put me in the cabin next to yours."

"Wonderful," Jake said, not bothering to hide his sarcasm.

He heard a rustling behind him as Sandy came out of their bedroom. In a sleepy voice, she asked, "Who's this?"

Still standing in front of Jake, Remulkin suddenly became animated. As Sandy stopped next to Giard, the portly man's face brightened. Extending a hand, he said, "I'm Lieutenant Remulkin Thramorus of the Galactic Defense Forces. Pleased to meet you, young lady."

"Lieutenant?" Sandy said as she shook the man's proffered hand.

"Uh, yes," Remulkin said. Jake saw his face redden again. "Recent ... uh ... developments required my return to active duty."

As the man released Sandy's hand, Jake saw him glance down. *Did he just look at Sandy's breasts?*

"What were you doing before those developments?" Sandy asked, either not seeing or ignoring the man's gawking.

"I'm a scientist. I was working at a polar research station when ..." The man paused, his smile faltering. His eyes clouded over, and he looked away. After a moment, Thramorus shook his head. "Anyway, my assignment there ended, and I found myself aboard one of the ships of the *Helm Warden's* fleet. When they found out about my previous military experience, they ..." The man's words trailed off, his gaze falling to the floor. Finally, he shook his head and looked up, glaring at Jake. "So here I am, stuck in a backwoods system and assigned as a liaison." Remulkin shifted his gaze to Sandra. His face softened as apparent embarrassment replaced his anger. Again he stared at her chest. Or was it even lower than that?

Jake and Sandy exchanged glances.

Colonel Giard made an adjustment to the edification encoder's interface. Cocking an eyebrow at the liaison, he shook his head. The holographic rendering of his brain mimicked the movement. "I have to get back to work, Lieutenant."

When Colonel Giard returned his attention to the edification encoder's hologram, Remulkin cast a meaningful glance at Major Fitzpatrick's abdomen and then nodded toward Colonel Giard, silently mouthing, "Does he know?"

The major's smile faltered, and her eyes widened. After a moment, she shook her head, a quick, barely perceptible gesture.

Remulkin glanced at Colonel Giard. The clueless asshole didn't even know his woman was pregnant.

The major gave him a pleading look.

Remulkin had seen the glow of pregnancy on his wife's face twice. The thought brought back the bitter pain of loss. Taking a deep breath, he smiled weakly at the woman and gave her a reluctant nod.

Colonel Giard looked from his work. "Is there anything else, Lieutenant?"

"No, Colonel," Remulkin said, barely able to refrain from calling the oblivious young man a knuckle-dragger.

"We have a fleet-wide training exercise scheduled for zero six hundred tomorrow morning. You'll ride along with me in the *Turtle* ..." Giard paused and gave him an embarrassed look. "That's what we call our GDF loaner. It's an Avalon-class utility ship."

Thramorus still couldn't believe Tekamah had handed these sub-Argonians the keys to a fleet. But he really didn't give a shit. For him, they were just a means to an end. He'd be fine as long as the knuckle-draggers stayed out of his way when the time came.

Colonel Giard continued his inane rambling. "Meet me in hangar bay one twenty-seven at oh five hundred hours, and you can demonstrate your liaising skills."

"Oh joy," Remulkin said.

Giard cocked an eyebrow. "Maybe there was a glitch in your language module. Otherwise, I might take your tone as sarcasm, *Lieutenant.*"

"Gods no, *Colonel.* Of course, I am sincere," Remulkin said in a tone that indicated anything but.

"Dismissed," the caveman said with a frown as he turned back to the encoder's hologram.

Remulkin shook his head and walked from the room. Turning left, he returned to his quarters. However, after the door to his cabin closed behind him, a chime rang out. He cursed in his native tongue and then switched to English. "Come in, Major Fitzpatrick."

The entrance membrane dissolved, revealing the young female.

"What can I do for you, ma'am?"

"How did you know?"

Remulkin rolled his eyes. In his mid-forties, he was young by Argonian standards, but even before his wife's two pregnancies, he would have spotted the woman's glow. Natural gestation was rare within the Argonian culture. When a woman took that path, it stood out. It certainly had both times his wife had been with child. He supposed that in this backwater excuse of a world, where every baby gestated within a woman's womb, the look might not stand out.

Remulkin shrugged his shoulders. "It seemed pretty obvious to me."

Major Fitzpatrick stared silently. After a moment, she said, "Please don't tell anyone."

Remulkin nodded toward the adjacent quarters. "Why don't you want him to know?"

Her face hardened. "I have my reasons."

Having had a very recent demonstration of the frailty of life,

Remulkin didn't think that even a knuckle-dragger like Giard deserved to be left in the dark about something this life-changing.

As if she had read his thoughts, Major Fitzpatrick's face suddenly softened. "I heard about your family ... hell, your whole planet. I'm sorry for your—"

Remulkin bristled. "I don't need your sympathy," he said, cutting her off. Grinding his teeth, he threw his arms up. "Keep your secret. Why should I care?" Turning from her, he walked toward the back. "You know the way out, Major."

Jake turned from the edification encoder as Sandy walked back into the room. She looked upset.

"Why did you chase after that asshole, Sandy?"

His words snapped her out of an apparent trance. She blinked and looked at him. "Uh, I'm sorry, what?"

"Why did you go after Thramorus?"

"Oh. I wanted to tell him I was sorry about the loss of his family."

It was Jake's turn to look confused.

"You didn't know?" Sandy said.

"Didn't know what?"

Sandy raised an eyebrow. "That was Remulkin Thramorus. The name didn't ring a bell?" When Jake shrugged his ignorance, she continued. "He was the sole survivor of the Chuvarti system. You know, the guy who watched his wife and three kids get vaporized by the fucking Zoxyth?"

"Oh shit," Jake whispered. "No wonder. What did he say?"

Sandy told him of their brief discussion. He felt like she was omitting something but decided not to push her on it.

Finally, she said, "So, you may want to—"

Jake held up both hands. "I know, kid gloves. Got it, ma'am, although I doubt the asshole will appreciate the sentiment."

Sandy smiled and punched his shoulder. "Be nice."

CHAPTER 24

Admiral Bill Johnston admired the crisscrossing pointed arches that decorated the high ceiling of the *Helm Warden's* long passageway. As he walked deeper into the ship, he saw the decorative casing of another doorway approaching on his right. A few steps later, the room beyond the tall arched entrance came into view.

Bill paused and stared inside, marveling at the collected flora and fauna that occupied the expansive terrarium. Unlike similar rooms within the Galactic Guardian, this one supported a desert ecology. Sandy hills interspersed with cactuses of varying sizes and types continued to the distant horizon.

He stepped into the room and blinked in confusion. The skyline was too far away. That far off horizon would fall outside the envelope of even this mighty ship. Then it occurred to him that at least part of the scene must be another manifestation of the holographic landscape they'd seen in Tekamah's command suite. He couldn't tell where the real part ended and the hologram took over, although the sand under the toes of his shoes was real, as were the two closest cactuses.

Suddenly, the nearest plant moved. The tall, prickly cactus with long saguaro-like arms reached down in a very un-saguaro-like style and grabbed a smaller plant. As it uprooted the little cactus a squeal echoed off the surrounding rocks.

Wide-eyed, Bill took an involuntary backward step. Behind the cactuses, he saw long trails traced by each animal's slow, almost undetectable conveyance. The troughs cut into the sandy soil behind each creature portrayed the aftermath of a slow-motion chase, one ultimately won by the marginally faster, long-armed cactus.

The saguaro-monster drew the squealing and struggling cactus toward an opening at the base of its branching arms. "Jesus wept," Bill whispered as he looked into its nightmarish mouth. The maw sported concentric rings of teeth and barbs that moved in oscillating waves. He watched in wide-eyed, shocked fascination as the smaller cactus slid into the saguaro's muzzle, its undulating teeth slowly drawing the still screaming animal deeper into the monster's gullet.

A new sound yanked Johnston from his horrified reverie. Unintelligible words from a distant conversation drifted into the terrarium. Blinking, he turned from the surreal desert scenery and looked down the hall toward Admiral Tekamah's office. Recognizing the voice of the GDF commander, Bill gave a final glance into the hazed atmosphere of the terrarium and then stepped from the room and walked toward the admiral's office.

As he drew nearer, a second voice said, "Yes, sir. He calls himself the Fifth Columnist."

Johnston froze, inadvertently eavesdropping, but considering the familiar term, unwilling to walk away.

"I can't believe there is a traitor," Tekamah said.

"It looks like we only have a few days to prepare," said the unknown voice.

Johnston couldn't believe what he was hearing. The Fifth Columnist was a human-coined name for a spy. It came from the Spanish civil war.

The men had stopped talking. Concerned they'd detected his presence, Bill stepped toward the door, walking heavily so that his footfalls announced his approach. Arriving, he knocked on the side of Admiral Tekamah's office door. He poked his head into the opening.

With raised eyebrows, he said, "Hope I'm not interrupting." He'd spoken in English, hoping it would dissuade them from thinking he'd overheard their native-tongue discussion.

Tekamah shook his head and gestured to Johnston. "No, no," he said in accented English. "Please, come in." Turning back to the man whom Johnston now recognized as the *Helm Warden's* communications officer, Tekamah nodded and said, "Thank you for your report. I'm glad the disruptor field is finally offline."

Johnston hoped he hadn't let the surprise reach his face. He was the senior human commander. Why in hell would Tekamah keep secrets from him, especially if it involved a potential spy?

The communications officer—Captain Regimus, if memory served—gave Tekamah an Argonian salute. He spoke in English as well. "I'll alert you of any, uh ... developments, sir."

Lowering his hand, the Argonian officer nodded at Johnston and then turned and left the room.

After an uncomfortable silence, Tekamah walked from behind his desk. He shook Bill's hand brusquely and then gestured to the floor. "Please, have a seat."

The GDF admiral remained on the same side of the desk. Behind each man, the floor raised to support them.

"Thank you," Johnston said. He recognized the Admiral's tactic. Wanting to treat him as an equal, Tekamah was addressing him face to face, without the barrier of a desk between them. It was a machination Bill had used on many occasions.

So why was the man keeping secrets from him?

Tekamah leaned back in his seat. Overhead, hundreds of holographic ships sprang into existence. Half rendered in aqua blue, the other half in lime green, they filled the cavernous room's upper reaches.

"Here we are, Bill," Admiral Tekamah said, pointing to the left group and then to the right one. "The *Galactic Guardian* and *Helm Warden* fleets. Thanks to your proactive steps, we have just enough personnel between the two of us to staff both task forces." He lowered his arm. "As we've already discussed, I am leaving you in charge of the *Guardian's* carrier group."

Johnston nodded. The move sent a spike of pain shooting through his head. Bill winced and began to massage his temples.

Seeing this, Tekamah gave him an empathetic smile. "I take it you've been hitting the edification encoder pretty hard."

Bill nodded tenderly. "You can say that again, Ashtara."

Tekamah gave him a perplexed look and then said, "I take it you've been hitting—"

"No," Bill said through a withering smile. He waved off the GDF admiral. "Sorry. It's a figure of speech. You're right. I've been hitting them hard, and I have a splitting headache to show for it."

The worst of it had subsided. However, the migraine's aftereffect had left a ghost of itself in his brain, like a sore muscle that barked with pain at the least provocation.

Tekamah's empathetic smile returned. "I understand. I know it is a lot to absorb, but we are short on time. How far did you get?"

"All of it," Johnston said through a pained grin.

"All? Even fleet tactics?"

"Yes," Bill said. "Even that."

Tekamah smiled. "Good, then let us discuss our tactics."

CHAPTER 25

Jake shook his head. This was getting really annoying. "Just activate the damned encoder, Lieutenant."

Thramorus gave him a condescending look. "Really? These are modules every child learns before they are six standard years old. How do you not have scabs on your knuckles?"

Jake ground his teeth but held his tongue. Finally, Remulkin activated the edification encoder's next module. Giard grimaced as the resultant disorientation washed over him. When it passed, he nodded to Thramorus. "Give me the next ..." He paused. The lieutenant's lips had spread into a stupid grin. "What?" Jake asked.

From behind him, Sandy said, "My, what a big brain you have."

Remulkin let out an uncharacteristic laugh. Reaching out, the Argonian made a gesture that sent Jake's holographic brain spinning. "I don't know. Seems like there is more hot air in there than anything else."

"Ha, ha, ha," Jake said, smiling. "Laugh it up, you two."

Remulkin looked at him as if he'd suddenly remembered that Giard was in the room. The idiotic grin fell from the man's face. "Who's laughing?"

Standing, Jake shook his head and turned back to Sandy. "Hey, baby. How's your training going?"

"It's good," she said. Wincing, she rubbed her head. "I've made lots of progress; got the headache to prove it."

Jake grimaced. "I know what you mean."

From behind him, Thramorus's annoyingly voice returned. "Uh, are you sure that's safe?"

Sandy tensed visibly. Confused, Jake shot a questioning look at the Argonian. Remulkin just frowned at him.

When Jake turned back to Sandy, he thought he'd glimpsed her giving Remulkin a curt head shake.

"What the hell is going on?" Jake said. "Are you okay?"

Sandy's face hardened into an expression he knew all too well.

Oh shit, Jake thought. They rarely argued, but when they had, it usually started in this manner.

"Of course, I'm *okay*," she nearly yelled. "I've told you not to treat me different, Mr. Giard. I'm not some helpless girl. I don't need rescuing. I'm an Air Force fighter pilot just like you. Anything you can do, I can do just as well, if not better."

Jake's eyes softened. He raised his hands. "I'm sorry, baby. Is this about what happened in California? I know that dealing with those assholes outside of your mom and dad's house had to have been traumatic. I—"

Sandy's eyes widened, her anger suddenly much more visceral. "And I don't need your God damned sympathy either!" Turning, she stormed from the *Turtle*. As she stepped into the open airlock, she shouted over her shoulder. "You don't know anything, Jake!"

Slack-jawed, Giard looked after her. He turned to Lieutenant Thramorus. "What the hell was that all about?"

A new emotion crossed the Argonian's face. He appeared to be struggling with a decision.

"What?" Jake said.

Remulkin's face hardened, and he shook his head. "You really are an idiot, *Colonel*," he said, pouring disdain into the military title. Still shaking his head, the portly man turned from Jake and reactivated the edification encoder. Another swipe of his hand sent the holographic symbols that represented the encoder's various modules scrolling like a hyperactive version of the wheel on *The Price Is Right* game show. As it slowed, Thramorus reached in with both hands and grabbed several virtual cubes.

Jake didn't know that was possible.

Looking at him with obvious disdain, the lieutenant shook his head. "You really are clueless," he said. Then he threw the collected modules into the holographic rendering of Jake's brain.

The rotating, disembodied brain shivered violently. As the modules disappeared into the pulsing mass, three oilcan pops echoed through the Turtle's main cabin.

Violent, disorientating waves of nausea swept over him. Jake had just enough time to register anger at the smart-ass's choice of material. Then the data dump of actual child-level learning modules overwhelmed his mind, and the black void of unconsciousness wrapped him in its cold embrace.

PART III

"The more you sweat in peace, the less you bleed in war."

— Norman Schwarzkopf

CHAPTER 26

The flight leader for the training mission's first wave, Colonel Jake Giard, flew the *Turtle* toward the hangar exit. As he neared the bay door, Earth's natural satellite slid into view. The Moon's scarred belly filled the bottom of the panorama, its night-darkened far side barely visible beneath the *Galactic Guardian*. In its opposition phase, the Moon was currently full as viewed from Earth, making its proverbial dark side truly dark.

With a sideward look, he regarded his crewmate. Remulkin sported his now familiar dour look. Jake grinned. He slid his hand back into the flight controller and gave it a quick twitch. In the blink of an eye, the *Turtle* flipped upside down.

Other than giving Jake a sour frown, Thramorus didn't react to the sudden change. "Are you finished?" he said sardonically.

"Lots of fun you are," Jake said returning his attention forward. He righted the ship. The moon rolled clockwise, falling from the top of the field of view and, with abrupt solidity, locking back into position at the bottom of the panorama.

To his right, Remulkin muttered something unintelligible. Ignoring him, Jake opened the squadron's EON channel. "Gunfighters, this is Six. Check-in."

"Gunfighter One," reported the first pilot.

"Gunfighter Two," said a second voice.

Several iterations later, the last fighter checked in. Jake nodded and guided the squadron into its assigned position behind the *Galactic Guardian*. Watching the final ship fall into formation, he reopened the channel. "The asteroid passed here about ten minutes ago. I've locked it into the *Turtle's* navigation system," he said.

While searching for training targets, Admiral Tekamah had identified an asteroid with a better than zero chance of leaving its mark on the planet in the next few decades. The elliptical orbit of this particular Aten-class Potentially Hazardous Asteroid or PHA had just carried it through the Earth-Moon system on its way outbound from its closest approach to the sun.

Jake had designed today's live-fire exercise to hit the targeted asteroid from several angles. However, the net force of the attack would send the rendered debris cloud along a new orbit that would take it into the sun on its next pass, forever removing asteroid 2015 MK132 from Earth's freshly overgrown list of concerns.

This was to be the first fleet-wide battle drill. In preparation for combat exercises, Admiral Tekamah had repositioned both fleets to the far side of the Moon. Ostensibly, the admiral had moved the fleets in order to monitor the live-fire training exercise. However, Jake was dubious about this assertion. Over the last two weeks, they'd completed several battle drills, the last few using their full complement of weapons. On those occasions, Tekamah and Johnston had monitored the exercises from Earth orbit. Jake shook his head. Those decisions were made way above his pay grade.

After checking the time, he activated the EON connection. "In ten seconds we'll begin. When we get to the release point, proceed to your initialization points as briefed. This will be a short flight to the RP. Keep it tight, folks. Watch your wingman, and hit your marks."

In short succession, the rest of *Galactic Guardian's* complement of fighters filed through the hangar exit. A moment later, Jake's Gunfighter Squadron, along with the rest of 6th Fighter Wing, rocketed away from the fleet. Two other wings followed in his trail.

Jake glanced toward the *Helm Warden*. Scheduled to start a few minutes later, its fighter wings and battlecruisers sat motionlessly, waiting for their timed release.

Suddenly, the *Turtle's* drive dropped offline.

"What the hell?" Jake said. He raised both hands from the console and visually searched its curved surface. All of the velocity and position data had frozen. He wasn't coasting: the ship had come to an instant stop. If not for the drive's inertial decoupling, he and Remulkin would have been turned into bug stains smeared across the *Turtle's* view-wall.

"What did you do?" the liaison asked in English.

Jake ignored him and scanned the tactical display. It showed that all of the fleet's ships had stopped simultaneously.

He tried to open the squadron's EON channel and found it locked out as well.

Within the overhead hologram, hundreds of ships now hovered motionlessly behind the *Turtle*, their hexagonal collection of diamond-shaped formations still hanging in perfect synchronization. Considering the screaming silence from the battle network, Jake knew the rest of his ships and those of the other squadrons must be experiencing the same communications lockout as well.

Suddenly, the *Turtle's* interior lights dimmed and shifted to red.

"Oh shit," Jake whispered. He watched the developments through widening eyes. The man had seen the Turtle respond the same way the first time a Zoxyth fleet had appeared in Earth space.

A cold chill ran down Giard's spine.

Without input from Jake, the ship's hologram suddenly zoomed out. As the entire Earth-Moon system filled the image, he took an involuntary backward step.

"Oh fuck."

With a horrified sense of déjà vu, Lieutenant Colonel Jake Giard stared at the pulsing red formation of fourteen enemy icons that now floated between the two planetary bodies.

The comforting sound of water droplets splashing against cold stone enhanced Lord Thrakst's meditation. It soothed him, helped the Zoxyth Warlord gather his thoughts while he genuflected before the Altar of the Forebearers. Another drop struck the floor near his feet. The staccato report echoed through the chamber. Thrakst opened his eyes and looked up at the giant sculpture of the Forebearer for which his ship had been named. Glistening in the room's soft light, a swelling droplet hung from one of Tidor's stony talons, just above where the Forebearer gripped the two severed Argonian heads by their hair. Then the droplet lost its battle. Surrendering to the ship's artificial gravity, it fell from the pointed stone talon. The report of its death echoed through the basilica. Closing his eyes, Thrakst tilted his head back. The comforting sound always reminded him of the home world, of a time before Tekamah had taken his wife and son.

Now thoughts of his lost family clouded his mind, threatening to undo him. Thrakst drew in a deep breath. After a moment, he released it in a long exhalation. Opening his eyes again, he glared into the pair of unseeing dead orbs carved into Tidor Drof's visage.

"Soon our revenge will be complete," he said through clenched teeth. His voice reverberated through the massive chamber, returning to him deep and distorted.

Then he heard familiar footfalls; a gait that belonged to the only member of the crew that would deign to intervene on his meditation. "Lord Thrakst," interrupted a voice.

Thrakst stared into the Forebearer's eyes a moment longer. Then he turned to face the back of the basilica. At the end of the long aisle that bisected the curving, concentric rows of pews, Raja Phascyre stood framed in the chamber's massive entrance, bracketed left and right by the headless and bound pair of sacrificial Argonians.

The Raja bowed and said, "It is time, my Lord."

Thrakst nodded. "Yes, it is, old friend."

The Lord walked up the aisle. As he reached the back, he cast a quick, over the shoulder glance at the Altar of the Forebearers and then turned back to Phascyre. "Walk with me, Raja."

The wizened warrior bowed his head again. "Yes, my Lord." Pivoting on a heel, he joined Thrakst as the Lord stepped through the exit. Together they turned and walked quickly down the passageway. The extravagant uniforms of the ceremonial guards posted at either side of the basilica's entrance formed a colorful blur in the Lord's peripheral vision.

As he and the Raja approached the lift that led to the bridge, its doors opened. The two ancient warriors passed from the stone, cave-like corridor into the lift's polished metal confines. A moment later, the opposite doors opened upon the bridge.

They stepped onto the command deck. Raja Phascyre slammed his massive staff into the rock floor. The thick iron of the ceremonial *Crozier of the Forebearer* rang in the ensuing silence.

All of the bridge crew members stopped moving and bowed their heads.

Thrakst regarded them for a moment and then nodded.

The Raja slammed his staff into the floor again, and the officers returned to their duties.

As he walked across the cavernous room, Thrakst gazed through one of the forward-facing ports, a large window that formed Tidor Drof's left eye. Ahead of his advancing fleet of fourteen ships, Earth's blue-green dot had swelled noticeably since he'd left the bridge. Its colorful orb sat centered in the brilliant sphere of light-speed-compressed stars ahead of the formation of warships. Above the window, a monitor displayed a countdown timer. As the last zyxyns ticked off the clock, Earth's blue globe began to swell, their rapid approach triggering an exponential ramp-up in its apparent size. Then the timer hit zero. The star field streaked from the central orb like falling rain, and the universe welcomed Thrakst's fleet back to real space, quickly wrapping the formation in its cold embrace of distant stars.

Three probes rocketed away from the *Tidor Drof*. Soon the sensors of the two that had headed toward Earth began to sweep the entire planet, probing for signs of either of the two lost fleets.

As the Lord moved to stand in front of his cathedra, the sensor officer looked up nervously. Thrakst opened his mouth to prompt the idiot to speak, but the hatchling finally found his tongue.

"Lord Thrakst, there's no sign of Commodore Salyth's fleet. The probes have circled the planet and found no ships, Zoxyth or Argonian," said the bridge officer.

Raja Phascyre growled. Batting aside the junior officer, he said, "Let me see that." Holding the hatchling at bay with his staff, the Raja scanned the console. After a moment, he began to tap commands into its interface.

"That's not the right probe, Raja," the sensor officer said. "What are you do—?" The officer's words cut out mid-question as a blur of movement passed between the two Zoxyth. The younger officer's head snapped backward. A trickle of blood ran from the point where the Raja's staff had smacked him.

Silenced, the young officer turned his stupid, confused gaze from Phascyre to Lord Thrakst.

The Lord's impatience boiled over. "Did Salyth hit this planet with a gene weapon?!"

While the device left no visible damage, the passage of its energy wave imparted a telltale quantum signature that the probes could detect.

After a quick scan, the officer looked up excitedly. "Yes, my Lord! It looks like he hit twenty points on the planet, all of them centered on highly developed areas."

"Search the planet's oceans for vessels," Thrakst said through a predatory smile. Perhaps Salyth had sent the emptied GDF fleet into the planet's watery depths.

As the officer went about his duties, the Lord contemplated the possibility. Phascyre had assured him that the Argonian fleet had not been heard from since arriving in Sector 64. But neither had Commodore Salyth. However, now he knew that Salyth had attacked Earth. So where was he?

The bridge officer interrupted his thoughts.

"Lord," he said shakily. "I have signs of one ship. It is …" He paused.

"Out with it!" Thrakst roared.

"There are fragments of a dreadnought in a bay near one the planet's biggest cities."

Thrakst's eyes narrowed. "And what about that city?"

The idiot stared blankly. After a moment, he said, "Its New York, my Lord."

Thrakst shook his head and growled. "Is its population of Forebearers-damned Argonians still walking about?!"

The officer swallowed hard and then nodded.

Thrakst roared. In one giant step, he crossed to him and batted the hatchling's head from his shoulders, a solitary, open-handed blow from his massive hand decapitating the idiot mid-nod.

"Admiral, the Zoxyth flagship and the remnants of its fleet just jumped into the system," reported the *Helm Warden's* sensor officer.

"Thrakst," the admiral growled under his breath. That sealed it. The spy was real. There truly was a traitor in the game.

Glaring at the pulsing red hologram of the enemy's fourteen dreadnoughts, Tekamah said, "Tactical, have they detected us?"

"Not as far as I can tell, sir. I haven't detected the quantum signature of a transplanetary scanner. It looks like the planet's moon is shielding us from their sensors."

Tekamah nodded. He had worried that the Zoxyth's recent advances in technology might have afforded them the same scanning ability as the GDF.

. Within the holographic display, three points of light streamed from the enemy formation. Two headed toward Earth. The curving path of the third brought it toward the Moon.

Tekamah pointed at them. "What are those?"

The man consulted his console. "Probes, sir. They're unarmed."

Captain Trent, the Commander of Tekamah's flagship, stepped

forward. "Send a single ship to intercept and destroy that thing before it rounds the moon." Looking to the admiral, the captain said, "Better they wonder if they stumbled on a patrol ship than know two fleets lie in wait."

Tekamah didn't say anything. Instead, he watched the accelerating probe. Suddenly, it winked out of existence.

Blinking, not believing what he'd seen could be true, he turned to the sensor officer. "Did our ship already fire on the probe?"

He shook his head. "No, sir. The *Kentrock* just broke formation. Why... Wait, where'd it go?"

Tekamah pointed to the officer's console. "I don't know, Lieutenant. Why don't you tell me?"

"Yes, sir," the officer said, a red hue creeping up from his collar.

After a moment, he looked up, confusion displacing his embarrassment. "It's gone, sir." He shook his head. "It blew up, nothing left but a small, expanding cloud of debris, Admiral."

Tekamah narrowed his eyes. After a slight hesitation, he nodded. "Recall the *Kentwood*."

Pointing to the communications officer, he said, "Order our fighters to hold." Turning to the helmsman, he pointed into the hologram. "Prepare to move the *Helm Warden* to block their advance. I want us between the bastards and the planet."

The officer nodded.

As the *Helm Warden* prepared for the micro-jump, Tekamah summoned the captains of his seven remaining battlecruisers. A moment later, the modeled enemy fleet dissolved and holographic renderings of all seven commanders stood before him.

Tekamah nodded to them. "Ladies and gentlemen, on my mark we will execute the planned micro-jump and surround the enemy fleet. Remember to maintain your assigned spacing. With the enemy's current formation, it will keep you out of the range of that gods-damned gene weapon. Our battle plan won't work if any one of you are out of position."

The officers nodded.

"Good luck, commanders. Dismissed."

All seven gave the GDF salute. Admiral Tekamah returned it, and the officers' holograms evaporated.

Tekamah cast a wary glance at the planet's moon hovering below the fleet. The jump would take them straight through its core. Aside from the ships traveling within it, parallel-space contained no ordinary matter. However, if the *Helm Warden* dropped back into real space during the transit through the moon, this would be the shortest counter-attack in military history.

He turned a meaningful look to the helmsman. "Coordinates in and confirmed?"

The officer gave an understanding nod. "Yes, sir."

Using his EON, Tekamah activated the Helm Warden's heavy-ship network. "Helm Warden fleet, move to intercept in three, two, one ..."

As Thrakst stood over the crumpled body of the dead bridge officer, a series of flashes flooded through the Forebearer's eyeports. The Lord looked up. When he saw the source of the lights, a toothy grin spread across his face.

Centered on the primary display, the magnified image of the *Helm Warden* hovered over Earth's blue and white surface. On the bridge's other monitors, he watched as the rest of the GDF flagship's armada joined the party. A final flash signaled the arrival of its last battle-cruiser.

The enemy fleet had popped out of parallel-space in a formation that enveloped his dreadnoughts. Thrakst's eyes narrowed, and he growled with frustration. Every one of the *Helm Warden's* ships hovered just beyond the range of his fleet's gene weapons.

Tekamah obviously knew their effective range.

"Curse these fools!"

"Deploy the disruptor field. I don't want them jumping back out."

Raja Phascyre leaned close. "My Lord, are you sure you want to do that? Remember how well your micro-jump attack worked against them in the Chuvarti system?"

"They escaped me that time. I'm not going to let Tekamah slip between my talons again."

"But, Lord, if you micro-jump all fourteen ships like this ..." He paused and brought up a hologram of the battlefield. A few commands later, each rendered dreadnought disappeared and instantly re-emerged closer to the enemy ships. They formed two concentric rings, one inside the surrounding enemy ships, the other outside it.

Phascyre pointed to the new formation. "If all of our ships deto-nate their weapons the moment we exit parallel-space, we'll hit all the ships simultaneously, regardless of which way they try to egress."

Thrakst studied the Raja's plan. Shaking his head, he said, "That will leave us close to their ships with no gene weapons in reserve. What of their fighters? They could exit the carrier any zyxyn now. If they've figured out a way to shield themselves from the weapon's effect, we'll be sitting drycats."

Looking through the Forebearer's left eyeport, Thrakst glared at the distant *Helm Warden*. He felt something gnawing at the back of his mind, something from a discussion with one of the weapon's key scientists. Then it came to him.

"Yes!" he roared triumphantly.

Spinning around, he pointed at another bridge officer and shouted, "Order all ships to weapons hold status!" His voice came back to him as it echoed off the bridge's damp stone walls.

"Yes, my Lord," replied the officer.

Pushing past Raja Phascyre, Thrakst ran to another console, his talons a blur as he entered data.

"I need another scan of surrounding space. Are there any other ships in this system? Where is the Forebearers-damned *Galactic Guardian* fleet?"

The Raja moved to the tactical console. "No, my Lord. There's nothing. Commodore Salyth must have succeeded. By now the unguided ships of Guardian fleet could have drifted well out of scanner range."

"Excellent!" Thrakst roared. He toggled the data on his console.

"Order the fleet to micro-jump to these new coordinates. I want them spaced at the precise intervals I've indicated."

The Raja studied the hologram. "My Lord, that will place the enemy even farther outside of the weapon's range."

"Do it!" Thrakst said. "And remind all dreadnoughts to maintain weapons hold until I say otherwise. I will have the head of every crewmember of any ship that fires without my order!"

~

Wide-eyed, Jake stared at the red holographic rendering of the Zoxyth fleet and the surrounding green octagonal formation of the *Helm Warden* and its seven battlecruisers. Suddenly, the image began to dissolve, its pixels flying apart. The swirling mass color-shifted and reformed into a familiar human face. Then it spoke.

"This is Admiral Johnston aboard the *Galactic Guardian*. We've detected a fleet of Zoxyth dreadnoughts. I've frozen all assets. Standby for orders."

Admiral Johnston looked off-camera, and then his visage faded. The holographic rendering of the fleet returned to the display.

Jake's heart raced. Adrenaline dumped into his system. As it had a couple of times in Afghanistan, the sudden shift from training mode to combat operations focused him. Narrowing his eyes, Giard reached into the hologram and zoomed out. The entirety of the ships amassed behind the moon slid into view.

"What the hell?" Jake whispered.

Remulkin ignored him. The scientist was busily tapping commands across the surface of the *Turtle's* console.

"This doesn't make any sense?" Jake said.

The *Galactic Guardian* still hovered over its fleet of fighters like a protective hen. However, where the *Helm Warden* had been, its entire complement of fighters still sat motionlessly. Apparently, all of its fighter wings had cleared its hangar just before the enemy's arrival. But they had remained behind the Moon when the carrier and its battlecruisers jumped away. Even now, they still hung motionlessly adjacent to the *Galactic Guardian's* fleet.

Remulkin took control of the display, zooming it out until the amassed ships between the Earth and Moon returned to the field of view. At this range, they were little more than a green ring around a red dot. The computer had exaggerated their size, otherwise at this scale, they'd be invisible.

Still looking at the idled fighters behind the Moon, Jake shook his head. "What are they doing?"

"I don't know?" Remulkin said with obvious anger.

Jake turned to see the scientist staring at the translunar Mexican stand-off. The scientist reached into the display and zoomed in on the scene. He magnified the largest vessel. With its sleek lines pointing directly at the enemy formation, the colossal *Helm Warden* blocked their path to Earth.

Cursing loudly, Remulkin resumed his manic typing.

Jake reached into the display and zoomed out until the hauntingly familiar asteroidal forms reentered the rendering. Judging by their apparent size, it appeared that the GDF ships were maintaining a respectable stand-off distance.

"It looks like Tekamah is staying outside of gene weapon range," Jake said.

Remulkin pounded a fist into the control console. "I can't break the control lockout! Why aren't we moving to help?!" he said in a tone boarding on hysteria. "What is wrong with your admiral?"

Jake shook his head. "I don't know," he said. He panned the display and pointed to the *Helm Warden's* idling fighters. "This doesn't make any sense."

Colonel Giard looked away from the display and switched to the command net. "Galactic Guardian Six, this is—" He abandoned the effort. "Shit! My EON won't link."

Remulkin growled and pounded the console again. "This isn't working! It won't take my commands. Why aren't they attacking?" He shook a fist at the hologram. "Kill the bastards!" Again, nothing happened. Thramorus threw up his hands and screamed, "Godsdamn them!" He shoved Jake aside. Caught unprepared, Giard stumbled backward.

The Argonian liaison rammed his hand into the *Turtle's* flight controller. He twisted and pushed it. No response. The ship refused to budge. "Damn it!" Remulkin said, hammering the console's surface with his other hand.

Recovering, Jake stepped back to the console. Placing a hand on Thramorus's shoulder, he said, "Lieutenant, we have our orders."

The scientist tried to bat his hand away, but Jake clamped down hard. He heard tendons in the older man's shoulder creaking and grinding. Finally, the Argonian released the controller. The man's bald head was as red as the ring of hair that haloed it.

"Where did they go?" Thramorus asked with renewed surprise and frustration.

"What?"

Remulkin pointed at the suddenly empty ring of green ships. He switched to accented English. "Tekamah let them escape!"

All of the Zoxyth dreadnoughts had disappeared from the display.

"What the hell?" Jake yelled. At the same time, Remulkin growled something similar in his native tongue.

Giard reached into the display again and zoomed back out. The enemy fleet slid back into view.

"There they are!" Jake said and released the breath he'd been holding. The enemy ships had fallen back, but they were still in system. They were in a new, linear formation a couple of hundred miles farther from the planet. Also, it looked like they had stopped their advance on Earth. Still expanding, the gap between their closest ship and the nearest GDF battlecruiser was equal to the entire width of the *Helm Warden's* formation.

In an apparent reaction to the Zoxyth's maneuver, the octagonal formation of eight GDF ships stopped as well, locking the gap at a safer distance.

Jake pointed at the spacing. "It looks like they fell back two hundred miles." Turning to Remulkin, he hoisted two hopeful eyebrows. "The *Helm Warden* and its fleet are way outside the range of the gene weapon now."

"I don't give a shit," Thramorus said, still in accented English. "Tekamah isn't going to fire on the family-stealing bastards, not unless they fire first." He shook his head. "Especially now that they're no longer advancing on your planet."

Remulkin paused. The anger drained from his face. Tilting his head like a perplexed dog, he reached into the hologram again. Looking at the enemy ships, he whispered, "That line. It looks like …" The scientist's words trailed off. Then his eyes widened. Remulkin slapped the curved top of the *Turtle's* control panel and started stringing together a fresh batch of Argonian curse words.

Jake turned toward him. "What?"

The man didn't answer.

Giard looked at the formation again. Remulkin's reaction had Jake's short hairs standing on end. In spite of the greater distance, the Zoxyth fleet's new orientation—in a line that pointed directly at the *Helm Warden*—suddenly looked ominous.

Shoving Jake aside, the portly man ran his hands across another portion of the panel's surface. Moving with surprising dexterity, the Lieutenant—Jake reminded himself that the man was firstly a scientist —entered a series of commands. In a few seconds, a holographic rendering of the two formations dissolved into a series of symbols. They still floated in the same arrangement as the opposing forces. However, instead of a ship, a small red satellite dish now sat where each of the enemy vessels had floated. On the left side of the display, a ring of eight discrete green spheres represented the ships of the Galactic Defense Forces.

Thramorus toggled a command, and concentric arcing rings began to emanate from the aftmost enemy ship like waves from a pebble dropped into a smooth pond. When the advancing front of energy fired by the first satellite reached the symbol for the next enemy ship, the second vessel detonated its weapon. Along the formation's axis, the energy's amplitude and speed appeared to double. Like noise waves from a cartoon megaphone, the lines fanned out as they traveled across the ships ahead of it. However, as the leading edge of the advancing wave reached the next ship in sequence, that vessel's satellite dish added its blast of gene weapon energy.

Jake watched the simulation in slack-jawed amazement. The wave's power appeared to double with each new squirt of energy. Twelve iterations later, the modeled wave burst forth from the lead element of the enemy formation and quickly crossed the two hundred-mile gap, enveloping the *Helm Warden* and its fleet of green spheres.

"Oh shit," Jake whispered.

～

Tekamah studied the new Zoxyth formation with growing unease. "What are you up to, Thrakst?" There was something familiar about the orientation of the ships.

"What are your orders, Admiral?"

He ignored the helmsman. Accessing the hologram's controls through his EON interface, Tekamah magnified the enemy fleet. All fourteen ships had reformed in a perfect line aimed directly at the *Helm Warden's* octagonal formation.

Something didn't add up, but this was no time to start changing his plan.

"Sir?" the helmsman asked again.

"Move the task-force to re-engage," the admiral said.

The officer nodded. "Yes, sir."

As the order went out to the battlecruisers, Tekamah continued to stare at the line of enemy ships. He rotated the display until his fleet came into view. It was like looking down the barrel of a lumpy rifle.

His eyes widened. "Oh my Gods." Turning to the helmsman, he shouted, "Belay that order!"

But it was too late. With its unmatched sub-light acceleration, the Helm Warden and her seven battlecruisers were already blazing toward the enemy fleet.

Suddenly, a brilliant flash shot from the aftmost dreadnought. Just like the directional old-world radio array Tekamah had belatedly remembered, the alignment of the enemy's transmitters focused the wave's propagation into a narrow, far-reaching linear beam as the next ship in line fired its weapon.

Tekamah watched with mounting dread as light sprang from the next ship and then the one in front of it. In accelerating fashion, the line of fire jumped from dreadnought to dreadnought, growing and speeding up with each new injection of energy.

Finally responding to his revised order, all eight GDF ships reversed direction in an instant.

Fearing he had reacted too late, Admiral Tekamah focused on the lead enemy ship as the advancing front of the energy wave raced toward it.

"Command all ships to deploy their weapons on my mark and in this sequence!"

"Lord Thrakst," the weapons officer said. "That will leave us virtually defenseless against the remaining ships."

The officer couldn't know of the tactic, so Thrakst decided to spare his life, for now. "If we fire in this order and this formation, the weapon's effect should be magnified and extended tenfold," the Lord said. Through a growl, he added, "Now send the order or die where you stand!"

"Yes, my Lord," the hatchling said and then transmitted the order to the fleet.

"Make sure they understand the importance of the firing sequence!"

Gazing through his view-wall, Thrakst felt his pulse quicken as he prepared to give the order that would finally avenge the death of his wife and son.

The officer nodded. "They're ready, my Lord."

Thrakst moved to stand in front of his massive stone cathedra. Raising both arms, he roared, "Fire!"

A glorious wave erupted from the *Tidor Drof*. Its galaxy-cleansing light flooded into the bridge, twin beams streaming through the Forebearer's eye portals. The glow emanated first from his ship at the back of the formation. The wave spread in its normal spherical pattern. However, when the white light reached the next ship in his linear formation, it distorted that ship's energy wave, focusing it into a beam. Then their combined energy raced to the next ship in line. Employing Thrakst's timing perfectly, dreadnought after dreadnought added the force of their gene weapon to the advancing front.

"Lord Thrakst, the enemy is moving to intercept."

Looking at the main display, Thrakst frowned. As they approached, the *Warden* and its ships began to spread apart, their closer proximity making their formation appear wider.

Too wide!

The beam was going to be too narrow!

The Lord spun toward the communications officer. "Cease fire!"

"My Lord?"

Not interested in leaving his fleet practically defenseless against Tekamah's more powerful ships, Thrakst knocked the officer aside, sending the idiot sprawling. He toggled the communications console, but a massive hand stayed his arm.

Without looking, Thrakst growled. "Release my arm or lose the hand, Raja."

Phascyre didn't release him, but pointed to the main display. "My Lord, they are retreating."

Freezing with his hand over the transmit key, Thrakst looked at the display. Seeing the apparent size of the enemy formation shrinking, he grinned broadly. "You're making this too easy, Tekamah."

Slowly withdrawing his hand from the console, he watched as the unhindered wave of cleansing light raced down the line of his ships, each flash bigger and brighter until the final wave erupted from the lead dreadnought with blinding intensity. The linearly focused wave burned across the vast void in a concentrated beam.

"Yes," Thrakst whispered, "Run, Tekamah."

Moments later, the wave washed across the retreating enemy

formation, its outer ships falling just inside the beam's narrow confines.

At that glorious moment, the enemy's precise octagonal formation began to dissolve into a drifting, disorganized group of unmanned ships.

CHAPTER 27

Aboard the Galactic Guardian and still hidden behind the moon, Admiral Johnston watched the eight green ships within the hologram start a slow tumble.

"Oh my God!"

The man on his right nodded. "As long as it's available to him, Thrakst will never stop using that godsdamned weapon."

"You're right," Admiral Johnston whispered.

The image of the emptied, drifting ships was too familiar, dredging up all too recent and horrible memories.

Intuiting the admiral's thoughts, the Argonian officer placed a comforting hand on his shoulder. "We can mourn our losses when the battle is over."

Taking a deep breath, Johnston turned to the man. "You're right, Admiral. I knew it was coming, but seeing those ships start their death tumble ... Well, it clarifies things."

"Yes, it does," Admiral Tekamah said, nodding. "This weapon is too dangerous, its masters too eager."

On the right side of the holographic display, the fourteen Zoxyth dreadnoughts, having regrouped into a diamond-shaped formation, began to advance on Earth again. Johnston watched them give a wide berth to the emptied *Helm Warden* fleet as if they did not completely trust the efficacy of their gene weapon.

"We have to remove both now before they get a chance to use it again," Tekamah said.

Taking his meaning, Johnston nodded as well. Checking his watch, he said, "Your gambit bought us a solid forty-five minutes. Let's see if we can convince them of the error of their ways."

The hologram panned to the moon. Admiral Tekamah swept a hand, gesturing to the holographic rendering of the GDF ships hovering over its pockmarked surface. "You have all of the Helm Warden's heavy-ship staff here, aboard the *Galactic Guardian,* and my entire complement of fighters at your disposal. The command is yours, Admiral. What are your orders?"

Johnston gave a slight bow to the Galactic Defense Force's supreme commander. "Thank you, Admiral Tekamah."

Taking control of the hologram, Johnston opened a fleet-wide channel.

∾

"Ladies and gentlemen, what you just saw was a demonstration of the enemy's unrelenting resolve to employ their gene weapon. What you did not see was the loss of human life. Contrary to what the enemy believes, we didn't lose a soul in that engagement."

Wordlessly, Jake stared at holographic Johnston. He felt the knot in his gut begin to loosen. Was it possible that he hadn't just watched another crushing defeat, hadn't just seen tens of thousands of beings erased from the universe? He looked over to the Argonian liaison. For a change, Remulkin was speechless.

"It took some last-second maneuvering," Johnston said, "but we baited them into firing their entire complement of gene weapons." The admiral appeared to consult his wristwatch. "We now have forty-five minutes to convince them of the error of their ways."

Johnston pointed at someone out of camera range. After a moment, he nodded and looked back into the holocam. "We just dropped a disruptor field over the entire system. When the time comes, we'll lower it just long enough to allow our ingress. After that, you won't be able to execute a parallel-space jump." The admiral paused, and a predatory grin spread across his holographic rendering. "But neither will the enemy. In the meantime, unless they try to make another parallel-space jump, the Zoxyth won't know the field is up."

"Obviously, we had foreknowledge of the enemy's arrival. Sorry for the subterfuge, I'll explain later. In the meantime, we've put you in the best possible position to win this battle." Johnston shook his head. "No. Make that the best possible position to win this *war*. With a few minor deviations, your assignments remain unchanged. The live-fire exercise you planned is no longer a drill. However, your target is now that fleet," the admiral said, pointing off-screen.

Johnston nodded to someone on his bridge, and a chime rang from the *Turtle's* console.

Both Jake and Remulkin looked at it and then back to the hologram.

The image dissolved again, but the admiral's voice continued to echo across the *Turtle's* spacious confines.

"We've just transmitted orders and autopilot programming to every ship."

The display reformed. Holographic renderings of the Moon and all of the ships—friendly and enemy—returned to their previous locations. Apparently unaware they weren't alone, the Zoxyth fleet remained on their Earth-intercept course.

"When we exit parallel-space," Johnston said, "I will demand their unconditional surrender. But make no mistake, if they don't capitulate immediately, we *will* destroy them. Failing that ..." The admiral didn't finish the sentence, but a sour look crossed his face. He just shook his head as if to rid an unpleasant thought.

After a moment, Johnston continued. "Weapons hold, ladies and gentlemen. Let's give them a moment—a very short moment—to do the right thing."

Admiral Johnston's face returned to the hologram. A predatory grin spread across the man's face. "Now, let's shock the hell out of those damned lizards."

~

Admiral Johnston turned from the holocam and pointed at the TacCom officer. "Drop the disruptor field, on my mark."

The officer nodded.

"I want it back in place the moment we reenter normal space," Johnston added. "Don't let them escape, Major."

The Marine officer smiled. "Not a chance, sir."

Turning from TacCom, Johnston gave the GDF supreme commander a hard look. "Admiral Tekamah, tell me again why you're so sure they can't have a gene weapon waiting in the wings, why I should bet the battle, hell, the war on that belief?"

Tekamah nodded somberly then pointed into the hologram. "There are two reasons, actually. The power output of those ships perfectly matches that of a ... standard—for lack of a better word—Zoxyth dreadnought, right down to their infrared signatures."

"Why's that significant?" Johnston said.

"Because the other thing we know is that that weapon requires a *lot* of power. So much power, in fact, that—without violating the laws of physics—their fusion reactors *can't* recharge faster than the observed time of fifty zurline or forty-five of your minutes."

"But what if they have more than one weapon aboard?" Johnston asked.

"They could have a hundred on each ship," Tekamah said. "However, they could only fire one of them every forty-five minutes."

"What if they added a spare, dedicated power supply?"

Tekamah nodded again. "That brings us back to my first point. Their IR signature would be different. You can't hide that much energy from the universe. We would see the extra heat leaking from their hulls, literally."

Johnston had heard all of this before, but considering the stakes, he needed the warm fuzzy of the admiral's assurances.

He took a deep breath and let it out slowly. Nodding, Johnston pointed to TacCom. "Drop the disruptor field in five seconds."

Shifting his gesture to the helmsman, Johnston locked eyes with the woman. Nodding to her in turn, he said, "Ok, Lieutenant Commander."

She moved her hand to the ship's drive controller.

The admiral looked into the holocam. Activating a fleet-wide broadcast, he said, "Parallel-jump in three, two, one, *mark!*"

Sandy gnawed her lips. Signaling their protest, they started throbbing, snapping the major from her thoughts. She hadn't realized she'd started chewing on them. A coppery dampness told her she'd been doing it for a while.

"Shit," she whispered.

Jake thought it was cute, but Sandy despised the nervous tell, although she supposed she could forgive herself this one. Calling the last few minutes an emotional roller coaster was an incredible under-statement. Seeing the enemy wipe out yet another GDF carrier group had crushed her, had made her physically ill. *Thank God for diligent nanobots.* Then the Admiral had revealed the whole thing had been a feint. Afterward, she'd oscillated between joy for the sudden reversal and anger for the admiral's deception.

Admiral Johnston's face suddenly returned to her EON's virtual hologram.

"Speak of the devil," Sandy muttered. Then fresh pain blossomed from her lips.

He said, "Parallel-jump in three, two, one, *mark!*"

The moon vanished from her field of view. As if someone had changed the television to a horror channel, the image outside swapped from the moon's pockmarked surface to the waking night-mare of the Zoxyth fleet.

Sandy's new position behind the advancing enemy formation painted a breathtaking panorama. Earth's blue-green sphere hung centered in the forward half of the fighter's spherical display. Eclipsing the central one-third of the planet, the massive *Galactic Guardian* hovered on the far side of the enemy's formation of asteroidal ships. Superimposed over the flagship's smooth lines, the rocky protuberances of the Zoxyth ships blotted out much of the *Guardian*.

Suddenly, every enemy ship seemed to tremor, a shudder passing like a ripple through all fourteen dreadnoughts.

The bastards had just tried to parallel-jump out of the battle!

Sandy grinned. "You're all big and bad when you have that damned weapon, aren't you?"

Her finger hovered over the trigger of her fighter's particle beam. In her mind's eye, she could still see the emptied San Francisco Bay Area. Thinking of the fiery, other-worldly depopulated aftermath of the Zoxyth's unwarranted attack, Sandy had to exert a massive force of will not to fire all of her weapons before Admiral Johnston could issue his ultimatum.

CHAPTER 28

In silent wonder, Lord Thrakst stared at the *Helm Warden's* tumbling ships.

After a moment, roaring laughter burst from his razor-sharp lips.

"That's it? That was all you had for me, Tekamah?"

He pointed to another officer. "Where is the Forebearers-damned Galactic Guardian?"

Nervously glancing down at his failed and very dead predecessor, the new sensor console operator consulted his displays and then shook his head. "There's still no sign of it, my Lord."

Thrakst grinned. He'd won this battle. He'd taken out an entire carrier fleet.

"My Lord," said the officer behind the weapons console. "Shall I destroy the empty ships?"

"No," Thrakst said. He pointed toward Earth. "Down there, a few billion Argonians await our attention."

The Lord moved to his cathedra. Standing before his throne, Thrakst looked across the bridge. A toothy grin spread across his face. In anxious anticipation, his pointed black tongue flicked and dabbed at his dripping fangs.

He laughed again. "Reassemble the fleet! I want to find out what happened to Salyth. Have one of the probes investigate the wreckage." Pointing to the officers behind the navigation and tactical consoles, he said, "Let's pick up where Commodore Salyth left off, starting with New York!"

As the ships returned to their diamond-shaped formation, Thrakst's smile faltered. He glared at the blue-green planet. Something about the situation had his spine scales oscillating.

The Lord pointed a talon at the helmsman. "Steer the fleet well clear of the enemy ships. Their auto-defense systems may be online."

He turned back to the image of the planet. *Is that you down there, Salyth?*

He couldn't understand how the commodore could hit so many of his assigned targets and not report back. It appeared he'd only lost one ship.

Narrowing his eyes, Thrakst shifted his gaze to the decapitated body of the failed sensor officer. "The worthless hatchling couldn't even manage three probes ..." The Lord faltered. His insides rolled as if he'd swallowed an unsedated drycat lizard. Slowly, he turned from the dead officer to Raja Phascyre.

The old warrior looked ... nervous?

Thrakst took the Zox's left elbow with his right hand and pointed a talon at the failed sensor officer with his other. "Raja, what had the hatchling done wrong? What did you do to his console?"

Did his old friend just flinch? Surely not.

"It was nothing, my Lord. He hadn't completed their calibration."

"Calibration of what, Raja?"

"Well, the sensor probes, my Lord."

Phascyre hadn't turned to face him. He still stared forward.

Thrakst's eyes narrowed. "All *three* probes?"

This time, the Raja did flinch.

"What about the third probe, Raja?!" Lord Thrakst said. The question repeated as his raised voice echoed several times, his barked question ricocheting off the cavernous bridge's rock walls.

Everyone froze, every crewmember casting a wary glance with at least one of their eyes.

Phascyre didn't answer.

The hard and soft tissues of the warrior's elbow creaked and popped as Thrakst's crushing grip elicited their protest.

"Phascyre? What happened to the third probe? The one we sent to check out this planet's moon."

The Raja stood motionlessly.

Finally, he spoke. "I don't know, my Lord."

Raising a scarred arm, the wizened warrior pointed at the dead sensor officer. Phascyre turned his mutilated face toward him. His lone eye burned with anger.

"Why don't you ask him, *my Lord?*" Phascyre said acerbically. Blatant disdain dripped from the words "my Lord".

Thrakst's head rocked back as if struck. A shocked moment later, he cocked his arm to strike the old Zoxyth warrior, but then white light flooded the bridge, streaming in from every port.

Breaking eye contact, the two Zoxyth warriors looked forward.

Thrakst released the Raja's elbow and shouted, "Report!" But as he said it, he saw the *Galactic Guardian* resolving from the fading light of its post-jump halo directly in front of the *Tidor Drof*.

Lord Thrakst knocked Raja Phascyre clear of the cathedra's right armrest. Slamming his fist down, he activated a fleet-wide broadcast. "All ships, fallback now, now, now!"

He pointed to the helmsman. "Parallel jump to the fallback coordinates *now!*"

The officer nodded vigorously and slammed his fist down on the emergency jump activator.

Nothing happened.

"Make the jump, idiot!"

The officer hit the button again.

Still nothing happened.

"My Lord," another bridge officer said.

Thrakst spun toward him. The officer punched in a few commands and then shook his head grimly. The Lord ground his teeth together. "What?!"

The hatchling twitched but held his ground. "There's a disruptor field over the entire system, my Lord. It just came up."

Thrakst pointed to the helmsman. "Reverse course! Get us out of ..."

Looking at the room's scattered monitors, he realized escape wasn't an option. The GDF had surrounded his fleet. And his ultimate weapon was fangless. He'd fired all of them against ... against what? A bunch of empty ships?

The Forebearers-damned mammals had lured him into it, and he'd taken the bait.

"Lord Thrakst."

"What?" he roared.

"The *Galactic Guardian* is hailing us."

"Let me hear it, incoming voice only. Do not transmit."

A squeaky voice burned into his ears. They folded flat against his skull, and the voice dropped to a slightly less annoying tenor.

He pointed at the communications officer. "Activate the translator, idiot!"

Mid-sentence, the enemy's rant changed to low-toned Zoxyth.

"...and if you fail to surrender, I *will* destroy your fleet!" After a pause, the Argonian said, "With extreme prejudice!"

Thrakst pointed to the weapons officer. "Pinpoint the source of that cursed disruptor field. I want to know the precise location of its transmitter!"

The officer nodded. "Yes, my Lord."

Lord Thrakst paused and pointed to the Raja. "Let me know when he has its position."

"My Lord," Phascyre said. "Are you sure this is a wise—?"

"Raja!" Thrakst roared. "You got us into this. I am going to get us out of it."

After a moment, the Raja bowed and then walked to stand next to the weapons officer.

Using the controls at his cathedra, Thrakst opened the full link, enabling video and two-way communications.

Two pale Argonian faces filled his main display. He recognized the man on the left. However, the older-looking one on the right was unknown to him.

He nodded to the one he knew. "Admiral Tekamah, I see you're back from the dead."

The admiral nodded and started speaking. The auto-translator quickly morphed his grating high-pitched voice into something intelligible. "Not for a lack of trying on your part, Thrakst."

The Lord gave the mammals a toothy smirk. The unknown Argonian flinched. This pleased Thrakst. So he widened the grin, exposing all of his silver teeth. Unfortunately, the man seemed to collect himself; his apparent fear morphed into anger.

Bristling inwardly, Lord Thrakst held his grin. He nodded to the stranger and said, "I don't believe I've had the pleasure."

"Jesus wept," Admiral Johnston whispered as the eight-foot-tall three-dimensional holographic rendering of the enemy commander popped into existence. Reflexively, Bill's right hand went to his hip. Grasping for the absent Colt 1911, his fingers closed on empty air.

The monster towered over them. Every time the beast took a breath, Johnston could see its individual scales undulate. Did the computer really have to portray the bastard as life-sized?

When Thrakst spoke to Tekamah, the EON automatically translated his words into Argonian. The rendered words sounded like an Argonian male. However, underneath it, Johnston could hear the combination of the low tones and high-pitched squeals that constituted the Zox language. The parts he could hear—the frequencies that fell within the audible range of human ears—sounded as if a roaring lion was arguing with a screeching parrot.

The beast bared his teeth.

Johnston flinched in spite of himself.

Was the bastard smiling? He was. The son of a bitch responsible for the loss of unknown millions was fucking smiling!

Johnston found the EON command he'd been searching for since the giant hologram had coalesced.

Thrakst shrunk to half his size. The now four-foot-tall lizard looked almost comical.

Johnston glared at the smiling bastard. For the admiral, seeing the being that had ordered humanity's death elicited unrealized emotions. When the beast asked who he was, a wave of raw emotions broke through the dam of a lifetime's worth of discipline and self-restraint.

With both hands clenched into fists, Johnston stepped to the holographic rendering. Through the EON interface, he adjusted the display settings, levitating the shortened reptile until they stood eye-to-eye.

In Argonian, he said, "The name is Admiral Johnston. I'm the one who's going to wipe that grin off your scaly face, you green-blooded piece of shit!"

The monster flinched. It had been small, barely perceptible, but there nonetheless.

Bill kept going. "You're going to surrender your damned fleet now, *Lord*," he said, pouring disdain into the bastard's title. He pointed toward Earth. "That's my home. You and your kind attacked it." Johnston lowered his voice and injected a practiced icy edge into his words. Through his own menacing smile, he said, "Feel free to decline, Thrakst. I'd welcome the opportunity to render you and every one of your ships into a boiling lump of molten slag; just like we did to the last Zoxyth that came this way."

Thrakst blinked. After a moment, he cut the connection, not deigning to address Johnston's demand or his braggadocious claim. Of course, the Lord had known the fate of Commodore Salyth the instant the *Galactic Guardian* had shown itself. "You'll pay for that one, Admiral," Thrakst whispered.

A hand grasped his upper arm, and Raja Phascyre whispered into his right ear. "Lord, we should accept his offer."

Stunned, Thrakst turned toward his old friend. After a moment, he knocked the Raja's hand from his arm. "You forget yourself, Raja."

Beyond the old warrior, the sensor officer looked confusedly from the Raja and back to him.

Thrakst pointed at the hatchling. "What?"

"Lord Thrakst, as I told Raja Phascyre, I have a fix on the disruptor's transmitter."

The Lord glowered at Phascyre then turned back to the officer. "Show me!"

The officer nodded and punched a command into his console. The Lord's personal display reactivated and zoomed in on a sensor blister that protruded from a corner of the *Galactic Guardian*.

Thrakst opened a fleet-wide channel. "All ships! On my mark, engage your nearest enemy ship, and then shift fire to this target."

He transmitted the coordinates and then reached for the controls on the arm of his cathedra, intent on reopening the GDF communications channel.

Raja Phascyre's hand shot out.

"My Lord, this is not—"

"Phascyre," Thrakst said through a low growl. Using his superior size and strength, he ripped the Raja's hand away from his forearm. As he held the warrior's hand in a crushing grip, Thrakst whispered into the Raja's ear. "The Forebearers may forgive you, but if you question my command again, I will free your shoulders from the burden of carrying your head."

Thrakst watched myriad emotions cross the Raja's sole eye. Finally, he bowed his head and retreated a step.

Shaking his head, Thrakst opened the communications channel.

The faces of the two Argonian commanders returned to his display.

"Well, *Admiral* Johnston," Thrakst said, pouring as much disdain into the title as had Johnston. "Since you asked so nicely, here's my answer."

CHAPTER 29

Sandy stared at the surreal Mexican stand-off painted across her fighter's immersive display. Almost two minutes had ticked by— an eternity when hanging on the precipice of battle. However, no one had fired yet. She toggled her radio. "Six, this is Seven. What do you—?"

Suddenly, the entire universe slid sideways, every visible point of reference jumping fractionally right. A brilliant beam of light visible as a white line outside the auto-darkened spherical display burned through the space that, a millisecond earlier, had been occupied by her fighter. If not for the drive's inertial dampening, the speed of the short, lateral leap would have turned Sandy into a red lump spread across the concave surface of the ship's interior.

In the brief moment that it took for Sandy to register the event, hundreds of additional white threads leaped from the enemy forma- tion. Like spokes of a wheel, they radiated out from the dreadnoughts, trying to impale the encircling ring of GDF ships on their burning spears.

However, every warship in the haloing formation of vessels easily evaded its assigned beam. Their virtually inertialess leaps kept them just out of the Zoxyth line of fire.

Sandy knew that the combination of superior weapons and drive technology afforded commanders of the Galactic Defense Forces the option of asking questions *first* and firing *later*.

However, the enemy apparently wasn't in a question-answering mood.

That was fine with Major Fitzpatrick. She smiled and fired all of her weapons.

"Looks like they aren't in a surrendering mood," Jake said.

Remulkin grinned menacingly. "Good."

"Gunfighter Squadron, on me," Colonel Giard ordered across the unit's EON channel.

Turning the *Turtle* toward their assigned target, Jake rocketed the fat ship at a Zoxyth dreadnought near one corner of the enemy's diamond formation.

As he led the squadron inbound on their first strafing run, a beam reached for the *Turtle*. Instantly, the ship leaped out of the line of fire. Then a brilliant light on Jake's left made his heart skip a beat. He feared that the aliens had fired another gene weapon. Looking in that direction, he saw a blindingly bright ball of fire. However, it wasn't growing; its size remained unchanged for the brief moment that he could stand to look directly at it. The intensity faded for a millisecond, and Jake saw the *Galactic Guardian* at the center of the glowing sphere.

He breathed a sigh of relief. The light hadn't been a gene weapon. It appeared that every enemy dreadnought had directed a portion of its firepower into the carrier. Under intense enemy attack, the *Guardian's* shields glowed so brightly that it looked like a miniature sun had taken up orbit around the planet.

Sandy opened their direct EON link. "I guess the assholes figured out which ship is generating the disruptor field," she said.

Jake heard something in her voice: a tone he normally associated with their intimate moments. *She's actually enjoying this,* he thought.

Subvocalizing, Jake said, "You're right; they're hammering the *Guardian*, but don't worry about them. Concentrate on yourself."

"Yes, Colonel," she said with the same excited tone and then cut the connection.

Giard grinned. Even his heart raced in response to the adrenaline pumping into his system. The imagery beyond the view-wall eclipsed anything he'd seen in the first battle. Brilliant plasma beams interlaced with flickering lightning bolts backlit by bursting nuclear bunker busters painted a mural of horrifying energies. No science fiction special effects artist had ever captured this level of intensity.

Looking down, Jake realized he had the console's edge in a white-knuckled death grip. During the last two seconds, the insane panorama had skittered across the view-wall five times. As Zoxyth lasers filled the space around his squadron, his ship's automatic defense systems had it jumping all over the place.

Grinding his teeth, Jake forced himself to focus on his next task.

As the *Turtle* reached the designated initialization point, it turned and rocketed directly at the targeted dreadnought. Over the squadron's channel, Jake said, "IP inbound. Gunfighters, cleared hot!"

Training his weapons on their designated target, Jake unleashed a devastating volley of plasma bolts and kinetic rounds. The *Turtle* shuddered as the massive release of energy momentarily overtopped the drive's inertial dampening.

The dreadnought's shields flared. Then the rest of Gunfighter Squadron added their firepower, and they collapsed. A fresh wave of spreading lightning bolts signaled the shield's death.

On cue, his squadron shot out of the ingress path, departing the plane of the attack on a perpendicular vector. Then Richard's Phoenix Squadron rolled in on the dreadnought.

While it continued to fire on the *Galactic Guardian*, the targeted Zoxyth ship shifted the weapons it had dedicated to self-defense to the new attackers.

Suddenly, one of Richard's fighters erupted in a brilliant detonation. It had jumped out of the path of one beam and directly into another.

"No!" Jake screamed.

Fresh gouts of molten rock shot from the asteroidal ship as Phoenix Squadron opened fire. Jake saw Sandy's jinking fighter on Richard's right wing.

"Thank God," he whispered and instantly felt guilty.

Additional jets of debris blasted from the enemy ship. Then Richard's squadron also vectored out of the attack path and out of the direct line of enemy fire.

Jake released the breath he'd been holding.

"Okay, Vampire Six," Richard said. "She's all dressed up for you!"

"Roger, Phoenix Six," said Colonel Newcastle. "I'm inbound now. Nuclear bunker buster armed."

For today's battle drill, Admiral Johnston had split up Newcastle's squadron. He'd assigned one of their nuclear-armed fighters to fly clean up for each of the starfighter task forces. As the Commander Air Group (or CAG), Newcastle had assigned himself to the one that contained Richard and Jake's squadrons. Now Giard saw the Texan's Vampire Space Fighter race toward the target.

With a mighty effort, Jake dragged his eyes from the image and shifted his focus to the task at hand. Directed by the autopilot and fire-control computer, the attack plan uploaded by Admiral Johnston already had his ship's weapons trained on the next target.

Consulting the holographic rendering of the battle and the plotted attack plan, Jake verified the vectors assigned to each of his fighters.

Nodding, he glared at the second Zoxyth ship and said, "You're next, asshole."

As if responding to his words, the targeted dreadnought redirected a portion of its attack away from the *Guardian* and fired on Jake's ship. The *Turtle* easily avoided each beam. Although the millisecond durations of those laser contacts had several hull temperature alarms flashing their warnings across the console's curved top. Jake had learned that the Argonian vessels didn't have foreknowledge of the laser's trajectory. They simply jumped out of the beam like a child who had touched a hot pan. However, the speed of the computer and the drive it controlled outstripped the ability of the laser. It moved out of the path faster than the weapon's energy could burn through the shields and the ship's skin. But it moved so quickly the human eye perceived it as precognition.

Suddenly, a new light source drew Jake's attention from his target. To his left, a web of glowing fissures spread across the first enemy ship. Then the *Turtle's* view-wall darkened as the brilliant light that streamed from every crack in the asteroid flared. Finally, each blade of radiation merged with its neighbor as the nuclear conflagration enveloped the entire enemy ship.

"Die, bastards!" Remulkin growled in accented English.

Jake looked at the now tumbling molten remnants of the first ship. "Oh shit!" Remembering Admiral Thoyd Feyhdyak's doomed effort to vaporize those same globs, he looked at Remulkin and said, "Run an orbital analysis of that debris. Where is it going?"

Remulkin grunted something unintelligible. It sounded derogatory, but the liaison bent over his half of the console, and his fingers became a blur of activity.

Strobing multicolored light streamed through every port of the *Tidor Drof's* bridge. The ship shook violently as wave after wave of enemy fire burned into its shields. It appeared Admiral Johnston intended to make good on his promise.

"Lord Thrakst, we just lost the *Forebearer's Redemption!*"

Shaking his head, Thrakst growled.

He refused to look at Phascyre. He wouldn't give the coward the satisfaction. Instead, he glared at the image of the *Galactic Guardian.* On the main display, the rocky profile of the dreadnought *Zoxa Prime* drifted across the *Guardian's* curved surface.

Staring at the *Prime*, Thrakst nodded grimly.

Intuiting Thrakst's plan, the Raja suddenly turned toward him. "No, my Lord. That is not ..." Phascyre began but stopped as Thrakst extended his forearm's dewclaw talon and gave him a final warning glance.

Nodding, the Raja retreated.

Thrakst opened a channel to the *Prime's* captain.

"Commodore Rasynth, I need you to ram the enemy's command ship."

"Lord?" The commodore blinked his confusion. "My ship is too slow. I'll never get close enough. I—"

"Vent your core, Rasynth."

The commodore blinked again, but this time with complete comprehension.

"The Forebearers demand it," Thrakst said.

Finally, Rasynth nodded and then bowed. "Yes, my Lord. May the Forebearers greet us with open—"

Cutting him off, Thrakst gave a curt nod. "Yes, yes, Commodore. Quickly, please. Time is of the essence," he said, then terminated the connection.

The scientist punched a final command into the console and then stood straight. A holographic rendering of the battle and the planet below popped into existence above the control panel.

Jake breathed a sigh of relief. A curving red line showed that the enemy fleet and the building debris cloud were in an orbital insertion trajectory. They wouldn't hit the planet.

Remulkin reached into the hologram, gesturing at the point of closest approach. "They're going too fast to enter orbit, but either by design or chance, the bastards are on a trajectory to skim the atmosphere. It's an aerobraking maneuver that will slow them enough for the planet's gravity to pull the formation into orbit."

Ahead of the *Turtle*, a plume of fire suddenly burst from the right side of his assigned Zoxyth dreadnought.

Jake blinked. "What the hell?"

As he watched, the torrent of fire continued to spread outward. Soon a massive jet of white-hot plasma streamed from a lake-sized hole in the largest asteroid of the ship's hull. At its perimeter, hill-sized boulders periodically broke free only to be vaporized in a brilliant flash when they drifted into the plume of fire.

"Is that a rocket motor?" Jake said.

"No. Not a normal one, anyway," Remulkin said without his characteristic snark.

The disruptor field had removed the parallel-space option. This rocket must be an emergency supplement to the version of the gravity drive employed by the Zoxyth. Jake could see that the combined effect generated significant thrust. The incredible acceleration was deforming the structural supports that tied together the ship's various asteroids.

"They're flying straight at the *Galactic Guardian*!" Remulkin said.

Looking at the hologram, Jake saw that the scientist was correct. With acceleration rivaling that of an Argonian battlecruiser, the ship rocketed straight at the carrier. Giard shook his head. Even he knew that flying straight into the muzzle of a carrier's main weapon was to ask for a quick death.

"Gunfighters," Jake transmitted across the EON. "Shift course and match acceleration."

Finally reacting to the new threat, the *Galactic Guardian* redirected all of its weapon batteries at the approaching Zoxyth ship.

"Same plan, new vectors," Jake continued over the squadron's channel.

In the hologram, he shifted the squadron's attack vectors to run perpendicular to the Guardian's laser attack. Caught between the lines of incoming laser fire and outgoing rocket thrust, the rendered enemy ship looked like a lumpy, cancerous tumor impaled on a spike of fire. Alternatively, the opposing beams looked like an axle rammed through the dreadnought, and the rendered equally spaced starfighter strike lines ran from it like the spokes of a wheel.

Through his EON, Jake sent the new discrete headings to each of his fighters.

Presently, several of the battlecruisers adjacent to the *Galactic Guardian* added their laser fire to the mix.

As Jake maneuvered to attack, he could no longer see the portion of the enemy ship closest to the *Guardian*. That half of its shields glowed like an umbrella-shaped star, obscuring the underlying dreadnought.

"IP inbound!" he broadcast over the EON channel.

The orientation of his attack run shifted the carrier to the top of the *Turtle's* view-wall. From this new perspective, it appeared that the *Guardian* was firing down on a speeding jellyfish. Undeterred, the dreadnought continued its incredible acceleration.

"That's suicide," Jake whispered.

"You're speaking of the dead," Remulkin said.

"What?"

The scientist shook his head. "All of them died when they vented their core. The instant they started to use it for thrust, it flooded the ship with enough radiation to immediately kill every one of them," the liaison said flatly.

When Jake looked back to the dreadnought, a storm of lightning bolts radiated downward from the shield's perimeter like tentacles, completing his earlier jellyfish analogy. One of the massive electrical bolts discharged across the *Turtle's* shields.

Then the force field collapsed. Instantly, the stone surface of the still accelerating enemy ship burst into white fire as rock sublimated directly into gas under the incredible assault.

Coming into range of the target, Jake fired his plasma and kinetic weapons. They blazed toward the doomed dreadnought. His rounds slammed into the unprotected ship, and it exploded, the combined multi-vessel assault converting its asteroids into gaseous and molten rock.

"Yes!" Jake screamed. Then he gasped. "Oh shit!"

The Argonian carrier tried to leap out of the way, but the incredible closing speed of the Zoxyth ship's remnants outstripped even the carrier's propulsion abilities.

The rushing, boiling mass slammed into the *Galactic Guardian's* shields, and the huge GDF carrier rocked. Its force field bowed inwardly. Electrical discharges spread across the shields. They glowed like a supernova again. Then they collapsed, popping like a bubble.

However, the force field had done its job.

The churning mass of molten asteroid now hung at a relative standstill, its velocity the same as the *Guardian's*.

"Thank God," Jake said, but suddenly, dozens of red Zoxyth lasers burned into a specific point on the enormous ship.

Colonel Giard's eyes widened as he finally understood the enemy's tactic. "They're trying to take out the disruptor!"

Remulkin nodded. Through a frustrated growl, he said, "If it goes down, the fuckers will escape!"

"Admiral Johnston, the disruptor field is collapsing!"

Bill turned and gave Tekamah a questioning look. The GDF supreme commander nodded gravely.

Returning a curt nod and pursing his lips, Johnston spun toward the weapons console and pointed to the officer manning it.

"Fire the weapon!" he said.

"Now!" urged Admiral Tekamah.

As the officer toggled the commands, Johnston stared through the view-wall.

"I hope we're not too late, Ashtara."

When the Galactic Defense Force's supreme commander didn't reply, Johnston stole a sideways glance.

Ash-white, the Argonian glared at the enemy formation, slowly shaking his head. Finally, Admiral Tekamah hoarsely whispered, "Gods damn you for making me do this, Thrakst."

"Direct all weapons onto the target now!" Thrakst said as the *Guardian's* shields collapsed. "Fire, fire, fire!"

Through slitted eyes, he watched the targeted sensor blister. First it glowed like a supernova. Then the image whited out as the brilliance of his fleet's combined plasma fire overdrove the camera's optical sensor. Finally, the display faded as that corner of the massive enemy ship dissolved into a cloud of expanding gas.

At the same moment, the sensor officer looked up excitedly.

"My Lord, the disruptor field is collapsing. We should be able to jump out of the system in a few zyxyns."

Thrakst nodded. The bubble of disrupted parallel-space spanned several light-seconds. They couldn't jump out until the collapse propagated throughout the entire sphere.

Outside, the battle continued to rage. Flashing, multicolored light still streamed through the bridge's various portals, bathing its interior in their stop-motion, strobing brilliance.

"Order all ships to jump the instant they get a parallel-space lock," Thrakst said. He started to grin, but in the bridge's strobing interior, the sensor officer's smile disappeared between flashes of light. The hatchling suddenly looked at him with confused eyes.

"My Lord!" he said. "I'm detecting an unusual energy signature coming from the *Galactic Guardian.*"

The warlord narrowed his eyes again as he turned back to the GDF carrier.

"This doesn't make sense, Lord Thrakst," the officer said. "It looks like a gene—"

A radiant sphere exploded from the center of the *Guardian.* As the expanding luminescent bubble spread across the battlefield, its brilliant, oddly tinged light flooded the bridge, eclipsing all other sources.

Thrakst exploded out of his cathedra, launching himself across the cavernous room. He slashed and pummeled his way through anything and anyone that blocked his path. Sparks flew from the steel-tipped talons of his feet. He crashed through the sensor board and its operator. Equipment and limbs flew as if thrown by an explosion. The warrior knew he'd already lost the rest of his fleet, but he had to live, had to avenge his family.

As he reached the weapon control station, he frantically entered a series of commands.

Too slow!

He was racing against time.

And losing.

The warlord's abdomen burned as if a million sletch-bugs were trying to dig their way out of his gut.

The Forebearers-damned Argonians had turned the gene weapon against him!

Move faster!

Moments slipped away from him, evaporating like wax in a blast furnace. As in his dream, the Zoxyth Lord felt as if he were wading through the thick mud of his home world.

He tapped out a final command and launched a specially configured missile.

Thrakst grinned through a grimace of pain as the weapon rocketed toward the *Guardian.* Then he lurched and doubled over as his body began to surrender to the reprogrammed gene weapon's molecular assault.

Around him, the rest of the crew writhed on the floor. Only the tough old warrior, Raja Phascyre, still stood upright.

Outside, ship after ship fell through the advancing wall of energy as its white curtain of insatiable light raced toward the *Tidor Drof.* But inside, the navigation panel still couldn't get a parallel-space lock.

No longer able to support his weight, Thrakst's legs surrendered to the ship's artificial gravity. As he collapsed, he saw the nav panel lock onto its fallback point. Still falling, the Lord fought to direct his body toward the navigation console. Black cave walls ate at the periphery of his vision. The whited-out control panel looked impossibly far away as if it sat at the end of a long, black tunnel.

His knees struck the stone floor, and Thrakst stretched out and swatted at the distant drive activator.

CHAPTER 30

"Oh fuck!" Jake whispered.

Somehow the gene weapon aboard the destroyed Zoxyth dreadnought must have survived the destruction of its ship. It had just fired. The weapon's energy wave blasted outward from the region where the melted dreadnought still hung next to the damaged *Galactic Guardian.*

"No!" Remulkin cried.

"Oh God!" Jake screamed. The weapon's ballooning sphere of light raced directly at the human-led task force. It closed the gap in milliseconds, too fast to evade.

Closing his eyes and grasping the console fiercely, Colonel Giard braced for the end.

Blinding light flooded through his closed eyelids.

Then it was gone.

However, to Jake's amazement, he wasn't.

Opening his eyes, Giard tried to blink away the blue spots that hovered in his vision, but as the external universe resolved, one of them refused to fade.

"What the hell?" Remulkin said in accented English.

Incredibly, all of the allied ships still appeared to be crewed. They continued to move in a controlled manner. However, each of the dreadnoughts now tumbled in an all too familiar fashion.

He wasn't sure what had happened to the enemy ships. But an educated guess told him that Tekamah had somehow turned the tables on the Zoxyth, had wiped them out with their own weapon, although a quick count revealed that another of the dreadnoughts had either been destroyed or had escaped.

Again, Jake tried to blink the last blue artifact from his vision, but it remained stubbornly present.

"That's a missile!" Remulkin said.

Jake blinked once more, and it resolved. The rocket had already crossed half of the enemy's dissolving formation. The blue fire of the rocket plume appeared to originate from the region of space previously occupied by the missing ship.

Inexorably, the weapon continued to accelerate past the last drifting dreadnought, the one closest to the carrier.

"It's aimed at the *Galactic Guardian!*" Jake said.

He began to open a direct EON channel to Johnston, but then several laser and plasma beams shot from the carrier and its complement of battlecruisers. However, the beams fell short of their target. They splashed against apparent shielding, soon cocooning the advancing missile in an opalescent egg of deflected light and plasma.

Suddenly, a voice blasted across the EON command channel.

"All ships, this is Admiral Johnston. Fallback to X-Ray, now! Do it now! That's an order!"

X-Ray? That was the designation for their position behind the Moon.

Colonel Giard opened his unit's EON channel. "You heard him, Gunfighters. Jump now!"

To his relief, he saw Richard and Sandy's starfighters exit the battlefield along with the rest of their ships.

Jake's hand hovered over the activator. While watching his squadron and the rest of the units within his wing slip into parallel-space in a series of ethereal flashes, he wondered why the admiral would have them jump to the far side of the moon for one missile. If the weapon was such a threat, why hadn't the Galactic Guardian jumped out as well?

A quick scan of the holographic display showed him that none of the GDF forces were following the human task force. Every Argonian fighter had turned to engage the onrushing missile.

As Jake watched the last of his starfighters disappear into parallel-space, Sandy activated their EON channel. He ignored it. Instead, the wing commander reluctantly followed the Admiral's order and punched his emergency egress button.

"Admiral Tekamah!" shouted an officer. He pointed into the holographic display. "Antimatter missile inbound!"

"Shoot the godsdamned thing!" Ashtara said.

"I am, sir, but it's shielded. And ours are still offline."

Tekamah turned to Johnston. "Get your forces out of here. Do it now, or we'll lose all of them!"

He saw questions forming on the admiral's lips.

Ashtara held up a finger. "No time, Bill. I'll explain later."

Johnston nodded and turned away.

Tekamah opened a direct link to the captain of every GDF vessel. "All ships, emergency—!"

"Admiral!" shouted the helmsman. "The parallel-drive isn't responding. It won't come online!"

As he spoke, the officer tried to activate it several times. Finally, he shook his head. "The Zoxyth attack must have taken it out."

Tekamah pointed at him. "Use the gravity drive; get me some breathing room." Then he reopened the command channel. "Ladies and gentlemen, I require your assistance."

A moment later, the battlecruisers and fighters began a sub-light speed retreat as they continued to pour fire into the enemy weapon.

Issuing an emergency command directly from his EON, Tekamah spun the *Galactic Guardian's* massive and mostly empty stern so that its bulk would shield the rest of the ship.

Two eternal seconds later, their incredible sub-light acceleration had the fleet pulling away from the missile.

Johnston stepped back to Tekamah's side and said, "The last of my ships just jumped—"

Blinding light suddenly flooded the bridge, and the floor smacked into Ashtara.

Then his whitewashed universe snapped to black.

As the *Turtle* slid into parallel-space, the outside star-field began to contract into a sphere off its bow.

Then the shrinking ball of stars flared white!

Reversing direction, the coruscating, blindingly bright sphere expanded and then engulfed the ship as if the *Turtle* had plunged into a sea of burning phosphorus. With a jarring snap, the vessel fell back into regular space.

Jake and Remulkin lurched from the floor of the ship. Thrown into zero-G, the two men ricocheted off one another violently. The collision sent each of them in a different direction. Tumbling, Jake flailed the air with windmilling arms and kicking legs. Then he narrowly avoided crashing head first into the right side of the view-wall. At the last moment, Jake tucked chin to chest, and his upper back crashed into it. The impact knocked the wind out of him.

Guppy breathing, he floated back across the cabin. Then the colonel heard a snap and a scream. He craned his neck and saw Remulkin flying away from the point where he'd slammed into the seam where the top left side of the display joined the ceiling. Below the man's left knee, his leg now jutted out at an odd angle.

Somewhat belatedly, a web of emergency restraints shot from the walls. Matching the system described by Richard and Sandy, the webbing wrapped each man in a protective embrace.

Dazed and still fighting to breathe, Jake looked around the cabin.

A few feet to his right rear and wailing in pain, Remulkin floated upside down. He hung between the left side of the view-wall and the console. Like a spiderweb, the restraining system held him immobile. It had arrested the liaison's tumbling flight just before he would have slammed head first into the pedestal's curved glass top.

Jake craned his neck, trying to look through the view-wall behind him. In brief glimpses, he saw a slowly rotating star field. The detonating weapon had left the *Turtle* dead in the water, had knocked the ship's systems offline and even degraded the emergency equipment.

He listened for the hiss of escaping atmosphere, but Jake could barely hear his own heavy breathing above Remulkin's cries.

"Lieutenant Remulkin! Shut the hell up!"

The Argonian stopped mid-wail, his head snapping back as if Jake had slapped him.

Giard held his breath, listening intently. Aside from the pounding of his heart, the cabin was silent. The hull seemed to be intact.

Remulkin began panting.

Jake looked at him. The Argonian started to struggle against the webbing. He screamed each time the shockwave of his movements reached one of the fibers holding his wounded leg.

The colonel activated his EON. Electronic noise like snow on a television screen flooded his vision. What kind of weapon could do that? Had they been nuked?

Every time Jake managed to turn his head enough to look outside, the webbing tightened and turned him away from the view-wall.

"Fuck!" he said between the scientist's yowls.

"Screw you, Giard!" Remulkin said. "This hurts like hell!"

"No," Jake said. "It's not you." He nodded toward the view-wall. "It's the other ships, the *Guardian's* fleet. They're probably in worse shape than we are, possibly a *lot* worse."

Jake saw the Argonian bite back another scream. Then the scientist gave him a quick nod. When he did, the sweat puddling on the man's face broke free and floated away in undulating blobs.

Colonel Giard struggled against the restraining system again. Finally, it loosened enough for him to turn his entire body toward the view-wall.

Parts of the wide display no longer worked. A checkerboard

pattern of card table-sized black panels obscured much of the outside world. As the sliding field of stars scrolled across the dead portions of the display, the points of light disappeared and then popped back into existence. Snowy video noise obscured a few other areas, but enough of the view-wall still worked for Jake to discern the outside world.

Remembering the *Turtle's* programmed trans-lunar escape route, he stared through the display. "Come on, let me see it," he whispered.

Finally, the Moon slid into the field of view. Soon, it filled the screen and just as quickly began to recede.

Jake focused on the movement of the background stars.

"Oh, thank you," he said as he released the breath he'd been holding. The weapon had knocked the *Turtle's* drive offline before it started to fly toward the Moon. They were adrift, but at least they weren't falling into the planetary body's gravity well.

The colonel continued to watch the precessing stars. Soon the ship's slow tumble should bring the *Galactic Guardian* and its fleet (or the remnants of both) into his field of view.

Jake glanced in the direction in which the Moon had scrolled. *Thank God you made it out, baby.*

CHAPTER 31

"Status?" Thrakst said weakly.

No reply.

He had collapsed to the floor after activating the micro-jump. Now he shakily rose to his knees.

"Status?!" the Lord said through a coughing roar. His head lolled. Using his arms, he pushed his upper body off the floor. Finally, the after-image of the Zox-focused gene weapon's molten lava pain began to release its grip.

Slowly, he lifted his head. As Thrakst scanned the bridge, he saw the reason for the silence. The weapon had almost completely obliterated his crew. A couple of officers started to move, but most had succumbed to it, had vanished. Only piled uniforms and armor remained where they had stood.

"My Lord," said a surprisingly strong voice.

Still slumped over, Thrakst turned to its source. Raja Phascyre towered over him, staff clenched in his fist. A stream of emotions burned from the old warrior's only eye.

"Raja, what is our statu—?"

Phascyre smashed his staff into the side of Thrakst's head. The blow sent the kneeling warlord sprawling across the bridge floor. In his weakened state, he struggled to regain his footing, but Phascyre was on him in an instant. The warrior assailed him. Each blow sent the Lord's head crashing into the floor. His world spun. Then he heard a growl from across the room.

The storm of impacts ceased.

Thrakst looked up in time to see his suddenly not so cowardly communications officer, fist raised high overhead, charging the Raja.

Turning from Thrakst, Phascyre rushed the officer. The gap collapsed, and the Raja slammed bodily into the aspiring warrior. The smaller Zoxyth bounced off of his chest like a balloon. Flying backward across the bridge, the young officer didn't stop until he slammed into his own console. With an audible crack, his spine snapped, and his body came to rest bent at an unnatural angle.

Roaring, Raja Phascyre raised his staff high overhead and spun it like a copter beetle. Taking a giant step, he lunged forward. With a single hand, the old warrior snatched the rotating staff mid-spin and drove it down into his prey. Contemptuously, he speared the junior officer's abdomen instead of his heart. The blunt tip of the ceremonial *Crozier of the Forebearer* passed through the hatchling's gut like a lance passing through putrefied fat.

Dazed by the Raja's attack and still lying prone, the Lord couldn't rise from the floor. As he watched Phascyre dismantle the officer, he tried and failed to comprehend the warrior's actions or understand why the enemy's repurposed gene weapon hadn't fazed him.

Phascyre wrenched the staff from the fallen officer. Tangled on the end of the square metal rod, his intestines scrolled out of his abdomen and followed the crozier across the floor.

Leaving the mortally wounded hatchling lying in his own effluence, the Raja slowly walked back to Thrakst. "Why can't you just die already?" he said with a snarl.

"What are you doing, Phascyre? Why?" But as he asked the question, Thrakst suddenly knew the answer. His eyes widened with understanding. "It was you," he growled. "You told them we were coming. You gave them your genetic code to make sure it spared you." He pointed an accusatory talon at the Raja. "Coward! Traitor!"

Again a storm of emotions streamed across the Raja's remaining eye. "No, old friend. It was you who betrayed the empire, you who led us into this unwinnable war, you who employed a weapon of genocide, and you who dishonored the Forebearers." Phascyre shook his head and swept an arm toward the distant battlefield. "And it was *you* who forced the High Council and me to sacrifice an entire fleet!"

Apparently registering Thrakst's surprise, the Raja nodded. "Yes, the High Council sanctioned my deeds." Then the warrior's scarred face darkened. "Those and more, old friend."

"Phascyre," Thrakst said. "How could you do this? How could you aid those who tossed a dreadnought into our planet, scarred Zoxa?" The Lord shook his head. "They took my family."

"No, Thrakst. You killed your family when you started down the path to genocide. When you wouldn't heed my advice, I took it to the High Council. I told them of your scheme to develop a gene weapon. They had begged you not to take the battle beyond our borders. When they discovered your plans to rain genocide down upon the Argonians, they ordered me to warn the GDF, to alert them of the location of your science team."

"You led Tekamah to the *Forebearer's Solitude?*"

The Raja nodded. "That was before I became the Fifth Columnist, but yes, I did."

"Fifth Columnist?" Thrakst said. Then deeper understanding washed over him. "You killed my family!"

"No!" Phascyre said. His face darkened again. "You killed them along with this entire fleet. I wanted to kill you sooner, but couldn't risk one of your dreadnought commanders escaping with a cursed gene weapon. Now that you are out of the way, the High Council intends to work with the GDF to suppress this genocidal technology."

"You are all fools!" Thrakst said in a roar.

Shaking his head, the Raja sighed. "This is futile. It is time to finish it."

Phascyre started spinning the staff above his head again. The last of the communications officer's innards flew from the end of the staff and fell to the floor. Glaring down on Lord Thrakst, he said, "If they will have you, old friend, give the Forebearers my regards."

The Raja snatched the spinning crozier with both hands and drove it down. According the Lord his deserved respect, he aimed for Thrakst's heart.

The warlord tried to roll out of its path. However, weakened by the enemy's gene weapon, he was too slow to avoid the Raja's lightning quick assault.

He was going to die.

Here!

Now!

At the hands of the traitor who'd cost him his family!

Suddenly, something flew across the bridge. With a thud and a muffled snap, a fist-sized stone slammed into Raja Phascyre's head. Having come from his blind side, the jagged rock knocked the polished black stone from the Raja's scarred eye socket.

Thrown off by the impact, Phascyre's thrusting blow ran wide. The staff gouged through Thrakst's chest scales and flesh but glanced off of the underlying bone plate, slamming into the floor with a spray of rocks.

Phascyre roared again as green blood spilled from the re-injured eye socket. Knocked loose by the impact, the polished rock and its long, gold anchor bolt fell onto Thrakst's chest. A snapped off, sharp-edged piece of the Raja's skull still clung to the gleaming bolt's threaded end.

Thrakst grabbed the polished rock and placed it against his palm. Slipping the bolt between his middle two talons, he clenched his fist and aimed the bony tip of the makeshift weapon at the Raja. Then he punched Phascyre in the face. With a satisfactory pop, the bone-tipped rod slid through the traitor's remaining eye. Finally, the Lord opened his palm and shoved the rock home.

The blinded, double-crossing bastard clutched his face and screamed. Blood poured between his talons.

"I seriously doubt the Forebearers will have you, *old friend*!" the Lord said, pouring derision into the familiar honorific.

Still lying on his back, Thrakst unsheathed his leg's dewclaw talon. "But if so, you can give them your regards in person!"

His foot shot out lightning-fast. Then fanning green gore sprayed the ceiling as the razor-sharp appendage separated the traitor's head from his shoulders.

~

Lord Thrakst struggled to his feet. His head spun, but through a force of will he remained upright, somehow holding onto the only thread of consciousness that the Raja had left intact. Some distance away, he saw the gutted communications officer writhing on the floor. The little warrior's innards lay strung across the deck in a trail of gore that extended to Phascyre's motionless remains.

Walking unsteadily, the Lord staggered across the bridge. Collapsing to a knee beside the fallen officer, Thrakst placed a hand on his chest.

"Thank you, warrior," the warlord said reverently. "If you hadn't thrown that rock, the Raja would've killed me. You have earned a seat with the Forebearers."

"I didn't do it for you or your damned Forebearers," the mortally wounded officer said with surprising strength. "I did it for my family." He paused and thrust a finger at the *Tidor Drof's* main display. "Tekamah killed all of them. When the bastard crashed the *Forebearer's Solitude* into our planet, I lost my entire village. And he did it with the Raja's help."

Thrakst barely registered the officer's words. He had followed the hatchling's gesture and now stared into the indicated display through wide, bloodied eyes. "I don't believe it," he whispered.

The ship's external cameras still tracked the enemy fleet. Several light-seconds away, the Galactic Guardian and its seven battleships tumbled across the backdrop of the nearing planet. His antimatter missile had found its mark. It had vaporized the back half of the carrier.

Still pointing at the display, the officer said, "It's beautiful, my

Lord. It's a ruined relic." Through gurgling blood, he added, "And I know you'll ensure that its masters follow it into oblivion."

A fit of coughs and spasms wracked the hatchling.

"We have won, my Lord. We have—"

He and his words died mid-sentence as Thrakst—weary of the officer's verbose passing—terminated the discussion with a swipe of his forearm talon. "Give Commodore Salyth my regards," the Lord said distractedly as he continued to stare at the display.

A moment later, the warlord dropped the officer's headless body to the floor and then wiped blood from his own face. "Thank the Forebearers," he whispered. Thrakst couldn't believe the missile had hit the carrier. He had fired it in a last ditch effort to keep the damned Argonians busy. The Lord had kept the heavily shielded weapon in reserve for just such an event, but he'd never imagined it would actually get close enough to faze the fast ship, much less destroy it.

Blinking blood from his vision, Thrakst dragged his gaze away from the incredible image. A sole Zoxyth officer stood nearby. His stupid, confused eyes stared at the two lifeless bodies.

With a mighty effort, the Lord climbed to his feet, steel talons scraping and clawing for purchase. Rising to his full height, Thrakst glared down at him. "Our work is not done," he said wearily. "Move to navigation. Transfer sensor data to the station and prepare to resume combat operations." When the hatchling still didn't move, the warlord yelled, "Now!"

The officer flinched and then dashed like a wetted drycat lizard. He scurried to the console and began scrolling through data feeds. The Lord knew that the officer was his last crewmember. They'd lost everyone aft of the bridge. Even on this forward-most deck, all of the Zoxyth stationed behind his cathedra had fallen to the repurposed gene weapon.

Thrakst staggered over to the throne and dropped into its cool, stony embrace.

The hatchling raised his head. "Lord, I'm detecting activity from the remnants of the enemy carrier."

On his personal display, Thrakst studied the fractured *Galactic*

Guardian. The largest piece of the broken carrier began to distance itself from the other sections, slowly increasing the gap between it and the destroyed scraps.

"That's their bridge," Thrakst said. His eyes narrowed. "Is anyone still alive?"

The officer scanned his instruments again and then looked up. "Possibly, my Lord. There appear to be weak life signs coming from all of their ships, but the sensors are having a difficult time penetrating the after effects of antimatter annihilation. There's too much interference to know for sure." He paused and tapped a few more keys. Then he grinned. "If there is anyone alive, they're defenseless. You fried all of their external weapons, my Lord."

"What about their gene weapon?" Thrakst said. "Could they fire another one?"

The officer shook his head. "No, my Lord. Even if they could muster the power to fire it again, the explosion's aftermath will suppress the gene weapon's quantum wave for at least as long as it will take our weapon to recharge."

Thrakst smiled and said, "Plot a micro-jump." He pointed at the carrier's bridge. "Plan to drop us in nice and close to that. I want to finish Admiral Tekamah!"

Lumbering out of his cathedra, Thrakst stumbled to the weapon control station. He kicked aside the previous operator's emptied uniform and activated the console. "I'll take care of the weapons," the Lord said through a cough.

Wiping green blood from his brow, he looked over to Phascyre's eyeless face. Thrakst growled, a low, rattling thing. "The High Council, huh? I think I'll pay them a visit when I'm through with your Argonian companions," he said softly and then grinned. "All of them will be joining you very soon, *old friend.*"

He turned from the dead traitor and pointed to his new helmsman. Raising his voice, he said, "Take us in! Now!"

CHAPTER 32

S andy's fighter dropped back into normal space at the designated fallback coordinates.

"Holy shit!" she shouted over her link with Richard. Trying to calm her overtaxed nerves, she took a couple of deep breaths. Then she said, "What the hell happened?! Did we hit them with a gene weapon?"

"I think we did," Richard said. "But I'm more concerned with that missile. Why did Johnston order us to jump out just as we kicked their ass?"

Sandy shook her head and took another calming breath. Jumping out of the chaotic battlefield into this tranquil, organized peace had shocked her system almost as much as if the reverse had happened.

Her sleek, silver-black Phoenix Fighter now hovered fifty thousand feet above the Moon's heavily cratered far side. Computer-controlled, every ship of each fighter wing had exited parallel-space in its previously assigned location. The entire air group had reemerged into normal space already arranged in a perfect formation.

"This is Commander Air Group. All units, check in," Colonel Newcastle ordered.

As Phoenix Squadron Executive Officer, Sandy visually scanned the unit's precisely arranged organized lines, making a quick headcount. Over the squadron-wide channel, she said, "All Phoenix Starfighters present and accounted for, Colonel Allison."

"Thank you, XO," Richard said.

After he had conferred with the commanders of the wing's other squadrons, he linked to Newcastle's command channel. "CAG, this is Phoenix Six. First Fighter Wing is a go."

As the accented voices of the multi-national commanders of 2nd through 4th Fighter Wings also checked in, Sandy ran her starfighter's diagnostics. All systems still reported green, fully operational.

After the Israeli Commander of 5th Fighter Wing checked in, a silent, pregnant pause screamed across the network.

"Sixth Fighter Wing," Colonel Newcastle said impatiently. "Check in, Colonel Giard!"

Sandy snapped her head to the left and looked wide-eyed at the wing's formation. Gunfighter Squadron's organized collection of starfighters sat at its farthest end, but even from here, she could see an obvious void in its ordered rows.

Jake hadn't returned!

Sandy opened her direct link to him. It connected, but an instant later, the link broke, and its icon grayed out.

"Sixth Fighter Wing," Colonel Newcastle said again. "What is your—?"

Suddenly, a brilliant light rose above the Moon's distant horizon like a second sunrise. Space itself seemed to glow.

"What the hell?" Newcastle said over the open EON channel.

Then the incredibly bright light whited out her spherical display. Sandy raised an arm to shield her eyes, but the billion-nanobot visual matrix painted across the sleeve of her suit beamed as brightly as did the inside of the sphere.

Then the light began to fade. Slowly, the external world resolved.

"Jake?!" Sandy shouted into their dead EON link.

As if someone had connected an untuned AM radio to the network, a faint rush of odd static started to stream through her EON's auditory feed. It had never done that during any of their live-fire exercises.

Colonel Newcastle reactivated the command channel. "Gunfighter Six, this is the CAG. Report!" he said, sounding as unnerved as Sandy felt.

"CAG, this is Gunfighter Seven. We are down one," said a distressed male voice. Sandy recognized it as belonging to Major Hill, Jake's wingman and second in command. "Gunfighter Six hasn't checked in, sir."

Wide-eyed and beginning to hyperventilate, Sandy screamed, "Jake!" It suddenly felt like there wasn't enough oxygen in her cockpit. Whipping her head left and right, she searched the entire formation for the Turtle's unique shape, but still didn't see it.

"No ... No ... No ..." Sandy whimpered between hyperventilating breaths. She swallowed hard, struggling not to panic. With her heart beating in her ears, Sandy activated her virtual hologram. Currently, it only displayed the area between the Moon and the formation. Aside from the collected fighters, no other ships occupied the region of space.

"Shit," she whispered. "God, please, no."

Major Fitzpatrick connected to the command channel. "CAG, this is Phoenix Seven," she said, not quite able to keep her mounting dread out of her voice. "The *Turtle* isn't here, and I don't see anybody else on this side of the Moon!"

As she spoke, she panned the display toward the battlefield, and a storm of disassociated multicolored pixels slid into view. Sandy couldn't see any ships. Instead, a psychedelic, three-dimensional version of white noise filled translunar space, obscuring the combat zone.

"I can't see anything beyond that, CAG. There's too much ... interference," the executive officer said, her voice hitching and cracking as it occurred to her that the multicolored storm might be a holographic rendering of a pulverized fleet.

"Roger, Seven," Newcastle said in a detached tone.

Sandy was about to shout at the CAG when Richard opened a link. "I'm sure Jake made it out," he said over their internal channel.

She connected to it and said, "You can't know that!" But as the words left her mouth, Sandy realized she *had* to believe it, *had* to own it. Otherwise, she would be useless to the unit, useless to the pilots depending on her to watch their backs, and useless to Jake.

"Sandy—"

"No, I'm sorry. You're right, Richard," Sandy said. "Sorry for snapping at you."

The command network reopened.

"We need to get back in there and find out what happened," Colonel Newcastle said. "I'm dissolving the task forces and returning all squadrons to their usual fighter wing assignments. First Fighter Wing, I want you to take up defensive positions on the far side of the battlefield."

"Roger, CAG," Colonel Allison said.

"Sixth Fighter Wing, I want you on the near side. Second through Fifth, set up a perimeter around the entire battlefield. Watch for the Zoxyth ship that jumped out. Scan your holograms if they'll work. Otherwise, do it the old fashioned way: use your eyes, folks."

In turn, each of the wing commanders acknowledged Colonel Newcastle's order. Then he continued. "I'll take Vampire Squadron into the middle. We'll assess the damage and marshal any disabled friendly vessels. Keep in mind: as we get closer, our EONs may experience the same interference. So be ready to switch to our tactical radios."

After a brief pause, he added, "Use your gravity drives to maneuver, no parallel-jumps until we know what's out there. I don't want anybody popping back into real-space in the middle of a drifting ship."

"Remember, folks: that Zoxyth dreadnought is probably still around, and it has a functioning gene weapon. By my watch, we only have thirty-five minutes before it will be recharged and ready to fire again."

"Good hunting, and Godspeed," Newcastle said. "Commander Air Group, out."

A few moments later, Richard activated the squadron's channel. "I've given the other squadrons their orders and loaded our ingress route into each of your autopilots," he said. "Acknowledge receipt and prepare for departure."

Sandy accepted the new flight plan. Her lips started to ache again. So she pressed them together and closed her eyes. Robbed of their usual chew toy, her teeth took to self-destruction and began to grind against one another. After taking a deep breath, she tried to release the stress and worry in a long exhalation. Achieving a modicum of success, she opened her eyes and focused on the distant lunar horizon, her hand hovering over the gravity drive actuator.

Richard reopened the unit's link. "Phoenix Squadron, this is Phoenix Six. Launch in three, two, *one!*"

Sandy slammed the activator forward. Their formation of fighters rocketed toward the Moon's limb, aimed for the exact point where the light of the detonating missile had formed a false sunrise.

Moments later, they zipped past its curved, gray surface, and the battlefield slid into view. Even from eighty thousand miles away, several chunks of debris glowed brightly enough to make it look as if a few small suns had taken up station between the two planetary bodies.

As she rocketed toward the scene, the bright lights blossomed from pinpoints into dots and then into angular, jagged chunks that drifted in all directions. Every second of travel added more detail as the gravity drive's incredible speed rushed them toward the carnage.

Sandy tried to activate her private link with Jake, but its icon remained grayed out. "Jake, are you out there?" she said to nobody. "Please talk to me, baby."

Only mounting white noise answered.

"Phoenix Six, this is Seven, are you picking up static across the EON?" she said over the squadron channel.

"Yes, I am," Richard said in a static-filled reply.

Then Sandy flinched as his actual voice entered her ears. "How do you read this?"

She toggled the radio transmit switch. "Loud and clear."

"At least these are working," he said. "All fighters, check in over the radio."

While they each replied, Sandy tried to tweak her virtual hologram. However, the colored points of light continued their disorganized dance, offering no discernible image.

Outside, something rocketed past her fighter. A moment later her ship jumped, just missing a large, glowing chunk of rock. Then another luminous boulder blazed across her spherical display, narrowly missing the starfighter.

Her heart went into overdrive as she scanned the region directly in front of the formation. They must be flying through the shattered remnants of the Zoxyth fleet! Space in front of them was choked with rocky detritus.

"Phoenix Six, we need to get clear of these asteroids!" The XO paused as her fighter did several evasive jumps. "This is starting to look like our flight over Europa," she said, recalling their doomed live-fire exercise over Jupiter's icy moon.

"I agree," Richard said. "Phoenix Squadron, turn to vector two-three-eight by three-three-six in three, two, one."

On his mark, Sandy turned her starfighter to the new, three-dimensional heading. Moving as one, she and the squadron made an instantaneous ninety-degree course change. The new route ran perpendicular to the original flight path. So several evasive jumps later, the swarm of glowing asteroid lumps thinned. The time between the ship's evasive skips doubled, trebled, and finally stopped altogether.

As they rose above the plane of the dusty debris field and reemerged into relatively clear space, three new light sources slid into view.

The XO squinted, trying to resolve the shapes. "What the hell are …?" she said in a whisper, but then her eyes widened. "Oh my God!"

She activated the squadron net. "The *Guardian* broke up!"

The carrier had fractured into at least three pieces. She wouldn't have recognized the ship if not for the size of the twisted and charred sections.

"Where are the hangar bays?" she asked, scanning the wreckage.

"Looks like they were vaporized," Richard said in a mystified voice.

Sandy saw that he was right. One end of the largest chunk of carrier glowed brightly. Along a sharply defined line, everything simply ended as if cleaved by a giant, white-hot knife.

"Seven," Richard said, calling her on their internal channel. "To the left of the Guardian, is that what I think it is?"

Sandy looked in the indicated direction. "Oh my God!"

Farther from the blast's epicenter, an organized swarm of scintillating points of burning embers tumbled through space.

"It is," Sandy said. Her voice cracked again. She scanned the debris field visually. "Please, God, don't let Jake be in there," she whispered.

"CAG, this is Phoenix Six," Colonel Allison said over the Air Group frequency. "It looks like we lost most of the Argonian fighters."

After a pause, Newcastle replied in a weary, strained voice. "Report received, Phoenix Six. Carry on to the far side of the combat zone. We still need to find that Zoxyth ship."

"Wilco, Six," Richard said.

Phoenix Squadron continued its trek through the battlefield. Its path would take them close to the remnants of the *Galactic Guardian*.

Sandy looked over her left shoulder, scanning space beyond the burning formation of Phoenix Fighters. She longed to guide her ship in that direction, wanted to search the area for Jake.

Then she traded one nightmarish image for another as the largest piece of the carrier slid across her field of view, blotting out much of the battlefield. Across the width of the ship remnant, every chamber lay exposed to hard vacuum. Between melted and charred bulkheads, Sandy could still see the interior's gothic pointed arches and ornate trim. However, instead of framing the entrances of grand halls and expansive terrariums, those tall arches now led only to empty space.

She flew past the still glowing remnant of the Guardian's bridge. Sandy flinched as a new static-filled transmission blared from her radio's speaker.

"Phoenix Six! This ... Galactic ... ian bridge on Guard frequency! Are ... reading this?!"

"All stop," Richard shouted across the squadron's frequency.

Switching to Guard—the universal emergency frequency—

Richard said, "Guardian Bridge, this is Phoenix Six. Have you weak but readable."

"Good to hear … voice, Colonel Allison," Admiral Johnston said, surging static clipping his words.

The squadron drifted closer to the hulk. Sandy checked her instruments and discovered that the carrier remnant was the one moving. Outside, she saw the space between the *Guardian's* bridge and the other sections grow.

"Good to hear your voice too, sir," Richard said. "It looks like you have some drive capability. What is the status of your personnel?"

"We have just enough gravity drive to move, but not enough to matter," Johnston said. "We have a lot of injured people in need of evac."

"Roger, Guardian Six," Colonel Allison said. "I'll relay your status to the CAG. We'll get help to you ASAP! Do you have—?"

Suddenly, a brilliant ray shot through the formation. Passing between the starfighters of Phoenix Squadron, the red beam cut a deep furrow across the Guardian's skin. A torrent of atmosphere and small cruciform shapes burst from the breach. Belatedly, Sandy recognized the writhing figures as bodies.

She spun her fighter toward the source of the attack and came face to face with the no longer missing Zoxyth dreadnought. Of their own volition, her fingers spasmed, launching a volley of kinetic slugs and plasma beams at the enemy ship.

The rest of the squadron's fighters fired their weapons as well. In a brilliant explosion, the munitions detonated against the enemy ship's shields.

"All fighters, execute attack plan Delta, anchor one-seven-eight by two-six-six!" Richard shouted over the radio. "Let's draw the bastards away from the Guardian."

With a quick EON command, Sandy entered the attack vector into her computer. It automatically uploaded the navigational data to her virtual hologram. Like a starburst, each ship flew away from the Zoxyth dreadnought on a discrete vector. As Sandy's fighter rocketed toward her assigned route, she saw that Richard's plan would keep the shots and resultant debris away from the remnants of the carrier.

Seeing the instantaneous reactions of the squadron's pilots made Major Fitzpatrick proud. With practiced synchronicity, every starfighter had jetted off within a second of receiving the command.

Ahead of her, the first wave of the hastily arranged ad hoc attack reached their assigned radial. They turned back toward the dread-nought and started firing on the enemy ship as they raced inbound.

Sandy reached her designated attack vector. At the initialization point, her fighter executed the programmed instantaneous course change.

"Second wave IP inbound!" Sandy said over the squadron frequency.

Then the forward portion of the starfighter's immersive display dimmed as the enemy's shields blazed white-hot under the first wave's volley. A moment later, the dreadnought's force field flared and then collapsed in a storm of discharging lightning bolts.

"Yes!" Sandy shouted.

They were hurting the bastards!

As she rocketed inward, the now unprotected enemy ship swelled, quickly filling the forward portion of her spherical display.

"Fire!" the major yelled and squeezed both triggers.

Her fighter shuddered as it, along with the rest of the ships in the second wave, simultaneously fired all weapons. Then the wave of starfighters executed an instantaneous ninety-degree, right-angle course change, vectoring out of the plane of the attack and the impending blast zone.

"Die, you son of a bitch!" Sandy said with a snarl.

Suddenly, the asteroidal ship vanished. In its wake, the plasma and particle beams sliced through empty space.

Sandy slammed her head back and screamed, "Shit!"

Then over the radio, someone shouted, "The bastards jumped out!"

The executive officer shook her head. "Thanks, Captain Obvious," she said through a frustrated growl.

∿

Remulkin still hung with his head pointed toward the floor. The gravity field had returned. So now blood pressure built as it pooled in his head. He tried to pull himself free of the webbing, but every movement sent a fresh wave of agony through his ruined leg.

Hanging opposite the scientist, the knuckle-dragger waged his own battle with the restraints. When they refused to release their grip, the colonel yelled, "Damn it! Let me go!"

Apparently responding to his voice command, the safety restraining system lowered both of them to the floor. Even the gentle touchdown sent an excruciating wave of incredible pain shooting up Remulkin's ruined leg. He tried and failed to bite back the scream.

With the side of his face pressed against the ship's silver floor, Remulkin watched the webbing dissolve back into the deck. It appeared to melt into the surface as the ocean of tiny machines assimilated the safety restraining system's constituent nanobots.

"Finally!" Colonel Giard said. Standing, the man ran back to the command console.

Fresh waves of pain swept over Remulkin as he struggled to rise from the point where the restraints had deposited him. Grimacing, the scientist swore profusely. He even threw in a few of his new English curse words.

As Thramorus hopped and cussed his way back to the console, Giard gave him a sideways glance.

"Are you going to be okay?" he said.

"No, I'll never be okay as long as these bastards keep kicking our asses."

The colonel shook his head. "I think the *Guardian* hit them with a reverse-engineered gene weapon. One dreadnought might have escaped. Even if it did, one enemy ship wouldn't be much of a problem," Giard said. "I'm more concerned with the carrier fleet. I think we just lost a bunch of people."

Remulkin glared at him. "You're clueless! No wonder Major Fitzpatrick hasn't ..."

Seeing the sudden fire in Giard's eyes, Remulkin didn't finish. "Hasn't what?!"

"Nothing," Remulkin said. He pointed at the console. "Obviously, the gravity drive is online. Why are we still sitting here?"

Colonel Giard glared at him for a long moment. Finally, he gestured at the pedestal. "Yes, the gravity drive is back online, but communications and weapons systems are dead."

Remulkin wiped at the sweat dripping from his brow. Then he pointed through the view-wall at the slowly rotating star field. "What happened to the ships? Where are they?"

Nodding, Colonel Giard activated the *Turtle's* drive. After arresting its rotation, the man turned the ship to face the battlefield.

A confused mess of burning embers and apparent ship remnants filled the field of view. "Oh my Gods," he whispered. Then movement near the center of the display drew his eye. Remulkin pointed at it. "What's that?"

Not waiting for the knuckle-dragger to respond, Thramorus tried to magnify the view-wall image with his EON. However, much of his network interface still wouldn't work. His link icons remained grayed out, and the rushing static noise continued to stream through the EON's auditory feed.

Apparently encountering the same disconnect, Colonel Giard began adjusting the display via the console's manual controls. A moment later, the central portion of the image zoomed in, expanding to fill the entire view-wall.

"There's the bastard!" Remulkin shouted.

The Zoxyth ship had returned to the battlefield. Suddenly, it fired a laser beam into a massive glowing piece of debris. When atmosphere and apparent bodies flew from the point of impact, the liaison belatedly recognized the targeted mass as a portion of the *Galactic Guardian*.

"No! You son of a bitch!" Colonel Giard screamed.

Then a squadron's worth of plasma beams burned into the dreadnought. As quickly as they had fired, the starfighters blazed away from the enemy ship in a starburst pattern.

Watching the small vessels maneuver, Giard pointed. "That's First Fighter Wing."

Remulkin nodded.

A moment later, its first wave of starfighters turned back inbound and began to fire on the dreadnought. Their salvo slammed into the asteroidal ship, and its shields collapsed.

The colonel pumped his fist in the air. "Get him, Sandy!"

"What are you waiting for?!" Remulkin shouted. "Let's get in there!"

Giard shook his head and slapped the top of the console. "I'd love nothing better, but our fucking weapons are down. We'll just get in the way."

"We don't need weapons. Hell, we can ram the son of a bitch!"

Colonel Giard looked at Remulkin as if the scientist had lost his mind. Maybe he had, but these bastards had killed his family, and now they were about to get away.

The idiot pointed through the view-wall again and said, "The Phoenix Starfighters are about to kill it."

Remulkin shook his head. "No, they're not."

The second wave of fighters fired on the asteroidal ship.

Then it winked out of existence.

Giard stared stupidly.

Remulkin glared at him. Then he said, "They can still hide in parallel-space."

"Oh shit," Giard said. His eyes widened. He looked at his watch. "They'll be able to fire the gene weapon in fifteen minutes!"

Remulkin nodded. "I think we will get another chance. The bastard has tasted blood. I don't think he's going anywhere soon, but when he returns, we need to hit him with everything we have."

"I know," Giard said. Then he pounded the control panel in frustration. "But the weapons systems still won't respond. At this point, I'd gladly fly the damn thing right into the dreadnought, but the *Turtle* is too small. We'd be nothing more than a bug stain on their windshield." He paused and again tried to reactivate the fire-control panel. A moment later, he shook his head. "We need firepower!"

The colonel's words triggered an epiphany. Grinning, Thramorus hunched over his end of the console and started punching in commands.

Next to him, Colonel Giard bent over, trying to see Remulkin's hands. "What are you doing?"

After hitting the last key, the liaison gently lowered himself toward a seated position. The floor matrix raised to support him and his injured leg.

Tenderly rubbing his busted knee, the scientist let out a long sigh. "You want firepower?" He gestured toward the console. "Activate that autopilot flight plan, and you'll have all you need."

Still bent over the console, Giard studied the plan for a moment. Slowly, a grin spread across the Colonel's face.

CHAPTER 33

"Damn it!" Jake said.

"Open it with your EON," Remulkin said impatiently.

"Don't you think I tried that already? Try it with yours."

"I … I don't have that range." Remulkin looked away. "Mine can only transmit a short distance."

Jake saw something new in the man's face. Was that sadness?

"What? Why not?" Giard asked. "I thought all you Argonians had the same EON. If it's limited to short range, how do you stay connected with your network backup?"

"I don't have one." The scientist looked away again, but this time Jake saw profound sorrow in the man's eyes.

Then his jawline hardened. He turned back to Jake.

"I don't want to talk about it." He gestured at the ocean of silver-black hull that filled the display's entire field of view. "How about we focus on finding a way into that ship."

Jake stared at the man for a silent moment. Finally, he looked through the view-wall and shook his head. "I can't. Admiral Tekamah has it locked down. And he's probably dead. Hell, even if that missile didn't kill him, there's too much electrical interference. I can't reach anyone over there."

He stopped and looked back to Remulkin. "You served in the Galactic Defense Forces as a younger man, didn't you?"

Remulkin nodded. "Yes, but that was a long time ago. Why?"

Suddenly, the *Turtle* slid sideways. At the same time, the shields of the empty *Helm Warden* flared again.

Apparently, some of the debris from the battle had tumbled into lunar orbit. Since they had approached the parked empty carrier—the lure that Tekamah had so effectively used to bait the Zoxyth into simultaneously firing all their gene weapons—the *Turtle* had made several lateral safety jumps. While the smaller ship relied on its maneuverability, the significantly larger *Helm Warden* simply let its force field deal with the incoming debris. Like camera flashes firing at varying intensities, it now strobed almost continuously.

"Why?" Remulkin asked again.

Jake pointed through the view-wall. "We're not gonna get through those blast doors."

Unlike the last time he had needed to get aboard a GDF carrier, the hangar bays weren't open on this ship. Tekamah had sealed them. The back of the massive carrier had the same smooth, silver-black skin as the rest of the vessel. Remulkin said they were blast shields that could open or close just like all the other openings they'd encountered to date, but these weren't responding to their attempts to gain access.

"Is there another way in?" Jake said. "A hatch? Anything?"

Remulkin was shaking his head but then stopped. "Yeah, just behind the bridge, there is an exterior access hatch that leads to a communications array. If you could get in there ..."

The scientist shook his head again. "But we can't even get past the shields."

The man was right. So far, the force field had stopped them from getting closer than a few hundred feet. Every time Giard tried to maneuver the *Turtle* closer, the ship just bounced off the invisible quantum membrane.

Jake checked his watch. "We're running out of time. There's less than ten minutes left before they can fire that damned weapon again."

Jake jammed his hand into the *Turtle's* flight controller. With the other, he pointed toward the top of the massive ship. "Guide me to the external hatch. I'll park us above it, just outside the force field."

"Then what will we do?"

"I have an idea," Jake said.

Precious moments later, he stopped the speeding *Turtle* directly over the bridge. The elegant lines of the massive ship's command deck protruded above the carrier's smooth skin like an aerodynamic submarine conning tower. Fore and aft, the structure tapered to points and blended back into the ship's mercurial skin.

As they approached the bridge's tapered aft end, Remulkin pointed. "There! There it is!"

Jake studied the area but only saw the lines of a small rectangle in the otherwise featureless skin. He gestured at it. "That's way too little to be a hatch."

Thramorus shook his head. "No! How many actual doors have you seen on one of our ships? It's a touchpad. Just place your palm against it, and the nanobots in your suit's glove will unlock the hatch."

Still more than a couple of hundred feet above the carrier, the *Turtle* hit the shields and bounced back. Arresting the backward drift, Jake brought it to a stationary hover.

Luckily, they were already in their Argonian spacesuits. Jake finished parking the ship across from the hidden hatch and then walked toward the *Turtle's* airlock.

"I still don't understand how we're going to get through the force field," Remulkin said plaintively.

Jake ignored him and stepped into the airlock. The Argonian followed.

Responding to the impending vacuum, nanobots flowed out of the thick collars of each man's spacesuit. By the time the outer hull dissolved, exposing the lock to the void, a clear helmet topped each of their suits.

As Jake turned to look at Remulkin, a directional light that tracked his head and eye movements shined in the scientist's face.

The Argonian squinted. "Would you mind not shining that in my eyes?"

"Sorry," Jake said, smiling in spite of himself.

Still standing in the airlock, he pointed at the distant touchpad. "I think the shield will let an Argonian spacesuit through." *At least, it did last time I tried*, Jake thought to himself.

Suddenly, the visible portion of the carrier's force field opaqued, flashing white and obscuring the *Warden*.

Another asteroid had impacted.

Thramorus pointed at the glowing membrane. "If that happens while you're passing through it, the force field will cut you in half," he said.

"That's not helpful, Liaison," Jake said sardonically. "Feel free to keep shit like that to yourself." He paused and pointed toward the hatch's smooth surface. "If the shields don't bisect us and we do get through, what happens when we get to the panel? What's to stop us from just bouncing off the skin?"

"There is a low gravity field over that part of the skin," Remulkin said. "Plus, there is a small handhold next to it." The scientist held both hands out. "Just go already. We're wasting time!"

Jake gave a quick nod and said, "We'll have to be careful. We never got around to upgrading the *Turtle's* spacesuits with the Argonian inertia-less EVM module. So we'll be free floating with no guidance."

Remulkin returned the nod.

Giard planted his feet like a man about to dive into a pool. He took a deep breath and then lunged toward the hatch.

Just as Jake cleared the airlock and approached the nearby shields, a bolide slammed into the *Helm Warden's* force field only a few hundred feet to his right. It detonated in a surreally silent flash. The shields flared white, and Jake crashed into them. The bone-jarring impact sent him drifting away from both ships.

"Oh shit!" Giard screamed.

"Gods damn it!" Remulkin said. "You bounced off the shields."

Jake swung his arms futilely, but in the vacuum, he just continued his slow drift.

"Fuck, fuck, fuck!"

Hearing a grunt, Jake stopped his rant. Looking right, he saw Remulkin had kicked off from the *Turtle*. He was flying straight toward Giard.

"What are you doing?"

"I'm saving your ass," Remulkin said.

The scientist slowly caught up with Jake.

They grabbed each other. Now both of them drifted away from the ships at an angle that was taking them higher, farther away from both vessels.

Giard suddenly realized they'd soon pass beyond the carrier's gravity bubble. Then, without the Argonian extravehicular mobility module, it would be a long drop straight down into the Moon's gravity well. With no atmosphere to slow their descent, the colonel and the scientist would slam into the surface. Their bodies would disintegrate. There'd be nothing left but a new crater.

Holding each other, they floated face to face.

Pale and sweating profusely, the chubby ginger looked straight into Jake's eyes.

"Make this count, Colonel."

Suddenly, the man shoved him, grunting with the effort. Using both arms and his one good leg, he had pushed Giard toward the *Helm Warden*.

The colonel flew backward. In his peripheral vision, he saw the shields strobe. Now only a couple of feet beneath his back, the glowing quantum membrane obscured the carrier. Jake gasped, but then it darkened, and he passed through unscathed.

Now above him, the force field flared again, temporarily obscuring the quickly shrinking Argonian.

"Remulkin! Why? We could have found—"

"I lost them," the scientist whispered.

"What? Who?"

"I lost my family," Thramorus said more forcefully, "lost them permanently! All because I was a hardheaded idiot."

Giard shook his head. "I don't under—"

"Shut up and listen to me. I lost my wife and kids, and I can never get them back. But you, Colonel, you have a family."

"What?"

"Sandy is pregnant, Jake. Go save her. Save your family."

In shocked silence, Giard stared up at the drifting scientist.

Suddenly, Remulkin dropped like a man falling off a cliff. With incredible speed, his figure accelerated toward the lunar surface. In moments, he dwindled and then disappeared.

Breathing hard, the scientist's voice came over the radio, weak and fading. "Now go kill the bastards, Colonel Giard."

Then he was gone.

"I will," Jake whispered.

CHAPTER 34

"Lord Thrakst, our shields are down," reported the sensor officer. "We may not survive another assault!"

From the safety of their fallback position, the Lord stared into the weapons console's display, studying the disturbed nest of enemy fighters that swarmed about his target. He smiled. His pointed black tongue nervously danced across his silver fangs. Dragging his gaze from the angry horde, he eyed the nearing planet.

Thrakst wanted to take the *Tidor Drof* down there and vaporize every Forebearers-damned one of them. But without shields, he'd be exposed to enemy fire, and that deep in the planet's gravity well, he'd lose the ability to parallel-jump. The Tidor Drof would be stuck, virtually defenseless.

No. He had to end this here, had to finish Tekamah now. After that, he'd take care of any stragglers. Then he could concentrate on the local Argonian infestation.

"I'm not going to allow Tekamah to escape me!" Thrakst said in a roar. He turned to the helmsman. "Take us in for three zyxyns. Then jump back out. I'll press the attack. I want to keep them pinned down until the gene weapon recharges."

He consulted the weapon's charge status. "One more attack should buy the time we need."

The officer nodded. "Yes, my Lord." The hatchling grasped the drive controller. "Parallel-jump in five zyxyns. Three, two, *one*!"

～

Breathless, Jake stepped onto the *Helm Warden's* bridge.

Fortunately, it had the same layout and design as the *Galactic Guardian*. Lowering his head, he sprinted to the marked lift point. As he slid to a stop in the pulsing ring of light, the lift grabbed his legs and hoisted him to the bridge's command deck.

At the top, Jake didn't wait to be deposited. He jumped onto the faintly glowing, twenty-foot-high translucent floor and jogged toward its center.

Using his EON interface, he activated the room-spanning holographic display.

Millions of multicolored pixels appeared to pour out of the bridge's antiqued bronze walls. A moment later, the swirling light storm coalesced into a model of the Earth-Moon system that slowly rotated over Jake's head. However, a vast region between the two planetary bodies refused to resolve. There the swarming pixels fell into disorganized chaos, like three-dimensional electronic noise.

Jake stared into the confused mess.

"Damn it, Sandy! Why didn't you tell me?"

The thought brought back the memory of Remulkin's death. The image of the man's plummeting body dwindling to an indiscernible point as it raced moonward ushered a fresh wave of guilt.

The son of a bitch had given his life, and all Jake could think of was Sandy and their unborn child.

He shook his head. If he didn't move fast, Remulkin's sacrifice would have been for naught.

"Pull it together, Giard!"

In his EON's virtual vision, Jake brought up the *Helm Warden's* communications control.

"What the hell?"

He couldn't activate any of the links. All of the communication icons were grayed out. Floating in his EON's visual feed, the symbols didn't respond to the tapping of his virtual hand. Jake's real hand twitched as the simulated index finger poked the icons again and again.

Nothing.

"Screw it."

Giard connected to the ship's sub-light drive.

Grayed out.

"Son of a bitch!"

But then he saw one icon rendered in brilliant gold.

Jake smiled. "What's this?"

The parallel lines of the twin-shafted three-dimensional arrow that represented the parallel-space drive slowly rotated in his virtual vision. It was available!

He could use parallel-space to jump the carrier into the combat zone.

"Thank God!" Jake said with a sigh.

He flicked his virtual finger through the menus. "One more thing …" Giard whispered as he searched. A moment later his hand gave the stop gesture. "There you are!"

Clicking the new icon, he activated the weapons panel.

"You're shitting me! Really?"

Now both of Jake's hands spasmed as he tapped multiple grayed-out icons, all to no avail.

Nothing.

He couldn't fire any of the carrier's weapons.

Tekamah had apparently locked out every system that could turn the unmanned *Helm Warden* into a weapon.

Grinding his teeth together, Jake stared into the electronic noise that polluted the battlefield.

"Screw it," he said again.

Reaching into the hologram with both hands, Jake grabbed the cloud, expanded it and then shoved it to the right side of the image.

Releasing it, he focused on the empty region of space to the left of the battlefield.

Colonel Giard poked the area with an extended index finger, and the autopilot accepted his command with its now familiar oilcan pop.

Another twitch of his virtual index finger activated the drive, and the *Helm Warden* snapped to the new location.

The world beyond the view-wall changed in an instant. Gone was the cratered surface of the Moon's far side. Now the wrath of battle painted its ugly face across the display. Black husks tumbled in the near field. In the distance, Jake saw the Argonian ship wink out of existence again. In its wake, another wasted volley of plasma and kinetic weapon fire burned through empty space.

Giard looked at his watch.

Five minutes!

Looking up, he stared at the protective shell of fighters swarming around the *Galactic Guardian*.

"Get the hell out of there, Sandy!"

The dreadnought suddenly flared back into existence.

Jake magnified the view-wall image just in time to see one of the Zoxyth lasers burn into the *Galactic Guardian*, cutting another long slice across its dark skin. Atmosphere and debris exploded from the opening.

Giard stared with mounting horror as again he saw that some of the detritus had flailing arms and legs.

"Damn it!"

Sandy jumped as the Zoxyth ship popped back into the battle. This time, it dropped in so close to her fighter, the dreadnought filled her entire field of view. Instinct took over; all of her weapons fired before she knew her hands were on the controls.

Between earlier attacks, Newcastle had pulled the other fighter wings off the perimeter of the combat zone and redeployed them in defensive positions around all of the battlecruisers. He'd placed 1st and 6th Fighter Wings around the stricken remnants of the *Guardian*. If the defenders could disable the dreadnought, Vampire squadron would swoop in and take out the floundering enemy ship with their slower but incredibly powerful nuclear bunker busters.

However, since the starfighters had repositioned, the enemy had adapted their tactics, shortening their attacks and varying their ingress locations.

Presently, volleys of weapon fire converged on the enemy ship, scoring multiple hits. Asteroidal debris rocketed away from its lumpy surface. Some of it flew straight at her starfighter, but it easily evaded the incoming rocks.

The outside world made another lateral shift, and her cockpit suddenly warmed.

"Shit!" Sandy said.

The Zox ship had fired directly at her. The fighter had dodged the worst of the laser's assault, but for the first time, its external skin glowed red. Multiple system warnings flashed in her virtual vision.

"Damn it!" she said in a frustrated growl. "That was close!"

Sandy canceled the alarms and scanned the systems. Nothing too bad. All of the critical ones still functioned. The plasma weapon's containment field had shifted to amber, but the rest of the armaments showed green.

Another brilliant river of light burst from the alien ship, slicing across the width of her immersive display. Barely missing her fighter, it tore another large hole in the unshielded *Galactic Guardian*.

Grinding her teeth, Sandy growled and fired another volley at the enormous ship's nearest asteroid, but the son of a bitch winked out of existence again!

Sandy's growl morphed into a scream. "Damn it!"

Colonel Newcastle's voice burst from the silent command net. "Report!"

"Gunfighter Squadron is down another man," said a nervous-sounding female. "We lost Major Hill, sir."

The news hit Sandy like a slap. She felt her face reddening as her anger boiled over. She knew Hill. He was a good man. But hearing the woman say they were down another man felt like they had already given up on Jake, written him off as dead.

Jake was fine! She would have known if he wasn't!

Sandy began to toggle her radio so that she could tell the bitch as much. But then Richard opened their personal EON connection. The interference had eased enough to permit limited, short-range use of the network. She still hadn't been able to link to Jake, but then again, neither had she with those in the *Guardian*.

"Let it go, Fitzpatrick," Richard said. "You and I both know he's out there, that he's okay."

Before Sandy could answer, he added, "And we will find him as soon as this battle is over."

Colonel Newcastle's weary voice returned. "Okay, Gunfighter. Is this Major Withers?"

"Y-yes, sir," the female said stutteringly.

"Thank you, Major. You're my new wing commander. Hang in there a little bit longer, and we'll get through this."

"Yes ... Yes, sir!" the woman barked, trying to put up a brave front. "Sixth Fighter Wing is a go!"

"First Fighter Wing is a go," Richard said.

The multinational commanders of 2nd through 5th Fighter Wings checked in. Then Newcastle opened the connection with the carrier.

"Galactic Guardian Actual, this is Commander Air Group," he said over the fleet-wide network. "All Terran fighter wings remain combat-effective. What is your status?"

"Roger, CAG," Johnston said. "I'm not sure how many more of those attacks this ship can handle."

"Copy that, Admiral," Newcastle said. "Is there any chance of bringing your gravity drive back to one hundred percent?"

"No. Looks like this is all we get. But that'll be a moot point soon," Johnston said. "We have less than two minutes before their gene weapon is back online. Admiral Tekamah and I want you to get your fighters to safety before that happens."

"But, sir, we're hurting the bastards. They'll have to—"

Admiral Johnston cut him off. "Zach, I appreciate what you are trying to do, but your pilots and their ships are our last hope. Fallback, and when the bastards deploy their weapon against us, you'll have a small window to jump in and take them out before they can parallel-jump out of the system."

"But, Admiral, there must be thousands of personnel still alive on the *Galactic Guardian.*"

"You have your orders, Colonel," Johnston said. Then his voice softened. "Go now, Zach. You've done all you can here."

"Yes, sir," Newcastle said almost too weak to hear. "It's been an honor, Admiral."

"It has been an honor for me as well, Colonel. You have less than a minute. Get the hell out of here! Galactic Guardian Actual, out."

"All squadrons!" the colonel said over the tactical radio, his voice back to full volume. "Fallback to point Alpha in three ..."

Trying to swallow down the huge lump in her throat, Sandy blinked away a tear. Reaching for her drive actuator, she counted down with Newcastle. "Two, one—"

Before she reached zero, the Zoxyth ship, already firing its laser batteries, dropped back into real space directly in front of Sandy's fighter even closer than last time.

The universe lurched sideways, but the fighter's interior atmosphere instantly felt like a blast furnace, as if Sandy had stuck her face into an oven.

She squinted against the radiant heat. In her virtual vision, she saw the fighter's entire complement of system monitors trip red and then die.

In an instant, her starfighter filled with swirling smoke.

As the blaring horns expired, a hissing noise slithered into her ears. Adjusting to the crashing air pressure, Sandy's inner ear popped like a machine gun. As the whistle ramped up to a piercing, high-pitched wail, the helmet flowed from her suit's neck and locked her into its protective atmosphere.

Sandy coughed, trying to clear her lungs. Then the suit's nanobots filtered the air, and she breathed easier.

Suddenly, her flight couch melted back into the bottom of the sphere. Then the last of the fighter's power core collapsed, taking the gravity field with it.

Sandy began to drift away from the floor. As she did, the forward half of the spherical display's concave surface started to balloon outward. All the cabin smoke streamed toward its top left quadrant.

Wide-eyed and beginning to float higher, she made a desperate grasp for the control console—the only cockpit element still protruding from the sphere's inner surface. Catching it with one hand, she pulled herself down and hugged the small pedestal with both arms and legs like a flood victim grasping the top of a telephone pole.

Looking over the top of the console, she stared at the visibly flexing wall. It undulated like fluttering paper. Even through her suit's helmet, the shriek of escaping atmosphere became an unbearable roar. Then the forward portion of the starfighter blew out, plunging Sandy into deafening silence.

After a moment, her traumatized ears registered the sound of her frantic breathing. The wet click of a nervous swallow interrupted her panting.

A nightmarish image stared back at Sandy as she looked through the huge hole left by the explosive decompression.

With gleeful malevolence, the sculpted alien face chiseled into the front of the Zoxyth dreadnought appeared to glare at Major Fitzpatrick. As she peered through the void, nothing but empty space sat between her and its monstrous, snarling, skull-chewing visage.

CHAPTER 35

J ake looked at his wristwatch.

Less than a minute remained before the enemy could fire their gene weapon!

A moment ago, the dreadnought had jumped out of the battle again.

The damn hologram was still of no use. Giard couldn't see where the bastards had gone, but he knew they'd be back.

He zoomed the view-wall image until the remnant of the *Guardian* filled the center third of the *Warden's* display. At that magnification, he could make out details of individual starfighters.

During the last engagement, Jake had seen the destruction of one of the dots he'd previously identified as a fighter.

Now that he'd magnified the image, he spotted Sandy's ship. "There you are!" he said. "Thank God!" he added as he released the breath he'd been holding since seeing the destruction of the unknown starfighter. "Now get the hell out of—"

Suddenly, everything changed.

Like high-speed action captured in a brilliant camera flash, three things appeared to happen simultaneously.

The dreadnought jumped back into the battle, lasers already firing.

At the same instant, Sandy's ship lurched sideways, and half of its exterior skin glowed like an autumn sunset.

Concurrently, all of the other starfighters vanished, only the after-image of their parallel jump's blue halo remaining in their wake.

"No, no!" Jake screamed.

Then the glowing skin of Sandy's fighter ruptured, exploding outward.

Even if she hadn't been cooked alive, her fighter was dead in the water.

"No!" Giard yelled at himself. He wasn't going to give up hope. They weren't dead! Sandy and their baby were on that starfighter.

Remulkin had been right. Jake needed to save his family.

He glared at the sweeping second hand of his watch.

The colonel had one option and only seconds to do it.

Reaching for the parallel-space actuator, he whispered a quick prayer.

"God, if this works, I'll never know it. Please watch over Sandy and our baby. Help her understand."

Jake closed his eyes. As he mashed the virtual button, he added, "Help her forgive me—"

CHAPTER 36

Through the hole in her fighter, the stone visage continued to glare at Sandy.

Now unopposed, the dreadnought hung motionlessly across from her as if savoring the moment.

She knew that the *Galactic Guardian*, also dead in the water, hovered just behind the husk of her destroyed fighter.

Still clinging to the pedestal, she raised her wristwatch to eye level.

As the final seconds tick, tick, ticked from her life, Sandy closed her eyes.

"Goodbye, Jake, I love you. I'm sorry I didn't tell you about our baby."

She felt tears puddling around her lashes.

"Goodbye, Momma," she said. A whimper escaped her lips as she added, "Daddy! I—"

Sandy flinched as white light flooded through her squeezed-shut eyelids.

Releasing the pedestal and floating free, she spread her arms wide and said, "I love you, Daddy!"

CHAPTER 37

The gene weapon bathed Sandy in its life-stealing effulgence. Wrapping her arms around her mid-section, the floating, unrealized mother hugged her abdomen and braced for the end.

An eternal moment later, her eyes snapped open.

Where was the pain? During her first brief encounter with the weapon over California, it had felt as if her insides were boiling. However, now she felt none of it. The only sensation working through her abdomen was that associated with weightlessness.

Somehow, she was still alive.

Brilliant light continued to stream through the blown-out wall, but its luminosity was already subsiding. Then the last of it faded, plunging Sandy into an inky blackness punctuated by blue afterimages. After another moment, she blinked away the last of the azure spots, but still couldn't see anything.

Sandy floated in complete, unrelenting darkness as if she'd fallen into a sensory deprivation tank. In her silent universe, each beat of her heart sounded like a thermonuclear detonation.

Finally, shadows began to emerge from the void. Adjusting to the dark, her eyes started to pick up shapes within those shadows. The ragged edge of the fighter's missing wall still hung ahead of Sandy. Through it, she saw ... nothing?

No, something was out there, a hint of stars, but too dark, as if seen through black tinting. Starting and stopping, the blacked-out stars appeared to scroll from the bottom of the field of view. Eventually, their zigzagging path carried them out of view at the top of the torn-out wall.

"Is that—?" Sandy said but then screamed as something touched the top of her helmet.

A few skipped heartbeats later, she realized that, still floating, she had bumped into the fighter's ceiling.

Releasing her abdomen, she extended a tentative hand toward the smooth featureless surface.

As her thumb and first two fingers touched it, they stuck to the surface. Sandy sighed and whispered, "Thank God."

Like smart velcro, the nanobots in the suit's glove gave her purchase on the smooth panel. Sandy began to walk hand-over-hand toward the jagged edge of the blown-out wall. When she tensed her hand to grip the ceiling, the nanobots held like glue. To let go, she simply relaxed her grip, and they released.

She reached the opening. A spectacular, surreal panorama blotted out half of the visible universe.

Like a hole in space, an incredibly dark and massive vessel now floated where the Zoxyth ship had been only moments before. But, as she'd seen earlier, the region wasn't entirely devoid of light. Now limited to the hole in the star field, the scrolling points still followed their zigzagging path across space.

Then she recognized the rotating shape. "Yes!" she said excitedly.

Slowly rolling along its long axis, the *Helm Warden* floated where the dreadnought had been. As the nearest side scrolled across her field of view, weakly reflected starlight undulated across the carrier's flowing, aerodynamic lines.

But the ship had been emptied. How did it get here?

Then she knew!

Sandy grinned. "Jake Giard! You perfect man, you!"

Her smile faltered as a jagged protuberance broke the lower profile of the carrier's smooth lines. The irregular outcropping rotated toward her. Earthshine from the nearing planet revealed the rust-red color of its cratered and charred surface.

Pent-up air burst through Sandy's lips as if she'd been gut struck.

"That can't be ..." Sandy started to say, but then the alien face rotated into full view, and she knew it was all too true.

Somehow, the Zoxyth dreadnought had melded with the *Helm Warden*. Like a nightmarish beast emerging face first from a pool of black mercury, the front half of the sculpted reptilian visage glared out into space from the smooth skin of the carrier's side. As the *Warden* continued to roll, the alien head's swept back, horn-shaped ears rotated out of view, and the monster appeared to scowl at Sandy as it regarded her over its slitted nose.

"No," she whispered, trying to wish the vision away. "Oh God. No, Jake."

Aboard the *Galactic Guardian*, Admiral Johnston stared through the view-wall and watched as the sculpted Zoxyth face scrolled back into view. "What in the hell happened?" he said in an astonished voice.

Beside him, Admiral Tekamah wavered unsteadily but didn't answer. Johnston extended an arm to the supreme commander, stabilizing him.

"Thank you, Bill," Tekamah said distractedly.

Johnston nodded. He cast a nervous glance overhead. Above them, the star field shone through a blown-out section of the bridge's ceiling. A few minutes earlier, an enemy laser had cut a long, straight-edged hole across it. Before the force field had sealed the opening, several officers had disappeared through it, carried to their death by the explosive decompression. Johnston had narrowly avoided the same fate. As he'd slid across the floor, Bill had grabbed onto a console. However, Tekamah had tumbled past him and then flown upward only to slam back down when the force field sealed the breach. Both men still bled from the multiple cuts and contusions they'd received during the event. And Bill suspected the GDF admiral had suffered a concussion as well.

Still a bit unstable on his feet, Tekamah gestured weakly at the hole. "It'll hold," he said too loudly.

Bill saw blood oozing from the man's ears. Johnston touched his own and found them bloodied as well. The rapid depressurization must have ruptured their eardrums.

He pointed a red-stained finger at the view-wall. "What happened, Ashtara?" he asked again.

The GDF admiral still didn't respond. Johnston gave the man an appraising sidelong glance. Tekamah blinked confused, unfocused eyes. Finally, his brow furrowed, and he yelled, "What?"

Johnston faced him and grabbed both of the man's shoulders. He gave the GDF admiral a gentle shake. "Stay with me, Ashtara."

Releasing a shoulder, Bill pointed toward the view-wall. "It looks like the *Helm Warden* jumped into the battle."

Turning from the surreal image, he studied Tekamah's eyes.

Still staring at the expansive display, the Argonian admiral blinked again. Then his eyes focused, and a haunted look chased out the confusion.

"Order your fighters to hold position!" Tekamah said in a suddenly animated voice. "Don't let them jump back in!"

Johnston nodded and made the radio call.

Then the hologram began to reconstitute over their heads. Apparently, the quantum storm whipped up by the enemy missile had finally relented. Outside, the protruding portion of the enemy ship rotated out of view again.

On the bridge, the GDF supreme commander grabbed the holographic rendering of the Helm Warden, stopping its modeled rotation. Then he turned the holographic version of the ship so that the Zoxyth face stared back at them.

Studying the miniature carrier, Tekamah shook his head. "I think their godsdamned gene weapon is still hot." He tilted his head to the model and said, "Watch this."

Suddenly, the holographic *Helm Warden* began to fade. Through the translucent carrier, Johnston now saw the complete enemy ship. The dreadnought remained intact. Except the portion of the face that protruded from the carrier's skin, its entire mass now lay encased within the structure of the *Warden*.

Tekamah expanded the image until it filled the overhead space. Looking up, both men stared into the paired ships.

Where physical material from one vessel crossed that of the other, the structures had melded together like a nightmare painted by Salvador Dali. Along their combined lines, smooth metal contours surreally flowed through cratered asteroidal surfaces.

Shaking his head, Admiral Johnston whispered, "Jesus wept."

"Roger, Galactic Guardian Actual. CAG, out," Colonel Newcastle said over the fleet-wide EON network.

Now that the hologram was working again, Richard studied its rendering of the battlefield. Somehow the emptied *Helm Warden* had jumped back into the combat zone. He stared at its smooth lines for a moment. Then comprehension washed over Colonel Allison. He smiled. "You son of a bitch! Way to go, Jake!"

"Sandy!" Richard said over their personal electro-organic network connection. Looking over his left shoulder, he said, "I think that's Ja—"

His voice died mid-sentence as he realized the link had failed and that Sandy's fighter wasn't with him. Nothing but empty space floated off his left wing.

Richard opened a squadron-wide channel.

"Phoenix Squadron, check in!"

One by one, every fighter save one sounded off.

"Where in the hell are you, Sandra?" he said, trying their personal EON link again.

Nothing but the perfect silence of a dead digital connection answered his query.

He reached into the hologram and magnified the battlefield again. As he zoomed into the image, a tiny dot between the *Helm Warden* and the remnant of the *Galactic Guardian* swelled into the husk of a destroyed but still recognizable Phoenix Starfighter.

"Oh fuck," Richard whispered. He started rocking back and forth. Subvocalizing, he began to repeat, "No! No! No!" in a constant loop.

"Colonel Allison? Are you still with me?"

Closing his eyes, Richard made a quick head shake. Then he opened them and accepted the connection.

"Sorry, sir."

"No, Richard, I'm sorry. I see it, too. I know you were close, but there will be time to mourn her later."

"Yes, sir," Colonel Allison said.

"Did you notice the *Helm Warden?*" asked the CAG.

Richard furrowed his eyebrows. Of course he'd seen the *Warden*. It was a damn big ship, hard to miss.

"Uh, yes, sir," Richard said after a brief pause.

A paternal tone entered the colonel's voice. "Son, did you also see the enemy ship?"

Allison blinked. He couldn't believe he hadn't given the bastards another thought, although he'd assumed it must be hanging near the battlefield. The weapon must still be hot. Why else would Johnston warn them off?

"No, sir," Richard said. "I don't see it on the display."

"You need to take a closer look at the *Helm Warden*, Colonel Allison."

"Okay, sir. Looking now."

He manipulated the virtual holographic model, stretching it until the carrier appeared to fill the fighter's overhead confines. Like the real ship, the rendering slowly rotated about its long axis. It still looked like a normal GDF carrier.

Richard started to reopen the connection but then froze.

"What the hell is that?!"

Two horn-shaped protrusions slid into view at the bottom of the ship. Impatient, Richard grabbed the virtual carrier. He rotated it manually and came face to face with their enemy.

"Son of a bitch!"

He reopened the connection. "How in the *hell* did that happen?" Belatedly, Richard added, "Sir."

"Damned if I know, son," Newcastle said through his East Texas drawl. "But you and I need to get in there."

The colonel's words barely registered. An epiphany had slammed into Richard like a sledgehammer: both of his friends were probably dead.

"Y-Yes, sir," Richard mumbled. Finally understanding the East Texan's intentions, Richard sat up. "Yes, sir!"

"Good," Newcastle said. "If they're not ... well, you know ..." He paused and then sighed. "If they're alive, you and I will find them, Richard."

Newcastle activated the fleet-wide EON connection. "On my mark, I want each fighter wing to jump to its newly assigned coordinates."

As the colonel spoke, several waypoints popped up in Richard's holographic display: one for their two starfighters and six others for the air group's fighter wings. The CAG had distributed them in a defensive perimeter that sat more than a hundred miles outside of the combat zone.

Newcastle continued. "That'll keep you outside of the gene weapon's range. Colonel Allison and I will jump into the battlefield and make sure the *Helm Warden* took out the damn thing. You are to hold station until you hear from Colonel Allison or me." After a pregnant pause, he added, "Or until you see the weapon's light wave."

"Vlad," the CAG said. "If that happens, I want you to take out the whole thing with a nuclear bunker buster."

"Da, comrade," the Russian officer said.

"If that weapon goes off, the bastards will have the still functioning parts of the *Helm Warden* at their command," Newcastle said. "Don't hesitate, Vlad. Don't let them escape. You won't be hurting my feelings. I'll already be long gone."

"Don't worry, friend," Vlad said icily. "I remember what they did to Mother Russia. I'll take care of them."

After a short pause, the CAG said, "We jump in twenty seconds."

CHAPTER 38

Sandy's heart raced as she stared across the kilometer-wide gap. A thousand-meter canyon of empty space sat between the major and Jake's likely location.

She had no idea if he was even alive.

Numerous calls using her suit's short-range radio had gone unanswered.

He could be trapped or hurt. Sandy shook her head. She didn't want to consider the other possibility, wouldn't consider it.

She had to find him, help him.

Now!

But she didn't have any means of propulsion, any way to get across the gap, not in a controllable manner, anyway.

The thought drew a leery eye to the fire extinguisher. Sandy had seen the hackneyed emergency employment of improvised thrust in enough science fiction movies to know it was a recipe for disaster.

Sandy shook her head. There had to be a better way.

Something flickered in her peripheral vision. As she turned in that direction, she saw a small piece of debris floating away from the fighter's floor. Then another light flashed from the gray surface.

"What the hell?" Sandy whispered.

A second chunk of debris—slightly larger than the first, but moving even slower—had ricocheted off of the floor. Concentric rings of blue light radiated from the point where it had impacted.

As darkness returned to her fighter, Sandy had an epiphany.

And a plan.

～

"I need to check Sandy's fighter, sir," Richard said over their direct EON link.

"Okay, Colonel Allison," Newcastle said hesitantly. "But you may not like what you find."

Richard nodded without commenting. He didn't want to dwell on the possibility.

A moment earlier, their two fighters had popped back into the battlefield. Both ships now floated side-by-side with their noses pointed at the *Helm Warden* and its conjoined alien tumor.

Richard started to turn his fighter toward Sandy's. Then he stopped.

As the flagship of the Galactic Defense Forces and its formation of ruined ships passed over China's southeast coast, entering Earth orbit, the sculpted alien face rotated into view. Illuminated from below, the nightmarish visage appeared to glare at Richard with all too real malevolence.

Tearing his gaze from the face, a face that looked exactly like the beast Jake had killed aboard the first alien ship, Colonel Allison shook his head and then guided his fighter toward the black husk of Major Fitzpatrick's ruined Phoenix Starfighter.

As he rocketed toward the ruptured hull, the small vessel swelled from a featureless point into an all too detailed image of charred destruction. Richard's entire body tensed in anticipation of what he might see within the burned husk. He stopped the vessel about a hundred feet from the remnant of her drifting fighter. From there, he could see about a third of its exposed interior.

It looked empty.

Like a reluctant family member drawing back a morgue shroud, Richard craned his neck, trying to see deeper into the cabin.

"Where are you, Sandy?" he said.

Colonel Allison still didn't see anything. He needed to reposition to a better viewing angle. His hand crept into the fighter's control interface.

Suddenly, the visible portion of the ruined fighter's floor convulsed.

"What in the—?" Richard started to whisper, but then a white blob flew out of the ship. He flinched, yanking his hand out of the flight controller. Luckily, he hadn't been gripping it yet, or his fighter would've jumped a few kilometers aft, out of the battlefield.

Moving from left to right, the egg-shaped blob sped across his field of view.

The speaker in his helmet sparked to life. "Richard?"

Colonel Allison blinked. "Sandy?!" he said over the suit-to-suit radio. "Where are you? Wait, is that you in the egg?"

"Egg? Oh, yeah. That's me!"

Smiling, Richard shook his head. "How did you ...? Where did you—?"

"No time," Sandy said, cutting him off. "Just meet me on the near side of the *Warden*."

Reaching back into the flight controller, Richard spun his fighter to face the carrier. Sandy's cocoon, or whatever the hell it was, shrank to a white dot as it continued to fly toward the silver-black skin of the massive carrier. Then it dwindled to a tiny point and finally disappeared altogether.

"You're going too fast!" Richard yelled. "You'll just bounce off the side!"

"No, I won't," Sandy said. "Unless I keep ... talking to ... you," she added through a series of grunts. Static filled the last words as increasing distance started carrying her beyond the suit's radio range.

Still staring after her, Richard shook his head.

His connection to Newcastle reopened.

"What's Major Fitzpatrick's status, Allison?"

Even though he'd also been fitted with an Argonian spacesuit, the colonel had been too far away to receive the transmissions of their suit radios. And without her ship's network connection, Sandy hadn't been able to activate an EON link.

"She's ... alive," Richard said haltingly.

"You don't sound so sure of that." Before Colonel Allison could reply, Newcastle continued. "Just get her out of there, and let's start working on getting to the *Helm Warden*."

"Uh, she's already there ... I think."

"You think? I thought you said you'd found her."

Richard slid his hand back into the flight controller.

"I did, sir." This time, Richard didn't wait for a reply. "Just follow me," he said as his fighter shot toward the Helm Warden. Belatedly, he added, "Sir."

After a pregnant pause, Newcastle said, "Okay," drawing out the word.

Within the holographic rendering of the battlefield, Richard saw the colonel's man-made space fighter fall into formation with his Phoenix Starfighter. The pair slowed as they approached the part of the ship that Richard estimated as her likely point of impact. Richard winced at the mental image elicited by the thought.

His suit speaker sparked to life.

"Over here!" Sandy said in a staticky shout.

At the same moment, he saw a flicker of light to port. Looking left, he saw it flash again. For a brief instant, a bubble on the skin of the massive ship lit up like a Chinese lantern.

Richard turned his starfighter toward it. Seconds later, the two fighters drew to a halt a few feet away from the blister that had generated the intermittent light.

Upon closer inspection, the Chinese lantern analogy persevered. Just aft of the protruding bridge section, it looked as if someone had glued the end of one to the skin of the *Helm Warden*.

On the side of the city-sized ship, it was impossible to judge the scale of the object, but then Sandy's head and shoulders protruded from its top. Floating in the open end of the roughly six-foot-tall by four-foot-wide lantern, she waved. The movement jostled the pregnant cylinder, and it strobed again.

"In here," she said, urging them with a beckoning gesture. "I found a way in!"

Shaking his head, Richard managed a smile. *Jake, you're a lucky bastard*, he thought.

Then the grin faltered as he saw that the icon for their direct EON connection remained grayed out.

"Giard! Are you there, buddy?" Richard shouted into his spacesuit radio.

Now close enough to access his fighter's network, Sandy opened a direct EON connection with him and Newcastle. "It's no use, Richard. I tried as soon as I got close enough. The *Warden's* network is down, and I can't raise him on the radio. He must be out of range."

"Okay," Colonel Allison said.

Just in case Giard could hear them, Richard transmitted again. "Hang in there, Jake! We're on our way, buddy!"

Sandy watched Richard slide through the hatch. Then she felt gravity begin to exert itself. All three of them glided to a soft landing on the floor of the small inner chamber.

Standing in hard vacuum, Sandy stared expectantly through the opening. She watched the field of stars rotate across the now empty airlock door. As the *Warden* continued its slow, axial roll, the hazy obscuration of Earth's atmosphere scrolled into view and slid down from the top of the opening. Then the planet's horizon streamed across the panorama. Less than a hundred miles below the formation of ships she saw the frozen landscape of Northeast Asia glide beneath them. Isolated white clouds hugged the permafrost of Northern Siberia like cotton balls resting on a field of snow.

Then, as if the planet's local weather had reached up into space, white skin propagated inwardly from the opening's perimeter like a time-lapsed video of frost spreading across a window. After several starts and stops, the hatch finally closed. When Sandy had opened it, the door had dissolved in the same halting manner. Viewing the stuttering movement was like watching a video feed that kept pausing to buffer.

A hiss leaked into Sandy's sound-starved ears. She twitched as all three of their helmets suddenly retracted, responding to the atmosphere pumping into the lock.

Richard turned to face her. "How did you launch out of there?" He paused, and then gestured to the exterior hatch. "And how did you find this?"

Sandy shrugged. "My ship was dead in the water ... space, whatever. Anyway, I remembered that the nanobots can draw energy from mechanical movement."

She looked around the room impatiently. Her inner ears popped as they equalized, adjusting to the ship's higher atmospheric pressure. That was new. It had never happened before.

Waiting for the internal door to manifest, Sandy turned toward Richard and Colonel Newcastle. "I didn't have gravity. So I grabbed the fire extinguisher and placed my back against the floor. Then I used short bursts to keep my body pinned down while I slid across its surface. As I did that, the suit's nanobots added mass like a rolling snowball. They also converted the mechanical energy into electricity and stored it for later."

"How in the hell did you think of that?" Richard asked.

"The GDF Liaison, Lieutenant Thramorus, told me what they could do. Once I had enough of the boogers, I had part of them attach to the fighter's floor and toss me out. The rest cocooned me and then acted as a smart, sticky spring to arrest my velocity and attach to the hull at this end of the trip."

"How did you find the airlock?" Richard said.

"I didn't. The nanobots took care of that one. After landing here, the cocoon slid across the hull like a speedy snail. It stopped over that small rectangle. When I placed my gloved hand on it, the hatch opened."

Suddenly, an inner wall disappeared. The three officers exchanged glances. Sandy craned her neck and surveyed the next room. "I keep expecting to see that damned gene weapon's light," she said in a hoarse whisper.

Standing to either side of her, Richard and Newcastle nodded.

"This close," the CAG said, "I reckon we'd never see it coming. One minute we're here, the next ..." He paused and then shrugged. "Pearly gates and blaring trumpets."

"He must be dead," Richard said, whispering as well. Seeing Sandy's angry reaction, he held up a hand. "The enemy commander. Otherwise, the bastard would've fired the weapon by now."

While he spoke, Sandy tried to open an EON channel with Jake. It still wouldn't connect; the icon remained grayed out.

God, please let him be okay, Sandy prayed.

Fresh lip pain blossomed.

With a quick head shake, she pushed away the thoughts. Her teeth clicked together as she clenched her jaw to prevent further lip chewing.

Sandy stepped into the next room. "Jake is here somewhere. We *will* find him!" she said, almost screaming the words.

Turning around, she saw Richard and the CAG exchange glances.

Newcastle raised his salt-and-pepper eyebrows. "I know better to argue with a woman when she uses that tone."

The two men joined her in the new room.

With uncharacteristic empathy, Richard squeezed her arm. "You're right. We'll find him."

Sandy gave him a curt nod. Then she turned and walked deeper into the unfamiliar room.

Judging by the airlock's position, they had to be just aft of the bridge. With a relatively low ceiling and plain white walls, this room was smaller than most she'd previously seen in either of the carriers. The trio walked down a passage that led to the chamber's far wall. They passed between banks of strange hardware. Like tiny streams of mercury, undulating silver threads of nanobots linked all of the components like a web spun by a metallic spider. With the smell of an impending springtime thunderstorm, cool, ozone-tinged air flowed across the racks.

"Computers," Richard whispered. "Must be a server bank or something like that."

Sandy reached the opposite wall, and an opening appeared in its smooth surface. For a moment, it halted halfway open. Frozen in the act of dissolving, the material at the edge of the narrow opening looked unfocused. The closer Sandy inspected, the blurrier it appeared. She tried to blink the image into focus, but it finished opening, and the edge solidified.

Pouring through the freshly minted doorway, a wave of warm, humid air washed across them. The acrid smell of burned rock assaulted her nose. A surreal scene revealed itself in the flickering light visible through the new opening.

"Oh shit!" Richard said.

Sandy stared in shocked silence.

The floor of the *Warden's* bridge was gone. Instead of gothic tiles, an uneven cratered rock jutted into the room. The asteroidal hull of the enemy ship dammed the lower third of the door and disappeared from view at its top right.

Sandy stepped closer and looked right and up, following the rock to its apex. The jagged extremity melded into the sculpted bird of prey that protruded from the ceiling of the bridge. Its bronze feathers now appeared to grow from fractured gray rock. She shifted her gaze back to the rock's base. Before an asteroid had merged with the ship, this doorway had opened onto the bridge's lower floor.

After the event, a chunk of asteroid must have broken off from somewhere above them. It had come to rest against the left wall, tucked into the acute angle where the down-sloping floor formed by the asteroid joined vertical bronze metal. She started to look away from the boulder, but then something about its shape drew her eyes back.

With sudden recognition, Sandy screamed, "Jake!" and then launched herself through the opening. She scrambled across the rock slope. Bracing her left hand against the tarnished bronze wall, she scurried along the rough, V-shaped seam.

"Jake!" she screamed again.

No answer.

No movement.

Closer now, she saw that he was face-down.

"Oh God, please," Sandy whimpered.

Scrambling across the uneven surface, she barely registered the gray powder that already covered the white skin of her spacesuit's legs. The same dust covered Jake from head to toe. That's why she had initially mistaken him for a broken piece of asteroid.

Reaching his motionless body, Sandy dropped to her knees. She grabbed his shoulders and pulled his face out of the dusty soil, launching a small cloud of the stuff. Rolling Jake over, Sandy dragged his upper body onto her thighs. She cradled his head with her left hand and gently brushed gray grit from his face with the other.

He didn't respond.

"Jake...? Jake...!" Sandy said, gently slapping his face with her open hand. Each pat launched a fresh puff of dust.

Allison and Newcastle stumbled up to her side. The Texan cast a wary eye about the room. Richard dropped to a knee. "Come on, Jake," he said. "Wake up, Colonel." He sounded way calmer than Sandy felt.

Her man still didn't respond.

"Baby," Sandy said through a sob. With the back of her right hand, she wiped at the tears streaming down her face. It came away covered in dark, gritty mud. In the hot room's unreliable light, she couldn't tell if Jake was breathing. Wanting to check for a pulse, but afraid of what she might discover, Sandy extended two trembling fingers toward his neck. Then, in the strobing light, she saw a small vortex of particles swirl beneath his nostrils.

"He's breathing!" she said.

Jake spasmed and coughed. His eyes fluttered and then opened. Confused, they darted across each of them. Then they focused on hers.

Jake smiled. "Sandy?"

"Oh thank God!" she said. "Yes, baby. It's me."

After another coughing fit, he looked around, eyes wide. "Where are we?"

He reached up and caressed her face. Then he sat up. Perplexed, he looked at the point where the jagged, colorless surface of the asteroid joined smooth golden wall. "What happened?"

Sandy gently wiped the dust from his face.

"Well, Captain America," Richard said. "You jumped the *Warden* into the battle."

Comprehension dawned across Jake's face. He stood and looked around the bridge. Gazing upward, his eyes followed the steeply sloping rock to the point where its buried apex disappeared into the bronze bird of prey. "Shit ..." he whispered, then smiled. "I guess it worked then."

"We don't know yet, son." Colonel Newcastle said gruffly.

Jake flinched, launching another dust cloud. He looked at Newcastle. "Hello, CAG."

The older Texan gave him a curt nod. "You did a brave thing, Giard."

Jake ran the fingers of both hands through his short hair, shaking them vigorously. The cloud that rose from him reminded Sandy of Pig-Pen, Charlie Brown's perpetually dirty friend. The thought made her smile in spite of their situation.

"Where's Thramorus?" Sandy said.

Her man froze with his fingers still buried in his hair. After a moment, he lowered his arms. As his eyes raised toward hers, they lingered on her abdomen.

He knows, she thought.

His gaze finally met hers. A storm of emotions crossed his face. Finally, he said, "He's ... gone." Then he glanced at her stomach again. A battle as intense as the day's worst raged across his face.

Sandy's heart hurt. There was so much they needed to talk about, but now wasn't the time.

Jake looked down. He took a deep breath and then looked up and stared into Sandy's eyes. The love and kindness in his made her melt inside. He mouthed, *I love you.*

Before Sandy could recover, much less speak, Jake's eyes widened again. He glanced at his watch and turned toward Newcastle. "What about the weapon?"

The CAG shook his head. "Still hot, we think. But we need to find out for sure."

Jake jiggled the last of the dust from his hair and then raised questioning eyebrows at the fellow Texan. "Then what the hell are we waiting for, sir?"

Newcastle smiled and said, "Follow me."

CHAPTER 39

C olonel Newcastle pointed to a flat section of wall on the right side of the long hallway. "There."

"Are you sure?" Jake asked. "So far, decorative casing or trim has framed every door I've seen on these carriers."

They walked up to the indicated point, but nothing happened. Newcastle reached out and tapped the wall. No opening manifested. "What the hell?" he said, his East Texas accent giving the last word an extra syllable.

Richard cocked a skeptical eyebrow. "I don't know, Colonel. I think Jake is right."

"Tekamah said it was here!" the CAG said plaintively, pointing at the wall. "It's supposed to detect my presence and open automatically." He pounded the bronzed surface with the side of his clenched fist. The third swing passed through empty air as the metal dissolved in stuttering, stop-animation movement. Inside, flickering, unreliable light revealed a small chamber.

Still standing in the long hallway, Newcastle looked into the room. Then he glanced over their heads at the flickering indirect lights that illuminated the hall's high ceiling. Finally, he looked at Giard. "Your stunt did a real number on the ship."

Jake nodded and gave him a withering grin. "You should see the other guy."

While they had worked their way deeper into the *Helm Warden*, toward this weapons cache, the CAG had briefed Jake on the situation. They'd told him about the visible portion of the dreadnought. (Thus his joke about the other guy.) The news of the melding of the two ships had shocked him most. Jake hadn't known it was a possibility. Considering the energies involved, he had thought they would both explode.

Sandy's heart had nearly broken when he'd told them of the events that led to his jumping the *Warden* into the enemy ship. Even now, it ached as she remembered the look on his face and how she'd felt when he told them about Remulkin's sacrifice. Then Jake had described the helplessness he'd felt upon seeing her ship hit by enemy fire.

After all that, when the unstoppable hand of time had removed all other options, he'd decided to sacrifice himself.

Sandy closed her eyes. Thank God that hadn't happened.

Presently, Jake nodded to Newcastle and said, "Maybe the enemy's systems are just as screwed up as ours."

"Well, I'd like to have a little insurance," the colonel said. Pointing into the new room, he added, "And I think this is just the ticket."

Sandy peered through the opening into the promised supplemental GDF armory. Racks of weapons lined shelves along both sides of the small chamber.

Admiral Tekamah had previously briefed the Terran fleet's senior commanders on its existence and had granted them unlimited access. Fortunately, Newcastle had been in the know, one of the few officers he'd trusted with the information and the access.

Sandy walked into the airlock-sized room.

"This is an emergency weapons cache for use in the event of an enemy boarding action," Newcastle said as he followed her in.

Behind them, Richard and Jake hung back, framing the left and right sides of the opening as they watched both ends of the long hallway. After checking his sector, Jake looked back into the armory and glanced at her abdomen again. Pursing his lips, he shifted his gaze to Newcastle.

She knew he wanted to tell the colonel, try to get someone to fly in here and whisk her away.

Waving a hand by her left hip, Sandy drew Jake's attention and shook her head, mouthing, "No!"

Myriad emotions scrolled across his face as competing priorities fought for dominance.

Come on, Jake, she thought. There was too much on the line, too much to lose. With pleading eyes, Sandy tried to will him into accepting the truth of their situation. The weapon could go off any second. It wouldn't matter if she were here or with the thousands of Argonians and humans still alive aboard the stranded remnant of the *Galactic Guardian.* Even if she could get outside of the weapon's range, she would gain nothing that mattered to her. Their child needed a father, needed a secure world in which to grow up. Any delay at this juncture could jeopardize all that.

Finally, Jake gave her a short nod.

Sandy sighed inwardly and returned the gesture.

Then Newcastle began pulling weapons off the rack. He handed each of them two firearms. "The stubby one is a plasma gun," he said. "Fires a beam like a laser on steroids. The long, heavy one is a kinetic rifle. It launches small pellets at hypervelocity."

Sandy took the pistol-sized weapon and placed it against her right hip. As promised, it stuck there, the suit's nanobots recognizing her intentions and holding it in place like velcro. Testing its security, she pulled it off. The nanobots released with a sound also reminiscent of velcro. She stuck it back in place and accepted the offered rifle.

She nodded to Newcastle. "Thank you, sir."

The colonel returned a very Texan-like nod and then handed the men their weapons.

Now armed like space cowboys, the foursome left the miniature armory and headed deeper into the *Helm Warden.* At the end of the long hall, they rounded a corner and pulled up short. Richard shook his head and said, "Damn it!"

Standing side-by-side, they looked up, scanning the rock that blocked their path. Craters covered its charcoal surface. From the tiled floor to the peak of the pointed arch sixty feet above their heads, the pitted rock formed a solid wall.

Sandy didn't see a way around it. They'd have to find another route. She tried to envision where they must be in relation to the sculpted alien head that formed the bridge of the enemy ship. Jake had told her they found the commander of the first Zoxyth ship on the top deck of that section.

"We need to go up a level," Sandy said. She pointed a thumb over her shoulder. "Let's go back to that service corridor. I saw a stairway there."

Jake nodded. "I think she's right. Their command deck is near the top of their bridge. From what y'all told me about the protruding part, that's at least another level above this one."

"Sounds like a plan," Richard said, nodding as well. "There was a bunch of portals around that deck. Maybe we can get into the dread-nought through one of them."

Sandy had already reversed course. Jogging, she quickly covered the hundred yards. As the men caught up, she stepped into the narrow corridor. Off to one side, a spiral staircase disappeared up a tube intermittently illuminated by flickering rings of light.

She pointed into it. "See—"

Suddenly, Jake's hand was over her mouth. He held a finger to his lips.

A bone-chilling screech followed by an impossibly low roar rumbled down the tube.

Having resisted him initially, Sandy froze. After a moment, the sound tapered off. She looked at Jake with wide eyes.

Hoisting his eyebrows, he gave her an okay sign.

Sandy swallowed but then nodded.

Jake looked at the men. He pointed two fingers at his eyes and then gestured up the stairs. Then he pointed at each of them in turn and signaled one, two, and three, Sandy last.

They all nodded.

Silently, the foursome stepped through the access hatch.

Jake slowly pulled the pistol off his hip, making sure not to let it make the tearing velcro sound. With a final, worried glance at Sandy, he started up the stairs. Then Richard and Newcastle pulled off their weapons and followed him.

After scanning the hall behind her, Sandy pealed the pistol from her side and placed a foot on the first step. As she extended a trembling hand toward the rail, a fresh roar caused the tread beneath her foot to vibrate.

Sandy flinched and thought, *Oh Jesus!*

CHAPTER 40

Holding his breath, Jake extended a leg over the broken rock. White-knuckled in the flickering light, his left hand gripped the curving stair rail. He shifted his weight to the foot that rested on the tread above the far side of the small boulder. A smooth, curving surface interrupted the rough, broken exterior of the wedge-shaped chunk of Zoxyth asteroid. Its radius matched that of the walls of the spiral staircase. This was the last of several pieces. Having dropped from the point where the tube's smooth walls had sliced through the dreadnought's outer hull like a cookie cutter, the pieces had rained down on the stairs below. The corkscrew-shaped formation of rocks sat precariously balanced on the rungs. It appeared that the slightest disturbance would send the whole mess careening down the tube.

Shortly after they'd started up the staircase, they began to feel grit underfoot. It had thickened as they climbed higher. Now a layer of tan sand covered everything.

Finally standing above the uppermost piece of broken hull, Jake helped Richard and then Newcastle over the rock. Sandy stepped up and extended a hand. He didn't want to take it. In his mind's eye, the image of Victor's head slowly sliding off of his neck replayed in an unending loop.

Anger flared in Sandy's eyes. She started to pull herself over the obstacle. Relenting, Jake took her hand and helped her climb into the portion of the staircase that extended into the enemy ship.

For better or worse, they were all in the dreadnought now. Jake closed his eyes for a moment, making a silent prayer for the latter half of that phrase.

Then he gave Sandy a hold gesture and silently mouthed, "Stay behind us."

Her eyes narrowed, but then she began to chew her lower lip. Usually, he adored that nervous tell. Today it deepened his worry. She blushed self consciously and quit chewing. Clenching her teeth, she eased the plasma rifle off of her back. After a deep breath, she gave him a short nod.

Already holding his rifle, Jake stepped past the other two men, cautious not to pivot a foot, lest grinding sand reveal their presence.

Approaching the top of the stairs, he found more of the gritty stuff. Now he could see it had poured in from inside the dreadnought.

That didn't make sense. Jake hadn't seen sand in the first Zoxyth ship.

He rounded the last turn, and blue sky came into view.

"What in the hell?" he mouthed silently.

Someone bumped into him. Jake looked down. Richard and Newcastle stood on the rung behind him. As they looked past Giard, the confusion on their faces matched his.

Beyond them, Sandy craned her neck. Then her eyes widened as another screech pierced the air.

All four officers flinched.

A clipped scream broke through Sandy's lips.

They froze.

The screech suddenly died. A deafening silence fell from the blue sky.

Then a roar like none before burst through the opening. Its vibrations sent a fresh miniature avalanche of yellow sand careening over the lip.

From the center of the tubular stairwell, the smooth, curving lines of four blue and silver GDF rifles now pointed toward the indigo sky like the stamen of a deadly flower.

The Zoxyth's roar continued but drew no closer. Jake kept expecting to hear the earth-shaking sound of the monster's running feet. A sound he'd heard before, the sound that had preceded the death of his young wingman.

When it didn't come, Jake pointed two fingers at his eyes again and then gestured toward the blue sky. The two men nodded, but looking at him with wide eyes, Sandy shook her head, mouthing, "No!"

Jake put on a brave face and winked at her. "I'll be okay," he mouthed back.

Turning from her, he started up the stairs.

A gust of hot air hit him. Then, flowing up the spiral staircase, cool air chilled the beads of sweat that had formed on his face. It ruffled his short hair.

Jake wiped the back of his gloved hand across his brow. The suit's nanobots soaked up the moisture.

Standing with his head just below the threshold, he took a deep breath. Giard's heart raced in response to the adrenaline dumping into his system. His ears rang with it.

Slowly, Jake raised his head until his eyes rose above floor level.

Under the overarching blue sky, the rippled surface of a desert floor extended to a distant horizon. He blinked as another hot gust peppered his face with sand. Giard struggled to comprehend the scene. Instead of a cavernous Zoxyth bridge, only sand-covered rock bluffs and green cactuses greeted him. Jake squinted into a mid-afternoon sun. It looked as if he'd emerged into the Mojave Desert.

Suddenly, the blue sky and sun disappeared, revealing a bronze ceiling. Overhead, islands of rock protruded from its otherwise smooth surface. Then the azure firmament flickered back into existence.

He had entered an Argonian terrarium.

When he'd jumped the *Helm Warden* into the battle, this part of the enemy ship had merged with a terrarium designed to mimic a desert environment.

A Zoxyth roar exploded from behind him.

Jake twitched and spun toward the noise. Grasping the kinetic rifle with both hands, he aimed it in the direction of the sound. His back slammed into the top few steps of the staircase.

Trembling, staring up through the long weapon's sights with one eye, Jake came to rest lying inclined on the stairs, a boot braced against one of the handrail's uppermost vertical support rods.

The beast was only ten feet away.

He was huge! Bigger than the last one!

The monster's roar tapered off, dying in a plaintive-sounding screech.

He came no closer. The Zoxyth only glared at him. Insane enmity burned from his red eyes.

Like the last Zox Jake had encountered, the reptile stood eight feet tall. Giard nodded as he realized that this must be the enemy commander.

Swallowing hard, Jake shimmied up the stairs, all the while keeping his gun trained on the monster. His shoulder blades skipped painfully over the stairwell's top step.

Now he saw why the beast hadn't attacked him.

The Zox warlord couldn't move.

Below its knees, the Zox's legs disappeared into a rocky terracotta bluff.

When Giard had jumped the Helm Warden into the dreadnought, the beast had melded with the terrarium's bedrock. Now he stood before Jake, stuck like a mouse in a glue trap.

He judged that at least a foot of the monster's full height extended into the rock, making him even taller than the beast Jake had killed.

Colonel Giard smiled. He knew exactly who this was.

Not taking his eyes or his weapon off of the warlord, he slowly stood. The boots of his spacesuit sank an inch or two into the sand.

Keeping the weapon trained on the Zox, Jake scanned the desert horizon. Squinting, he gazed up at the deep blue sky. Again it flickered out of existence. Now he could see that when the sky vanished, it took the horizon with it. They were actually in a room roughly the size of a skating rink.

Sky and horizon reestablished themselves. Once again, Jake stood in the middle of a vast desert. Cactus of varying sizes dotted the landscape. Some were part of the holographic horizon. However, several persisted even when the artificial horizon didn't.

The overarching indigo sky winked out again, revealing a wall that was half antiqued bronze, half stone. In that direction, the rock floor of the Zoxyth bridge rose above the desert floor in a gradual incline.

The monster continued to glare at him. Like demonic dewclaws, those damned forearm blades kept sliding in and out of the bastard's arm.

The beast they'd found aboard the first Zox ship had used his dewclaw blade to kill Victor. The razor-sharp appendage had cut through the young lieutenant's neck like so much smoke.

A deep rumble accompanied the Zox's every breath. It reminded Jake of the time when, as a kid visiting the circus, he'd stood next to a winded elephant following its performance under the big top. Like the circus animal, the Zox's massive chest rose and fell with each respiration. Green blood oozed from a deep gash in the beast's side. Through the open wound, Jake saw overlapping boney plates instead of ribs. They appeared to slide and articulate with each breath.

Giard scanned the desert floor. He tensed and did a double take. Two additional Zox—one almost as big as the Zoxyth commander— lay partially buried in the sand. However, these were not warriors waiting to pounce on him. Both had been decapitated. The empty eye sockets of one of the severed heads appeared to glare at him.

He turned back to the surviving alien. Around the standing beast, several consoles protruded from the desert floor. Those still upright listed, leaning left. They stood perpendicular to the buried, slanted floor of the enemy's bridge. The consoles looked similar to those Jake had seen on the first ship. Some of them appeared to be inert, their electronic displays black. In front of the Zox commander, a dead, toppled pedestal lay in the sand. Jake studied its fractured top and sides. It looked like the beast had pounded it into submission.

To the left of the Zox commander, but well out of its reach, a green icon pulsed on the tilted surface of another console. Just behind it, one of the terrarium's native rocks stood ten feet above the sand. A green plant hung from its near side. Jake blinked as he saw scales on its surface. He smiled as he belatedly recognized the shape as an arm. There'd been an alien standing behind the control panel and its flashing green icon. When the two ships had merged, that one had received a lethal dose of mineral poisoning.

Ten feet beyond that console, a leaning, black stone throne jutted from the sand. On a display attached to its side, Jake saw Newfoundland's triangular island scroll under the formation of battered ships. It looked like they were now in the lowest part of the orbital insertion.

Their fifty-mile altitude had the formation skimming through the top of the atmosphere. Earlier, Remulkin had assured him that they had plenty of speed. Soon, as they continued along their southwesterly course, the formation of ships would pass through perigee and begin rising, having only lost a little velocity as they grazed the planet's upper atmosphere.

Training their weapons on the beast, Richard and Newcastle looked over the edge of the opening, scanning left and right. Giard stepped aside, and the two men climbed from the mouth of the spiral staircase.

Jake gave Sandy a reassuring nod and gestured for her to come up as well.

Her head emerged from the floor. Sandy froze as she and the monster locked eyes.

"Say hello to Lord Thrakst," Jake said.

Apparently hearing his name, the warlord turned his gaze to Giard with an indignant roar. The howl shifted to the mixture of screeches and rumbling roars that constituted the Zox language.

It was hard to read the reptile's facial expressions, but the bastard's indignant tone was unmistakable.

Jake held up a hand and spoke in Argonian. "Yeah, yeah, we hear you. Shut the fuck up, asshole!"

The monster's head snapped back is if Giard had slapped him.

Jake kept his rifle pointed at the bastard and looked at the CAG. "The prisoner is secure. What are your orders, sir?" He nodded toward the reptile. "*Lord* Thrakst isn't going anywhere," he added in Argonian, pouring disdain into the asshole's honorific.

Richard smiled menacingly. "I'd be more than happy to test fire my weapon. That big mouth would make an excellent target."

Newcastle glared at the monster. The muscles in the big Texan's square jaw rippled. "I'd gladly do it myself," he said.

Jake saw the colonel's index finger longingly caress the trigger of his weapon.

After a pregnant pause, the digit fell away from the mechanism. The CAG sighed. "But that'd be too good an ending for this bastard," he said, lowering the weapon.

He turned to Sandy. "Major, make your way back to my fighter. Use its radio. Let Admiral Johnston know that we've secured the enemy bridge. Tell them to bring in the space fighters and muster a few troops. Also, tell them we'll need some technicians. They can use the Phoenix Fighters to ferry personnel."

The colonel paused and pointed at the console that had the flashing green icon. "I'd bet a dollar to a donut that's the gene weapon's actuator. We need someone that can disarm the damn thing."

While the CAG spoke, Jake watched Thrakst. The beast kept looking over his own right shoulder, appearing to gaze at that icon.

Then the monster's eyes shifted from the console. He glared at the throne and its monitor. On it, the hooked shoreline of Cape Cod streamed into view.

Thrakst's tongue flicked again. Its pointed black tip dabbed at silver fangs. Jake had seen the apparent nervous twitch several times since he'd emerged from the stairwell.

After glaring at Giard for a moment, the Zox looked right again. With apparent longing, he stared at the flashing icon.

His tongue flicked again.

Jake's eyes narrowed. It looked like the warlord was getting excited about something.

As the formation of ships passed into the Earth's shadow, the lights of a vast city rolled into the monitor's displayed image.

Thrakst looked at it. His tongue flicked again and again. Spittle now flowed freely from the tip of each fang.

"Hey," Richard said, pointing at the monitor. "There's New York."

He was right; they were about to pass directly over the city.

Newcastle continued to give Sandy her orders.

Jake stepped closer to the beast. Still standing well out of its reach, he continued to aim his weapon at the reptile's ugly head.

"Something's going on here," he said over his shoulder. "*Lordie* here is getting awfully anima—"

Suddenly, Thrakst bent at his waist as if trying to touch his toes. His right arm made a violent right-to-left sweep.

Green mist sprayed the sand.

Somehow the beast's forward motion continued. It somersaulted straight toward Jake. In its wake, the stumps of the Zoxyth's lower legs protruded from the desert rock.

As the shortened beast lunged at him, Jake aimed at its center of mass and fired his weapon. A storm of sparks exploded from the rifle's side as it spat out a silver pellet. With a pitiful click, the kinetic round bounced off of the beast's massive chest.

An incredible impact launched Jake. Knocked from his feet, he drifted backward as if in slow-motion. As he flew through the air, sparks of other malfunctioning weapons flashed in his peripheral vision.

Then, with extreme prejudice, the universe reasserted its normal playback speed. Jake slammed into a hard patch of desert floor. It knocked the last remnants of air from his crushed chest.

An inky blackness flooded his peripheral vision.

Above him, the unreliable blue sky winked out again.

Suddenly, Sandy's wide-eyed face filled his narrowing field of view. Her lips moved, but he couldn't hear her over the roaring jet that seemed to be landing right next to his head.

Jake focused on her face. He fought to hold onto the narrowing thread of consciousness.

No! No! No!

The thread snapped.

Like a drowned man, Jake sank into the black void of unconsciousness.

CHAPTER 41

"Jake!" Sandy screamed again.

His eyes lost focus.

"Jake!"

She slapped his face, harder this time, not the gentle pats she'd given him on the *Warden's* bridge.

"Come back to me, baby!"

He didn't respond.

Sandy looked across the stairwell opening. Richard and the colonel were hammering the monster with their rifles. Their plasma guns lay on the ground where they'd landed. The two men had thrown the pistols at the beast after they had misfired as well.

Sandy had already tried to fire both of her weapons. They had malfunctioned, too, apparently falling victim to the same malady that had the ship's systems on the fritz.

Green blood continued to spurt from the end of the reptile's legs. Obviously weakened, the beast now crawled toward the gene weapon's activation button.

The impacts of their rifles weren't going to be enough. Somehow, the bastard kept moving forward.

Newcastle slammed his kinetic rifle down on the beast's head again. The long weapon broke in half. The colonel threw it aside. The big Texan took a step back and then lunged at Thrakst, slamming bodily into the side of the beast.

The Zox commander almost toppled. Recovering, he braced himself on two stumps and one clawed hand. His other shot out lightning-fast, backhanding Newcastle across the room.

The unconscious man crumpled to the ground next to Major Fitzpatrick, launching a spray of sand across her.

Jake coughed. His eyes opened. Looking sideways, he saw Newcastle. The confusion there evaporated. Her man scrambled to his feet.

Standing unsteadily, he grabbed the business end of her rifle and ran to Richard's side. Jake hoisted the inert firearm high overhead and began raining blows down on the bastard's head. Richard had taken to hitting the monster like a batter trying to hit a home run, but the warlord's head barely moved under the continuous blows.

Thrakst kept inching forward, a trail of green blood in his sandy wake.

Nearing the weapon console, he raised up onto his knees. Even under the continuing rain of blows, the bastard jammed one stump and then the other into the sand.

Even shortened, the monster still stood a foot taller than the two men.

Jake and Richard made a last-ditch effort. They threw themselves at the beast.

Thrakst knocked each man aside. They flew like rag dolls.

As he took a lurching step toward the console, Sandy desperately looked for something to use as a weapon. The only thing in reach was a small cactus, a round collection of green spines that resembled a yucca plant.

She grabbed one of its pointed green spikes and yanked the cactus out of the ground.

Screaming, it squirmed in her hands.

Wide-eyed, Sandy looked at its base. Instead of roots, three rows of sharp teeth gnashed. As she held the squirming yucca plant-thing out, it contorted its body, trying to bite her.

"You'll do," she said and hurled the snarling thing at Thrakst.

It landed on the bastard's head, teeth first.

The warlord roared and batted at it. He forgot about the console, grabbing the little yucca plant-thing with both hands.

The tenacious little bastard refused to let go.

To either side of him, Jake and Richard scrambled back to their feet and started to run toward the monster.

To Sandy's horror, Thrakst gave up on the plant-thing and reached for the gene weapon's flashing icon.

She held out both hands and screamed, "No!"

Suddenly, a fifteen-foot-tall saguaro cactus that stood near the console folded in the middle. The long, three-armed plant would have looked perfectly at home in Arizona's desert.

Not anymore.

As the cactus bent over, a gaping maw appeared between its branching arms, revealing several rows of insanely sharp teeth.

With incredible speed, the arms appeared to wrap around Thrakst. The yucca plant-thing disappeared into the saguaro plant's nightmarish mouth.

Then the tall cactus snapped back to its upright position.

A deafening silence fell across the surreal desert scene.

In front of the gene weapon's console, Thrakst stood motionless for a moment.

Finally his footless—and now headless—body fell backward.

CHAPTER 42

Across the dust cloud that the dead Zox's collapsed body had launched, the three of them stared in silent amazement.

After a long moment, they started laughing.

From behind Sandy, Colonel Newcastle's gruff voice spoke up. "What in the hell is so damned funny?"

Richard gave the saguaro-thing a wide berth and walked to the CAG. Jake and Sandy ran toward one another. She leaped onto him, throwing her arms around his neck and her legs around his waist. He wavered under her, but remained on his feet, hugging her tightly.

Sandy soaked it up for a moment. Then she leaned back and grabbed his face with both of her hands. After staring into his smiling eyes, she pressed her lips to his.

They kissed passionately.

Afterward, Jake lowered Sandy to the ground. They walked over to Richard and the CAG.

Allison helped the big man to his feet and finished updating him. With wide eyes, the Texan looked at the room's numerous cactuses. "I'll be a son of a bitch," he said. Glancing at a particularly tall one that stood nearby, Newcastle added, "What do you say we get the hell outta here?"

EPILOGUE

"Do you want to know who you are? Don't ask. Act! Action will delineate and define you."

— Thomas Jefferson

EPILOGUE

"What's that, Daddy?"

"Well, pumpkin, it's a monument," Jake said.

"What's a mom-u-ment?"

Jake smiled and looked down on the small spacesuited figure that stood on his left. Then he looked over the child's head and linked eyes with Sandy. Behind her visor, a tear breached the levee of her lower eyelid. In the moon's low gravity, it started the long, slow trek down her cheek.

His wife's chest raised and hitched. A small patch of her visor fogged. The news of Remulkin's sacrifice had hit Sandy hard. Five years later, the anniversary coupled with this stark reminder of that fateful day's events elicited strong emotions for both of them.

Sandy put on a brave face and winked at Jake. Then she looked down at the little girl between them.

"It's something we build to honor ..." Sandy paused and shook her head. "To help us remember something or someone *real* important."

"Oh!" Candace said with a child's awe. "This must've been something or someone *really* important."

Jake and Sandy smiled.

"Both, pumpkin," Jake said.

The trio stood side-by-side in front of a gymnasium-sized white block. The massive cube matched the office building-sized monument erected in front of the United Nations. That monument honored the millions of lost souls as well as all who fought—both Argonian and Earthling—to save humanity from annihilation. However, this smaller —but still massive, considering the logistics of its construction at this site—monument stood in honor of one man's sacrifice.

It stood atop a small, five-year-old crater. The moon had gained many new craters that fateful day. However, this one held special meaning.

Remulkin Thramorus's final resting place lay almost perfectly centered within an ancient twenty-kilometer-wide crater. The monument erected above it honored the scientist's final act. Had he not given his life to get Jake into the ship, humankind might have ceased to exist on that fateful day.

Suddenly the top of the block blazed like burning magnesium.

Jake's visor darkened to compensate for the influx of light.

Candace started to hop with excitement. Because it took her longer to land in the weaker gravity, her feet pumped an extra time between each jump. "It's here! It's here!"

Jake shared a melancholy smile with his wife. Squeezing his daughter's hand, he said, "Yes, it is, pumpkin."

The monument stood taller than the distant crater rim. When the light of a new four-week-long lunar day rose on this portion of the Moon, it hit this high point first. Now sunlight began to illuminate the upper reaches of the lip as well.

Spinning, Candace excitedly pointed at the distant halo of white light. "Look! It's Remulkin's Eye!"

Jake and Sandy both nodded, but at that moment neither of them could speak.

Viewed from above, the white point of the monument now shone from the center of the brightly lit rim of the newly renamed Thramorus Crater.

Jake and Sandy had seen Remulkin's Eye from orbit, but this was their first time to see it from ground level.

After a long silence, he picked up Candace. Jake held her in front of him and stared into her beautiful blue eyes—she'd gotten those from her mother.

"I love you, pumpkin," Jake said. Then he wrapped his arms around his daughter and hugged her tightly.

Opening his eyes, he looked over her shoulder at the monument.

Thank you, Remulkin, he thought. *Thank you.*

Candace's little feet started scissoring.

"Do it again, Daddy! Do it again!"

Jake looked around at the gathered tourists. None of them seemed to be paying particular attention to his family. With a crooked grin, he hoisted Candace over his head.

"Really high this time!" she urged.

Jake lowered her and then tossed Candace up into the star-filled, airless sky. She continued up and up, giggling the whole time.

"Jake Giard!" Sandy said with mock exasperation.

A new gruff voice joined the conversation. "She's definitely another daddy's girl."

"Just like her mother," Jake agreed.

"Listen here, Mr. Giard," said a scratchy female voice. "You damn well better not drop my granddaughter!"

"Mother!" Sandy said with genuine exasperation this time. She pointed up. "Language!"

"Darn it, Firecracker! You keep chewing on his ear like that, and he just might drop her."

Candace glided down into Jake's waiting hands.

"Do it again, Daddy!"

"No, honey. We have places to go."

Holding hands, Sandy's parents walked up to them. The taller figure had a slight limp.

Jake pointed at the man's lower half. "How's the new leg, John?"

Sandy's father reached down and rubbed his right knee and then looked at the sky. "Feels like it's gonna rain."

Jake smiled.

∽

"I can't believe you two are leaving me stuck on this rock."

"You're the one who took the UN presidential adviser job," Sandy said.

"Besides, with your years of Washington, D.C., experience," Jake said, "you should feel right at home in New York."

"You'll just have to leave galactic exploration to us peons," Sandy said.

"Galactic exploration?" Richard said with a chuckle. "Let's not get too full of ourselves. You're only going next door."

"Calling eight light years next door might be stretching the term a bit," Sandy said.

Jake smiled. "It's a start," he said. Staring past the hologram of Richard, he gazed through the ship's view-wall. Earth painted a beautiful panorama across its width. He returned his focus to his old flight schoolmate and pointed at the planet. "But we'll miss that rock."

Richard waved a dismissive hand. "At your ship's cruising speed, you'll only be gone a few months."

"Who says we're coming back?" Sandy said.

Richard cocked an eyebrow. Through his crooked grin, he said, "We'll see."

Jake smiled at their unending banter, another thing he'd probably miss.

He couldn't believe they were about to leave the solar system. He wondered what waited for them at their destination. After the trials and tribulations of the last five years, it was nice to look forward to something for a change.

Depopulating many of the world's capital cities had left a huge power vacuum. However, Ronald Reagan had been right. The polarizing effect of an external enemy had united humankind.

With its New York headquarters untouched and its infrastructure left largely intact, the United Nations had filled the void. Capitalizing on society's newly realized external focus, the U.N. became the face of humankind. Now they even had delegates in the Senate of the United Galactic Federation.

After five years of recovery and rebuilding, they still had a long way to go. They would never know the total number of lost lives with certainty. Estimates ran upward of 170 million dead. Aside from the instant deaths inflicted by alien gene weapons, untold millions had perished in the aftermath.

Massive waves of aid, coupled with huge infusions of technology and rapid training, had elevated humanity into the galactic culture almost overnight.

Cramming the last decade of a galactic integration program into a period of months hadn't been without its problems, both culturally and economically. But after five years, Earth society was poised for unprecedented expansion and development.

Now it was time to move some of our eggs out of Earth's basket. The Argonians had set aside Galactic Sector 64 for human settlement, said humanity had earned it. Thanks to those same Argonians, humankind had the technology to begin journeying to the stars in earnest.

No longer a warship, the *Helm Warden* had been rebuilt in Earth's first orbital shipyard. Recommissioned as the *Terrestrial Explorer*, the massive vessel now served as a colony ship. After a hiatus of tens of thousands of years, the descendants of the Argonians that had long populated Earth were finally about to continue their journey to the stars.

A new world awaited them.

"Wow, Richard," Sandy said in reply to something Jake had missed. "You're sounding more and more like a politician every day."

Jake smiled. "You'll probably be running for U.N. president soon," he said.

"All right, all right, let's not get carried away again," Richard said with a laugh. "Don't you two have somewhere to go?"

Jake consulted his EON. "It is about that time." He paused and saluted his friend. "Take care, General Allison."

"You take care of your family, General Giard." Richard's face became uncharacteristically serious. "And stay safe," he said, returning the salute.

Then Richard smiled and pointed to Sandy. "And you, Colonel Sandra Fitzpatrick-Giard, please make sure my boy here doesn't run off on any more glory hound missions. He's already quite the folk hero down here. We don't need his head getting any bigger."

"No promises," Sandy said. She gave her cheesy ba-bye wave and then closed the holo-link.

Jake squeezed her hand.

"Are Candace and your parents all set?"

Sandy nodded. "Candace is hanging with Grandma and Grandpa in their quarters." She paused and pointed to the cameras. "I imagine they'll be watching us."

"Yeah, them and ten thousand others on the ship." He gestured through the view-wall. "Not to mention a few billion down there."

"No pressure," Sandy said. She squeezed his hand and mouthed, "I love you."

"I know," Jake said with a wink.

They released hands and walked to their assigned consoles.

After a brief visual scan of the bridge crew, Jake consulted his EON. All of the colony ships had checked in as ready for departure.

As the Commander Air Group, Jake opened an EON channel to the fleet's fighter escort. "This is the CAG. All squadrons, check in."

While Jake received the status updates, Admiral Johnston turned to Sandy. "Colonel, is the *Terrestrial Explorer* ready for departure?"

"All stations report a go status," Colonel Fitzpatrick replied.

Johnston nodded.

Knowing the eyes of the world were on them, Jake turned to the fleet commander. "Admiral Johnston, *Terrestrial Explorer* and fleet are ready for departure."

"Thank you, General Giard," Admiral Johnston said.

The fleet admiral turned to face the view-wall.

Jake knew the man's image now filled billions of televisions across the world.

"We take this first step for all humankind," Johnston said. "Today, we carry its hope and its children to the stars."

After a brief pause, Johnston nodded to General Giard.

Jake opened a fleet-wide EON connection. "*Terrestrial Explorer* fleet, parallel-space in three, two, *one!*"

Thank you for reading the Sector 64 series! Want more?

Hi, folks. Dean here. What a ride, huh? I hope you enjoyed reading *Retribution* as much as I enjoyed writing it. As I continue to work on my next novel, I also hope you'll take a moment to pop in and let me know what you thought about the Sector 64 series. I'm writing a new trilogy within this universe, bringing back some of your favorite characters. What do you think? Would you like to ride along with Jake, Sandy, and their family as they explore our little corner of the galaxy and its yet to be discovered alien races?

Visit deanmcole.com/notify to get alerted when I have a new release.

On another note, have you ever wondered where I got my idea for the movement of the Argonian fighters? You might be surprised to find out that I modeled the flight profile of the Turtle after that of an object I and several other Army helicopter pilots saw flying over Fort Hood, Texas. You can read all about it in my blog. It's on my website: deanmcole.com

Lastly, you will be helping me immensely if you take a moment to rate and review *Retribution* on Amazon.

If you're wondering where to go now, might I suggest *Solitude*? It's the first book of my *Dimension Space* series which includes *Multitude* and *Amplitude*, all of which are available as ebook and paperbacks. Continue to the next page for cover images, more information and links.

Thanks again for reading. I couldn't do this without you. Now don't forget to post your review.

Warmest regards,

Dean M. Cole

Seabrook, Texas

Solitude: Book One of Dimension Space

The Martian meets *Gravity* when Earth's last man, Army Captain Vaughn Singleton, discovers that the last woman is stranded alone aboard the International Space Station. Commander Angela Brown could reverse the event that swept humanity from Earth's surface ... if only she could get there. If you like action-packed, page-turning novels, you'll love the electrifying action in this award-winning, apocalyptic thriller.

SOLITUDE: SNEAK PEEK

Angela looked down to see the familiar horseshoe shape of Hudson Bay glide beneath her white boots. She shifted her gaze to the south and spotted Canada's biggest annular lake. It ringed Manicouagan Crater—one of Earth's largest asteroidal scars and easily visible from space.

"Uh, Commander Brown, if you're done sightseeing, I could use a hand here."

Angela smiled. Mindful of the ever-watchful eye of Mission Control, she resisted the urge to, playfully, hoist her middle finger.

Instead, the commander gave him her cheesiest smile and said, "How may I be of assistance, Major?"

Major Peterson did a double take. He floated a few feet across from Angela. Behind the visor of his helmet, a crooked grin spread across his ebony face. "Really, Commander Brown? Assistance? What happened to, 'What can Brown do for you?'?"

Angela sighed and rolled her eyes. "Don't you start, too." Inside her helmet, her head shook side-to-side. "Crack one public joke, and it follows you around for the rest of your life."

"That'll learn ya," Bill Peterson said with a smile.

Angela ignored him and continued. "That was 2018. It's been two years. I mean, really?!"

Paying no heed to her, the major wrapped his gauntleted hand around a coffee cup-sized white cylinder. His body writhed as he struggled with the stubborn electrical connector.

The pair of astronauts floated near the left or port end of the International Space Station's 300-foot-long solar array truss. The structure supported all sixteen of the station's main solar panels. To Angela, the long edifice looked like the mutated body of a dragonfly with way too many wings.

"This thing doesn't want to budge," he said with a grunt. The man's entire body lurched as he tried to force the electrical connector to turn.

"Is that Charlie Eight One Niner?" Angela said.

After giving the connector's three-inch-thick barrel a final fruitless twist, he released it with a frustrated growl. "The one and only!"

The two spacesuited figures floated in the shadow of the station's outermost solar panel, but sunlight reflected off the truss, illuminating the major's face. He looked from the cylindrical connector and winked at her. "Got a can of WD-40?"

Angela smiled and held up a large set of white pliers. "Nope. But I do have the convincer."

She tilted the joystick grasped in her right hand. The bracket under her feet vibrated, and the robotic manipulator arm attached to the bottom of her boots moved the commander toward Major Bill Peterson.

A moment later she released the controller. Now they floated face-to-face: Angela standing on the end of the long manipulator arm, Bill clipped to the array's hard points, the offending power coupling between them. A metal label riveted to its side read:

C819

Angela grasped its outer ring with the convincer—a tool specifically designed for stubborn connectors. In the zero-G environment, she relied on the stability of Canadarm2, the manipulator arm strapped to her feet, to give her the leverage that she needed to apply a twisting force to the wrench.

The sticky connector finally broke free on her third attempt.

With a crackle of breaking squelch, a new voice blared from the radio speaker. "Great job, Commander."

"Why, thank you, Houston," Angela said. "While I have my tools out, is there anything else ... *I* can do for you?" She glared at Bill and silently mouthed, *Thanks, butt hole!*

In 2018, when UPS had brought back their old slogan, she'd asked a pesky reporter, "What can Brown do for you?" The S.O.B. had run with it. His editor had even made it the title of the front-page article. It had stuck, and now two years later, even she had almost uttered the damn thing!

"Actually, Commander Brown, there is something you can do for me."

Angela suddenly realized that the voice belonged to Randy McCree, the director of Mission Control.

"Oh ... hello, Director. To what do we owe the pleasure?" Angela said, wincing inwardly. She resented the nervous feeling in her gut. The young physicist hadn't asked for this assignment, hadn't wanted it. In fact, Angela would've been happy if they'd left her to her experiments.

Ahead of the space station, Iceland appeared on the eastern horizon. Behind them, the inverted white triangle of Greenland's southern tip retreated, slowly sliding behind the curving line of the planet's western limb.

"Got something I'd like you to take a look at," McCree said.

Angela's head moved back and forth as she scanned the long solar array. Great! The woman had only been mission commander for a week, and on her first spacewalk, she'd already screwed up so badly that someone had summoned the director.

Apparently, NASA's ever-watchful eye was focused on her at that moment. Randy McCree chuckled. "It's nothing to do with your work. You'll need to look a little farther away to check this issue."

"Okay," Angela said, drawing out the word. "What do you have for us, Director?"

"Need you to take a look at Europe."

"Europe? Have you guys misplaced France ... again?"

After a pregnant pause, the director's voice returned flat and humorless. "It seems we might have."

Commander Brown and Major Peterson exchanged confused glances as their smiles faded.

Randy McCree didn't wait for her to reply. "A few minutes ago, several data centers went quiet. Our hackers can't get anything from them, either."

Angela knew that by hackers he meant Information Technologies, or I.T. for short.

"Did they lose power?" Major Peterson said.

"No. There just isn't any new or active data coming through them. Since then, the problem has only worsened."

"Um, Houston, I'm not sure what we can see or do for you from here. I mean, Teddy is pretty good with computers. But—"

"All the servers are in Central Europe," Randy said, cutting her off. His voice had acquired a frazzled edge. "But there's more. We can't raise anyone on the phone either. And all of the region's news networks went silent, too. There's a satellite looking at the area." He paused as if searching for words. "But what we're seeing ... It doesn't make sense."

The cold blue waters of the North Atlantic scrolled beneath the ISS. Their current track across the planet would soon take them over Ireland, Britain, and indeed, France.

"I need human eyes on this thing," Randy McCree said.

Commander Brown knitted her eyebrows. "Thing? What are you seeing, sir?"

"Well, it almost looks like an aurora."

Angela and Bill exchanged concerned glances. Exceptional auroras usually signaled the arrival of particularly energetic solar discharges—something that could prove fatal to astronauts not within the metal walls of the space station.

"Is it a coronal mass ejection, sir?" Commander Brown said calmly, relieved that her concern hadn't crept into the words.

"No, no, no. We haven't had any CMEs in the last several days, and certainly, nothing pointing toward Earth. No, this is something else."

Angela started breathing again and opened a station-wide channel. "Teddy, I need you in the Cupola."

"What's up, Command-Oh?" the Russian crew member said, his mock SoCal surfer boy accent lilting each word.

Angela looked ahead. Beneath the aft end of the port or leftmost forward-pointing solar panel, she watched Ireland's rocky shoreline crest the blue horizon. Overhead and to her right, the long, articulated truss that connected all sixteen of the station's main solar arrays extended 150 feet to the structure's midway point. There it connected to the line of modules that formed the body of the ISS. Between her and the intersection, banks of solar arrays extended left and right like mirrored wings.

The woman looked forward again. As they continued eastward, she glimpsed an upside-down reflection of Ireland on the bottom of the outermost solar panel.

Movement to her right front drew her eye. In the faceted windows of the Cupola, a blond mane drifted into view. Even from 200 feet, she could see it filling a significant portion of the station's observatory.

"Jesus, Teddy! I told you to tie that back," Angela said and then reopened the connection with Houston.

"Hey, man. Don't be hating on the 'fro."

The commander cleared her throat. "Um, Mission Specialist Theodore Petrovich, we're on with Director McCree."

Teddy donned a navy blue baseball cap that sported the circled red chevron of Roscosmos, the Russian Federal Space Agency. The hat reined in his blond mane. Inside the observatory, the man held up his palms in a what-gives gesture. His mock Valley intonation morphed back into his almost clichéd Russian accent and dropped an octave. "Da, Commander. I'm in position." After a brief pause, he added, "Good morning, Director McCree. What can *Brown* do for you?"

Angela shot him an angry look that went unnoticed by all but Major Peterson who chuckled lightly by her side.

"Telemetry shows that you are about to pass over Ireland," the director said. "There's an atmospheric anomaly we'd like you to take a look at. It's over England now and approaching their west coast. So you should—"

"No way!" Teddy interrupted, the return of his Russianized SoCal accent drawing out the words. After uttering a few others in his native tongue, he said, "What in the *hell* is that?!"

To Angela's right, Bill twitched. "Son of a ...!" he said with a tone of shocked awe. After casting an embarrassed glance toward the commander, he pointed east.

She looked forward, and her eyes widened.

A curtain of white light was rising above the horizon.

"Oh my God," Angela said in a whisper.

The commander could see why the director had compared it to an aurora. In the upper reaches of the atmosphere, its light faded to black in undulating feathery fingers.

Then the full height of the thing rolled into view, and the comparison collapsed. The colorful sheets of the aurora borealis usually ran in faint curving lines that never quite reached the planet's surface. However, this thing's light extended all the way from the edge of space down to the ground.

"That's no aurora," Bill said.

Angela nodded wordlessly, unable to speak. This was wrong, very wrong.

The curtain of white ... energy? ... appeared to run in a perfectly straight line left and right until it disappeared over the curve of the north and south horizons.

What the hell could create something like that? she wondered.

The director's voice snapped Angela from her reverie. "What are you seeing, Commander?"

"Houston, we've spotted the ... the anomaly." Breathlessly, she added, "It looks like a wall of light!" Her respiration rate had doubled. The astronaut swallowed, trying to rein it in. "But not like an aurora. The light reaches all the way to the surface. I-I can't see through it!"

The damn thing was high, too high!

"Houston, I'm not sure we'll clear it!" Bill Peterson said. "Looks like we're flying straight at it."

The ISS's ever-arcing orbital path sent them careening toward the white wall. Its upper reaches extended high above the planet. The opaque curtain concealed everything beyond it. It looked as if the space station was rushing toward the energetic rampart like a doomed moth on a collision course with a planet-sized windshield.

Angela's entire body tensed. Pain radiated from her clenched fists. Then the planet's eastern horizon slid into view over the energy curtain's upper reaches, and she relaxed a shade. If they could see the horizon beyond the anomaly, they must be above it. Right?

As their path carried them closer to the wave, Europe and then England and even the Isle of Man slid into view behind the wall. In the highest reaches of the ever-thinning atmosphere, the anomaly appeared to fade and then disappear completely. But the commander had no way to know if its effect—whatever that effect might be— extended above that point.

Angela's body began to tense again as the thought took root like a weed.

Inexorably, the ISS continued east, racing toward its date with the anomaly.

Looking down now, she watched the base of the wave move across the surface, advancing westward, moving in the opposite direction of the ISS. The wavefront raced across the Irish Sea. As the station passed over the Cliffs of Moher on Ireland's western shore, the curtain of light swallowed Dublin ahead to the east.

She held her breath as they sped toward the upper reaches of the anomaly.

"Here it comes!" Teddy shouted.

The commander crossed forearms in front of her helmet. To her right, Bill had the same involuntary response. "Oh God!" he yelled.

Head turned slightly, Angela watched through narrowed eyes as the wall rushed at them. North and south, its extremities appeared motionless, but the central section rushed at them with impossible speed, closing the gap in milliseconds!

Find out what happens next. Get Solitude: Book One of Dimension Space Today!

ABOUT THE AUTHOR

Amazon Top 20 and Audible Top 10 Author Dean M. Cole, a retired combat helicopter pilot and airline pilot, has penned multiple award-winning apocalyptic tales. Solitude, book one of Dimension Space, won the 2018 ABR Listeners Choice Award for Best Science Fiction. Previously, IndieReader named Dean's first full-length novel, Sector 64: Ambush, to their Best of 2014 list. His sixth book, Amplitude, the third Dimension Space novel, is now available.

Follow Dean on BookBub!
bookbub.com/authors/dean-m-cole

For More Information:
www.deanmcole.com
dean@deanmcole.com

facebook.com/authordeanmcole

twitter.com/deanmcole

instagram.com/deanmcole

Printed in Great Britain
by Amazon